PRAISE FOR

The Reason Is You

"The book's opening reads like women's fiction—a freshly impoverished and romance-challenged heroine moves back home and reinvents herself, finding love in the process. But by page two I knew Lovelace was going to yank that expectation away from me and shape it into something astonishing and glorious, then thrust it back at me and dare me not to love it. And I did. I loved it . . . *The Reason Is You* is a splendid debut and all-consuming reading experience."

—*USA Today*

"A spot-on debut novel, Sharla Lovelace's prose is smart, witty, funny, with a hot, sexy edge that makes *The Reason Is You* an oh-so-tantalizing romantic journey, without any gooey gushiness oozing too-sweet sentiment. She takes us through the lives of Dani and a fascinating cast of characters and—lucky for readers—the line between our world and the mystical one is deliciously blurred. I could not put down this book, devoured it quickly, and can't wait to see what the author comes up with next."

—Kathryn Magendie, author of *Family Graces*

"A romantic story about love, ghosts, and second chances. But under all of that, it's a story about redemption. This novel is the definition of a page-turner."

—Therese Walsh, author of *The Last Will of Moira Leahy*

Berkley Sensation titles by Sharla Lovelace

THE REASON IS YOU
BEFORE AND EVER SINCE

The Reason Is You

SHARLA LOVELACE

BERKLEY SENSATION, NEW YORK

THE BERKLEY PUBLISHING GROUP
Published by the Penguin Group
Penguin Group (USA) Inc.
375 Hudson Street, New York, New York 10014, USA

USA | Canada | UK | Ireland | Australia | New Zealand | India | South Africa | China

Penguin Books Ltd., Registered Offices: 80 Strand, London WC2R 0RL, England
For more information about the Penguin Group, visit penguin.com.

THE REASON IS YOU

A Berkley Sensation Book / published by arrangement with the author

Berkley Sensation Books are published by The Berkley Publishing Group.
BERKLEY SENSATION® is a registered trademark of Penguin Group (USA) Inc.
The "B" design is a trademark of Penguin Group (USA) Inc.

For information, address: The Berkley Publishing Group,
a division of Penguin Group (USA) Inc.,
375 Hudson Street, New York, New York 10014.

ISBN: 978-0-425-25486-8

PUBLISHING HISTORY
Berkley Sensation trade paperback edition / April 2012
Berkley Sensation mass-market paperback edition / May 2013

PRINTED IN THE UNITED STATES OF AMERICA

10 9 8 7 6 5 4 3 2 1

Cover art by Danny O'Leary.
Cover design by Lesley Worrell.

To Troy, Amanda, and Ethan.
Because touching your dreams is only as sweet
as the people who touch them with you.
Thank you for sharing this journey with me.

ACKNOWLEDGMENTS

First of all—wow. I'm still in awe that this long-standing dream is actually coming true. It's been a crazy ride to get here, but I haven't been riding alone.

Thanks to my family, the Lovelace and Scroggs clans who have listened to me drone on and on about this "writing thing" for years, smiling and nodding and humoring me. The only reason I made it this far is because of your faith, love, and support! I know everyone's family is amazing, but mine truly rocks. (wink.) I love y'all with all I've got!!

To my kids—Amanda, you are the light of my life, you smart, wonderful, witty, exasperatingly mouthy, beautiful girl. You were there ten years ago when it started with the Snuggly Ready Writey Club, complete with English accents. (You had to be there.) Now here you are, a stunning young woman, a writer in your own right, and I'm so proud of you. I love you, boog. Ethan, I've watched you grow from boy to man, and the trip has never been boring! LOL! I love the memories we have of just us (Evil Cult Children) and Sharla Warla Barla Darla Biscuit Muffin. Your spontaneity makes me crazy and makes me laugh and I love you so much. You are a one-of-a-kind individual, and I'm so proud to call you my son. Amanda and Ethan—I would never truly understand sullen, snarky, moody, make-me-gray teenagers without inspiration from the two of you. Riley came honestly. (love you!!)

I thank Troy, the love of my life, and the man who makes me smile. You let me share this with you, and actually let these characters have life, talking about them with me like they were real people. (they're not?) You will never know how special that is for me. Every writer needs someone who loves them enough to tell them when something sucks, as well as when it's good. That's luuuuuurrrv, baby! You're my other half, my love. And that's forever.

My brothers, Randy and Marty, and their families, who are now saying, "Really? My sister wrote a book?" Yes I did. Hopefully, I got the fishing part right or I'll never hear the end of it. (laughing.)

My parents, June and Buddy—who are in here as Nathaniel and Helen June. (sorry, Mom!) You supported every single crazy idea I ever had with vigor and love, and I wish you were here to celebrate this one with me. I love and miss you both every day, and while we can't sit on the porch for coffee, I know you are up there on our three stars smiling down. Hopefully not fussing at each other. Be nice.

Big thank-yous go to my awesome friends and coworkers who've been bouncing with me the past year—thank you for listening to me rant and sometimes lose my mind. Especially Renee, who has learned more about the book industry than she probably ever wanted to. (ha!!) I love you! To my crazy TCPT friends (www.tcptexperience.org) who taught me about physical, emotional, and spiritual strength, and then made me go home and write and quit talking (lol). To all my online writer friends—I would not be able to stand the voices without you! ☺ To my fellow RWA-WFers for being a daily source of inspiration and support. Writing is so solitary, especially in a small town, and connecting to all of you keeps the sanity! On that note, I want to shout out to a particular group near and dear to me because it was the first time I met other writers in person. My friends from the DFW Writers' Conference (2010 and 2011)—Maria Ghiglieri, Stephanie Hollis, Kimberly Rood, Ellie Soderstrom, Janet Butler, Dawn Alexander, Candie Campbell, Lindsay Cummings, Roni Loren, Piper Bayard, and Kristen Lamb. *Love. Y'all. So. Much.*

To my agent, Jessica Faust of BookEnds—you are a Godsend. Seriously. Thank you for all your support and calming influence when sometimes I need to be talked down—LOL! I am so blessed to have you in my corner. Thanks to my amazing editor at Berkley Sensation, Wendy McCurdy, for having the eye of an eagle and making this as perfect as it could possibly be, and to the art department for conceptualizing such a phenomenal cover. I'm so excited to work with such a great team.

Huge thank-yous to the authors who took the time to read my book and give me their quotes. A special nod to Jodi, who took my pages with her on a European vacation, and then wrote me the most fantastic letter about leaving little bits of it behind as she went, in six countries. Love it! I thank you all so much.

And finally, thank you, God, for reminding me every day to let You drive. For continuing to kick me in the butt when I need it. And for not giving up on me.

Chapter 1

STARTING over sucks, but at forty it sucks the life out of you. This thought squeezed my brain on the six-hour drive to Bethany from Dallas. I second-guessed my decision for the ninety-ninth time, eyeing every exit ramp as a potential escape hatch. As we got closer to the dark clouds looming above my hometown, in a Ford Escort with no air-conditioning and my sixteen-year-old daughter hanging her naked legs out the window to dry her pretty little coral toes, I felt the options slipping. One by one.

Not that I wasn't grateful to have a destination. My dad loves me, and he's never judged. But this time was no visit. It was the real deal, with bath towels and Tupperware and everything that would fit in a U-Haul trailer. My head started to bang out a rhythm just thinking about it, but I knew it was the smart thing to do. I'd tried everything after losing my job, and despite the number of times I pushed reality aside, it kept waving at me.

I had Riley to think about. I had to keep a roof over her head, and I couldn't afford to be choosy on what roof that was. We would be okay. I glanced over at her, eyes closed, jamming to whatever her iPod was pumping into her head, and I prayed she would be okay. That she wouldn't be tainted by association with me.

"So, when do we get to Podunk?" she said after we drove through Restin, the nearest big town. Not big like high-rises. Big like it has a Walmart.

I cut my eyes her way. "Wow, that's nice, Riley. Good attitude."

"Well?" she whined, holding her cell up to the window. "I barely get a signal when we go to Pop's. It's like the world falls into hell at the city limit."

"Sorry. Make do."

She rolled her eyes with a smirk, then pulled her dark hair down from its ponytail and fluffed it out before tying it right back up again.

"It's so sticky," she muttered.

I scooped my own hair back. "Rain's in the air," I said. "Get used to it."

The scenery turned from flat and drab to rolling hills of pine trees and underbrush. I knew we were close. I knew my dad had probably adjusted and readjusted the furniture on the wraparound porch. Probably checked out my old bedroom and the extra bedroom just one more time. It was one in the afternoon, and he most likely had dinner planned for that night and the next two.

The sign came closer as we topped a hill, barely visible under the neglected tree branches. The paint was worn off to nothing, and the words were just a darker shade of old.

Riley squinted as we approached.

"Never noticed that sign before. What does it say?"

"Welcome to hell."

That won me a fun look. On the downside of the hill, the town came into view, but not before a few straggling old houses made their unfortunate presence known. Riley turned in her seat as we passed an old wooden house with an iron rooster on top and three broken-down trucks out front.

"Was that a toilet in their front yard?"

"Uh—yeah, I think so," I said.

"It said FOR SALE."

I looked over at her. "You in the market?"

"Somebody's actually going to buy a used toilet?"

I bit my lip to keep from smiling. "Makes a dandy barbecue grill, I've heard."

She rubbed a hand over her eyes and slumped in the seat. "Oh God."

"Yeah, good luck with that."

We drove past the embarrassment, into the timeworn little town of Bethany. Past the different levels of new, getting progressively older as we reached the center and drove halfway around the circle before we veered off to the right. Past the old market and then past the Bait-n-Feed. I eased to a halt at the stop sign, and stared ahead. It was the last one.

Riley pulled her feet in, and I felt her eyes on me.

"So—" she said, letting the word hang.

I tugged at my bottom lip with my fingers. "What?"

"Just wondering how long we're gonna sit here?"

I took a slow breath and let it out. "Just thinking."

"About it being final?"

I stared at the blue eyes so much like mine. Damn, that kid could hit a nerve when she wanted to.

"It's not for a weekend this time, Mom," she continued, her voice smaller. "When we get to Pop's, that's it."

My eyes burned and I had to look away. I grabbed my lipstick from my purse and blindly swiped some on as I contemplated being Worst Mom of the Year.

THE house waited as we rounded the gravel driveway, like it knew we were coming. Faded and solid, with memories soaked into the solid oak beams, it was home. I wanted so badly to give Riley that feeling. All I'd managed so far was three apartments with thin walls and a key to the pool gate.

True to my guess, my father sat in one of the porch chairs, nursing an orange soda. His blue fishing hat looked newer than usual, but the blue coverall jumpsuit and ragged work boots were the same.

Riley stretched her way lazily out of the car and met my dad halfway up the steps.

"Hey, Pop," she said, winding her arms around his neck.

He did his little growl that used to make her giggle when she was little, and lifted her off the ground. Barely.

"You're getting tall."

"I put an extra inch on this morning, just for you," she said as she tugged on his short white beard.

I gave the trailer a look and then decided to come back later for all that. Pretend it was temporary for a few more minutes. Instead, I let my dad suck me in for a giant hug. I closed my eyes and breathed in the smell of tobacco and Steen's pure cane syrup that I would know in my sleep if I was struck deaf and blind.

"How was your trip?"

"Peachy."

My voice was muffled into his chest, but the answer didn't matter.

"Just glad y'all are here and made it safe before the rain hits."

I couldn't tell him that I knew we would. The rain always waited for me. I looked around. The only new addition was a weather vane in the form of a B-52 bomber plane, metal propellers and all, flying above the house, giving sound to the breeze as the little blades caught it.

"Everything's pretty much the same."

"Just older and creakier, like me," he said, laughing.

We shuffled into the house, and I braced myself for the horse that bounded across the worn hardwood floor.

"Bojangles!" Riley exclaimed, hitting her knees like a little kid.

But the five-ton black Rottweiler only had eyes for me. For some damn reason, that beast loved me and felt the need to share the joy every year when we came. His big feet landed on me with the momentum of a subway train, and down I went.

"Bojangles," I grunted.

"Sit!" Dad said.

Bojangles sat.

"Can you get him off me first?" I asked through my teeth.

Riley giggled and pulled him off, jogging to the kitchen with Bojangles at her heels to get a treat. After all, he'd performed so well. Dad helped me up and looked over his shoulder.

"She seems okay."

"She's used to disappointment, Dad, she rolls with it."

He winked at me. "Come on."

I heard the back door screen bang and knew they had headed out for a rendezvous. The dog might love me, but he knew who to hit up for the party. With the exception of one unfortunate goldfish, he was the closest thing Riley'd ever had to a pet.

"At least it's summer. She has some time to get settled in and meet people."

I looked away. "Yeah."

"Quit worrying."

"Yeah," I repeated.

"It'll be fine, Dani," he said, touching my arm so that I turned back. "She's tough."

"Tougher than me."

"Tougher than you used to be. But you're a different person now."

I smiled and looked around me. At the room that never changed, the furniture that never moved, everything still in its place. The same pictures adorning the wall, the same clock ticking in the corner over the rarely used fireplace. The same soft rug on the floor. Everything freshly dusted.

I felt like that room. All the same but freshly dusted.

"You'll be fine once you start working and get your feet under you."

He headed to the kitchen and came back with two waters, handing me one. He started to say something, when I heard Riley outside.

"Hang on." I held up a finger as the back of my neck tingled and I leaned out on the porch.

I walked around to the side steps and stopped cold. Leaning casually against my car, in his usual all black and sunglasses, arms folded across his chest, was Alex.

Sweet God.

I was sixteen when I met Alex. He appeared at my car as I left a party I'd only been invited to as entertainment. I was drunk and hysterical and attempting to open my car door with a house key, and he charmed me with his arrogant good looks and convinced me to walk home instead. We took the long way by a diner and he sat with me as I bought a hot chocolate and a muffin.

He was old, I thought at the time. Thirty-one, he told me. Almost twice my age, but he had that sexy, confident, hot-as-hell older-guy thing going for him. He laughed at my bumbled attempt at flirting and told me to drink my hot chocolate. I was too buzzed to notice the other patrons that cut their eyes my way and whispered about *that loony Dani Shane talking to herself again.* Or maybe I was just hardened to being the town joke.

Call him my guardian angel, or whatever, but he probably saved my life that night. And unlike the others, he didn't move on. He became my only friend. I won't deny that my hormone-ridden brain played out more than a few fantasies involving Alex. He was hot for a dead guy, and funny, too. It was easy with him. Instant. Like I'd known him all my life.

When I left for college at nineteen, he left a white rose on my windshield, and that was the end of it. At the time I thought I'd at least see him when I came home to visit, but no. He was done with me.

Until that moment, when he chose to chat it up with Riley as a grand entrance.

With Riley.

My head said to walk forward, but my feet went numb. Then he looked my direction, and suddenly I was head-to-toe buzz with blood rushing in my ears. I took a deep breath and attempted normal as I made it down the steps without tripping.

Riley saw Alex. Riley wasn't supposed to see people like Alex.

She had her usual folded-arms-with-one-hip-jutted stance, looking annoyed as hell, while Bojangles circled the yard in a frenzy with his nose to the ground. Alex slowly took off his glasses and locked his blue eyes in on mine with that arrogant little smile of his. I felt heat radiate from every pore.

"Dani," he said, low and smooth, and all the breath left me. "My God, look at you."

I opened my mouth to say the same thing, that after twenty-plus years he still looked exactly the same, hot enough to melt my shoes. But then the mommy gene stood up and waved and I remembered Riley was there.

He laughed, a deep throaty sound, as he pointed at Riley. "I knew it had to be."

A nervous noise squawked from my mouth. Nothing profound like I always imagined it would be.

"The eyes were the first clue," he said with a wink.

Riley frowned, her expression a mix of disgust and wariness.

"God, you know this perv? He was here on the car watching me and won't tell me who the hell he is."

He smirked. "The sweet, gentle nature was the clincher."

I couldn't quit staring. Alex—right there in front of me. My whole past poured down over me in a whoosh, as I locked eyes with the one person that had made it all bearable.

"Mom!"

Riley's voice jolted me back and I jerked her direction. "What?"

Her face screwed up in disgust as she studied me. "Ew."

"What?" My eyes widened as I imagined boogers on my face or something.

"God, Mom, could you be more obvious?" she said under her breath as she looked from me to Alex. "What, did y'all date or something?"

Alex laughed, and I felt my jaw drop a little, and I briefly wondered if my deodorant would hold up to the nervous breakdown coming on.

"Not exactly, sweetheart," he said, his gaze hardwired into mine.

The disgust came back again, as I knew it would.

"I'm not your *sweetheart*, and you can do googly eyes with my mom all you want but stay away from me." She turned to go and then threw back over her shoulder, "By the way, it's summer. The all-black thing is a little Goth."

I stared after her, trying to process it, then closed my eyes and willed it all away. I had never once had a three-way conversation with Alex. No one had ever seen him but me. That whole circus act with Riley had my brain on meltdown.

"Surprise."

His voice was soft and low and when my eyes popped open, his expression had gone just as soft.

"What?"

"Apple doesn't fall far from the tree."

Chapter 2

"WHAT the—" I blinked, turned and walked a few steps, and turned back again. I suddenly felt too hot, and my hair smothered me. I lifted it from my neck and held it there.

"Evidently, you didn't know."

"No," I whispered. It wasn't meant to be a whisper, but that's all that came out. "How—did I miss it?"

"You need to talk to her."

I laughed weakly at that. He wouldn't blink and it gave me a twitch.

"Oh sure. 'Honey, see that girl over there? Yeah, I know you like her shoes but don't go tell her that because she's dead and people are watching.'" I rubbed a hand over my eyes. "God, I shouldn't have come back here."

"It's not geography."

A fat, random water droplet landed on my arm and I cast my gaze toward the heavy grayness rolling overhead. "Maybe not, but it's stronger here. Like a magnet." I looked back at Alex. "She never did this before."

"Coincidence."

The panic rolled over me as I checked my watch for a reason I didn't really have. "Maybe we can still go back to Dallas. I'll—find something."

"Dani."

"I don't want her to have to live this life," I said as I bit my lip and lowered my voice. "I didn't come back to have to worry about her, too."

"Keeping it from her doesn't protect her, Dani, it makes her have to struggle like you did."

Looking into his eyes as he said that brought back those memories in a rush. Things I'd locked away and put behind me. The weight of the soggy air pushed at me, and my frayed nerves pushed back.

"Talk to her."

"Okay, okay. I get it, *Dad*," I said, folding my arms tight around myself. "Hi, by the way. Nice to see you again. Get lost, did you?"

His mouth twitched into a smile and he pushed off the car, resting both hands in his pockets.

"Walk with me."

Of course. What the hell else would I do? Typical Alex diversion. I fell into step beside him, glancing around for Riley. I heard the dog bark inside so I figured she'd gone back in with him. My head spun as the thoughts bombarded me. What had I come back to?

"By the way—the *dad* comment? Math doesn't work that way anymore, Dani." He leaned closer and whispered, "You're older than me."

I made a sound of disgust. "Oh, that's just wrong."

"I've always thought older women are hot."

"No, you didn't."

He laughed again. "No, I didn't. But—" At his pause I looked up and his eyes set me on fire again. "I do now."

I stopped, ignoring the need to fan myself. The buzz—

the rush that always pulled at me when around him—was the same, but I didn't remember being *this* drawn to him before. Maybe because back then he was old.

"Where'd you go, Alex? Where have you been?"

There was the intensity in his eyes that I remembered, playful and dead serious at the same time. Infuriatingly hard to read. An almost-smile pulled at his lips.

"How was college?"

I blinked. "Uh—two decades ago," I said, laughing for the first time since I'd seen him talking to Riley.

"Okay, how are you doing since the layoff?"

I felt my smile dissipate. "How do you—" I stopped and licked my lips. He wasn't a mind reader. He wasn't God. He never just *knew* things like movies portray. "Been keeping tabs, Alex?"

He didn't respond, but his expression turned soft. His left eye twitched, a sign of failing composure for him. He turned to face the water ahead of us, and I followed his gaze to the dock. Sporadic sprinkles dotted the river, and the smell was unmistakable. I looked back to see that his eyes had gone hard and faraway. He was done talking; I knew the signs. Just as I knew as I resumed walking down to the dock, he wouldn't follow me.

The ground was spongy under my feet, leaving impressions that got progressively soupier as I approached the shoreline. I didn't care anymore about the raindrops. I had only about a half hour, maybe less, to feed the itch the storm was causing in me. I closed my eyes and inhaled the undeniable aroma of the Gulf. The storm was pushing it up the river. I loved the saltiness of it on my lips. The heavy feel of it pressing through the air, like it was pushing against me and pulling the breath out of me at the same time. It was exhilarating, like it was just for me to absorb. When the wind picked my hair up, though, I opened my eyes. I knew it was time to go in. Everything after that always scared the hell out of me.

* * *

I rinsed dishes blindly that night while the thunder rattled the window in front of me. My dad had a dishwasher, but living plate by plate didn't warrant much use of it. I felt the need to make it feel loved.

Riley was up in her new room, formerly the guest room, trying to get a cell signal or channel ghosts maybe? God, I didn't know, but the whole thing had my stomach in knots. Dad morphed at my side and leaned against the counter.

"You didn't talk much at dinner."

I smiled up at him and looked away again quickly. I was afraid he'd see my struggles again, and I was afraid to let him down. Lightning flashed through the window and I winced as I waited for the next rumble. *One . . . two . . . three . . .*

"Just tired, I guess."

"A lot on your mind."

"Yeah. Thanks for all this, Dad." I put a dish back in the sink and gave him my attention. "Getting Riley's room ready like that, it's great."

"Well, I just want her to feel at home."

At home. "Thank you."

"I'm proud of you, you know."

I gave him a hug around his bulging middle and picked the dish back up.

"Saw you outside today."

I froze in mid-rinse and looked forward, focusing on a tile with a red teapot stenciled in it. The warm fuzzy of the previous moment vanished and the familiar tension settled in my bones.

"Okay."

There was a long pause, and I wanted to nudge him so he'd get it out there.

"Is it—" He stopped and fidgeted with a dirty fingernail. "Are they back, Dani?"

"They?"

"The—whatever they are."

I had to chuckle at the simplicity of that. Another flash lit up the yard like daytime, and I put the dish back down, wiped my hands, and faced him. *One . . . two . . .* I felt the vibrations ripple from my ankles up, like the house was welcoming me home.

"Dad, it's not a group that—follows me around."

He rubbed at his face, his beard. He looked like I felt, and it made me realize what he must have gone through with me.

"Well, I don't know that much about all this, and it's been a long time, so bear with me."

I looked around to make sure Riley wasn't anywhere nearby.

"People just—stick around sometimes, you know? Afterward. They don't even have to be local. They're just—there." I looked down. "And for some reason, I can see them."

He nodded and narrowed his gaze. "And someone was here today? I saw you talking to nothing."

I closed my eyes. *Talking to nothing.* "Yes."

"I don't know, Dani." He pushed off the counter and picked a coaster off the table absently and balanced it on its side. "I guess when you did so well up in Dallas—you never talk about it anymore. Not even on visits. I guess I thought it was over."

I laughed softly. "Not over. Just new, and I knew how to hide it there."

Bright white light flashed along with a concussion that shook the earth, and I jumped. The storm was on top of us.

"What about Riley?"

I looked away, feeling the burn in my chest. "Yeah, about that."

"Aren't you worried about her seeing you?"

I bit my lip. "I was out there today because I found Riley talking to someone."

His look was blank.

"An old friend. The dead kind," I added.

He flinched as if I'd poked him with a lit match. "What?"

I pointed at his face and chuckled. "Yeah, that's probably what I looked like." I nodded. "She could see him, talk to him. Freaked me the hell out."

My dad looked gray. "She—can see them, too?"

The deep rumbles resonated through the walls, making the countertop buzz under my fingers. The air itself felt unstable.

"Evidently. But I've never seen her do it till now."

"She didn't say anything?"

I shook my head. "I don't think she knew." At his bewildered expression, I continued. "They look like we do, Dad. It took me years to figure out the difference."

"Which is what?"

I shrugged. "Eye contact. Intensity. Hard to explain. Plus I get all skin prickly when one of them is nearby."

He blew out a breath. I felt bad bringing this all back to him. "What are you gonna do?"

I rubbed my arms and watched the sheets of water transform the window. I had no idea.

I sat with the car in park, cold air on full blast for the moment after my dad semi-rigged it. I stared at the building in front of me, at the faded brick, the windows dulled by twenty years of dirt with plastic sale signs taped to them.

My dad heard talk that they needed help booking the fishing guide boats for Sabine Pass. Scheduling the routes and selling the tackle. And since I knew the river and swamp from the shoreline pretty well once upon a time, evidently it was the natural progression of things.

My head throbbed to the point I felt it might push my hair out, and I flipped an air vent to blast right at my face. From a promising future at a hot graphic design firm in Dallas to booking boats at the Bait-n-Feed.

"How sad is my life?"

The rap on my window answered me. I jerked to the side and looked into the face of warm brownies and ice-cold whole milk. A big porch painted green where I sat cross-legged with a giant stainless-steel bowl and snapped beans while Miss Olivia LaChance spit sunflowers seeds into a paper cup and quizzed me about her dead relatives.

Miss Olivia was maybe the only live person I could talk to openly about my "situation." That's what she'd call it. Miss Olivia wasn't known for subtlety and hated gossip, so she paid no mind to the townsfolk yapping about me. She just out and out asked me one day why I was so odd and wasn't going anywhere till I told her everything to her satisfaction.

That became a habit, a habit I came to like because it was like unleashing a flood. I didn't have to filter my words first with her to make sure they made sense or keep my secret to myself. My "situation" wasn't creepy or contagious around Miss Olivia. It was interesting. Sometimes too much so.

She was widowed with no children, so I helped her out and she got some company. She must have had a million people die in her lifetime, because there was always an endless list. I never could quite convince her that it was a random thing. That I didn't see every dead person in the world and I couldn't summon them up. They were just there when they wanted to be.

"My own momma don't come see me," I told her once. "Why would yours?"

She squinched up her eyes, shaded by the brown straw hat she always donned. "Why do you think that is, Dani girl? That your momma don't make herself seen for you?"

I never answered that question. It was the one thing that seemed the most unfair.

As I looked into those same old eyes outside my window, I felt the familiar surge of relief. Miss Olivia was the only person in all of Bethany I ever bothered to look up when we came in. No one else would have cared anyway.

She tapped on the window with a pale pink painted fingernail, and I quickly obeyed, rolling it down. The heat rushed in and settled on me like a wet blanket.

"Yep, I knew that was you, Dani Lou Shane." She rapped knuckles on the door, which meant I needed to get out of the car, so I did and closed the squeaky door behind me.

"Hey, Miss Olivia," I said, giving her a hearty hug.

"You haven't changed one bit, girl," she said as she pulled back to study me.

"You just saw me last year," I said, squeezing her arm.

"Yeah, but I keep getting a different perspective." She laughed and adjusted her giant bag. "The rate I'm shrinkin', I'll probably need a booster seat in a year."

Miss Olivia was a frailer, thinner version of the woman she used to be, but the eyes never changed. Full of piss and vinegar, she'd say.

"You should see Riley now," I said. "This past year, she went from skinny with braces to a body that scares the hell out of me."

"I imagine I will at some point, eh? I heard you were back. Back for good?"

My mouth opened to form the words, but oppression that had nothing to do with the heat weighed me down. I looked around at the dusty building, the cracked pavement, the handwritten scribble on a piece of notebook paper in my hand telling me about this job—and just smiled. What the hell else could I do? Cry? Not in public.

"Looks kinda that way," I finally forced out. "I'm here to see if they'll give me a job."

Miss Olivia paused on that a second, then nodded and patted my arm. "Well, things do as they do, you know? All we can do is hold on and hope for a good seat."

I chuckled. "Guess so."

"Well, let's get in out of this sun, girl. I don't need more spots, I'm speckled enough."

"Yes, ma'am."

We walked in together; I took her bag that seemed to lob her to one side and smiled in spite of it all. If anyone could see the sunny side of a pile of shit, that woman could.

I followed Miss Olivia to the counter and hauled her bag up for the lady to see when she gestured for me to do so. She upended it, and handmade soaps of every possible color and scent tumbled out, each meticulously wrapped in plastic wrap and tagged with a pink ribbon.

"Got a good batch here, Miss O," the lady said, inspecting each one. "Last one went in a week. Think you can churn out some more?"

"I got nothin' but time, Marg. Nothin' but time. My great-nephew is comin' to spend the summer with me in a couple of weeks, so I won't even have yard work to do."

Marg rested on her elbows. "Really? What's that about?"

"Hell if I know," Miss Olivia said, shaking her head so the straw hat wiggled. "My brothers are still overprotective, I guess. Think I'm gonna kick the bucket if I do any work, so they send slave labor."

Marg looked at me. "Who's this?" Marg was heavyset, in a solid sort of way, weather-worn, tanned, but still a relatively pretty face with very white teeth and icy blue eyes.

"Oh, sorry," I spoke up, wiping a hand on my capris before I offered it. "I'm Dani Shane, Nathaniel's daughter?"

Marg's eyes lit up at that. How interesting. "Nathaniel, huh? How's he doing?"

"Great. I was told to ask for—" I checked my paper. "Margie Pete?"

"You found her."

"About a job opening you have?"

Marg threw some cashews in her mouth as she sized me up. *Foo-foo, soft little corporate female.* I'm sure that's what registered. What registered with me is that she didn't appear to know me. That was always a plus.

"I need somebody to schedule the fishing guides and the bait runs," she said and paused as though it were a waste of time. "Answer the phone and work the store."

"Okay."

"I've got two guides and a guy who does the bait runs, but all that needs to be scheduled now, all formal. Didn't used to be, but we got a new owner. Chuney got too old and sold out to a guy from the Midwest." She scratched her head. "A lot of structure with this new owner."

No bitterness there. "Gotcha."

"And if a guide bails at the last minute, it's you."

That got my attention. "Come again?"

She smirked. "Tell me what you know about the river."

My thoughts scattered into panic mode, then gathered back again to hold hands and shiver. Surely, the likelihood of me having to do that had to be pretty slim.

"Well, enough to get around. I've walked it a lot. Fished off a lot of points."

She nodded and wrote something down. "You'll need to go out with a guide and get the scoop."

My hair started to sweat. "Um, don't they need to know things like what bait to—"

"Yep. Ask whoever brings you."

I smiled as I felt my ears catch fire, and I tried to catch Miss Olivia's eye, but she was focused on unwrapping a peppermint she snagged from a bowl.

"Uh—I—don't know."

Marg leaned on her elbows again, piercing me with a hard stare. "You got other options?"

The weight of that reality settled on me like wet concrete. "No."

"Neither do I." She ripped a blank application off a pad. "I need help, and you're all I got. Call it bonding. Here, fill this out, I need it for payroll."

I felt sick. But I grabbed a pen and filled out my information blindly. Previous work history—*seriously?* I left it blank.

"Are there really that many people that want fishing guides here? I mean, don't most fishermen already have their own spots?"

Marg sorted out Miss Olivia's soaps. "You'd think, huh? You'd be surprised what people'll throw money at."

She perched tiny glasses on her nose and scanned my application quickly, looking up at me like I'd secretly plotted to kill the president. "No previous work history?"

I smiled. "Nothing relevant."

"Hmm," she grunted and looked back down. "Be here tomorrow at six."

"In the morning?"

"Very same."

I turned for the door and somehow made it out. Miss Olivia and Marg exchanged a few more niceties and then Miss Olivia followed me out. I leaned against my car door as she stopped to face me.

"I'm in hell."

She laughed softly as she ambled on to her car. "Get some rest tonight, you got an early day tomorrow."

"So I heard." I licked my lips. "I have to go out on the river."

She nodded and her hat bobbed with it. "You'll be okay. Just breathe."

I lifted my hair off my neck and inhaled the scent of old dust. "Yeah."

"Gotta go cook me some beans, now."

I blinked my drama free. "Who's snapping them for you, now?"

She waved me off. "Girl, I buy 'em in a can now. Don't got time for all that mess."

I smiled as I sunk into my car, cranked the ignition, and listened as the air conditioner groaned its death rattle.

"Of course."

Chapter 3

BOJANGLES met me at the car, all tongue and wet slob-bery love. At that moment I could have ridden him into the house. No one was home, and I was so grateful. I didn't need any more witnesses to my pathetic state. I just wanted to go have a meltdown.

My clothes felt oppressive and sticky. I stripped on the way up the stairs, and was down to my bra and panties and almost out of them as I walked toward my bed.

"Nice."

I whirled to see Alex draped in the chair by the window. His old spot. He had a half smile on his face but new interest in his eyes as he panned down.

"Shit!"

I stumbled backward over a pair of shoes, missed the bed, and landed flat on my ass on the floor. I yanked at a corner of comforter and pulled half the bedding over me while he tried really hard not to laugh.

"Damn it, Alex, you can't do that."

He grinned, and my insides went all wobbly. "Do what?"

"Just—be there like that. Without warning."

"Never bothered you before."

"Well, I was a kid then. Probably didn't do much parading around in the buff, either, I don't think." I blew out a breath to calm my heart rate. "Oh, that's a lie. I probably wished you'd catch me."

His eyebrows raised. "What?"

I struggled to sit normally while still covered. "Hey, I was a hormone-ridden teenager and not exactly on anyone's A-list."

He grimaced. "God, please stop there."

I laughed. "Why?"

He shook his head and held a hand out. "Because that's just—no."

"What—you were hot. You don't think girls fantasize about—"

Alex stood up and waved both hands at me, his face taking on a look like he'd just inhaled vomit. "I don't want to know this. That's just—" He did a body shiver.

I grinned. "You never thought about me like that?"

He turned a look on me. "When you were a kid? Do I look like a pervert to you?"

I sighed dramatically. "Joking, Alex, you can quit the panic attack." He rubbed at his face and sat back down. I had to laugh, in spite of my predicament. "Look at you, all shivery. You sure weren't that turned off when I walked in here."

"You're an adult. And half naked. It's legal."

"Well, unless you plan on watching me sit on the floor all evening, I need to get up," I said, waving a corner of comforter.

He gave me a long look and then put his head down. "Get dressed. I'll wait."

I smiled and took my time pulling clothes from the dresser to put on. *Mess with me, will you?*

"Okay."

He sat back and tilted his head to one side as I dumped my bag out, found some aspirin, and downed it with the previous night's bottle of water that sat half full on the nightstand.

"Bad day?"

"Surreal."

"Tell me."

My head was too clogged. The room felt still and jittery at the same time, like the air was nervous. I tugged on the ceiling fan cord to stir up some breeze.

"Do you know where Riley is?"

Minimal movement of his head. "She didn't check in."

"Alex, please don't mess with me today."

He sat forward again and rested his forearms on his knees.

"I haven't seen her. Your dad is out. Now breathe and talk to me."

I dropped forward onto the bed on my stomach and grabbed a small pillow to hug. I swear I was sixteen again.

"Mom?"

I dropped my head into the pillow. Correction. *She* was sixteen.

"Mom? You upstairs?"

My head jerked upward. "Go! She can see you."

Alex stood with a tired sigh and walked around a corner of the room and was gone. He never just went poof. He always walked away.

"What the hell?" Riley said just outside the door.

"I'm here, boog."

She entered holding the clothes I'd discarded on the way up, looking around the room.

"Do I want to know?"

I shook my head. "I was hot and disgusted and couldn't get them off fast enough."

"Okay." She dropped them as if they were covered in slime and flopped onto the bed next to me.

I handed her a pillow. "What's up?"

"This town is so lame. I don't know how you grew up here."

"I was lame."

She rubbed her eyes. "I walked around today, it's like freakin' Mayberry."

I laughed bitterly. "Not quite."

"Seriously, there's nothing to do."

"You know the rules. Keep saying that and I'll find something for you to do."

The famous eye roll and she flipped over on her back to stare at the ceiling.

"I'm sure Pop could use a duster, maybe a raker, most definitely a mower—" I began.

"Think he'd pay me?"

I glared at her. "He's *feeding* you. You have a bed and a shower. That's payment enough."

She focused back on the ceiling. "So what's got you so grumpy today?"

"Irony." That earned me a blank look. "I went off to college for higher education so I would never have to grovel at this town's feet again."

"And now you're groveling?"

I closed my eyes as my brain put the words together. "Got a job at the Bait-n-Feed."

Her face scrunched up. "Wow."

"Yeah. At six in the morning."

"For real?"

"Doesn't get more real than that."

She fiddled with her pillow. "Sorry, Mom."

"It's life, boog. Not always how we plan it." Sounded all parental, but I didn't buy it. I thought it pretty much sucked.

She sat up. "Well, don't wake me up. That's still night as far as I'm concerned."

"Maybe I'll come climb on your bed and put my makeup on," I said, shoving her.

"You need makeup for that place?"

I dropped my face into the pillow. "True," I mumbled. "Maybe I'll just stay in my pajamas. Save time."

She shoved at my arm and I felt her get up and leave. If I hadn't been starving, I would have stayed in that spot all night.

"Alex, I don't suppose you deliver?" I attempted.

Nothing. He was gone. Oh well, it was always a fifty-fifty shot.

My alarm clock sung at five a.m., but I'd stared at it through two, three, and four as well. I'd forgotten the energy of that house. The feeling of never being alone in my own skin. I cleaned up, threw on jeans and a stretchy T-shirt, brushed my hair into a ponytail, and called it good. Then I went for a little mascara and lip gloss only because my inner girly girl said to quit being pathetic and step it up a little.

I backed up and surveyed myself in the big, oval gold-leaf mirror that had hung in my bathroom since I was seven. My outer forty-year-old told me I needed some powder, maybe some Botox, a little Sheetrock spackle.

I smelled coffee, which meant Dad was up. As if on cue, Bojangles bounded in all a-wiggle and stuck his nose right up my ass.

"Okay!" I moved quickly. "I'm coming."

He followed me down just to be sure.

"Hey, sweetheart." Dad looked up from the crossword puzzle he pulled from the newspaper. Already in his blue hat.

"Morning." I headed to the coffeepot. "Although Riley says this doesn't qualify as morning."

He chuckled. "I used to agree with that. Now, I'm up before five whether I want to be or not." He pointed to the cabinet. "I got you some creamer. I know you like that better than milk."

I chuckled silently. "Thanks, Dad."

I sank heavily into the worn wooden chair, as Dad peered at me over his reading glasses and set his pencil down.

"You look like you've been beaten with a stick."

"Not yet, that's later."

He sat back and took his glasses off.

"Dani, I know coming back here wasn't in your life plan. And this job is ridiculously beneath you." He rested his arms back on the table. "But, honey, this is temporary. You'll get your feet back under you. Life's not perfect."

"That much I know."

"Do you? Because you sure keep expecting it to be."

I frowned into my coffee. "I just get tired, Dad."

"We all get tired, honey." He got up and poured himself another cup, then turned slightly, his thick white eyebrows raised. "But you have to put that weight down sometimes. You carry it around with you twenty-four-seven."

His chair scraped the wooden floor as he sat back down, and I closed my eyes.

"I'm sorry. I'm just a little bitter right now, okay? I just have to get through some things and then I'll be fine. I'll make peace with it."

He squeezed my hand. "What about Riley?"

"I'm terrified."

"Of?"

"Of my crap landing on her. Of this town drowning her in it."

He toyed with the rim of his cup. "What about—"

"Yeah. Now she's got her own. And people will look for something odd because of me."

"So, don't you think we need to talk to her?"

I rubbed my eyes. "Yeah, that seems to be the popular vote."

"Or lock her in the attic."

I smiled in spite of the turmoil sucking my brain cells. "Riley would just carve a hole in the roof."

* * *

MARG was making a second pot of coffee when I arrived. Or it could have been the fifth for all I knew. She gave me a once-over when I walked in and chuckled as she turned back to the coffeepot.

"Wasn't sure you'd show."

"Why's that?"

"You weren't exactly doing cartwheels about it yesterday."

I laughed and panned the room. "I'm too old for cartwheels, Marg." I met her eyes. "I'm here because I have to be. I need the job."

Her sharp gaze narrowed for a moment, then nodded almost imperceptibly. "Fair enough." She lifted the hinged countertop piece to allow me in. "Come on back here."

Guess I passed.

"We have two guides, and they'll be here shortly. You'll go out with one this afternoon and the other tomorrow."

"Just two?"

"Well, there's Bob that makes bait runs every morning, and technically could do any of the river with his eyes closed if he wanted to, but that's not his thing."

"Okay."

"He's not much of a people person. You'll see later."

I ran a hand along the counter as I panned the walls so thick with merchandise, I couldn't tell what color the room was. "So he's already out today?"

"By five every morning; that's why I'm here. He lives next door."

I vaguely recalled a mobile home and a golf cart next to the store. I smiled. "Why not just give him a key?"

"He steals." The coffeepot beeped. "You want coffee?"

I blinked. "Um, sure."

"Cups are underneath. Help yourself."

It went on from there. I learned where the fishing licenses were and how to do them. I learned how to run the register, look up and post the daily tides. Sabine Pass is a saltwater connection between the Neches River and the Gulf of Mexico, so where many rivers aren't affected by tides, ours is. I was shown where the guide schedules were (on the wall), where their rate charts were (in a drawer), and all about the five different types of deer corn. Okay, maybe that's an exaggeration, but I don't think so.

And bird feed. And garden supplies. And of course, all the fishing gear a small country could possibly need.

The phone interrupted her spiel on jigs, sinker weights, and swivels, and I took the opportunity to find the bathroom, which was down a hall marked by door beads. At least it wasn't fish hooks.

When I returned, Marg told me that I would work till three every day so to bring my lunch or eat chips out of the machine. And that after a couple of days I'd be on my own after twelve, because that would be her new hours.

"We close at three?" I asked as I counted suet trays.

"No, but the new owner comes in from noon till six. Noon to three gets busy, needs two people. He'll make sure the bait's okay for the night."

I turned midway through counting. "The bait?" I checked out the multicolored wall of faux fish. "Do they do something?"

Marg laughed like you do when a child says something cute. "Not *that* bait, back here."

She headed down the same hallway, past the bathroom, which she pointed out wasn't open to the public, through another door to a small room that opened to the outside and reeked so badly I stepped backward.

"Oh—wow."

"You get used to it," Marg threw over her shoulder. Two large vats filled with what appeared to be thousands of mud minnows and live shrimp squatted like giant moonshine stills. These I'd fished with as a kid, but I'd evidently either blocked out or entirely missed the LIVE BAIT sign out front.

"Bob pretty much keeps this all maintained," Marg hollered over the noise of the aerator churning oxygen through the water. "You just have to come fill people's buckets."

I stared at the scene in front of me and crossed my arms to keep the sanity in. "Groovy."

There were a couple of random customers that morning, but when the bell jingled later and Marg told me to handle it alone, I bit at my lip. Especially when I saw it was a girl I knew from school. Sort of.

She smiled sweetly at Marg and I remembered that same smile next to five other clones, giggling at me behind my back while their boyfriends openly leered behind theirs. I may have been too weird to talk to, but I still had tits and an ass and they all wanted a piece of the unknown.

"Hi, Marg."

Marg looked unaffected by the charm. "Lisa. What can I help you with?"

Another smile and a glance at me. Curiosity. Vague recognition. A plus B equals—bing!

"Um—" The gaze flickered back to Marg. "Fifty-pound bag of wild bird feed and twenty-five-pound bag of cracked corn." She flitted a hand toward the door. "My son's out there to help load."

The focus came back to me, much to my joy. The smile again. Unsure.

"Dani Shane?"

Act surprised. "Yes?"

"It *is* you. Wow." She laughed, and I watched as memory dawned. It was in the eyebrow. "Do you remember me? Lisa Lowe? We graduated together."

We did nothing together, but being a grown-up now, I pushed away the anxiety that broke me out in a sweat the instant she walked in. Instead, I feigned thinking about it. Former popular kids still need that rush, and I wasn't about to give it to her.

"Doesn't ring a bell, but your face does look kinda familiar." I smiled back. "How are you?"

She blinked rapidly, obviously thrown off by someone not remembering her glory days as one of Shelby Pruitt's groupies.

"Good!" All the teeth came back on cue. "Really good. I'm Lisa Marlow now, married Dr. Marlow's son, Carson. Do you remember *him*? He was a year ahead of us." She fidgeted with a bracelet and tucked her hair back. Twice.

I smiled back as I refused to remember him and shook my head. "Honestly, that was too long ago. I do good to remember last week," I said, laughing, forcing her to laugh with me.

"Well—yeah, I guess. Me, too." Another laugh, although not a convincing one. "And we hung in different circles, so—"

I nodded. She nodded. We were bonding, I suppose.

"So, you're back here now?"

"Yes. Me and my daughter."

Eyes lit up. "Oh! How old is your daughter?"

"She's sixteen."

"So she'll be a junior? So will my son." Lisa pointed at the door where the elusive son supposedly waited anxiously to load bags. "Maybe they can meet up this summer so she'll have a friend to start school."

It was everything in my power not to burst out laughing at that one. "Absolutely. I'm sure she'd appreciate that. It's so hard to start over, especially at that age." Or mine.

"Oh, I can just imagine." I saw the questions whiz through her little bottle-blonde brain.

"So, what made you work *here*?" she whispered after Marg had left earshot. "I mean, didn't you have some bigshot job in Dallas?"

The hair on the back of my neck suddenly stood on end, my neon sign that a spirit was nearby. When my heart rate sped up as well, I knew it wasn't just any spirit. Great.

"Um—yeah," I said, wanting to look around but stopped

myself. "Layoffs. And in that world, when you make too much, no one under that wants to hire you because they know it's temporary."

I knew that was condescending, but I couldn't help myself. Ugh. She nodded and looked sympathetic, although I knew she didn't really understand. Staying in Bethany, there's no way she could.

"So after a while, I had to suck it up. Had Riley to think of."

Her son came in and waved. A big guy, six foot–ish and buff.

"Mom? It's in the car."

"Okay, coming."

"Ask his age, Dani," Alex said to my left, and I had to struggle not to jump and turn his way. I didn't need that.

"Uh—wow, he's only sixteen?"

She blinked and licked her lips. "Yeah, well, he—we held him back in junior high to help him out a little."

I nodded the mom nod of compassion. "Oh, okay."

"Well, good to see you again, Dani," she said, now needing to exit before she divulged any other not-so-glorious tidbits.

"You, too."

"And I can keep my ears open; if I hear of anything better, I'll let you know," she whispered conspiratorially.

I just smiled. She left. I blew out a breath slowly and looked around for Marg, who hadn't come back in yet.

"What are you doing here, Alex?" I whispered toward the counter.

"Come to check on you," he said over my shoulder.

"Well, quit. I don't need anyone being reminded about me."

"You needed to put that bimbo in her place."

I chuckled. "Yeah, that part was kinda cool." I touched my hair. "But I wish I'd gotten a little more ready this morning. I look like a ragdoll."

He leaned over on the counter in front of me so I had to look at him. "You blow her away just getting out of bed."

My stomach twisted like a teenager with a crush. How did he have that effect on me?

"Yeah, yeah."

"Have fun," he said with a wicked grin, and he disappeared down the hall.

I scarfed down a bag of chips just as one of my mentors arrived. He was at least six foot five with whacked-out curly red hair peeking from beneath a Dallas Cowboys cap. His face glowed almost as red as his hair, and his belly strained at the buttons so hard I cringed every time he moved.

Marg introduced me as Nathaniel's daughter, and I held out my hand.

"Hi, Dani Shane."

He did that barely-grab-the-fingertips thing that men sometimes do to shake a woman's hand. Revolting.

"Hank Turner, sugar." Oh yeah, that made it better. "Didn't know Nathaniel had a little girl."

That made my heart hurt a little for my dad.

"I've been living in Dallas for the last twenty-one years, so—"

Hank took off his cap and scratched through his curls. "Oh, well, I've only been around for a couple of years myself, and usually only see your dad when we're launching or docking. So what brought you back here?"

God, evidently. "Life just worked out that way," I said, grinning.

"Well, sugar, I look forward to showing you the south end tomorrow." He winked.

Ugh, a winker. I couldn't stand men who wink. Except Alex. Somehow, my clothes wanted to fall off when he did it.

"Sounds like a plan."

"It's a date then, sweetheart," he said as he pointed a finger at me. "Hey! What's a minnow and a flounder have in common?"

"Jesus," Marg muttered.

I just raised my eyebrows and smiled.

"They're both dinner for somebody." He slapped the counter with a big beefy hand, and his whole belly shook with squeaky laughter over his joke. His face turned even redder.

"Cute," I said, winking. Why the hell not.

"Oh, I got a lot more. But I'll save them for tomorrow."

Lucky me. "Good deal."

"Not for you," came another voice I didn't recognize and briefly hoped was alive. It was.

Hank wheeled around as what I'd call the anti-Hank strolled through the door. The smaller, older man gripped Hank's hand and slapped him on the back, then turned to Marg and myself.

"Ladies."

Marg laughed, and he pretended insult.

"You're so full of shit, Jiminy."

He shook my hand for real, and I liked him instantly.

"You would be Dani."

A laugh escaped my throat as I tried to figure out what was familiar about him. "Yes, sir, I believe I would be. And you're—Jiminy?"

His eyes narrowed in his weathered face and sparkled with amusement. "Yes, ma'am."

"You can call him Cricket," Hank said, sidestepping.

"Not if you want me to answer," he said, turning on Hank. Hank laughed and held his big palms up as Jiminy turned back to me. "Last name doesn't matter. Jiminy works just fine."

The bell jingled behind them and I looked over their shoulders to see two guys walk in with a five-gallon bucket. Oh joy. Everybody did the manly shake and pump, exchanged greetings, found out how the kids were, threw out all the appropriate fishing lingo on what was biting where.

It's a small town. Of course they knew them. I knew them, too. Once upon a time, they were the leering boyfriends.

Chapter 4

ONE of them, Blaine (or as I'd now refer to him, the pudgy balding one), hadn't changed his ways. The whole time he talked, he kept cutting his eyes my way. Oh, the memories.

Hank bid his good-byes, promising great adventure for the next day, while Jiminy leaned on a shelf. He was a watcher, I noticed. Blaine finally made his way to "talk" to Marg and pay for the mud minnows I would be lucky enough to collect.

He leaned forward on the counter. "How's it going, Marg?"

"Just peachy, and you?"

"Can't complain." He looked my way as I tried desperately to not notice. "Sure got some good scenery in here today."

Okay, seriously? It was everything I could do not to hit the floor in hysteria. Even Marg's expression reflected something similar, and she coughed behind her hand. I laughed lightly and held a hand out for the bucket. He took it instead and squeezed.

"Blaine Wilson."

I smiled through the repulsion. "Dani Shane."

His slimy smile twitched a little as the name floated around the memory bank.

"Dani Shane—didn't you—" fumbled the other guy, otherwise known as Ricky. Or maybe it was Rick now, or Richard, or hell it could be Dick for all I knew. He left the question unfinished and pointed.

"Yes, I did."

Blaine let my hand go and stood back upright. He maintained his smile but I guess he didn't want to be infected by the suddenly tainted scenery. Ricky-Rick-Dick was a little less rotund and a little more couth.

"Hey, I didn't know you were back in town. How've you been?"

"Great." I looked down, not interested in catching up. "Just the one bucket?"

Blaine came to his senses and cleared his throat. "Just the one."

"Five dozen," Marg threw over her shoulder. "Fill the bucket half full and there's a net on the wall."

I grabbed the bucket and headed back, with Jiminy on my heels. I looked back at him as I was enveloped by stench.

"Come to see if I can manhandle some fish?"

He shook his head. "Nah, saw you do that when you were seven. I figure you have it under control."

I stopped in mid-grab for the green mesh net dangling from a rusty nail.

"What?"

Jiminy grinned at me and then took the bucket from my hand and proceeded to fill it with water from the tap off the minnow vat.

"Your dad and I are old friends. Used to go fishing now

and then, sit around and make our own lures. You were always around."

"Really?" I racked my brain. "I don't remember. I'm sorry."

"Remember throwing the casting net for minnows off the old point?"

I smiled. "Wow, that's going back."

He chuckled. "I taught you how."

I was mortified not to remember him. How embarrassing. "Oh my lord, I'm so sorry I can't remember that."

"Don't sweat it," he said and waved it off. "Hell, I don't remember anything before age sixteen myself. And that's just because I got my license and the good life began."

I laughed. "My daughter's sixteen."

"She driving?"

"Technically, but I had to trade down and my current car embarrasses her, and then we moved here so she has nowhere to go."

I wielded the net and scooped up some of the panicky minnows, letting them slither through my fingers one at a time as I counted them into the bucket. If Dallas could see me now.

"So, what's that story out there?" Jiminy asked, thumbing behind him. I scooped up some more, wondering what he knew.

"Just people I went to school with."

"Friends?"

"Hardly."

He chuckled. "Got that impression. They're both assholes, but they got what they deserved." When I looked up, he continued. "Their wives are both uptight and bitchy and put them so far in debt they can't find their ass with both hands."

I giggled at that and nearly dropped a wiggly one.

"Oops, crap, I lost count."

He peeked in. "Throw in half a dozen more and it's good."

I looked up. "You counted?"

"No, but do you really think they're going to? They'll be drunk in an hour, anyway."

I shook my head and laughed. "You're bad, Jiminy."

WE headed out on the water, and I closed my eyes and gripped the edges of my seat, focusing on breathing. It wasn't the time for anxiety to win. The smell—the spray on my face—the electricity on the water—was everything I loved about the river. Everything a storm would bring to me, like a teaser. It was exhilarating except for the bouncing movement across the waves that told me we were getting farther and farther from land. I opened my eyes and willed my morning coffee to stay put. We were out in the middle. I zeroed in on a bushy island to the left and counted the waves till we slowed up next to it.

"You okay?" Jiminy asked.

"I'm good." I tried a small grin.

He touched my arm. "Dani, you're clammy and shaking. That's far from good. What's the matter?"

I laughed, and it sounded weak to my ears, as the familiar buzzing rush that the river always brought me sang louder than my voice.

"Nothing, I'm just—" I shrugged and tried to shake it off. "I just get nervous out on the water."

Jiminy chuckled. "You grew up on the water."

"Over there." I pointed at the shore.

"You went fishing."

I pointed again. "From over there."

He sat back and studied me for a second. "Hmm. Never realized that."

I shook my head, just wanting to get on with it. "Okay, teach me something."

Jiminy gave me a fish chart, a bait chart he'd made of what was biting on what, and a hat that said "Captain J" on the front.

"Wow, you're really organized." I flipped through the laminated pages. "You update these every time it changes?"

"Yes, ma'am."

"That's a lot of work."

He adjusted his hat. "People pay a lot of money."

We hit every possible cut and cove and sandbar on the north end of the pass. Jiminy didn't say anything else, but he drove slower and closer to shore. I loved him for that.

We saw Bessie Heights, Stutes Island, Coffee Ground Cove, among others. I knew them all, since they were on our end and accessible by land—sort of. Some of them were swampy. Saw a cute little houseboat docked right around the cove from my dad's house. Then what was left of Coffee Ground Cove, which was my hiding place when I was a kid. It had an old abandoned dock and low-hanging trees, and I could disappear in there and pretend the world was beautiful.

He told me what fish were where and why. Where the ridges were and where the breeding happened, and why the tides were important. He made me cast a couple of times, I guess to prove I could, and actually looked impressed that I remembered the big alligator that once resided in the second cut of Bessie Heights.

"I named him Herman Munster when I was little."

He chuckled and then looked back at me again. "Sounds like something your mother would say."

I almost fell out of the boat. "What?"

He nodded, still looking amused. "You're Nadine, made over. Look and talk just like her."

My fingers went numb. "You knew my mother?"

"Went to school together."

"So did my dad."

"Yep."

I was amazed. "What was she like?"

Jiminy flipped over a laminated map and studied it, then grinned up at me. "I'm sure your dad's told you all that, girl."

I shook my head. "I mean from someone else's point of view. What do you remember about her?"

His face got a faraway happy look as he looked away. "Her laugh. It was infectious."

There was a moment when the only sound was the water lapping the sides of the boat and a nearby frog doing a throaty warble. Then he came back to the present.

He gestured toward the steering wheel. "Can you drive?"

I raised my eyebrows and coughed. "On land."

He chuckled. "Want to give it a shot?"

"Not even a little bit."

"Come on." He got up and pointed for me to take the captain's chair. "Face your fear. It's easier than a car. No lanes."

Shit, shit, shit . . . "Is it really necess—"

"Call it an adventure. Come on."

I made it without sinking us or running up on a sandbar, but I wouldn't go look to do it again on purpose, either. Ever.

Back at the shop at nearly closing, I was met at the door by Bob the bait guy. Marg told me that Bob was unique, and that was an understatement. Bob grinned up at me from all of five foot two, with a large gap between his front teeth and tattoos all over his body. But that was nothing. Bob was a one-legged, very hairy, weather-worn man in blue jean shorts, a metal fake leg, and sneakers. Oh, and he had a hump on his back. I kid you not.

"Nice to meet ya," he said in the gravelly voice of a life-long smoker, shaking my hand like a man. I couldn't help but like him.

He loaded up the bait vats, saluted me with a smile, and headed to his trailer, squeaky pole leg and all.

I closed up shop according to Marg's notes and thought she was awfully brave to leave that to me on the first day. Guess I made a good first impression. Well, to be fair, she'd already taken all but one hundred dollars to the bank, so it wasn't like I was left with Fort Knox.

I knew where I was going when I left, and it was the opposite direction from home. Within minutes, I wound through the neatly graveled figure eights, eventually landing at the end of a small rise. I got out and walked back two rows to the pinkish gray granite stone that sported my mother's name and date of death. April 16, 1970. The day I was born.

My dad never let it be that way. Never once was my birthday anything other than my birthday. I only knew that my mother lived in the cemetery instead of at the house with us, and we kept flowers there for her and frequently went through the scrapbook she made when she was pregnant. I was six when I really noticed the date, and my dad explained it casually as being insignificant because she was just happy she got to see and hold me there at home where I was born, before God took her to heaven.

I never wondered if I killed her.

I did wonder why she never came around to tell me that herself. A million other people felt the need to tell me their postmortem thoughts.

"But not you, huh, Mom?" Nope. Never her. I took a deep breath. "We need you—me and Riley."

It felt awkward to say that, having never known her or had any kind of relationship with her. I always visited, always talked to her about what I was doing as if she couldn't possibly know otherwise. But I never asked for anything. Not even advice. Not even back then when I really needed a mom. I didn't know how to have one.

"I'm back in this messed-up place again, and—" I blew out a frustrated breath. "You didn't—or couldn't—keep them off me, but I'm begging you. If you have any pull whatsoever. Please keep them off Riley." My voice choked. "She doesn't deserve this. She didn't ask for this."

My eyes burned with tears, and the back of my neck prickled. Not like with Alex, which always felt like electric current, but just enough to make me react. I turned to see a redheaded older lady approach. She wore a lemon yellow pantsuit and carried a large orange purse that matched her orange shoes. How unfortunate to spend eternity in such an awful wardrobe choice. But, hey, when she put it all on, she probably didn't realize there wouldn't be a do-over.

I swiped at my eyes and smiled, looking back at the stone where the silk daisies appeared to morph from the top. That hadn't changed. For forty years, my dad kept her favorite flowers on her grave. He never let them fade. He changed them out before they could.

"Nadine Danielle Shane," the lady read as she stood next to me. She jutted her head that way as she turned to speak to me. "That your momma, there?"

"Yes, ma'am."

She nodded and squinted at the date. "Gone a long time. You aren't old enough to have had too much of her."

"None."

She clicked her tongue, shaking her head. "Shame. Damn shame. Your daddy raise you?"

"Yes, ma'am. He's all I had."

Her head swiveled and she faced me with a snort. "Seems to me you obviously have more than most."

A smile tugged at my lips on that one. "You have a point, there."

"Damn right I do."

"So, where are you from?" I asked.

"Arkansas," she said proudly.

"How long have you been—"

"Couple months, I guess. Keep ending up in different places. My family's all spread out, so I guess I have to go get closure with all their deadbeat asses before I can relax."

I laughed. "Good luck with that."

She grinned then and brandished her ugly orange purse. "Thanks for the company. Even for just a minute. It gets lonely where I am."

I focused back on my mother's headstone. "I understand that all too well."

AT a little after midnight, I was tired of being wide awake horizontal so I tiptoed downstairs. Got a glass of milk and a leftover roll from supper and headed out to the porch. Bojangles lifted his head in interest of the dinner roll, wiggled his nose a bit, then decided it wasn't worth the effort. Meat might have been a different story.

I settled onto the porch swing with a blanket I hadn't brought for warmth—there was plenty of that. I needed the comfort in whatever way I could find. In the night sounds of the breeze turning the metal propellers of the weather-vane plane and the crickets and locusts and whatever else was out there partying in the thick air. Probably big tree roaches, too, but I chose denial on that one and it was too dark to prove otherwise.

My dad was so happy about my job. I didn't have the heart to tell him how much I dreaded dragging my ass down there again to field crap from old "friends" that probably wagged tongues all over town. Tomorrow would bring a whole new shift of the newly informed pretending to be surprised.

I knew I felt sorry for myself and part of me despised that but the other part was PMSing and didn't care.

"What the hell am I doing?" I whispered to the night.

"Whatever you have to," it whispered back as the skin on my neck burned.

I jumped and jerked to my left to see Alex lean against the rail. I licked my lips.

"Guess I have to get used to that again."

"I have faith in you."

He crossed the porch and joined me on the swing, careful not to touch me. People touch ghosts all the time and don't realize it. Feelings of déjà vu, confusion, random illogical thoughts, losing your way midsentence. Longer contact is more intense, for both. You feel everything they feel and vice versa. All I know is Alex always made it a point to avoid it, so I assumed it wasn't a good thing for them.

"So, what brings you out here where there might be cockroaches?"

I shivered. "Was trying to block that, thank you."

"Just saying."

I sighed. "Can't sleep. Too excited about work tomorrow—today—whatever."

"Your dedication is inspiring."

I sighed. "Yeah, I'm all that."

He was quiet for a moment, probably to let my self-pity firmly root itself.

"It's just temporary, Dani."

"Really?"

He sighed impatiently and looked away.

"No, seriously, Alex. Really? Because my dad sings that same song. Do y'all see a lot of upper-level jobs around here? Maybe one day I can be police chief?"

He sat quiet again, and I felt the flood come.

"Shit." My voice quivered and I hated it. But he'd been there before.

"I know."

"I got away from this place and the claws it has that drag you down and rip you up. I made sure I'd never be at its mercy again." The tears overflowed. *"Never."*

"I know," he repeated.

"I know you do. You're the only one that does." I gulped air. "Now I'm back, forced to kiss ass to stupid, closedminded people that I wouldn't wipe my shoes on a year ago."

He looked at me in the dark, and I felt the intensity of his eyes more than saw them. They glistened.

"They aren't all that way, Dani. Don't brand them all."

I shook my head. "No, I know. I just—" I blew out a breath to try to calm down. "I just can't stand the thought of Riley taking the crap for this. They're gonna fuck with her, Alex, and I don't know what I'm gonna do."

"You'll be a mom. That's all you can do."

"Yeah, I've been such a stellar example of that so far."

"You have. Look at her. She's a strong, smart-ass young woman that doesn't take any crap."

A laugh broke through my snotty hiccups. "Yeah."

"So keep doing what you're doing." He leaned slightly toward me. "Start with telling her so she has something to arm herself with."

I closed my eyes. "Yeah."

"Seriously."

I nodded and mopped at my face. "I know."

"You're going to tell her?"

"Yeah."

"Really?"

I sniffed. "At some point."

"Wuss."

I chuckled a little in spite of myself. Only Alex had that power. "I went out in a boat today."

There was a pause. "Really?" His voice sounded odd. He knew my crazy fear, he'd seen my reaction before.

"Drove it, even."

"How was it?"

"I didn't throw up."

He laughed and I pushed the swing softly as the thoughts zipped through my head ninety miles an hour. I closed my eyes and tried to let the quiet noise settle the buzz. After a moment, I peered sideways out one eye to find his steady gaze on me.

"Hey," he said, his voice soft.

"Hey. Just checking if you were still here. Never know with you."

"I'm not going anywhere."

* * *

I stepped up the appearance meter a little the next day. Just for my own vanity. I couldn't bear any more "friends" witnessing my downfall without at least good hair and makeup to buffer it.

It would be okay. It would be a good day. I had the right outlook, I was thinking positive. No more whining and bitching and moaning. I was done with that.

Even at ten till six in the morning, it was already muggy, so I rolled down my car windows. Not that that really helped anything, just gave some circulation. I drove past the two other streets that led down to the river, both of which held a couple of houses. I always liked that the river area didn't get too populated. I liked the remoteness. There were only a few cars in front of me this early, probably leaving for Restin. I remember being psycho enough to leave that early for work once upon a time. That was another lifetime ago.

We crept up to the stop sign, one at a time. My phone buzzed on the console next to me, buzzing itself onto the passenger floorboard.

"Crap."

I leaned over and groped around with one hand, my fingers blindly flailing through old receipts, a pen, and evidently an old pair of sunglasses I'd lost. I looked down for a second. Just long enough for—*bam*.

Not a big bam. More of a crunch that involved stopping without the use of my brakes. Enough to make me suck air so hard I almost choked as I jolted forward. I sat there in disbelief at the view of my rattletrap kissing the bumper of the white BMW in front of me.

"Son of a bitch."

The guy that got out of the car with aviator sunglasses had a set to his jaw that clearly mirrored my response and probably a few more.

"Shit, shit, shit," I mumbled as I got out and attempted a smile I didn't feel. "Hi."

He stared at his bumper and caressed its new wound, which I noticed was very minor, thank God. Unfortunately, my *black* car made the union not so pretty, minor or not.

"Hi? That's what you get out and say?"

I backed up a step, taken aback. "Yeah, that's what I usually start with. You didn't let me get to—"

"Do you even have insurance?"

Okay, officially insulted. "Yes, of course I do." I took a breath to slow the adrenaline. "Look, I'm really sorry. I got distracted." I checked out the damage again, caressing my dirty bumper so I could show I cared, too. "It doesn't look bad. We'll get it fixed."

"Not bad for you." He pointed at my car with a lip curl. I swear, I didn't imagine that. "This car is two months old."

I imagined it being born, slapped on the ass. "I understand. I'll take care of it. I'll call my insurance company—"

"Well, give me your information," he said, pulling his wallet out. I noticed his hands were rough. The wallet was worn. Not like someone you'd expect to drive a white cushy car. "I have to go into Restin this morning, I'll get an estimate."

I went back for my bag as two other cars crept by. *Really? That interesting?* I prayed that I had the most updated card.

"Please, God, don't let me be a dumbass," I whispered. God answered me with favorable results and I breathed a sigh of relief as I handed it to him. "Okay, here you go."

He took off the sunglasses and peered at it, then me. I proceeded to write his info on the back of an old receipt I'd pulled from the floorboard with my phone. He pulled out his cell phone, took a picture of my card, and handed it back to me.

Well. Okay then.

"I'll be in touch," he said and strode back to his chariot and pulled away.

"Great," I muttered, looking down at my scribbles. "Fucking great."

I went to work, stocked lures, fielded phone calls, posted tide information, told some guy that speckled trout were biting on Rat-L-Traps and buzz tail grubs, and hoped no one was around to hear and know that I pulled that out of my ass.

On my non-lunch break as I munched a bag of Cheetos, I called the insurance company to tell them I was an idiot and that a Jason Miller would contact them. He already had. Of course.

I went out on Captain Hank's boat. I'd never seen the south end of the river, so it truly was a tour. I didn't get a hat or a list or anything laminated. What I got was a play-by-play of everything Hank had ever caught, tried to catch, or wanted to catch, with eighty-five "sugars" in there to sweeten the pot. On the bright side, the water was calm and flat and Hank was all about trolling the sides, so I did okay.

By the time we got back, I was grateful to check the bait vats and sweep the floors. I went in the back way and checked the critters first and came up through the hall. I rounded the corner through the beads, smack into a hard body in jeans, T-shirt—and aviator sunglasses.

"Oh!"

"Jesus," he muttered as I stepped on his foot.

"What the—are you following me?" I exclaimed as he took off the glasses. "I told you I'd take care of it." It unnerved me that he was behind the counter with me.

Hard green eyes glared at me. "I just got here. What the hell are you doing here, and coming up the back way?"

"I *work* here, asshole." I walked toward him, hoping to be intimidating. "You want to get on the other side of the counter, please?"

But he stopped, very still. "You what?"

Just then, Bob wobbled in with his heavy side-to-side gait, grinning. "Hey, Dani. Hey, Mr. Miller."

"Bob." His face visibly softened to nod a sideways grin

at him, and in that tiny instant when he wasn't scowling, he struck me as good-looking.

"Got everything set for the night, Boss. I'm gonna head over."

I felt my eyebrows raise. "Boss?"

He turned back to me, and the troll was back. He held a hand out, his face set in stone, his eyes not blinking. It was like looking at a cyborg.

"Jason Miller. Owner. Manager. Asshole. I believe we've met."

Oh, just beat me with a fucking stick.

"Dani Shane." I shook his hand. "Am I still employed?"

He let my hand go and turned to run a report on the register. "So far. If you work better than you drive."

I closed my eyes and focused on breathing. Tried not to be swayed by the thoughts that descended upon me, saying, *You don't need this. You are above this. You don't have to take shit from this petty peon.*

Because I did. I wasn't anymore. And I had to. End of story. *Move on, Dani, suck it up.*

"Okay," was what I managed to say instead, and I grabbed the broom so I could take my frustrations out on the floor. We did our things in silence till I left. Then I said good-bye, as I swung the door open.

"See you tomorrow," he responded without looking up.

I let the door close behind me and thought about jumping in the river.

LESS extreme measures called for junk food. Tapioca pudding. Chicken and dumplings. Cheese. Ice cream. Not necessarily in that order, but I needed to go to the store. There'd be a bigger store or even Walmart in Restin, but I was not in the mood for a twenty-minute drive up the highway with no air. The Market would have to do.

The bell hanging at the top of the door jingled as I went

in, making me wonder if those things were required door attire. What stopped me short was the sight of Riley behind the counter.

"Um, hey."

Riley lifted a hand lazily. "Hey."

"Get bored at home?" Home. That just fell out of my mouth, and sounded so strange.

"Epically." She looked around her. "Walked down here for some chips and ended up with a job."

"You—really?"

At that moment a boy and girl appeared from around a corner. She swiped quickly at her mouth as he fidgeted with his clothing and walked as if there were crawlies in his floppy jeans. The girl was blonde and pretty and probably perfectly figured, but it was hard to tell with the man's overalls she had on.

"Hi, can I help you?" she asked, her voice soft and drawly.

I smiled. Or grimaced, maybe. "I'm good."

"Why not?" Riley was answering. "Get some spending money. Not that there's much to spend it on around here," she added, nudging blonde girl so that she laughed as she took a seat next to Riley.

I stared at the girl, somewhat stunned into silence, then forced my attention back to Riley. "Okay."

That's all I could come up with. I stood rooted to the spot, not quite sure what to make of it. Not sure if it was a good thing. Money wasn't a bad idea, but with Riley's new bag of tricks, I wasn't sure if being so *in public* was a good idea. Of course, not being such a chickenshit and telling her about it would have been a grand idea.

"I work noon to six every day but Sundays, so I'm almost off now." She consulted her little black-and-white-checked watch. "Carmen's been training me."

Oh good. Blonde girl had a name and trained my Riley in what? Smiling? Fashion tips? How to blow the stock boy?

"Okay," I repeated.

"So are you buying something, Mom?"

I felt the familiar prickle, and looked around. Nothing. No one.

"I—yeah. Chicken and dumplings tonight."

"Cans are over there." Carmen pointed to her right.

"Did I say in a can?"

Riley laughed. "Come on, Mom, really. Cans are over there."

Ugh. I sucked. I rotted. I was the mother from hell. I snatched up a basket.

The store hadn't changed much over the years. Low aisles you could almost see over. Odd organization of items, which when I was growing up, I didn't realize was odd. I was amazed in my twenties to find out that chain grocery stores didn't stock toilet paper next to the dairy items.

I grabbed chips, doughnuts, chocolate, ice cream, pudding, and every other kind of crap I could find. And finally the damn chicken and dumpling *cans*. And brought them up front just in time. To come eyeball to eyeball with the surprised snarky sideways smirk of Shelby Pruitt.

"Well, I'll be damned," she drawled. "Dani Lou Shane. I heard you were back."

I had a quick thought that the day couldn't get any worse, and I immediately shoved it away for fear that it might. *Nice thoughts. Nice thoughts.* I smiled, painfully aware of Riley's gaze narrowing. She was too old, sometimes.

"Hey, Shelby. How are you?"

"Great. Married almost twenty years to Matty Sims. You remember Matty, right?"

Here we go again. I got a memory recall of Matty Sims and me in the nurse's office. He was on the cot, and when she walked out, he pulled his dick out and wagged it at me. Wasn't much to wag.

"Kinda."

She chuckled the amused noise of someone who knows

you're lying. She was smarter than Lisa Lowe-whoever-she-was-now. Bitchier, too.

"So, what made you want to crawl back to Bethany?" she asked in her saccharin-sweet way. "Weren't you some big shot somewhere?"

I scratched the back of my neck, that tingle still present, but there was no Alex or anyone else around.

"Yeah, well, I'm relocated now."

"Relocated? At the Bait-n-Feed?" Then she giggled. I held on tight to my basket.

"Well, nice to see you again, Shelby," I said as I moved forward. She looked down.

"Wow, a junk-food fest? I'm coming to your house." Another giggle and an arm touch to show sister solidarity. Ya-ya. "Oh, that'd be your dad's house, I mean."

"That's for me," Riley chimed in, eyes ablaze.

I closed mine and prayed for that to go unnoticed. I loved her for catching on to the cattiness, but it wouldn't go well. Shelby's head swiveled to Riley and back to me. Ding! Ding! Ding!

"Oh wow, this is your daughter?"

"This is Riley."

Shelby smiled at her then at me as if we were admiring a teapot. "She's beautiful, Dani."

I threw a glare at Riley, so she choked out, "Thank you. Nice to meet you."

"Oh, you, too." She looked at the counter with disdain and then lowered her voice. "Do you work here?"

When Riley just smiled and nodded, she added, "How sweet. How old are you?"

"Sixteen."

"So's my daughter, Micah."

Of course she was. Evidently, we all popped them out the same damn year. I saw Carmen nudge Riley.

"She's on the varsity cheer squad. We're so excited."

"I'll bet."

She turned back to me. "And did I mention that Matty is the coach?"

Shook my head. Nope. But we got it now. I tried again to move on and put my basket on the counter.

"So who's the lucky guy?" Shelby asked, leaning over to check out my hand. "Oh," she said then, lowering her voice. "This was a divorce move?"

I pasted a smile on. I knew damn good and well that she knew damn good and well that I wasn't married. I may not have made the rounds every year, but if she knew I was a big shot somewhere, then she knew the rest.

"Good to see you again, Shelby," I said as I pulled items onto the counter.

There was a snarky little sound, and then, "Yeah, welcome back."

I looked Riley square in the face when I answered, "Uh-huh."

"What a bitch," Riley whispered when Shelby had moved out of earshot.

I stopped, mid-grab to my wallet. "Watch your mouth."

"Micah's just like her, too," Carmen said. She cast her eyes down as I met her gaze, as if she didn't mean to spew forth sound.

Riley took her time ringing me up, a snarky grin on her face as she handed me my change.

"Wow," I said, holding up the bills. "There's something new, you giving money back."

The bell jingled again, and in walked Miss Olivia, sporting a white pantsuit with her straw hat.

"How goes it, Dani girl?" she asked as she rested her giant purse on the counter.

Riley sat back in her chair and looked amused. I took a breath and then just laughed. I had to.

"That good, huh?" she continued. "The job?"

"It's okay." I patted her arm. "It's all okay."

She did a double take when she saw the girls. "My God, you weren't kiddin'. This girl looks twenty-one or more."

Of course Riley beamed on that. "Hey, Miss O."

"And how old would you be now?"

"I would be twenty-one or more."

Miss Olivia guffawed at that, throwing her head back. "Oh yeah, girl, you are your momma's offspring."

We all laughed except Carmen, who sat there looking sweet and confused. Probably bummed that Riley wouldn't be going to school with her now that she was suddenly an adult.

"Well, my nephew'll be here in a few days, and he's *only* seventeen, so try to go easy on him, all right?"

"You have a nephew my age?"

Miss Olivia opened one of her bags and tossed a few seeds in her mouth. "He's my niece's son. Just sounds less 'old woman' than great-nephew, don't you think?" She threw the bags on the counter and dug for money as Riley rung her up and Carmen continued to smile pretty. "You two need to come over for supper when Grady gets here. I'll call you." And she was gone.

Riley looked at me. "Grady? Really?"

I gave her a look. "It's after six; are you off?"

She looked at Carmen, who nodded and yawned. "I am, too, but I'll wait for Mrs. Shumaker to come back and relieve me, go ahead. There's nobody in here but Micah's mom, anyway."

"And the guy in the flip flops."

Carmen frowned. "Who?"

"Blue shirt and flip-flops, beard, spiky hair." Riley gestured to the back corner. "He was back there looking at magazines, probably still is."

She shook her head and shrugged. "Never saw him. Oh well."

Hello. My alert went up, and as we exited, I knew I was

on borrowed time. That clock would become a bomb if I didn't take some action.

And right on cue, there was my action. Alex strolled up as we approached my car, and my heart jumped so hard I felt the knock.

"Ladies," he said softly, smiling that way of his that made me sweat. This time the sweat was for a far different reason, as I whirled in place to see if we had an audience.

"Mom, what are you doing?"

"Nothing," I breathed. "Alex, what are you doing here? Are you trying to kill me?"

"Not today." He sat on the hood of my car with his shit-eating grin. Cute. He was in a playful mood. Groovy.

"You again?" Riley asked.

I ignored her. "Well, Shelby's in there, so—" *So please take the hint and scram.*

"Shelby! Damn, that's been a while."

Riley looked from me to Alex and back again. "Please stop talking in code," she said loudly, then gestured toward him. "And what, do you just really like that outfit?"

He gave her his full mischievous attention, eyes flashing. "Men don't have *outfits*, sweetheart, but yes, I do, matter of fact. Do you?"

"Not particularly."

He laughed. "What do you prefer?"

"Something this decade."

I was in full meltdown, and I faced her so it would look like she was talking to me.

"Riley, keep your voice down. Alex, please don't do this today. I'm begging you."

"Do what?" Riley asked.

"None ya," I hissed.

"None ya?" She backed up a step. "My God, that's so eighties."

"I don't really give a shit what decade it is, Riley. Not everything is your business."

She held up a hand. "Damn, Mom. Chill."

I was about over the top, stepping forward to tell her just how chilled I was, when Alex said calmly, "Maybe you should get in the car, Riley."

"Excuse me?" she asked, bowed up. "Who the hell—"

Shelby walked out at that precise moment and that was it.

"Get in the car," I said, my voice cracking. "Now."

She knows that sound. The sound of my sanity scratching down a chalkboard. She huffed and sulked and slammed the door.

"Looks like you got your hands full with that one," Shelby said as she sauntered to her car.

Adrenaline shook me head to toe, and I turned and got in the car without another word.

"Mom," Riley said when I started it up. "Is he not gonna move?"

"He'll move." And as my car went in motion, he smoothly stepped away and walked down the street.

She scoffed as she turned to watch him. "What is his problem?" she asked. "What is *yours*, for that matter?"

"Just too much, okay?" I said as I ran my fingers through suddenly sweaty hair. "Too much of this day. I've had enough."

"What's with this guy, Alex?"

"Nothing."

She blew out a breath. "Whatever."

"Yeah, whatever." Okay, jump the shark. Rip the Band-Aid off. "Do you ever notice—people that others don't seem to?"

"What?"

"Like the guy in the store? Flip-flop guy?"

She blinked a couple of times and stared at me like I was insane. "I don't know."

"You don't know?"

She shrugged. "Maybe, I don't know. I'm more observant than most people."

There's a spin. "More observant."

"Yeah. Why?"

"I—never mind."

My head throbbed, my stomach was rebelling against the Cheetos, and I didn't have the stamina.

"Mom, you're acting like a freak."

I rubbed at my face. "So be it, Riley. I've earned the right."

We pulled through the drive, and I stopped, got out, and went in. I was done. For starting on such a good note, the day had officially kicked my ass.

Chapter 5

I spent the evening out on the dock alone, sort of. On purpose. I'd had enough of other people for one day, and just
wanted the quiet sounds of the water trickling through the
cattails and swamp grass.

I wandered down the road first, to my old cove, Bojangles
at my heels. It was clear that not too many others shared my
feelings about Coffee Ground Cove because it was highly
overgrown and difficult to get through the vines and growth.
There was one path down to the dock, and only one side of
the dock that was still sturdy enough to hold weight. As I
looked around, I tried not to let disappointment settle over
me. You can never go back, I guess. But in my heart it would
always be magical.

Bojangles, on the other hand, kept staring at the ground
as if ticks were ready to ambush him, so we headed back to
our own dock. He looked tickled shitless to have company
at his favorite spot. He lay at my side, sprawled on his belly
with his head slightly over the edge of the dock so he could
watch the ladyfish and shad swim just under the surface.

If I'd had bread crumbs to throw out, the water would churn in a frenzy and he'd jump up and wag his tail and bark at them. But today, there was no bread, no frenzy, no barking. Just peace. He seemed good with it. I was envious of that.

Simple lack of activity, and he was fine either way. No stress. No decisions other than where to walk, where to pee, when to sleep or eat.

"Damn dog."

Bojangles lifted his head at the sudden break in the silence and tilted it. His tail wagged a couple of strokes, slow as if unsure. I dug my fingers in the soft hair of his neck to relax him back down before he decided to come sit on me. A long cattail swayed next to the dock, and I plucked it from its mucky roots. Letting the furry end just touch the surface, I skimmed the calm water, watching the resulting ripples resonate out. Forever changing something's world for that one second.

I felt the footsteps behind me, and Bojangles's tail went into full thump mode as he flopped awkwardly to his feet. I turned to see Dad walk up with two Cokes and a bag of pretzels.

"Hey."

"Hey, yourself." He scoped out the options, then groaned as he lowered himself down to sit as Bo danced around him and then sat between us. "Lord, I remember when getting on the ground didn't require premeditation."

I laughed and reached into the bag. We sat in silence for a bit as the duskiness fell over the water. Bojangles watched the pretzel bag till his eyes got heavy. Then I felt the gaze and looked to the right to catch my dad studying me.

"What?"

"You tell me."

I shrugged. "Nothing."

"*Nothing* doesn't usually have you out here hanging with Bo."

"He twisted my arm."

Bojangles let out a long snore right about that time.

"Well, no one can deny his charm."

I laughed a pretzel right out of my mouth on that one, and Bo simultaneously woke up and snatched it out of mid-air before he flopped back down to munch sideways.

"Wow."

Dad held out the bag again. "Saw Marg today. Said you're doing good. She likes you. And she doesn't just like every-body, so that's saying something."

"She likes *you*."

He took the bag back and shook his head. "Don't be silly."

"I'm saying she lights up like a Christmas tree when it comes to you."

"So what happened to your car?"

I smiled. "Subtle."

"Made a good impression on the new boss, huh?"

I blew out a breath and looked back toward where my car sat guiltily. "God, can't anyone keep their mouth shut around here?"

"Pretty much no."

I rubbed at my face, feeling the day's twitch coming back. "You wondered why I sat with Bo? He wasn't quizzing me."

Dad chuckled. "Sorry."

I ran a hand through my hair and let it fall. The dark swallowed up the water in front of me and I remembered being seventeen and wishing it would swallow me with it. I was careful not to look down, straight into the water beneath me. Night water was like the rain. Just waiting for me to succumb to it. Waiting for me to fall in so it could suck me down.

I shook my head free of the vertigo pulling at me. "Went out on the boat with Jiminy yesterday."

There was a pause before he laughed. "No kidding?"

"Went out with Hank today."

"Well, aren't you just stepping outside your box?"

I grabbed a pretzel. "I think my box stayed in Dallas."
At his chuckle I added, "Jiminy knew me, by the way."

He nodded. "He knew you when you were little."

"He said you and him and Mom used to hang out."

Another chuckle. "That seems like a hundred years ago."

"Everything changed when she died, huh?"

He nudged me. "Just got busy. You know as well as I do
how life changes when you have a baby. Everything you
used to think was important becomes trivial."

"Especially doing it alone."

"Especially."

"Still miss Mom?"

He took his time letting out the next breath. "Every day."

"Me, too," I said, although it barely came out. "I mean,
it's odd to miss someone you've never met. But I guess I miss
the idea of her."

"How does Riley handle that?"

I looked at him, confused by the turn.

"About her dad—"

"Oh." Strange, that I'd never seen it as similar. "She—
really hasn't brought it up in a long time. She used to."

"You still tell her you bought her at a store?"

"Hmm." I laughed. "That was easier, wasn't it?"

Funny that I could laugh about it now. Riley was five
when I had to tell her she wasn't *bought*. She had seen past
that ruse and wanted the skinny. At that time, the story
became that there was once a daddy but that he had to leave.
It was always lame.

But how do you tell a child that the man who helped make
her was a loser asshole who charmed her gullible mom? The
kind of loser who says all the right things and drops hope
and affection and "L" words in your lap and to someone as
love-starved as I was, seemed to be lined in gold. The kind
of loser who talks you into futures and picket fences and
letting go of friends and possessions and everything to move

into his fancy apartment, getting rid of your own stuff because it doesn't match.

And then when you get pregnant, he looks at you, smiles, kisses you off to work, and while you are at work happily caught up in thoughts of a wedding and a family in your rosy-tinted world, he packs up everything and vanishes.

No clothes left behind. No toothbrush. No hair in the sink or drool stain on the pillow. Because there was no pillow. He took that, too.

No proof that he was ever there except for what you have cooking inside you. How do you tell your child that? That I know I'm not important enough to be graced like the Virgin Mary, I know I didn't imagine six months of my life with this man, but he evidently fabricated a job, a name, an identity that I found out was all false.

An acquaintance of mine that had met him once at a restaurant with me did at least verify in my mind that he was real and living and that I hadn't completely crossed over reality. But it didn't matter. He left me without a trace. No note. No savings. No furniture or appliances. Just college loans and an apartment I couldn't afford to keep.

Yeah, that was pretty real.

When Riley was twelve, she bluntly asked me, *So, do you really know who my dad is or was it a one-night stand?*

Too much TV. Definitely.

A one-night stand, I told her.

I just couldn't bear to tell her that he was Houdini in Armani and escaped when told of her existence. Let her think I was just sleazy. I just couldn't tell her the truth.

Kinda like now.

"I tried to tell her about—the ghosts—today."

I felt his head swivel. I swear. "Really."

"Yeah." I shoved another pretzel in my mouth and proceeded to talk around it. "Didn't go so well. She thought I was a lunatic, which in hindsight she was probably right."

"So she knows?"

"No. She didn't catch on. I was a babbling idiot."

"Do you—think you should, really?"

I blew out a sigh. "I'd love not to have to, but—" But what? My invisible friend tells me I should? "—But I don't know. I'd rather she heard from me."

He looked down. "Yeah. You're probably right."

"She tell you she got a job?"

"No."

"At The Market. Just walked down there today and decided what the hell, I guess."

"Hunh." He chuckled. "Y'all have had a full day, haven't you?"

"We had something. Well, at least she has the desire to get some money. That's the first sign of ambition I've seen, yet. Usually she just holds a hand out."

"What does she want to be?" he asked.

"A mooch, so far. She's so lazy."

He elbowed me, getting up slowly. "So were you, and you turned out okay."

I rose with him, and Bojangles looked disappointed that the party was over.

"Yeah, I'm just the poster child for success."

He gave me a look. "Quit being so hard on yourself. You're doing fine."

I looked out at the water, surrounded by dark, lit only by the partial moon and a radio tower in the distance.

"I don't know, Dad. This brand of *fine* is beating me up."

I sat cross-legged in the big chair in my room, looking out the window at the dark. I barely recall sitting there in earlier years. I was usually slung across my messy bed. Besides, it was Alex's spot.

I ran a finger along the worn, fuzzy arm, tracing the pattern in the gray fabric.

"What are you doing?"

I looked up, proud of myself for not jumping. My old skin was coming back. But I wasn't in the mood. Alex strolled closer and leaned against the window.

"Mad at me?"

I followed the lines with my finger. "Did you know this was a maze? Inside—"

"—A bigger maze." He nodded and gave a sideways smirk. "Spent a lot of time there."

I met his eyes. "So you should know better than anyone how hard I'm trying here. Trying to make things good for Riley."

"Yes."

"So popping up in public to make me dance like that was not cool."

"Dani—" he began.

"You knew she'd see you and talk to you. You pick The Market parking lot for that? My God."

His expression didn't change. "If you were honest with her, you wouldn't have to dance."

I got up and stood just inches from him and stared up into his face. My head started buzzing at the proximity, and I had to back up a half step before I—*before I what?* I shook my head clear.

"I've had to dance my whole life. Knowing doesn't make it easier."

"You can't be with her twenty-four-seven to protect her, Dani. I'm sure she's done it before now, she's just been damn lucky no one has noticed. She needs to know how to react to this, how to protect herself. Why don't you want to give her that?"

"Because she's sixteen. She shouldn't have to *protect herself.* She shouldn't have to worry about her reactions and who's watching." I hugged my arms in front of me, trying to stem the emotion rising up like the noise ringing in my ears. "Because once I tell her, the life she knows is over. Nothing will ever be the same for her."

He frowned. "And you think you're the only source? You'd rather she found out like you did? Have some stranger point it out?"

"So that's what that whole dog-and-pony show was about today?"

He crossed his arms and looked at me in disbelief. "What are you so angry about?"

I felt my resolve snap. "Because that's crossing the line, Alex!" I yelled in his face. Too close. His eyes flashed and his jaw tightened. "That's screwing with my life. And hers."

"I'm not screwing with you or anybody else, Dani," he shot back at me through clenched teeth. "I want you to open your damn eyes. Why are you so hardheaded?"

"Why do you care so much what my daughter knows or doesn't know? It's none of your business."

His face went stony. "Fine. Figure it out."

He walked out the bedroom door into the hallway and was gone. My adrenaline pumped so fast, I could hear my heartbeat. I walked to the bed, sat down, and crumbled. Too many sleepless nights and the exhaustion of the day settled on me like a heavy fog, and I couldn't fight the emotion anymore. I closed my eyes and fell over on my side, the stress shaking my body.

I jerked awake hours later, still lying in the same spot, still in my clothes. Judging from the bowling balls on my eyelids, I gathered my pre-slumber crying jag had done its typical number.

"Shit," I mumbled as I rubbed them and pushed myself up on a groan.

"Welcome back."

I jumped. "Damn it, Alex." I couldn't pull the cobwebs out. "See, that's what my life is about. And that's what Riley gets to look forward to now. People morphing out of the walls."

"Yeah, your life sucks so bad."

I dropped my head and sighed. "I didn't mean to get all over you like that, earlier. It was a bad day."

He rose from his chair and crossed the space to kneel in front of me. "Tomorrow's another day."

I stared at the window, black and solid. That's how I felt. "I tried, Alex. I tried talking to her and I choked." Tears burned the backs of my eyes. "I don't want this for her."

"It's not your choice, love," he whispered.

I closed my eyes and let the tears come again. I was so tired of tears. Alex never left. He watched me cry in silence, unable to touch me or hold me or wipe my tears away. He could only be there. Like always. Or almost always.

"Where did you go?" I rasped finally, when I was spent.

His eyebrows twitched together in question.

"When I moved away."

He paused for a second. "I was there. For a while."

I perked up. "Where?"

"Around."

"But—"

"You needed to learn how to interact with the living, Dani."

"Without you."

He nodded almost imperceptibly. "Without me."

My lip quivered again. "I missed you."

Something in his eyes flickered. "I missed you, too."

There was a long, intense gaze between us that was new. Felt like a hole was burning through the back of my brain.

"And when I got pregnant and lost everything? And raised her alone?"

"You had friends."

I scoffed. "Not close ones."

"That was your choice."

How did he know that? "I was alone."

"You were never alone." His jaw twitched but his eyes bored into me, hard. "Riley was born on a Friday night, after six hours of labor, seven o'clock straight up. She stopped crying as soon as she saw your face."

My skin prickled and his image swam before me. "You were there."

"Of course I was."

Several moments of silence passed. "Why?"

"What?"

"Why did you stay? Why me? Every other spirit comes and goes. Not you. You stuck."

He blinked and looked away, which told me the subject was about to change. He was uncomfortable. Any other time, he'd outstare a mannequin. I watched him reestablish his control as he met my eyes.

"You kept things interesting."

"That's all? I kept you from being bored?"

He laughed. "In a sense." His smile remained, but his eyes got serious. "You're my friend. You matter."

The air got thick. It needed to be lightened up.

"So, if you were *around*, did you watch me do *everything*?"

The corners of his mouth turned up.

"You did? You watched me?"

He laughed and shook his head. "Come on, what do you think I am?"

"A man."

"But not a pervert. I do believe in privacy."

I raised my eyebrows. "This from the man who pops up in my bedroom with no warning."

"Here is different."

"How so?"

"Just is."

That actually made me laugh, and I wiped my drippy face. "So now you'd think nothing of watching me?"

"Not with another man. I wouldn't want to see that."

My stomach did a shimmy. He'd be jealous? "So, then—"

"Let's talk about the shower."

"The shower?" I laughed again. "You saying you want to see me naked?"

He chuckled. "Uh, what did you call me a minute ago? Oh yeah. A man."

"But not a pervert."

He laughed lightly again and crossed the room to sit in "his" chair. *To get away from me? Too hot in the room? Hmmm.*

"I'm saying you're beautiful. What man wouldn't want to see you?"

I grinned. "Well, maybe I'd want to see you, too."

"Love to help you out with that, but this doesn't leave." He held out his jacket and dropped it back to rest against his body.

"Damn."

"Yeah."

"Bet you'd be hot." Did I just say that to Alex? It was a weird turn. Even weirder, and not unnoticed by me, was that he'd called me *love*. That was new, too.

A smile pulled at his lips and he gazed unblinking at me. "If memory serves."

Heat ran straight to my face, but I laughed out loud. "Well, don't hold back the confidence."

"You know, you could have it worse. I could have been ugly."

"True."

His expression lit up the room. "Good to see you laugh again."

"Oh God," I said under my breath. I rubbed my swollen eyes and groaned. "I'm too old for all this drama."

"HAVEN'T seen the boss around lately, have you?" I asked Bob one day a few weeks later as I helped him load the vats. Actually, I just held the door open for him; he seemed to do better without me in the way.

"Think he's out of town."

"Hmm."

Not that I wanted more of Jason Miller and his insults, but I did want to know the status on the car damage and how much that would cost me. His insurance hadn't called mine back with the estimate, so I was in limbo.

"Boat's there, but car's gone, so I assume."

"Boat?"

Bob jutted his head to the left as if that nailed it. At my vacant expression, he said, "The little houseboat in the cove around the point from here? You've seen it, right?"

"That—that's his?"

"Yes, ma'am. He lives there."

And drives a BMW. "Where does he park his car?"

Bob looked up patiently. "Next to the dock."

Stupid points for me. "Who lives on a boat?" I said absently.

"A guy whose ex-wife took the house."

I stared at Bob, or actually at his hump, since the way he leaned over I couldn't see his head.

"How do you know all this?"

Bob stood upright and stretched, adjusting his metal leg. "He talks to me."

"Really?"

Bob's grin displayed his many gaps. "Guess I just have one of them faces."

I laughed. "I guess you do. So what else did you find out?"

"He gave up everything except his boat and his car, let her have it all, then she sold everything and moved to Texas."

"Here?"

"Hour from here. That's where he goes when he takes off."

"To see her?"

He stood upright and gave me an exasperated look. "To see his son."

I felt my jaw drop. "He has a son?"

Bob shook his head and laughed. "Do you talk to anyone?"

"Clearly not enough."

We finished up and I locked the place down, filled with anticipation for the evening. Riley and I had plans to go to Miss Olivia's for dinner. The elusive Grady had arrived, so she was ready for company. I was ready to relax and let my guard down a little.

Riley, on the other hand, acted like I'd signed her up for the army.

"God, it's a setup, Mom," she said as she stomped back and forth from her room to mine. Mine had the better bathroom.

"No, it's not."

"Bullshit."

"Watch your mouth."

I got a disgusted sigh as she tossed her mascara on the counter.

"Please! I mean she seems nice and all, but I am not going to go sit on the porch and drink lemonade with some hayseed hick."

I choked back a chuckle. "Who said anything about lemonade?"

"I'm just telling you—"

"Look, we are going because my oldest, dearest friend invited us to dinner. I never asked you to wear a party dress and pearls, okay? Go Goth and scare the crap out of him, I don't care. But act right."

"Whatever," she mumbled. "Where *are* all your friends, by the way?"

I stopped, straight iron halfway to my head. "What?"

"I haven't seen you talk to anyone or run across anyone other than Miss O. You never have, come to think of it. That you appear to like, anyway. I mean, everyone couldn't have left like you did, did they?"

I blinked and opened my mouth to say—something. But that something told me we had ten minutes and it wasn't the time. Again. I went back to mauling my hair.

"Yeah, I guess they did."

"Well, I can't say I blame any of you."

Standing on Miss Olivia's still-green porch with my sulky daughter was surreal. Like I'd stepped back in time. Except for the lock on the door. That was new.

The hunk that appeared on the other side of the screen was new, too. I bit my bottom lip to keep from laughing as I watched Riley's eyeballs fall out of her head. He held open the screen door for us, and I winked at her as I walked past her and touched her cheek.

"Close your mouth, boog," I whispered. "Mosquitos are bad."

Chapter 6

I didn't even get an eye roll. I think all her body parts were in shock. So much for hayseed.

"You must be Grady," I said, offering my hand to the at-least-six-foot-or-more beautiful boy-man in front of me.

"Yes, ma'am."

Which was good until he just squeezed my fingers.

"Oh no." Couldn't help myself. Must have been that house. "Look, sweetie, take my hand." I grabbed his hand and showed the stunned kid how to do it properly.

"Oh, kill me now," I heard Riley mumble behind me.

"Careful what you wish for," Miss Olivia said as she entered the room with a plate of warm brownies.

Grady took his bewildered look to his aunt, who gave him no slack.

"Learn something there, boy." She gestured to me. "Shake a woman's hand like you mean it. Not like she's some frail, inferior creature."

All his good looks dissolved into panic mode. "I—I wasn't—"

"I know all that, boy. Just relax." She shoved the plate at him. "Now go on and introduce yourself proper."

He grabbed the plate and stared at it as if it could rescue him. I held out my hand again.

"Hi, Grady, I'm Dani Shane."

The poor guy grinned crookedly and grabbed my hand in a death grip. "Grady Grader."

I heard Riley's brain whirl, I swear I did. She wouldn't be able to resist it.

"Seriously?" she piped in from behind me.

He pried his fingers loose and I watched his eyes do a similar dance to hers as he settled on Riley. Except his went north to south and back again. I turned to see a mischievous light spark up in her face as she did the up-and-down thing right back at him. His crooked grin got bigger and he laughed quietly.

"Yeah. My parents thought that was cool."

"Drugs?"

"Psychosis."

They laughed and were instant friends. I watched her in awe. Even in the presence of a guy that turned her insides to goo, she was savvy and witty and sharp. I envied her that. I would have been a babbling idiot.

"Y'all want some lemonade?" Miss Olivia asked.

I looked at Riley and chuckled to myself. At that point, she would have drank motor oil hanging upside down from a tree if he asked her to.

"How's the car?" Miss Olivia asked, yanking me back to my misery.

Riley followed Grady and the brownies to wherever he was going and I snagged one off the plate as they passed. I'm not sure either of them was aware there even still was a plate.

"How did you know?"

She gave me a look that called me stupid. "Dani girl, I probably knew before you got out of the car."

"Sad, but true."

"Plus, I hooked Grady up with him a couple of days ago to do some maintenance on his boat, and he mentioned it."

"What?"

"He's good with that stuff. Wants to work on engines and parts and things. Gives him a chance to do something other than piddle around here."

I shook my head. "Jason Miller has this whole town in his pocket."

"Hey, now hold on there, girly," she said, as she placed a gnarled hand on my arm. "So far, he hasn't done a thing to bother anyone. Well, except Marg, and that's just because he changed some rules. You got issues with him because he got under your skin."

I flinched at that. "No, he didn't."

She flicked a hand at me. "Please. I can almost see the bumps."

I scoffed at that. "Let's set the table."

I passed Riley in the kitchen and thumped her so that she didn't sprout roots as she chatted up Adonis.

"It's set," Miss Olivia said as she led the way into the dining room and settled into her chair.

"Oooh, fried corn," Riley said as her eyes took in the spread of fried everything and veggies soaked in butter. "Like a real supper."

I turned to stare her down till she looked up at me and laughed. "Just kidding, Mom."

"Yeah."

"He's good-looking, too," Miss Olivia said as she speared a chicken breast.

I frowned. "Who?"

"Jason."

I slumped. "We're still there? Really?"

"Who's Jason?" Riley asked.

"Mr. Miller?" Grady asked, looking at his aunt, who dutifully nodded and grinned at me. "He's nice, but kinda scary."

"Ain't no *kinda* about it," I said, and then froze as I replayed it. *Ain't no kinda?* Dear God, I was regressing. The culture peeled off me by the minute.

"Who's Mr. Miller?" Riley asked, looking at each of us.

"My boss," Grady said as he piled a precarious amount of food onto his plate.

"My boss," I echoed.

"You know, boy, you can have seconds," Miss Olivia said. "You don't have to hoard it."

He glanced at her as he scooped more. "I'm not. This *is* the first helping."

"Lordy, lordy," she mumbled.

"Wait. You and Grady both work at the bait shop?" Riley asked.

"No," he answered. "I help out on his boat. Fix stuff, keep the engine maintained."

"He lives on that boat," Miss Olivia said, with a direction to her tone that I knew had a look to go along. I refused to look up and acknowledge it.

"That's what I've heard," I said, picking at my green beans. "No grass to mow, I guess."

"Oh yeah, there is," Grady answered. "He has me mow all around the dock."

"So, how is he scary?" Riley asked.

"Just intense. He never stops."

"Never smiles, either," I said.

"Oh no, he can be funny, you just gotta catch him in the right mood."

I raised an eyebrow. "Guess I haven't caught that mood."

"Well, you did rear-end his car," Miss Olivia said to my immense delight.

Riley nearly spit out her lemonade. "You hit your boss?"

"That was you?" Grady asked.

I glared at both of them. "So, where are you from, Grady?"

He looked at his aunt, then back at me and chuckled, wiping his mouth. "Denton, ma'am."

Riley snickered. "That means the subject is changed."

"You here all summer?" I asked as I slathered real butter on a real potato—as opposed to the pretend ones in a box.

"Yes, ma'am." He looked at Miss Olivia again, who smiled back at him and winked.

"Mm-hmm," I said. "So what did you do to piss your parents off that bad?"

His head jerked around along with Riley's. Miss Olivia just chuckled.

"Ma'am?"

"Mom!"

I laughed and snagged a roll out of a red basket. Grady's face went just as red.

"What was the crime?"

"Oh my God, Mom, I swear," Riley muttered, and if looks could've killed me, her bright blue eyes would have turned me to dust.

"Don't swear at my table," Miss Olivia said, making Riley pink up as well.

Grady focused on his plate.

"Go ahead, boy. Get used to this town knowing your business," Miss Olivia prompted.

No kidding.

He pushed some food around and didn't look up. "I took my mom's car out one night with some buddies. Got drunk and—hit a building."

I blinked. Riley closed her eyes, probably seeing her prospective summer go up in smoke.

"A building?"

"Yes, ma'am."

I looked at Miss Olivia and worked at not smiling, which was hard because she was having too good of a time.

"Wow. Anyone get hurt?"

"Just the car."

"And now here you are."

"To help out Aunt Olivia."

I nodded, not that he could see it since he only had eyes for the center of his plate.

"I have apple pie and ice cream for dessert," Miss Olivia said in an attempt to finally bail him out so he could eat in peace.

"You made pie?"

She shook her head. "Hell no, Dani girl. I bought it frozen and stuck it in the oven."

Well, finally. "Works for me."

The kids went out on the porch with their lemonade after supper, and the irony cracked me up. Riley wasn't happy enough with me to crack up with me so I let that go. Miss Olivia put food away and I washed dishes in the sink like no time had ever passed.

"She is you made over, that's for sure, yeah."

"I like to think I wasn't that mouthy."

"Mmm—not to me. But you did have an edge to you."

"That was just survival."

She looked sideways at me, and her wise old eyes saw more than she let on. "How you doing with that now?"

I paused, feeling the slippery soap run over my hands, watching the water clean the plate free. I'd never be cleansed free like that.

"It's just my life, you know. Never known it any other way."

"And now?"

I tilted my head. "Now, Riley has to learn that, too."

She put a finger to her cheek. "Wait—why?"

"Ah, yes. There's that. Do you remember about Alex?"

"Hard to forget that," she said. "I wish some hottie would come visit *me*."

"Well, Riley can see him, too."

Miss Olivia took a step back. "Holy smokes, girl."

"Yep," I said, handing her a plate to dry. "Don't you just want to be me?"

"So the hayseed hick wasn't a complete waste of time?" I asked once we got in the car.

She gave a little groan. "Is it possible for you to walk away from this conversation?"

"Not even slightly."

She sighed, but I saw the smile. The glow. She was smitten. "Look at you. You're all googly."

She ran fingers through her hair. "Please don't say that word, Mom. It's disturbing."

"Googly, googly, goog—"

"Why don't we go by Ella's?" she interrupted.

"Who's Ella?"

"It's a restaurant on the river—they have really good desserts."

I pointed at the house we were still parked in front of. "We just ate our weight in pie."

"Yeah, but they're supposed to have this phenomenal hot banana pudding crunch, and we can bring Pop some."

"How do you know about this place?"

"Carmen told me."

Oh yes, Carmen. Yay.

"Okay," I said as I pulled out of Miss Olivia's curvy, hedge-lined driveway, onto the gravel that lined all the river-access roads. "So where is this place?"

"Instead of turning at Pop's road, keep going—"

"At the boat launch?"

"Yeah, down close to there."

"Have you been there already?"

She turned my way. "Yes, in my invisible car."

"Don't act like walking is out of the question," I said. "You walk everywhere else."

"So speaking of that, when do I get a car?"

Something fell out of my mouth. Something like a laugh. "With my invisible money? Let's go look tomorrow."

I'm sure there was an eye roll, but I couldn't see it in the dark. We pulled up and parked, and I admired the pastel lighting that oozed from the multicolored windows.

"This is cool. How long has it been here?"

We got out and strolled along the wooden boardwalk that flanked the perimeter of what was essentially an old boat-house revisited.

"Carmen said it opened last month."

Just inside heavy double-oak doors was a giant framed chalkboard that looked to weigh a thousand pounds and sported several specials in different-colored chalk. The floor appeared to be the original planking, and stainless steel buckets lined the wall, filled with napkins and wrapped silverware. A waitress snagged a bucket and nodded for us to follow her.

"We're just getting something to go," I said, pointing at the menus under her arm. "Could we just—?"

The perky little blue-eyed blonde glared at me as she handed us the menus.

"Thanks."

I opened one and we perused with our heads together. Bread pudding. Key lime pie—yum, but already had pie. Already had lots of things, but somehow still ended up with my nose in the dessert section. Giant brownie volcano. Sopapilla cheesecake.

"Oh, now that has possibilities." I pointed at what was likely death by butter.

"I recommend the banana pudding."

The voice came from behind and over my head, and I spun around to see Jason walk past us and up to the counter.

Riley's eyebrows shot up. "Who's *that*?"

"Satan."

"He's hot."

"Like I said."

Jason turned around and leaned against the counter as the hostess disappeared for parts unknown.

"It's served hot instead of cold. It's unusual but really good," he continued.

It took me a second to remember what the first part was about. I just nodded.

"Just my opinion," he said with a shrug.

"Told you," Riley said, still engrossed in the menu.

The hostess came back with a bag of something warm and steamy and handed it to him.

"You just get back in town?" I asked.

His eyes narrowed. "You knew I was gone?"

"Um, you weren't at work. Bob told me you were visiting—"

"Yeah," he said, cutting me off. "Just got back."

Okay then. "Supper?" I asked, with a gesture toward the bag.

"Most nights."

"You eat here that much?" Riley piped up. Never one to be shy.

He looked amused. "I'm not much of a cooker, and I get tired of nuking ramen noodles and ravioli."

"Dude, there's other things you can do."

I put a hand on Riley's back and prayed for her to shut up as he chuckled. An actual smile—wow. Must have been what Grady was talking about.

"This is my daughter, Riley. I'm sorry."

"No problem." He stepped forward with his free hand and shook hers. "Jason Miller."

"Jason—" She threw me a questioning look. "Your boss? Grady's boss?"

"Yes."

"This is the guy you rear-ended?"

There are moments I wish her to be sucked away with a giant turkey baster. That was one of them. A small grin played at the corner of Jason's mouth, however, and his dark green eyes actually looked kind of happy. From that perspective, I could see the "hot" comment. Normally, I just got the scowl.

"You know Grady?"

"Miss Olivia is a very close friend. We just ate over there, actually."

"And it was bad?" He gestured at the menu.

"No," I said, laughing. "Riley just wanted to come get some dessert."

"Well," he said as he turned to leave and the businessman morphed back in front of me. "Like I said, you can't go wrong with the banana pudding."

I was pretty sure that was the most conversation we'd had outside of the bump and grind with our cars. We'd managed to keep work talk to the bare minimum of nods and grunts.

"Jason?"

We all turned to see Shelby Pruitt Sims, in the perfect little blue workout suit. With the perfect little head tilt and the perfect amount of lowered zipper.

"Hey, Shelby."

"You eating here again?" she said, touching his arm and smiling.

"Evidently."

She turned to Riley and me as if we had just sprouted there. Perfect smile was accentuated with perfect nails as she flipped perfect hair out of her eyes.

"Hey, Dani," she cooed, looking from me to Riley and back. "What are y'all doing tonight?"

I held up the menu. "Ordering."

Riley pulled it back down, as I interrupted her. "Mom."

Shelby's eyebrows twitched ever so slightly. "She's just a little firecracker, isn't she?"

Riley looked up and smiled, unsure. "Ma'am?"

Shelby switched gears. "How's that little job going, Dani?"

I smiled as best as I could around the acid that churned in my stomach. "It's doing just fine, Shelby. Thanks for asking."

She turned to Jason then, head tilt still in play. "You know, Dani and I went to school together."

"Really?" he responded, going on automation. Disinterest settled on his face. This was the guy I knew.

"Yes, we did." She smiled back at me as if we were co-remembering. "I was a cheerleader like Micah is now, and Dani was—what did you do, Dani?"

The heat rose up through my neck to my scalp. To hell with Jason being there, Riley was witness to this fiasco. Watching this bitch try to step on me like it was twenty years ago.

"I graduated," I said on a laugh that I crafted from somewhere in my core. "That was all that mattered. All the rest faded off once the real world kicked in."

Shelby's smile disintegrated into what was just a twist of her face. To downplay her golden days was tantamount to blasphemy.

"Yep," Jason said, which snapped Shelby's head around. "High school is only interesting in high school."

Shelby's mouth worked a smile back out. "Well, of course," she said with a nervous little laugh. "But it's still fun to remember."

"Depends on what you're remembering," he said, peeking into his bag. I'm sure he wished he was eating it. "For me, college was better."

"Ditto," I said. "College was awesome."

Jason smiled, and his face transformed again. "I have to leave you ladies. Supper's getting cold." He did a chin lift at me as he passed that I took to signify an all-out good-bye.

Shelby's face was priceless. She'd been dethroned and flicked aside. But before she could turn that prissiness on me, Pissy Number Two walked up. The perky little blonde waitress we had so rudely put out sidled up next to her mom and yanked her hair down from its ponytail, fluffing it out.

Shelby composed herself. "Have you met my daughter, Micah?"

I held out a hand. "Hi, Micah."

"Hey." Limp hand. Disinterest.

"Hey, I'm Riley."

"Hey."

The girls smiled and sized each other up, and I felt a second of pride as I watched Riley. She had no outward sense of inferiority. She stood there eyeball to eyeball with Shelby Junior with no reason to feel less than.

"Micah made varsity cheerleader for next year," Shelby said again.

Micah sighed and looked around. "Mom, quit."

"That's cool," Riley said.

"Whatever."

Micah pulled off her work belt, which sagged with napkins and straws and an order pad, and dropped it on the counter.

"Can we go, Mom? I'm exhausted."

The prom queen smile returned. "See y'all later."

"Yeah, much," Riley muttered after they were out the door.

"Riley."

"Seriously, Mom, that woman is—messed up."

The snicker came out. Couldn't stop it. It just bubbled up and fell out of my mouth.

"And I don't see all this evil you talk about with your boss. He seemed okay to me."

"Well, he was a little different tonight."

Or a lot different. A whole new side of him kind of different. The kind of side that interacts with other humans instead of looking to feed.

"He kinda defended you."

I frowned. "You think?"

"Yeah, he sure put Miss I-Used-To-Be-A-Cheerleader in her place."

"Yeah, I guess he did."

"She was your *friend*?" Riley asked.

"No." I studied the menu again. "Can we pick something now? I didn't know this was going to be a long-term event."

Right on cue, the new hostess appeared and looked from Riley to me. "So, are you ready?"

"What do you want, boog?"

She rolled her bottom lip between her fingers. "I guess he kinda sold me on the banana pudding."

"You already wanted it."

"Yeah, but I was considering my options."

"Well, I'm going with that, too."

"Aw, you'll have something to talk about at work so maybe he won't be so mean," she said, with an elbow to my ribs.

I gave her a double take. "No, no, no, my girl. It's nothing like that."

She held up a hand. "Whatever, I'm just saying he's better than that Alex dude that keeps popping up."

And then I broke out in a sweat. We got our order and left, and once we were on the road and immersed in banana pudding aroma, I threw it out there.

"About that Alex dude—"

"I know, y'all have a thing."

My mouth went dry. "What? No, there's no thing."

"Please, it's so obvious."

"How?" How was I having this conversation?

"Mom, you choke whenever you see him. You don't breathe. Clearly, you have something heavy with the guy, and he gets all—zoned or something."

Zoned or something. Oh man. "I totally breathe. It—it's just more complicated than that."

"Whatever. I don't care. I don't want to know about your love life; I'm just saying it's no secret you have the hots for each other."

I rubbed my face. "Oh God."

"Don't be such a prude, Mom. I mean, he's cute, too. Just a little—weird."

"Yeah, well."

"New wardrobe would probably help. Satan just seems more normal."

Cute. "Mr. Miller."

"You have to call him that?"

"*You* have to call him that. He's my boss."

She opened the door. "Whatever."

Chapter 7

Iᴆ I concentrated, I could follow one ceiling fan blade around and around. I kept losing it, though, and had to start over. I threw the covers off and spread out. It was a muggy, sticky night, ticking with energy. I could almost feel the hairs on my arm move. Not unusual, but I was tired of staring at that damn fan with its whisper that always sounded like voices to me. At the bookshelves holding books that hadn't moved in twenty years. At the design on the far wall made from the faint nightlight. At the ninety-two plastic slats of the window blinds, the three bottom ones bent.

The clock glared at me with its stupid blue numbers. To think I'd almost bought one of those clocks that shoot the display up on the ceiling. I would have been homicidal.

I needed sleep. I needed peace. I needed sex. Probably sex would get me the other two, so I thought about that. Because if it was just the release, the shower massage and some dirty thoughts would join me in that little party and take care of that. But I had the feeling that was too much of a quick fix. I needed the real thing. The full treatment. I needed a warm, hard body.

"Okay," I said to the fan as I swung my legs all the way out of the covers. "I'm officially frustrated now."

Which brought my thoughts to Jason, completely unbidden. I pushed them away and thought about his scowl and grunts and his dented freshly birthed car instead. But then, there were those aviators and those green eyes—

"Oh my God, really?" I slapped a hand over my face.

Was I really that hard up that one fifteen-minute session of civility with Castro had me humping my pillow?

I looked at the extra pillow.

And then I got up.

It's no secret you two have the hots for each other. Oh, Alex. The "hots" was an understatement. That man could make me sweat from fifty yards away. But there was history there, too. Years of in-depth conversations and friendship. And who the hell was I kidding? His smile could reduce me to goo. I would bet that he could have had any woman he wanted before he got married. Married. Funny that I never thought of him as married. He didn't wear a wedding ring. I never gave much thought to Alex's personal life when I was younger. About him being someone's husband and father.

That made my heart lurch. He had a daughter, too. I wondered if it was hard for him to see me with one, now. They all died together, that's all I knew. For as much as Alex knew about me, he was very private about himself.

"How sad is it that my hottest fantasy is with a dead man?" I looked around. "And that I'm talking to myself?"

It was a pity party, I admit it. Sleep deprivation brought on by worry brought on by Riley's new networking—plus the fact that I kind of wanted to see my boss naked and trying to hide the fact that I'd always wanted to see Alex naked—piled up on me.

I flicked the lamp on and flopped into Alex's chair. It would have been a good night for him to show up. Keep me company. Then again, no. I'd have probably broken all the rules and jumped him and given us both seizures or something.

Antsy, I got back up and snagged the stack of clean clothes still on the dresser. A corner of color in the closet caught my eye and I moved some boxes aside to see my baby box nestled back there.

I called it my baby box. My dad always called it that—it had my mom's scrapbook and my first everythings. And my favorite, most precious possession. A picture taken of my mother and me. In that very room, right after I was born. Both of us all messy and exhausted, our heads close together. My dad said the aneurysm burst about an hour later. He wasn't in the room, he'd left for just a few minutes and came back to find her still holding me. And gone.

I sat cross-legged on the bed, my faded orange-and-red fabric-wrapped box in front of me. I lifted the lid, browned on the edges from time and handling, and peered inside at my treasures. My mom's love in a box. Dad told me that she always took pictures, even when she was young. That she was a born photographer but didn't have those options.

I pulled out her scrapbook she made when she was pregnant, the plain cardboard covered in mosaic tile so that it weighed a ton. When I was little, I thought it was jeweled. But back then, I thought everything about her was magical because she was such a mystery to me.

I opened the book, careful not to crack the worn spine. Faded photos with colored paper accents, her little remarks and funny sayings written randomly everywhere. Arrows and hearts and smiley faces. She and my dad and their beagle, Bevo, grinning as they pointed at her flat belly, with a bubble cloud drawn to the left that said *puppy in the oven*. A list of possible name considerations on another page, with scratch outs and scribbles to the side. *Samantha* was clearly a contender, as it had four stars and a bubble drawn to it that said, *Nate's*. *Danielle* had three stars and a *mine* next to it.

Several pages in was Christmas, my mom holding a decorated stocking next to her tiny baby bulge.

This was how I knew my mother. How I learned about her. Through all her quips and quirky comments that were never intended to be studied and analyzed so that even the handwriting was committed to memory. I used to wish for some new nuance of information, some snippet of photo to jump out at me, something new. I felt that same old feeling as I looked through it all now. Hoping that my wiser adult eyes would glean something not seen before.

I needed something new. I needed my mom to jump out of the book and tell me what to do. How to do it. I wanted my picture to do its magic. Something like—

"Where the hell is my picture?"

I turned the page back to the one of all the shots of my room done up in black-and-white checks and stuffed animals, and then back to the one afterward of my dad holding me at the funeral, in front of all the flowers. It wasn't there. I touched the yellow spot on the page where it had once been.

I set the book on the bed and dug in the box, rooting through finger paintings and brightly colored lumps of clay that were supposed to resemble something. I thumbed through cards and many other loose photos that never made it into the scrapbook because Dad did good just to get them into the box.

But it wasn't in there.

I closed my eyes and listened to the whisper of the fan above me and played my old game of pretending it was my mother talking to me. *Where is it, Mom?*

Nothing.

I got up and pulled the other boxes out of the closet till the floor was cleared. Nothing. I felt gypped. Like my mother had left. Again.

"This is silly," I mumbled.

I shoved all the boxes back in and just stood there, too

wound up to get back into bed. My gaze fell on a drawing among the mess on the bedspread. Of me and my dad on a dock, him with his blue hat. And my anxiety started to melt.

I picked up the drawing, with its ceiling-flat blue sky and blue choppy water around a brown dock with fish swimming in a see-through bucket. Red-mouthed smiles on both of us as a huge fish with an identical smile hung from my fishing line waiting to nestle in my dad's net.

I walked down the hall to Riley's room, careful to sidestep the creaky spot just before her door, and peeked inside. Covers were inside out and wrangled around her like something you'd see come out of a swamp, but she slept like an angel. I wondered if she'd look through her old drawings one day and feel that same sense of love and security.

My luck, it would be the one she made of being bought at a grocery store.

DAD and Bo were already coffee'd and gone by the time I dragged my dead ass downstairs the next morning. I tried to leave myself a mental note to ask him about the picture later. I probably needed to write it on a wall or something. In permanent magic marker. My brain wasn't on its best game.

The shop door did its jingle when I entered and I gave it a little finger wave. And then stopped when I saw Jason at the counter.

"Hey."

"Hey," he said, glancing up, then back down at a notepad. "How was dessert?"

"Um. Fine." I lifted the counter and joined him. "Since when are you here this early? Where's Marg?"

"On vacation."

"What?"

"For two weeks."

Two weeks of full days with Jason Miller. That must have shown on my face, because he looked almost giddy.

"That a problem?"

I recovered quickly. "No, of course not."

He chuckled. "Of course not."

I looked at him curiously. Weird turn of personality.

"Okay. So—I'll get on the tide reports then." I turned to the coffeepot and stopped. "You didn't make coffee?"

"Don't drink coffee."

I rubbed my eyes. "God."

He laughed softly again from behind me and I shook my head as I pulled out a filter and the Folgers and numbly went through the motions.

"I take it you missed your morning fix?"

"This is my morning fix—most days. I can sleep later if I don't stop to worry about coffee."

"And today was a sleep-in kind of day?"

"Huh?"

He gestured to my white T-shirt and gray sweats, topped off with a ponytail and no makeup. I made an irritated sound and went back to the coffeepot.

"Haven't slept much lately. Wardrobe wasn't a priority."

"Did you get confirmation from Hank on his booking this morning?"

My hand stopped mid-scoop. Hank had a booking? I called somebody. Didn't I call somebody? It was a couple of days ago.

"Um—no. I'll check in a second." I stared at the scoop still in my hand, unable to remember how many I'd done. "Oh, what the hell," I mumbled, throwing in another two. Wouldn't bother anyone but me anyway.

I turned to pull the tour schedules out of the drawer but Jason was in the way. Standing there in his tight blue jeans and black pullover T-shirt. Jesus, I was hard up. He looked up from his pad and I pointed.

"Need to get in there."

His eyebrows shot up, and I realized where I pointed.

"The—the drawer. The schedules are in the drawer."

He looked down. Then back at me and stepped aside. "Sorry."

I yanked the drawer open so he had to move a little farther and stared at the day's schedule in dismay. Had I called Hank? Crap. I snatched up the phone and dialed his number.

"Yello."

"Hey, Hank, it's Dani."

"Sugar, it's a bit early, don't you think?" he drawled.

I watched the slow drip of the coffee and closed my eyes. It was too much.

"I know, I'm sorry, but I need to check that you're lined out for a half day'er this morning."

"This morning?" There was a shuffle as the phone slipped. "Sweetheart, I got nothing today but whatever's on ESPN."

Crap.

"Well, you have a booking—looks like from a couple of weeks ago." I peered closer at the information. "Looks like two kids and an adult at eight o'clock."

"Sweetheart, my boat battery's on charge and I got no time to charter anything on this short notice. Call Jiminy."

I hung up and cursed the day, my life, and the zit I felt growing on my nose.

"Problem?"

I scrolled to Jiminy's number with one hand as I maneuvered the coffeepot with the other.

"Not if Jiminy comes through for me."

"He's out of town."

I set the phone and the creamer container down together with a thud.

"Bob?"

He picked up the sheet. "With two little girls on board?"

I blinked. "Is he gonna eat them?"

"He's a little crude, Dani. He pees off the side of the boat no matter who's around. Doesn't matter. He's out on a bait run anyway."

Jason set the sheet aside and pulled out a bait catalog, as I stared him down. He finally bent to my psychic ability and turned.

"What?"

I downed three big gulps of coffee for bravery. "Who else can we get?"

He smirked. "I was told we have you."

Another swig and then I chuckled. Tried to appear nonchalant. "That's really kinda just a—theory."

He flipped a page. "Well, theory or not, you're all we've got. Should've called Hank ahead of time."

I laughed nervously. "No—see, I know and I'm sorry, but you don't understand."

"Don't understand what?"

The coffee sat like acid in my stomach. "The—the boat—doing a tour by myself. I can't."

"What do you mean?"

"I can't drive the boat. I mean, technically, yeah, get me out in the middle of the river and I can probably steer it. But—getting out there—" I licked my dry lips and tried to breathe normally. "Launching and docking? No. Trolling? Not a chance in hell."

He stared at me. "Marg told me you were backup."

"Well, my guess is none of us thought it'd really come up."

His jaw twitched as he turned and leaned against the counter.

"Well, my guess is you better figure out how to pull this bluff off."

I felt a fine sheen of sweat pop out and I laughed. "Seriously, come on. If Hank can't put a charter together this fast, what am I supposed to do? We have to cancel."

"They'll be here in an hour. It's too late for that."

I peered closer at him. "Why are you so calm?"

One side of his mouth drew up. "What do you mean?"

"You should be panicked, too. You're all calm and—pleasant."

He chuckled and averted his gaze. "My son turns ten today, I guess it's a good day."

"Oh. Well, that's cool." I put aside my misery for a microminute. "Doing anything special?"

A shadow passed through his expression and I instantly regretted the question. Of course *he* wouldn't be.

Jason shrugged. "He probably is. I already had my time with him, sort of. Doesn't matter, though. Still a good day."

I set my cup down as he walked into the back, and in walked Blaine Wilson with Matty Sims. Lovely. I pulled out every drawer I could get my hands on, tugging maps from everywhere. Shit. I was so screwed.

"I'll be damned, my wife wasn't shittin' me," Matty said slowly. A little too slowly.

I attempted a courteous smile through my pending panic, four different maps clutched close. Surely two little girls wouldn't be that hard to buffalo. If I could just get the dad to drive the damn boat.

Matty sauntered to the counter, Blaine tagging behind like his pet ferret. He nodded at the maps.

"Whatcha got going here?"

The fumes that emanated off him pushed me back a step.

"Arranging a fishing tour," I tossed back as I snatched a couple of Jiminy's extra hats from an upper shelf. "Can I help you?"

Matty leaned forward on the counter. "You do tours? I'd go on one of your tours." His speech was slow and drawly and matched his foggy eyes. Still, he grinned like he'd said something fabulous.

I set down the hats and put a finger under my nose. "Wow, Matty, that's some powerful—breakfast—you had."

His grin turned into something snarkier. "Well now, didn't you just turn out all cocky?"

"Can I help you with something?" I didn't have time for all that. I didn't have time for anything.

"Came for some deer corn, but I don't know—" he

slurred. He dragged his eyes around and then back to me. Head to toe. "What else you got?"

I looked at Blaine, who turned his smirk away. I grabbed a nearby pad, refusing to be baited.

"How much corn you need?"

Matty ran a finger down my neck and I swatted it away.

"How. Much. Corn." I stared him down with everything I had.

For about two seconds, we were back at school with me cornered under the stairwell. His body pressing mine against the tile. Same breath. Then I was back. His arrogant sneer was so repulsive, I almost felt sorry for Shelby. Almost.

"A little strange on the side might be fun, don't you think?" he said, his voice raspy. The look on his face said he thought it was sexy.

I felt the familiar prickle on the back of my neck and I almost groaned. *Please don't be you, Alex. Not now.*

"And you always were that."

My head pounded on no caffeine, and an old lady in the corner caught my attention. She wore a blue T-shirt and black stretchy pants on her frail frame, black slip-on tennies on her feet. She had salt-and-pepper hair and was really unremarkable in appearance except for the mischievous twinkle in her blue eyes that hinted at trouble. She winked at me. Great. Another dead winker.

I slugged back more coffee. The old lady came to stand next to Blaine, close enough to make him fidget. It was hard to keep a straight face.

"Corn?"

"Aw, come on." He dropped his voice. "Bet it'd be freaky with you. You still freaky, Dani?"

I blinked and put the pen down, leaning into his stinky breath.

"You still dick-less, Matty?"

Blaine snickered and moved like there were ants in his

shoes. The old lady followed him, so that every place he landed, he had to instantly shuffle again.

Matty puffed up like a blowfish. "You're just jealous, freak show, because you never got you a piece."

I nearly upchucked my coffee. "A piece? Really?"

The old lady walked up close to him and whispered something in his ear that made him quickly grab his crotch and then relax again. I laughed.

"You know what? I think I'll let Shelby have all your *pieces*, okay?"

"Coach Sims!"

Matty whirled wobbly around to greet the voice with a car salesman grin and a shaky hand. A boy of about twelve rattled on to Matty about football while the dad stood proudly by him and held the hands of two younger girls.

Two little girls. Crap.

I turned to grab all my papers, and was about to go look for Jason to ask questions, when he walked through the hall entryway.

"Oh hey," I said, "I think they're here. Early."

"Got it under control?"

"Do I look under control?"

One of the maps slipped free, and he bent to pick it up. As he handed it to me, he leaned to look past me at the group by the door.

"They don't look too scary."

"I want to throw up."

He laughed. A genuine laugh, which I noted as the second one I'd seen in two days.

"You'll be fine."

"No. I won't. I'm gonna make an ass out of myself and then follow that up with probably killing us all." I pulled out their paperwork for the dad to sign. "But hey, if you're good with that, then what the hell."

My pen clattered to the floor, shattering what was left of my composure.

"Shit."

I squatted to pick it up, and suddenly the old lady was squatted in front of me, directly between me and Jason. Her skin was deeply etched and kinda saggy, but her light blue eyes could have been that of a twenty-year-old.

"Just watch," she said in a soft, muted voice.

I opened my mouth but then looked up at Jason by the counter, and I rose, carefully stepping to the side so as not to touch her.

"So what boat do I take?"

Jason shook his head as you would to a child that just wears you out and opened a cabinet with keys dangling from hooks.

"This one is already out and docked," he said as he pressed the key into my hand. "No launching required. Just go in reverse first."

I stared at the key and wished for another life.

"And since when do we call customers 'dick-less'?"

That brought my head back up, and heat rose up my neck. But irritation won over embarrassment.

"Since he wanted to get in my pants and I've seen what's in his."

The corner of his mouth twitched into an almost smile. "Oh?"

"And not in a fun way."

"Oh."

"He's just an older drunker version of what he was twenty years ago."

"Shelby's fortunate."

I just raised my eyebrows at that. I didn't have the fortitude to get into a Shelby discussion.

"Okay." I rubbed at my face and felt lost. "He needs deer corn. I'm gonna go—deal with this. If you hear a loud bang, or we don't come back tonight, send out a search party."

"I'll take care of the corn," he said. A knocking noise

came from the bait room, and Jason frowned his way back that direction.

The girls' names were Celeste and Carole. Eight-year-old twins, but not the wear-the-same-clothes-and-fool-the-teacher kind. The brother left for some kind of practice, while Daddy-O and the rugrats were left with me, all signed in and donned with Jiminy's caps. Celeste didn't look impressed with the hat idea. She appeared to be the potential high-maintenance future cheerleader. Carole, however, promised to follow a more library-aide-slash-valedictorian route.

Celeste kept taking her hat off and tucking her hair behind her ears and replacing it. She had a neon pink rod and reel. Carole brandished a blue one. They were ready to go.

Okay. I downed two more cups of coffee before I remembered I would be out on the water for four hours. *Four hours.* Crap.

"Okay, let's head down to the dock," I called with enthusiasm. Hoping I fooled the dad. I carried the tackle box full of lures and Jiminy's notebook of laminated fish pictures and notations. I would cheat my way through.

I watched the water approach, watched the boat bob gently, and felt the familiar buzz of anxiety fill my body. The sound of distant wind sang in my ears, and I shook my head clear of it. Then, as we reached the boat, the unexpected happened. I heard it. That unmistakable sound of body functions starting to churn, reroute, and spew. I pivoted just in time to see little Carole pull a Linda Blair and blow forth half her body weight in vomit.

I jumped back. Celeste screamed. The dad cursed. Poor little Carole just turned green at the sight of what she'd done all over the dock, and did it again. Thankfully, she missed the boat. And the old lady sitting in it. She winked at me again.

The dad apologized and I turned the whole stinky crying procession around, with promises to reschedule when Carole felt better, and to please keep the hats. I breathed a sigh of relief and told them I'd meet them there in a moment.

When they were out of earshot, I turned back to her.

"What did you do?"

"No offense, but I'd rather my grandkids not be run up on a sandbar or impaled with each other's hooks."

She finished with a gravelly cough. First time I'd ever heard a spirit cough. Kinda figured that went by the wayside with that whole death thing.

"Your grandkids?"

"Yes, ma'am."

I began to laugh. "Oh, that's just priceless."

"They can come back another time," she said. "Maybe I will, too. This looks like fun."

"You made her throw up?"

She shrugged and her eyes lit up again. "You learn things." She got up slowly. "And now she'll go home and be allowed to curl up in bed and read all day."

I narrowed my eyes. "What she really wanted." She shrugged again and smiled. I pointed a finger. "You're good."

"You're welcome."

I laughed nervously. "That, too. I was petrified, thank you."

We walked back up the dock, and I was careful to face forward like I'd long trained myself to do.

"By the way, what did you say in Matty Sims's ear?"

She chuckled and coughed again. "I told him his penis was out."

"And he heard you?"

"Nah, just gives him the idea."

"Man, where were you when I was in high school?"

"Breathing."

* * *

THE back door was open as I walked back up, and the banging noises I'd heard earlier were noticeably louder.

"I'm back," I said, peeking in. "Holy crap."

"Can you hand me that wrench?" he said, his voice strained from what appeared to be a nearly upside down position he was in.

I followed his finger to a rusty tool on the floor in front of the minnow vat. A floor now evenly covered in about a half inch of water. I handed him the dripping wrench and gingerly spattered my way around him. He had the cover off the water pump by then, and the motor made sounds like a giant card caught in a wheel spoke.

"What happened?"

"A hose ruptured, I think. There's some electrical tape up front in the drawer. Go get it so I can wrap it before it completely pops."

"That's making the noise?"

"No, that's making the mess."

I smirked behind his head. As I turned, the noise stopped. "Hey, you fixed it?"

"Temporarily," he said with a grunt as he tightened something a little more.

He was still on his knees in the water, and his jeans soaked it up. His hair stood out on end. It dawned on me that I'd never seen him messy.

"Hmm."

"This thing needs to be replaced, but for now all I have are Band-Aids."

"It's pretty old."

"It's ancient," he said, blowing out a breath. "And if I turn it off, it may not come back on, so can you please go get that tape before I prune up?"

The question barely crossed his lips when it happened.

The hose burst under the pressure and whipped out, catching him across the side of his neck before he could duck.

"Jason!"

He fell sideways and attempted to grab the wildly gyrating hose as it blew fish water like a power washer.

"Crap!" I lunged and tried to grab it, too, but it sliced across my legs and arms faster than I could move. "Ow! Shit!"

Jason scrambled for it and his angle hit the hose so that water spewed directly up my nose at two hundred psi. I half screamed, half choked as I fell backward onto my ass with a splash. The burn made my eyes water and I coughed as I groped blindly.

"I got it," he yelled, but it slipped past him and walloped me upside the head.

"Ack! Geez!"

Suddenly it hit my hand at just the right millisecond, and I wrapped my fingers around it. Not a great moment, because the power pulled me with it. Right into Jason. We went down like dominoes, me on top of him, nose to runny nose.

Chapter 8

Two seconds later, the water stopped. Just stopped. We both head-snapped toward the offending hose—and past it to where Bob stood, his hand on the switch. His mouth twitched with the effort not to laugh.

"You turn the water pump off, it'll stop," he said.

Jason and I both sucked air, and as we faced each other again, I was suddenly acutely aware of his arms around me and the fact that I was sprawled against him. I let go of the limp hose and pushed myself awkwardly off him, till I could sit. In water. But there reaches a point when you can't get any wetter.

"Holy crap," I sputtered.

Bob gave in and let out the laugh. "I heard the screams, thought I'd come check."

"That was him," I said, pointing.

Jason sat up and gave me a look, then managed a laugh through his recovery. He swiped a hand through his wet hair, then got to his feet. He held out a hand for me, but I was already on my way up, courtesy of the minnow tank.

"What a mess," I said. "Is there a drain in here?" I surveyed the concrete floor.

"There is, but it's old. It'll drain slow," Bob said as he pointed at some random holes.

"It's done this before?" Jason asked.

"Once or twice."

"Great."

Bob and Jason surveyed the water pump and the health status of the shrimp while I plucked up random floating garbage.

"I'm gonna run home and shower this funk off me if you don't mind," I said, drawing attention back to me. "You should, too, this reeks."

I pointed to his soaked clothes that clung to his body. Then following his gaze, I looked down at myself and instantly brought my arms up. My drenched thin white shirt and equally thin white bra now outlined everything. In vivid detail.

Bob quickly excused himself and wobbled away, while Jason, who was only a foot away, lifted his gaze to my face.

"That might be a good idea. Need a jacket?"

I raised an eyebrow. "Cute. No, thanks. I'll be back in thirty minutes."

But then he raised a hand to my hair, which temporarily paralyzed me until he pulled away a shrimp whisker.

"Oh God." I cringed and attacked my hair.

"Wait." He brushed fingers against my right cheek. "Was that me or the hose?"

I touched the bruise gingerly. "Same guy that got you."

Taking his cue of brave moves, I touched the side of his neck softly where a giant red welt raised.

"It's okay, I'm good."

"Hit you pretty hard."

He smiled. "I'll live." His eyes fell to my shirt again, which this time was only inches away. "Go get changed."

I slogged into the house, met by Bo and his very curious nose. He stuck to my leg as I stopped short at the foot of the stairs, when I noticed Riley curled up in my dad's ragged brown recliner.

"Hey, boog, whatcha doin'?"

She looked up from the album in her lap, and then did a double take. "My God, Mom, did you fall in the river?" Then she put a hand to her nose. "Or the sewer?"

"Neither. The shrimp vat had some issues. Why are you still home?"

"Am I not supposed to be?"

Bojangles let out a loud snort against my thigh, then swung his tail hard as he appeared to grin up at me.

"Don't you work now?"

"At noon." She gestured toward an old wall pendulum clock. "It's only eight fifteen, Mom."

I rubbed my face and winced at the contact with my cheek. "Is that all?" I pointed at the yellowish brown photo album. "What's this?"

She shrugged. "Thought I'd blow some time with a nostalgia kick, but this one was on top of the other ones." She nodded toward the wall of shelves that had every nuance of our lives. "Don't think I've seen it before."

Neither did I. And I had made them all. The one she held was older and unfamiliar.

"What's in it?"

She flipped a few pages carefully. "Most of them are black and white. Old people pictures."

"Really?" I sat on the arm, then remembered my state and got back up.

She flipped back. "Looks like Pop when he was young, see? And your mom?"

Funny how calling her Grandma or something similar was as foreign to Riley as "Mom" was to me. Hard to name someone you've never met.

I'd seen old pictures of my parents before, even a few of these pictures. But not in an album like this, with notes and comments like my baby album had.

"Put it in my room when you're done, okay? I want to look at it later."

"When you're not covered in shrimp slime?"

"Pretty much."

Bo jammed his nose into my crotch right then, and that was enough.

"Seriously! Go eat something!"

I must have been at least semi-menacing, because he semi-ducked.

"Hey, can I go hang out with Grady after work?"

"Grady?"

"Mm-hmm." She continued to slow-turn the pages. I stood there and waited her out. "I'm not gonna look up for you to make this cute, so you may as well give it up."

"Then you don't want to go badly enough."

That got me the look I so richly deserved. "Mom?"

"There, I feel better now."

"God, you're so weird."

My shower was too quick to really enjoy, but I refused to throw my hair up and go again. I blew it out and dressed at least in jeans. Then grabbed the mascara on the way out.

Of course, Alex waited at my car. I looked back over my shoulder.

"Riley's in there."

He held up his hands. "And I'm not doing circus tricks."

"Well then, feel free to get in, because I've got to get back to work."

I grimaced as my door groaned so loudly I thought it might jump off and die.

"Such dedication," Alex said with a grin as he just—ended up in the front seat. I prayed that Riley didn't see that.

"So—bored today, are you?"

He looked me over with that sideways sexy way of his and I tried not to listen to my libido.

"Aren't you just all fresh and perky for work in the *mid-*

dle of the morning?" he asked, then frowned as he leaned forward. "What happened to your face?"

I putzed down the gravel road that led off the property. "The shrimp vat blew a hose and flooded the bait room. I was in the way."

"I didn't realize you had such a dangerous job," he said with a crooked grin.

"Me, either," I said on a laugh. "Ugh, the whole back is drowned in funk."

"Was it just you?"

"Me and Jason."

I refused to look. I swear, I felt his eyebrows raise, and I wouldn't look at him. It reminded me of Riley just moments earlier, and suddenly I felt her pain.

"Jason. That was the Nazi, right?"

I pulled my bottom lip between my teeth. "Yeah."

There was a pause. "You didn't look this good the first go-round this morning."

I frowned at him. "Thanks. And you weren't here this morning."

He shrugged and looked forward. "Hmm."

I shook my head. "Some people call that stalking, you know."

"They don't have a sense of adventure."

I laughed. "Oh, okay."

We were nearly to the shop when a memory hit me.

"Hey, remember those old family pictures? Of my mom and dad?"

He pulled out his sunglasses and put them on. God help me. "In your box?"

"No, the other ones. They were just loose. Come to think of it, I never did know where they came from. I guess my dad just had them out—handed them to me." I shook my head. "I can't remember."

"Don't know. Why?"

I flipped a hand to wave it off. "Riley just had an old album I don't remember seeing before."

Alex looked at me. "Really?"

"Mm-hmm. I'll check it out tonight if I don't fall into a coma first."

He randomly touched buttons on the dashboard console that did nothing. "So, what's the deal with Jason?"

"He's my boss."

"And?"

I feigned major interest in a road sign. "There is no *and*. That's all."

I felt his eyes bore a hole in the side of my head, but I swore to hold out. My right ear started to twitch.

"Hmm."

Thankfully, we arrived, and in typical Alex fashion, he gave me a sideways almost smile and walked around the side of the building as I went in. I took a deep breath and pulled my head back to the world everyone else lives in. I strolled in for the second time that morning and threw a casual smile out to Jason and two female customers who were clearly throwing pheromones to him.

"I'm back. You can go."

The ladies turned around with an expression like I'd just killed their dog. They were obviously immune to the smell. Jason looked a little grateful for the interruption, which I had to laugh about a little inside.

"They want to book a fishing trip for their boyfriends," he said, nodding at the schedules he had on the counter. "I'll be right back."

"Okay."

He gave me a once-over as he began his exit. "You look better this time around."

Geez. "Get going, will you?"

He laughed and was out the door before the two women could bat their highly packed eyelashes.

"Okay," I asked, "so are the guys serious fishermen, or just want to go have a good time?"

I got blankness.

"If it's serious, they won't have a good time?" the blonde with pink stilettos finally asked.

"Of course. If they are into the fishing, that in itself is a good time," I responded. "But if they aren't into meticulous fishing and high-tech tips, and want something more casual and laid back, then I'll know how to match them with a guide." Yin or yang. Jiminy or Hank.

"Mark'll want the real deal," the brunette with drawn eyebrows and D cups said as she fished out a red leather wallet from her Dior clutch. "He can do casual on his own."

"Yeah, whatever," said the blonde. "Tony'll roll with it."

I nodded and pulled Jiminy's book out on top. "Will this be paid together or separate?"

Brunette looked at blonde. "I'll get this, and you get the body wrap and wax this afternoon."

"Cool."

"Cool," I echoed. Wow.

I took care of three more bait orders, which I did very carefully since the room still had about an inch of standing water. Then I had a bright idea to aim an oscillating fan down that hallway to send the smell the other direction. Jason would think that was smart.

And that thought halted me as I stooped to plug it in. Why did I care what Jason thought? Maybe because being sprawled on top of him earlier was the closest thing I'd had to sex in years. Maybe I needed to break the other hose.

Lord.

Jiminy came by. Lisa Marlow and her giant son came by, which was actually helpful because without Jason, I needed some muscle to move some feed. Fifteen other people came by. Still no Jason.

After two hours, I started to wonder. Was he so high

maintenance that it took him that long to get ready? Surely not. Was he the type to ditch responsibility and think of ten other things to do before returning? He didn't strike me as irresponsible. He struck me as anal. He was so OCD on rules and procedures, I couldn't imagine he'd just bail.

I didn't have his cell phone number. Well, I guess technically I did somewhere on a random piece of paper from the fender bender. But I wouldn't be able to find that again if my life depended on it. I dug around the counter a little, looked on the board by the register, for a Post-it or something that might sport his number. Nothing.

Three o'clock, my quitting time, came and went. Something was definitely not right.

I picked up the phone to let Riley know I'd be late—when there it was on speed dial.

JM HOME

"Well, kiss my ass."

My elation was short-lived, however, because the number rang unanswered till it rolled to voice mail.

"Jason. Leave a message."

"Hello? This is Dani. That's one heck of a shower you took. Are you okay? Are you even hearing this?"

Crap.

I went ahead and called Riley and Dad, then dialed Jason at least twenty more times as I fumbled with the afternoon register report and counted the money. Because the later it got, and the more empty ringtones I listened to, the more agitated I got. And the more worried I got. Not sure why I was worried about a man I barely knew, except that it seemed very out of character from what I could tell.

My mommy paranoia began to build, with images of his pristine pampered car rolled into the river, or wheels up in the big ditch around the corner. I worried he would boil to death in a too-hot shower. Lying there alone. Wet. And naked.

And that's when I knew just how pathetic I'd become. And that I was closing early at—I glanced at my watch—4:24.

I checked the bait vats and sloshy floor, kept the fan on, bagged the report and the money, put it in the safe I'd been told about under threat of death and dismemberment by Marg, and locked the door behind me. Anyone in need of bait or feed or Miss Olivia's soaps that desperately in the next hour and a half needed a life more than I did.

Halfway down Jason's road, my stomach tightened. What did I expect to find? What right did I even have to go check? When the boat *and car* came into view, however, my head went back to the shower scene. And not the pleasant version.

"Shit."

I slammed my car into park, ignoring its rock-and-roll groan, and broke into a trot down the narrow dock. There was an old bell on a pull string on a wooden pole. My hands shook as I yanked on it, sending the thing into a frenzy. I already had the next plan in play as I scoped out the boarding ramp leading to his door.

I abandoned the useless bell—because obviously if he was dead or dying, what the hell good would the stupid bell do—I boarded the ramp, crawled over the rail, and gave one cursory look toward the water as I knocked and grabbed the lever at the same time.

The door swung open out of my hand as I recoiled and just about swallowed my tongue.

"Jesus, Dani, what the hell?"

Jason stood there with a wild and somewhat bewildered expression.

"Um, exactly!" I sputtered.

"What?"

I rubbed at my face and then patted my chest, telling my heart to slow down.

"Shit, I thought something happened to you. I thought

you died in the shower or something." Then I caught a whiff and wrinkled my nose. "Then again—"

His face went dark and he turned from the doorway. "I never made it there."

Okay. Didn't know bathing was so stressful. I felt awkward and uninvited there in the doorway, as he fiddled with mail on the table. A quick look around told me that it wasn't a typical bachelor pad on a boat. He'd made it a home. The small wooden table to the right held a three-wick candle in a pewter bowl. A tray of mail and a brown paper–wrapped package sat to one end. Built-in shelves framed a window, and held a multitude of books and pictures. Beyond that appeared to be a small efficient kitchen, and the walls I could see from where I stood sported a variety of more photographs. Black and white, mostly.

I blew out a breath and backed up a little. I was bewildered by the whole scenario. He was there all day, changing from Jekyll to Hyde instead of cleaning up. He wouldn't answer his phone. He didn't come back to work.

"Whatever," I said, flailing a hand as I turned. "Glad you're alive. See you later."

"Hang on," he said, his back still to me. His tone was irritable, as if he'd really rather I *not* hang on.

"It's good, Jason." I headed for the rail.

"Dani."

It was just my name, but the tone and reverberation of it made me turn. His expression made me stay there.

His eyes were red and angry, his jaw hard. He looked as if every nerve ending might pop all at once. But behind the anger was something almost palpable, even from several feet away. Something raw.

He gestured jerkily toward the door. "You can come in if you want."

Did I want? Hell, I had no idea anymore.

"Um—"

"Please."

I met his eyes and frowned slightly. "What's wrong?"

He shook his head and motioned for me to come in again. Crap. I walked past him slowly, past the festered shrimp funk, and looked around again. There wasn't much more to see except a hallway that I assumed led to bed and bath. From that angle, there was another wall of built-ins with doors. The whole thing was a genius use of space, giving a sense of more than was really there.

Jason shut the door and rubbed at his face and hair absently, shoving a lock of hair up. I thought he looked disheveled back in the bait room, but he was definitely on a downslide.

"What's going on? Why didn't you answer the phone?"

He reflexively looked down at his cell clipped to his jeans.

"No, your home phone. I couldn't find your cell."

"I wasn't here," he said. "I just got here about ten minutes before you did."

I opened my mouth to ask the next obvious question, but he held out a hand.

"Can you give me a minute?" He reached behind his neck and pulled his shirt off before I could blink. "I need to go get this off me, I can't stand it anymore."

I just nodded. My tongue tied itself in knots at the sight of him shirtless. He was muscled and hot and at that moment I didn't even care if he'd rolled in pig manure first.

"Just—sit down." He motioned to a comfortable chair in front of a TV. "I'll be back in a second, and I'll explain it all."

"Okay."

Not that I had many options. I could leave, but then I'd miss the encore. And I cared much less about where he'd been all day than I did about seeing him come out shirtless and clean and smelling good. Maybe even in a towel.

"Jesus, Dani, get a grip," I mumbled as I sank into the chair.

Water came on down the hall, and my eyes fell on one of the photographs across the room. A black-and-white one of a little boy gazing out a window. I got up for a closer look. Same dark hair, intense eyes staring out at the world. To the right of that photo was another one of the same boy, grinning at the camera with construction-paper bunny ears.

As I moved around the room, to the wall photos, the framed ones on the shelves, all the pictures contained some version of Jason's son. Alone, with friends, with grandparents, with Jason. Nothing with his mother, I noticed.

I stepped around the table and my hip nudged the package. When I moved it back, I noticed it was addressed in black Sharpie from Jason to Connor Miller in Kenington. That was about an hour west of Restin. An equally black stamp RETURN TO SENDER was plastered across it.

"Oh no," I said softly as I ran my fingers over the offending words. I didn't know the details, but I was pretty sure this was the root of it.

I picked up a framed photograph of the two of them in baseball uniforms, Jason's arm across his son's shoulders. Jason was evidently the coach, and they posed all serious and manly.

"That's the last picture we took together."

I whirled around and jumped so hard I was lucky not to drop it.

"Shit, you scared me." I returned the frame to the shelf, careful to fit it back to the faint shape in the dust. "Sorry, didn't mean to snoop."

He was shirtless again, God help me, in a pair of jeans, barefoot, and his hair still damp.

"Actually, when people say that, they just didn't mean to get caught."

I held up my hands. "Swear to God, I didn't steal anything. Your photos just sucked me in." I motioned around the room. "I love pictures."

He nodded and walked to the fridge. "All I have is water and orange juice. Want something?"

"I'm fine."

He snatched a bottle of water for himself and took a long swig, then looked at me.

"Time got away from me today, I'm sorry."

"It's okay. I just have an overactive mind, I guess."

His eyes narrowed. "You were actually worried about me?"

I felt my neck heat up. "I was *concerned*. You did get walloped with a pissed-off hose today, after all."

A small smile softened his face. "Well, thank you for the *concern*, then. How's the bait room?"

"Still a little soggy, but better."

Jason nodded absently. His face went dark again as he ambled toward the table. He touched the name written on the package and landed heavily in the nearest chair.

I wasn't sure what I was supposed to do. Leave him with his thoughts? Sit down with him? Offer a body massage? I pulled out a chair and sat.

"I didn't believe it when his present showed up back here today," he said finally, not looking up. "Thought there had to be an explanation."

I waited.

"I was there day before yesterday. He was distant but at least past hating me. I told him something special was on the way." He ran a hand across the package. "I couldn't wait for him to get it. Then it showed up here."

"Did you call?" I asked.

"Yeah. Told him happy birthday and that for some reason his gift came back."

"Didn't he understand that?"

"He hung up." Jason's jaw tightened. "Shocked the hell out of me. I called over and over and finally got his mother. She said she'd sent it back because he didn't want it."

I closed my eyes. That wouldn't be good.

"So, I just got in the car and went there. Just like I was—not thinking. He was at a swimming party with a few kids and of course I embarrassed him."

"He'll get over that."

"I won't," he said flatly. "He used to be so proud to be with me. He was my little man. We were tight. And now—he's so angry. He was *embarrassed* of me."

"It's the age," I attempted.

"No. It's his mother." He looked back down at his hands. "When we first split a year ago, he was okay. Sad, but okay. They moved to Texas to be closer to her family, so I followed to be closer to him."

"Understandable."

"Something happened after that. He won't take my calls. And she won't talk to me about it. I don't know what the deal is; they're both avoiding me."

I smelled a new man in the picture.

"Do you think he's just mad about the divorce?" I asked. "I mean, sometimes kids act out and then blame the one who left."

"I didn't leave. She did."

I bit my lip. "Oh. Sorry."

"He might not realize that, though. I tried to make it easy on everyone. I never made a fuss over it. I didn't fight her. Maybe I should have. Maybe he thinks I didn't care."

"Jason, I'm sure he knows—"

"Really? How are you sure?"

I was taken aback. "What?"

He shook his head and rose from his chair. "I don't know why I'm telling you all this. I've never told anyone my private business."

I frowned. "I didn't ask you to tell me anything. I was just listening."

"Well, I'm sorry I bothered you with it."

Clearly, I was dismissed. "Bother me? I'm getting whip-lash right now. That's bothering me."

He rubbed at his eyes. "I'm not good company right now. It's been a long day."

I glared up at him and got up. "Really now?" I dug my keys from my pocket and turned for the door. "Sorry for your day."

I was out and down the ramp and across the dock before he could say another word. I kicked myself for caring. For feeling bad for him. For letting my guard down.

I threw my car into gear and drove the minute around the cove to my dad's house, blind with annoyance. Bojangles met me at the door again, but he didn't get the love he wanted.

"Men are pigs, Bo. No offense." He didn't look offended.

No one was home yet, and that was a good thing. I needed to unwind. Look at that album, maybe take a nap. But it wasn't in the living room or on the shelves. It wasn't in my room or Riley's.

"What the hell?"

Irritated but too tired to spend more time on the chase, I flopped onto the living room couch. I only remember one or two thoughts before I succumbed to the black hole. And both of them involved Jason.

I awoke to the smell of cornbread, but I couldn't pull myself out. Lack of sleep had a firm grip on me and it tugged me back down. It took Riley's laughter in the distance to finally pull me out of my coma. I sat up and got my bearings, which threw me when the windows were all dark.

I wandered into the kitchen to see my dad ladling chicken gumbo into bowls for Riley and Grady. Oh yeah. Memory dawned. Hanging out after work. God, I felt like I'd slept for a year.

"Hey."

All three heads turned my way.

"Hey, sweetheart," my dad said, nodding my direction. "My gosh, what did you do?"

I rubbed at my face and winced at the bruise. "Oh yeah. Little equipment malfunction at work."

He put down his ladle to come tip my chin up like I was eight and peer at my war wound. "You feeling okay?"

"Yeah, just finally gave in to sleep deprivation, I guess. God, I feel drugged."

"Hey, Mrs. Shane," Grady said as he waved a spoon at me. "Riley invited me to eat."

I gave him a thumbs-up. "Cool." I remembered the album. "Hey, Ri, what did you do with that album today?"

"Put it in your room," she said around a sneaked bite of cornbread.

"I didn't see it."

Riley shrugged, and I was too foggy to care. I grabbed a bowl and decided I needed sustenance. I went out on the front porch with it and a glass of sweet tea and settled into the swing. I breathed in some of the best night air we'd had in a long time. Dry and humidity free. A full moon lit up the porch. It was beautiful.

"Yes, it is."

I turned to my left to see Alex against the rail.

"You read minds, now?"

"Just a guess." He pushed off and came to join me on the swing carefully. "It's a great night."

I took a big bite of butter-soaked cornbread. "To follow up a sucky day."

"Sorry to hear that."

"Men are assholes."

Alex started to laugh. "Cut to the point, there."

"It is what it is."

He looked down wistfully. "Supper looks good."

"Mm-hmm. Dad's gumbo is the best."

"I miss food."

I looked at him. "Can you smell it?"

He shook his head. "No, but I remember smelling it. Tastes. Touch." He met my eyes.

I swallowed, and it had nothing to do with the food. We sat in comfortable silence as I ate, and I couldn't help but wish for that in a real way.

"Did you used to do this sort of thing with your wife?"

Alex looked at me like I'd sprouted wings. We never talked about his life much. Or at all, really. It always turned back to me.

"What?"

"This." I held my hands out. "Just being together sharing space."

He smiled and looked off where the darkness soaked up the trees, lost in his memories, I guessed.

"Yeah, I guess we did. We had a back patio we used to sit on. We'd put bird food out and watch the birds and squirrels fight it out."

I was stunned. A piece of Alex's life. I was almost afraid to acknowledge it for fear he'd realize the blunder and stop. He caught me staring and did a double take.

"What?"

I looked away and laughed lightly. "Nothing. You just— never talk about that."

"About birds?"

I gave him a look. "You know what I mean."

He let out a sigh and looked away again. "That was so long ago, Dani." He got up slowly. "Walk with me."

Chapter 9

WE strolled down the steps, through the yard, up the gravel road. The stars were pale with such a bright moon, but the sky was perfect.

"What was her name?" I finally asked.

Alex put his hands in his pockets, eyes focused downward as if he were studying the dirt pass under our feet.

"Why?" he asked, his voice quiet.

"Because in all these years, I've hardly learned anything about you."

"You've never asked."

I shrugged. "I was young, Alex. Selfish." I peeked at his profile. "I'm asking now."

We walked a few more feet and I felt his eyes on me. "Her name was Sarah."

I felt a lump harden in my stomach. Sarah. Sarah and Alex. Alive. I cleared my throat as my ears started to ring a little.

"How did you meet?"

"At work."

"At—I don't even know what you did—God, how horrible am I?"

Alex laughed. "I had two jobs, actually. I worked at a bank during the day, and a boat shop most nights."

"Wow, that's pretty different."

"Well, the boat shop was my dad's, so I grew up in there." He chuckled. "Later on, I did it more as an apology than a need."

"What do you mean?"

"I was supposed to take the business and I caved to the white-collar world instead."

"Ah."

"Yeah." We passed a few more steps in silence.

"Are your parents still alive?" I asked.

"I'd be in my seventies, Dani."

"Oh yeah, guess not." I toed a rock. "So you were a banker."

He laughed. "Hardly. I was a peon."

"And that's where you met Sarah?" That was weird, to say her name. His expression showed the same thing.

"Yeah."

I let a moment pass. "What was she like?"

At his pause I chanced a look, and saw the trace of a smile on his lips. I was instantly hit with a pang to the heart. Then he looked at me and I looked away.

"Funny. Beautiful, and completely unaware of it. And infuriatingly hardheaded at times." He made a random move as if to twist at a wedding ring, and then glanced down as if he just remembered it wasn't there.

I laughed to myself. "Sounds like Riley."

"Sounds like you."

We had made it to the main road, toward Ella's, and I could see the warm glow from the windows. Back in the public eye. So I made sure to keep my voice down.

"What?"

"Evidently, I'm sucked in by stubborn women."

"Excuse me, I don't think I sucked anyth—" I had to stop, but the connotation was already there. Alex started to laugh.

"No, I'm sure I'd remember that."

I blew out a breath. "Yep, it's certified. Men are assholes."

He laughed again and spun to walk backward in front of me.

"So do you miss her?"

The question was across my lips before I could even form the thought. *Why did I say that?* He stopped and therefore I had to as well or run into him. He never flinched, just trusted that I'd stop. We were only inches apart. He stared into my eyes for a moment before closing his, and I wanted to pull it back.

I was mortified that I'd hurt him. *Did he miss her?* How stupid of me. I opened my mouth to take it back, but he opened his eyes then and they were clear, like the conversation had never happened.

"Alex, I—"

"Shh," he whispered. "Go down there. Relax. Have a beer. Have some pudding."

I blinked. "Beer and pudding."

"Don't knock it." He smiled. His poker face was back on.

But not for me. I shook my head. "You know everything about me, Alex. My weaknesses, my secrets, *everything.* You know down to the second my daughter was born and what I had for dinner that night. I care about you. I just want to know you like that."

His jaw twitched, and he looked away.

"I didn't mean to hurt you," I continued. "I'm sorry I went too far."

He met my eyes instantly, with an intensity that made my toes tingle.

"They were my family, love." His voice cracked a little, and my stomach flipped over. "I miss them like I miss breathing. But that is my cross. And it was a long time ago. Please leave it there."

I felt hot tears burn the backs of my eyes. "I'm sorry."

He shook his head and inched closer. "You never have to be sorry that you care about me."

"What do you mean, 'your cross'?"

He dropped his head. "Good night, Dani."

"Too much again?"

He smiled and winked at me, but the playfulness was gone. "Good night, Dani."

He turned and walked away. I stood there, stunned. I'd never heard so much of Alex's life. Sarah. Alex loved a woman named Sarah. The name made me feel weird. What was that feeling in my stomach? Jealousy? No—I didn't think so. Not so much jealousy, as maybe a reality check. The reality that he wasn't Superman or something invincible.

Or all mine.

He'd had a life, and love, and family and friends, all before I entered the picture. And lost them. And for reasons I'd never understood, he never crossed over. I assumed that they did, or he'd be with them.

Alex and Sarah. And a daughter with no name.

For now, I stood in the middle of the road alone, pondering questions that no one was there to answer. So I decided to go for the pudding.

I pushed open the heavy wooden doors of Ella's to muffled music and a troubled mind. And I realized with a start that it was because for the first time in my life I was sharing Alex. As stupid as that may sound. Not that his past was something not there before, but it wasn't there for *me* before. My selfishness claimed him for myself, like all he existed for was me. Granted, he only talked about me and always turned subjects off himself so he was a coconspirator in the madness, but still. As an adult, I should have seen past it. I should have realized that there were at least two others that occupied his heart and mind that were far more than just names.

"Hi. Do you have a pickup or are you meeting someone?"

I blinked and found myself face-to-face with a flushed heavyset girl with the prettiest dark eyes I'd ever seen.

"Um—" I guess eating alone wasn't one of the choices. "Just ordering some dessert."

She took my order and asked if I wanted to wait at the bar or there in the lobby.

"There's a bar?" I looked around and only saw buckets.

She smiled. "Yes, ma'am. It's seafood buffet night and we have live music on weekends and Tuesdays." She pointed to a hall on the right. "We'll bring your order to you if want to go check it out."

Wow. Like a real grown-up with a life. What a concept. Halfway down that hall, I caught a glimpse of myself in a huge mirror with a jolt. Holy crap? Straight from a drooling nap to walking all the way here with mascara smeared, a bruise on my cheek, no lipstick or blush or even my hair brushed.

I did a quick hair repair, smoothed it down, swiped under my eyes, and bit my lips to give them some color. I stepped back to survey the effect.

"Hope for dim lighting, Dani," I whispered.

The next set of doors opened to a whole new world that fortunately for me did include dusky lighting and an eighties cover band.

I wasn't the type to go sit at a bar alone, but this was technically a restaurant, right? Just happened to have entertainment there. And as I looked around, I noticed it also happened to have a large majority of the town. Apparently, this was the hot Saturday-night ticket in Bethany.

Tables overflowed with diners as they mauled barbecued crabs and sucked on crawfish heads. Beer flowed and personal garbage buckets filled up with mangled shellfish parts.

I saw way too many familiar faces, so I turned to find a corner of the bar I could hide in, and ran smack into Jason. Again.

"Oh crap."

"Hey." His face didn't say *hey*. It said *beat me with a stick*.

"Hey," I said back.

He backed up a step and ran a hand through his hair and down across his eyes as if I'd just worn him out all over again.

"Saw you come in and I was gonna tell you to come sit down but I don't know if that's safe."

I gave him a smartass look and took a quick inventory of the bar. There were three empty stools in the corner. Nice, dark, and wouldn't have to stay long anyway.

"I'm just waiting for dessert, I can sit up here."

He gave me a don't-be-stupid look. "Come on."

He turned and clearly meant for me to follow. I opened my mouth to protest, but he was already halfway back to a table. I could have ignored him, but I did have to work with the guy, so with that justification I trudged in his wake.

He sat at a tall table with stools, facing the band, and so I took the chair to his right. He had a mug of beer in front of him that looked relatively untouched. Unfortunately, the timing wasn't great because the band was on a break, and a spooky Evanescence song was on so we had nothing to pretend to focus on.

"Want a beer?"

I shook my head. No matter what Alex said, beer and pudding just sounded nasty.

"Have you eaten?"

I nodded. I was acutely aware of two tables of "problem people" to my right, and I felt the heat rise in my neck as I heard my name mentioned in their chatter.

He looked frustrated with me. "Okay, next question." Then he dropped his eyes to the cardboard coaster in front of him. "I'm sorry about today."

I blinked. Was that a question? "Um, okay."

He kept his eyes cast down, tracing the pattern of the coaster with a forefinger. "It was a really bad day today, but that's no reason to—anyway." He shrugged and stood the coaster on edge.

"It's okay."

"Not really. I shouldn't have been like that. Guess I'm not used to having anyone care enough to listen—much less come check if I'm alive."

I laughed at that. "Call it morbid curiosity."

"Call it what you want, my own wife never took that much time to see what I was doing."

I studied him as he balanced the coaster and then leaned it against the glass. His vulnerable side peeked out, and the last time it did that, he yanked it back and barked. I didn't have a great record so far that night with "wife" conversations, either, so I proceeded with caution.

"I'm sorry."

Jason looked up, narrowing his eyes slightly. "How's your face?"

My hand went up automatically to check it. "Oh, it's okay."

He nodded and I had the distinct impression that small talk was about to run its course. "Your daughter seems all right."

I smiled and pulled a packet of sugar from a square plastic cup so I'd have something in my hands.

"She's my everything."

Which reminded me to send my everything a quick text about my whereabouts, in case they got worried. I had just gone out on the porch to eat, after all.

"I take it her dad isn't around?"

A small laugh came up unbidden. "No."

"Do they still have a relationship?"

I knew he asked to get some bearing on his own situation, but there was no comparison. It was like apples and elephants.

"She never knew him."

He frowned, and I could imagine the thoughts going

through his head. But his eyes weren't defensive for once, the walls were down, so I decided to go for broke.

"Look around this room, Jason. I grew up here and can name at least fifteen people in here close enough to eavesdrop on us, but did you see anyone speak to me?" Jason's eyes did a quick scan of the room. "I got away from here and moved to Dallas for twenty years, but that didn't change anything. Riley's dad was no different than anyone else."

"He left you?"

"That's an understatement."

Jason took a swallow of room-temperature beer. "My wife left me. Not for anyone else, she just didn't want *me*. How do you make that logical for a ten-year-old?"

"How do you make up a father for a child who thinks she was bought at the grocery store?"

He chuckled. "Okay, you win."

"Her dad was a con man. And yet I still tell her it was a one-night stand with a great guy I never saw again."

"Why?"

"So she doesn't feel like half loser." I waved at a waitress and ordered a beer after all. "We haven't had that many men around, so she doesn't relate easily to them anyway. The last thing I want is to add 'sired by a troll' to her insecurities."

A smile played at his lips as he focused back on the coaster. "I know where she's coming from." At my quizzical look, he continued. "I grew up in three different foster homes."

That got my attention. "Wow. Really?"

He nodded. "Fell into the system when I was seven, and aged out at eighteen. People want babies, not kids old enough to remember their baggage."

"Man, I'm sorry. That sucks."

He sat back and pondered that. "I don't know. It was better than where I started out."

"I can't imagine not growing up with my dad."

"What about your mom?"

"She died when I was born."

"Sorry."

I shrugged. "What about yours?"

"My mother was an addict. Never knew my dad."

"Okay, you win."

He laughed, a genuine laugh that was infectious. "One of my foster dads always said that what doesn't kill us makes us stronger."

My beer arrived, and I raised it to him. "Touché. You know, that applies with your son, too."

He looked back down at his hands, and I wondered if I was back on foreign ground again.

"It will get better, Jason. It just may take some work. And some time."

He nodded slowly. "Yeah." Then he scanned the room. "What's the story here?"

"You mean with me?" I smirked. "I'm surprised that they haven't already bent your ear."

"About what?"

I took another swallow. "I never quite fit in when I was a kid. And small-town minds never let that go."

Those green eyes of his locked in on mine, and for once in my life, I didn't look away. It was liberating.

The band came back and broke immediately into a fair rendition of an REO Speedwagon song. Two couples got up to dance in the small square of floor. I sat back and enjoyed the music. Enjoyed being out. In public. Without scrutiny.

They played an Elton John song next, and then Foreigner's "Waiting for a Girl Like You." Three more couples locked up. And before I knew it, Jason was up and pulling at my hand.

"What—no—" I laughed. "I don't dance."

"What doesn't kill us—".

"Oh, but it might." I tried to pull my hand free but no luck.

"You've plowed into my car, landed on top of me, and

tried to break into my home. You owe me." Then he just put on an endearing expression that I didn't know he was capable of. "Come on, don't shoot me down."

"Oh crap." But I was on my feet, and in four more steps, I was in his arms.

Everything in me stiffened. "How do you know I won't step on your feet now?"

"Instinct."

I felt the low rumble of his laugh.

"Relax," he said low above my right ear. "It's just dancing. Nothing scary."

"Um—" I could hear my heart thump in my ears. That seemed kinda scary.

"Just relax."

I closed my eyes and tried. Concentrated on the music and the fact that his body was tight against mine. A body I'd seen part of and knew was as good as it promised to be under the pullover shirt and jeans. Focused on the warmth of his hand that wasn't sweaty and prayed that mine wasn't. Thought about the interesting proximity and angle of his head to mine, and how he smelled like soap and wood.

"I don't even remember the last time I danced," Jason said after several moments.

I did. "Riley is sixteen. So that makes seventeen years ago, probably."

He laughed and leaned back to see my face, I guess to see if I was serious. "Okay, you win."

I laughed with him, and it happened. I felt every muscle unlock and let go. I even let go of the breath that felt stuck in my chest.

The song rolled to an end, and Jason did a finger twirl and turned me with a flourish.

"Well, look at you," I said with a grin. I felt more female than I had—ever. Light. Sexy.

"Whoo-hoo, Dani Shane!"

And it all tumbled down with one voice and one set of

hands clapping right behind me. I twisted to see Shelby Sims's inebriated face. I felt them—all the little muscles and nerve endings in my body—as they got reacquainted and braided themselves into the intricate knots I was so familiar with.

Shelby's normally perfectly applied eyes were smeary and smudged in the corners, and her lipstick was left to remnants in the cracks.

"Well, don't y'all just look all sweet," she gushed, her eyes noting that Jason still had hold of my hand. She tilted her head all cute. "Hey, Jason."

"Shelby."

She touched the sleeve of my nothing-special T-shirt and cooed, "Wow, Dani, you just look so pretty. Step out for a big date, tonight?"

I felt the heat come up through my ears. Why did she make me so defensive?

"It's not a date—"

"Where's your husband, tonight?" Jason interrupted.

A fake laugh accompanied a smile that seemed too slow on the take.

"He's doing his thing, I'm doing mine," she drawled, doing her best to lock eyes with him and be sexy.

I wondered *who* was doing Matty's thing. Another slow song came on, and I saw her eyes light up.

"Well," she said slowly, like her mouth got stuck. She sidled up to him, unconcerned with me. "Since it's not a date, how about my turn?"

A laugh escaped my lips, as I turned to walk back to the table, but Jason still had my hand. He pulled back and I turned, surprised.

"I wasn't done," he said, his gaze fixed on me. "Sorry, Shelby, some other time."

I was speechless. Shelby backed up and walked away without a word. I'm sure she was boiling, but I never saw her face. I was too in awe.

"Wow."

A mischievous smile tugged at one corner of his lips, and he pulled me tighter than we were before.

"They're going to talk anyway," he said in my ear.

I managed to peer sideways enough to see Shelby sit down in a huff at a table of her cohorts. I had a flashback to the high school cafeteria. I cleared my throat.

"She's not gonna take that gracefully, you know that, right?"

"Do you care?"

"Only if it affects Riley."

He nodded slightly as if he just remembered that. We were so close, my face was in his neck and he smelled delicious. I avoided the urge to lick him.

I knew all my tension had returned but I didn't realize it showed, till he jiggled my hand and squeezed me. He lowered his head so that his mouth was against my ear.

"Relax."

Jesus. Just his lips against my ear nearly had me on the floor. How's that for relaxed?

"Thank you, by the way," I said after a bit. He lowered his head again to hear me.

"For what?"

"For that back there with Shelby." I laughed. "I mean, we're gonna pay for it, but that was—really nice."

He tilted his head to look at me, which put our faces so close, I could have twitched and touched him.

"Who said I was being nice?" he said with a smirk. "Maybe I was selfish."

I let the smile come that wanted to and watched his eyes drop to my lips and hold time still in that moment that could go either way.

The song decided it for us. It came to an end and lights changed, as a more upbeat one replaced it. Our eyes met again, and we both blinked away the intensity as we let go of each other and made our way back to the table. My heart pounded five hundred miles an hour, making me almost light-headed. Lord, I hadn't experienced all that physical rush stuff in a long time. A *long*, long time.

We sat and both grabbed our mugs for a quick swallow and something to do. A waitress approached with an apologetic smile.

"I'm afraid they lost your ticket when I checked on your dessert, so they're fixing you up right now. Sorry for the wait."

I gave her a wide-eyed look. "No problem."

Jason set his mug down. "You totally forgot about that, didn't you?"

"Completely."

We both smiled. It was different then, like we'd crossed a line, but yet not. And things felt very blurry. Till I caught Jason's expression as he looked past me and frowned. I turned to follow his gaze and that was a mistake. I met with an entire plate of shrimp scampi across the right side of my face, shoulder, and down the front of my shirt.

"Oh!" I was on my feet in seconds and turned to look face-to-face with Matty's sidekick, Blaine.

"Oh damn, Dani, I'm sorry," he said, his mouth oozing the words but his droopy eyes darting.

I heard the snickers behind him, and I leaned to my left to give them my full attention. Everything went red in my brain. Lisa Marlow and another woman looked down at their plates, as if hoping I wouldn't turn them into lizards. I walked around Blaine to Shelby, dimly aware of Jason on my heels, and it was everything in my power not to yank her up by her hair. I flicked a shrimp on her instead.

"Seriously?" I said in a low tone as I attempted to contain the humiliated rage boiling within. "You're really this childish?"

Shelby held up two hands. "I don't know why you're being ugly to me, Dani, but lord, what a mess." She eyed me up and down slowly. "Maybe one of your little voices had it out for you, huh? Tripped Blaine up?"

I stopped breathing and time stopped with it. I was back

in high school. Then another voice intervened, one that wasn't there back then.

"What's wrong with you people?" I heard Jason say, from what sounded like a mile away. "Grow the hell up."

I turned to look up at him, amazed. No one had ever stood up for me before. No one alive. Tears came to my eyes and some of the anger dissipated.

I grabbed some napkins off their table and swiped at my face as I walked away. I met the mortified waitress at the door, pulled a twenty from my pocket to trade for the beer and the dessert she held, and walked blindly back through the hallway, avoiding the giant mirror. I shoved the heavy wooden doors open into the night, and stood on the board-walk trying to push back the emotion.

Seconds later, Jason was by my side.

"You all right?" he asked.

I took a deep breath and forced a grin I didn't feel. "Can't you just see the appeal in coming back here?"

"Why *did* you come back here?"

"Got laid off from Cairn Design and jobs were scarce. Finally had to suck it up."

"Cairn Design? You worked for an ad agency and now you're at a bait store."

I slung scampi from my hair. "Yep. Thanks for nailing that down." I left the boardwalk and hit the road at a clip, wishing I'd ordered five more desserts.

"No, Dani, I didn't mean—" I heard him actually jog to catch up with me. "I'm sorry."

He circled in front of me so that I had to stop, ironically in the same spot that Alex had done that. I couldn't help scanning the area.

He put a hand on my arm. "Seriously, I didn't mean it like that. I don't—always say things right."

"Hmm."

"My people skills aren't the best, and my communications skills are even worse, so—"

"So you're a real catch, huh?" I said in an attempt to lighten up the turmoil in my gut.

He blew out a breath. "I guess."

We stood there awkwardly for a moment, then I gestured toward the road ahead. "Need to get back home."

"Did you walk?"

"Yes." With one of my little "voices." God, I hoped he hadn't heard that.

"So did I; I'll walk with you. You don't need to be out here alone at night."

It was very déjà vu–ish to walk there with one man and back with another.

"Sorry you had to witness that," I said after a bit.

"Seems you're just destined to wear shrimp today."

"Oh God," I said on a laugh. "Yeah, I guess so."

"You handled it gracefully," he said looking sideways at me. "Better than I would have."

I felt the familiar stomach twist of the outcast. "Lots of practice."

"They're idiots."

I nodded. "Yes, they are."

"What was that 'hearing voices' comment about?"

My throat clenched and I broke out in a sweat. "You know how kids are," I said, hearing my voice shake a little. "And Shelby's still the bitch she was back then."

We reached the gravel drive, and I could see the glow from the windows.

"I'm good here, Jason. You don't have to walk me all the way."

"You might get attacked by a bear, you know. You do smell pretty good."

I laughed. "Plenty of garlic."

"You're safe from vampires."

"Well, that's important."

As we approached the porch, I heard voices and realized that Riley and Grady were there. Oh joy.

"Well, hey, Mom," Riley said, laden with innuendo.

"Well, hey, Riley," I shot right back, tilting my head at the sight of Riley draped sideways on the porch swing, her legs across Grady's lap. "Grady."

To his credit, he shoved her legs off of him so hard she nearly fell off the swing, and he got up to stick his hand out.

"Mr. Miller."

Tough choice, going for the boss first or the mom.

"Grady."

"Did you get my text, boog?" I asked.

Riley got up and perched on the porch rail. "Yeah, but Alex had already told me."

My whole body failed me. I rooted to the spot and I seriously wanted to throw up right there. Thank God we were lit only by moonlight, because I was pretty sure I glowed red.

"Who's Alex?" Jason asked.

Grady shrugged. "I didn't see anybody, I guess I was inside."

Riley looked so mischievous, thinking she was playing coy between Alex and Jason. She had no idea.

"Friend of my mom's," she said with a grin at me. "He came by and saw me out here and said you had gone to Ella's for pudding."

I held up the bag. It was all I could do.

Riley sniffed the air. "I don't smell pudding." She sniffed again. "I smell shrimp. Again. But in a good way."

"She had a run-in with a plate of scampi," Jason said.

Riley looked amused. "You sure know how to live it up, don't you, Mom?"

"Yeah, I'm a regular party girl."

She tugged on Grady's sleeve. "Let's go down to the dock."

He followed her like a smitten puppy, and Jason turned back to me.

"Well, I'm here," I said quickly. "No vampires or bears in sight, so I think I'm safe."

"So—Alex is your—what?"

Right now? My aneurysm. "My best friend." Wasn't a lie. And it was the best I could do considering I never normally acknowledged his existence.

"Mmm."

"Thank you," I said quickly before he could analyze and start interrogating. "For tonight. For what you did. And also for the company."

"Ditto. You made a bad day end good."

I smiled. "Now, see *that* was the right thing to say."

We stood there on the second porch step like awkward teenagers till I broke the barrier and reached out and hugged him. He stiffened; I guess it was different being there alone as opposed to a noisy dance floor.

"Relax," I whispered, and I felt him loosen up as he chuckled. "We're on my father's porch, with my daughter right down there. It doesn't get any safer."

His hands came up my back to return the embrace as he laughed lightly. It felt good. He felt good. Really good.

"Have a good night."

"You, too."

And then he was on his way down the long gravel drive. I peered over the azalea bushes trying to see Riley in the night glow, before I gave up and trudged into the house.

For the first time in my life, I hoped Alex wasn't upstairs. I really wanted to do the girly basking thing and think about the odd evening with Jason. Before crustaceans got involved.

Chapter 10

EARLY mornings on the dock were a favorite of mine as a kid. For the solitude, I guess. Not that there was a lack of that in my life, but there was something about the fog on the water, a hint of light glowing through it, water still as glass. Even the animals were still asleep.

Bo was spread across my bare feet as I leaned against a piling. The coffee in my hand still had wisps of steam, but I knew not for long.

When Bo lifted his head and his ears twitched, I followed his nose to see Alex. He was leaning up against a tree, hands in pockets, typical stance for him. Also typical was his distance from the river. The one place I could count on him *not* being.

I knew he would stand there all morning waiting for me, so I tugged my feet loose and hauled myself up. Bo took off ahead of me, running right past Alex. His head swung from left to right, nose twitching. Poor guy could never quite get that he'd spend the next half hour sniffing the yard and never find what he sought.

Alex turned to watch him run. "I had a dachshund named Brandi. I miss her when I see dogs play." He pushed off the tree. "Especially with kids."

Okay, that was new. "What happened to her?"

Alex shook his head. "I don't know. I guess my parents probably got her."

"You never went back to, like, check on things? On people?"

He smiled as if amused and started walking, knowing I'd follow. "It wasn't a chosen vacation, Dani."

"Well, I realize that," I said wryly. "I'm just saying, I mean—you came *here*."

"That wasn't a choice, either."

What? "What?" I assumed he came and went anywhere he pleased. I felt stupid over the amount of things I didn't know about him.

"Brandi was the best dog I'd ever seen."

"Nice dodge. Subtle."

"She could throw her own tennis ball," he said, ignoring me.

I gave him a look. "Of course she could."

He laughed. "No, seriously, she'd roll over and get it out of her mouth with her front feet and shove it. Then get up and chase it before it went under the couch."

A moment went by, and we made it to the porch and sat on the steps.

"Your daughter's dog?"

I felt the tension set up like concrete between us.

"Yes."

I played with a fingernail. "So will you tell me her name?"

"We're doing this again?"

I laughed to keep it light. Or that was the intention. "What? You know my daughter's name."

He got up and stared out toward the water, although it couldn't really be seen from there.

"Your daughter's not dead," he said.

Well, so much for light. "Okay, sorry. I just thought—we share everything else. And yet the most basic things about you are a mystery."

He turned and studied me for a second. "Not a mystery. Private."

A cough came out of its own accord. "Private? This from the man who morphs out of the wall with no notice." I met his hard gaze, determined not to look away. "Fine, never mind. I just thought—whatever. But then don't go chat with mine when I'm not around."

"Oh, that's what this is about."

"No, that just came to mind, actually, but it's relevant."

"So is telling her the truth."

"Oh, wow, that's new." I rubbed my eyes.

"Time's running out, Dani."

"For what? Is she gonna blow up?"

He shook his head. "Don't play that. You know what I'm saying."

"Whatever." I got up. "You want to keep your memories and your life to yourself and play the privacy card, fine. Then mine is private, too. I'll tell her when the time is right."

"Yeah, I can see that's your priority," he said softly.

I frowned. "What does that mean?"

He looked away. "Nothing. You just seem busy."

"You mean last night."

"Nah, you just went for pudding last night." He said that like it was a dare.

I blinked. "Yeah, I did. Got the beer, too."

He rested one foot on a step. "How'd that work out for you?"

"Not bad."

He nodded, but the tension set in his jaw told me that he wanted so badly to say something. There was the sound of movement inside the house and he nodded again toward the door.

"Your family's up. Better go take care of them."

* * *

IT was cool outside, and that was the first hint. The second was that I had on a halter dress. A yellow one. I knew it didn't add up, but dreams have a way of just pulling you along, whispering in your ear to just go with whatever is unfolding in front of you.

A breeze stirred a big tree swing ahead of me, and I walked toward it, curious. We didn't have a swing. As I looked around me at the big rambling trees and spongy earth, I realized we didn't have this yard, either. The swing's ropes were thick and braided, matching the mass of the tree it hung from, and the seat looked to be three inches of thick hardwood and long enough for two people.

As soon as I grasped the rope—which surprised me in its smoothness—I felt fingers brush the back of my neck, moving my hair. Without looking, I somehow knew it was Jason. But why? Why would Jason touch me like that, and— oh—run his lips down my neck like that? My breathing quickened, and I let the delicious sensation tell me that dreams can be fun that way, so I reached behind me to pull his head down as I twisted mine up to meet his lips.

I turned in his arms, wrapping my fingers in his hair, searching those hot green eyes for answers that didn't appear to have questions. We were just there, kissing long and deep and enjoying the feel of each other's bodies—something my nerve endings were vitally awake and aware of.

My skin felt hot against the chilled breeze, and there was a random thought that asked me why I wore a halter dress in cool weather, and actually why I wore a halter dress at all. Then Jason sat on the swing and held it steady as he pulled me onto him, staring at me with a smile and eyes that had changed to blue as I straddled him on the giant swing. More odd random thoughts flitted across my brain that the green actually suited him better and how much easier it was to straddle a man with a dress on.

I felt him hard against me, and that sent a rush of heat through me, but that had nothing on what jolted through my veins when he ran his hands up my thighs. All the way up. Oh, the dress idea had definite advantages, I decided, my head swimming with desire. I closed my eyes as he ran his lips down my neck to my cleavage, kissing the insides of my breasts.

I dropped my face to his hair, and inhaled deeply the aroma of him before he lifted his face, his expression heavy and aroused. And belonging to Alex.

I sucked in a breath and froze, but he just whispered, "It's okay, love."

It was okay? It—it was okay to touch him? Feel his hair in my hands, his body against mine? I lowered my mouth to his and kissed him softly, tentatively. He made a little noise in his throat and kissed me back, working those hands that used to belong to Jason. I pulled back a little and stared at him. *It was the dream thing,* my brain told me. *Roll with whatever unfolds.* But—nothing felt dreamy. It was cold and breezy and the wrong time of year for a dress I'd never wear, in a yard I'd never been to, making out with a man I could never touch, but other than that it was all pretty damn realistic.

I closed my eyes, feeling very awake and yet afraid to wake up, not wanting to lose what I had in my hands. I could smell him, feel him, feel his mouth travel down my neck again. Feel one of his hands come back up to move fabric aside so that he could feed my breast and nipple into his mouth.

"Oh!"

My eyes flew back open, and for a split second I was afraid he'd be Jason again. Then I felt guilty about that. Then I didn't care who he was, because his other hand was between my legs and the thumb was under my panties, mimicking the tongue motion at the same time.

"Oh my—G—"

It was exquisite. And I'd never known the sensation before, yet my body seemed to. I knew exactly how to react, how to move, and another random thought rolled by as I wondered why I'd be wearing panties in a sex dream. I mean, really? Why?

It wasn't Jason. It was all Alex, and I couldn't take my eyes off the sight of him doing what he was doing, my hands clenched in his hair, and I lifted his head and kissed him deeper than I'd ever kissed anyone in my life. I dove deep as his fingers did the same. It was erotic and passionate, and oddly familiar. I tasted his mouth, tasted his skin, I would have taken bites if I could have, just to remember it all.

"Let's go in, love," he said, his voice husky and thick with sex.

I didn't have to agree, we were just there. Dream magic— I loved it. My dress was gone and his pullover and slacks were gone, which I realized in a flash hadn't been black. We were as naked as naked could get, on his chair, but it wasn't his chair. It was bigger and red, and I couldn't care less. I took him in my mouth before I could possibly wake up and not get the chance, and he grabbed my head and moaned. God, he was large and hard and before I could even get the thought of wanting to ride him completed, I was there. Lowering myself onto him and watching his face tense up with ecstasy and want. The chair was perfect for us. I rode him slow and tantalizingly as he worked me with his thumb and made love to me with his eyes.

Once again, my thoughts went to the bed and we were suddenly there. He started low on me, his tongue taking up where his thumb had left off, teasing me till I snatched handfuls of the sheets that weren't my sheets in my hand. Then he was inside me again, and I wrapped my legs around him, caressing his chest, his arms, anything I could touch. I breathed him in, trying to memorize the smell, the feel, the taste of him. I couldn't get enough. And it wouldn't last. Somehow I knew that.

"Oh my God—Alex—"

It was there, it was going over the top, and his eyes—oh God, his eyes wouldn't blink. They burned into mine as he pumped me harder. Like he'd miss that nanosecond of watching me come.

"Baby," he growled through clenched teeth, drawing out the word as if he needed to hold on to it.

His fingers tangled in my hair and his whole body tensed in motion. I shut my eyes to absorb the wave that rolled over me, but then popped them open again. I didn't want to miss this, either. It would never happen again. His eyes burned, as if he knew that, too. Of course he did, I dreamed him that way.

"Love—" It ended in a roar as he drove harder and pressed his forehead to mine.

That did it, I was done. Sounds, sensations, everything crashed around me in one giant rush and I just held on to his ass and rode it out, moaning his name.

"Dani."

I couldn't speak, I couldn't catch my breath. Everything went dark, so I must have closed my eyes.

"Dani."

"Mmm?"

I didn't want it to be over. I didn't want to open my eyes. He felt wonderful, his body felt like heaven under my hands, inside me. Finally. I smiled as he touched my face softly. It felt like petals from a flower. And when I opened my eyes to look into his—it *was* a flower.

Just a flower. A white rose.

"Dani," he whispered, his voice cracking.

He was next to me on the bed, staring down at me like a deer in the headlights. Fully clothed.

"What—" I blinked and licked my lips, still tasting him. "I don't understand."

Then my nerve endings came back to life and I became aware of the air on my bare breasts and the fact that I was on top of the covers with my panties at my ankles and just exactly where my hands were.

"Oh my God!" I bolted upright, yanking my tank top back into place and rather ungracefully pulling pillows over me. "Oh my—holy shit—what the hell?"

Alex toyed with the rose, his gaze still locked on mine.

"Good dream?"

I know my mouth moved—I felt it. But I was way more aware of all the other sensations still tingling to be able to say anything more. A dream. Yeah. That's what it was. Jesus Christ. And he was right there, inches away. Okay, maybe several inches, but the heat from that dream sucked up the space.

"I—uh—wow." I scooped my hair back from my face, and it was damp. Of course it was. I'd just had wild monkey sex with Alex. Oh God. And his expression made my stomach dance. "What?"

"You—that was—" He closed his eyes, looking almost as flustered as I was. "I didn't mean to watch that. I just—"

I covered my face. "Oh God, what did I do?"

"Made me want to really be doing all of it."

I dropped my hands and stared into eyes so full of heat that tingles went to important places all over again. My breathing quickened.

"God, so do I." What? Did I just say that to him? The world wiggled underneath me. His face was right there. I heard a whimper come from my throat as I leaned up at him, and had to stop. Had to fight the urge to kiss him. "I want—I want more."

"More of what?"

"All of it. Your mouth." I was so close.

His jaw tightened and his gaze fell to my lips. "Do you know how long it's been since a woman moaned my name like that?"

I blinked myself a little closer to reality. I would have to guess twenty-five years? Probably nothing on my puny little five. But still, his voice was low and husky and sexy and I was fighting logic. I could still feel his hands on me and the delicious tongue thing.

"Do—do you think we're a little too close to have this conversation?"

A smile pulled at one side of his mouth. A mouth I wanted to get back to and get to know much better. A mouth I could *never* get to know better.

He leaned closer and his eyes danced. "Don't trust yourself?"

I met those eyes. "Not even a little bit. Two seconds ago, you were—" I pointed at nothing, but I needed to do something with my hands. "After that, I'm a little shaky." Certain places still pulsed from the orgasm from hell.

"So am I." His eyes got serious again as he trailed the rose gently over my lips. He stared at its path and said almost to himself, "I'd give anything."

"Me, too," I whispered. Or tried to. A little squeaky noise came out instead. "Even just to—" I trailed off. My heart pounded in my ears.

"Just to what?"

I took the rose from him carefully and studied the petals. "Just to kiss you." I closed my eyes and ran the flower along my own lips. I wanted it back. "I got to kiss you. Feel you. It was so hot. I knew—I knew it was a dream, it had to be just—" I swallowed hard. "But it was so real."

There was a long moment of silence, and when I opened my eyes, the look on his face made my breath catch. Desire. Heat.

"It was—pretty intense."

"Looked like it."

Inner groan. "So, I—I—moaned?"

"Among other things." He blew out a breath and blinked as if shoving the memory back.

"Care to share?" My voice didn't sound like me.

"No."

"Really?"

"You had the good side; I want to hold on to what I saw. Forever." I felt heat warm my ears, and I covered my eyes, but I heard the smile in his voice. "I couldn't help myself, Dani, I couldn't look away. That was the hottest thing I've ever seen."

I dropped my hands. "You know, a gentleman would have."

"Bullshit," he said with a smirk. "A beautiful naked woman having sex with herself and moaning *your* name— there's no man on earth that'll walk away from that."

"Oh sweet God, stop now!" I pulled a pillow over my head.

His laughter, deep and warm, filled the room. How sad that I was the only one to feel its resonance.

"So."

I pulled the pillow down. "So?"

It was new—the expression on his face. Intimate. Familiar. Like a lover. Well, hell, I guess we were. Or as much as we could ever be.

"Were we good?"

"Well, you were here for the audio version, you tell me," I said with a laugh, trying to lighten the air.

"You tell *me*," he said in a voice so low I swear I got wet again.

I licked my lips, and got a little rush when that caught his attention.

"It was—phenomenal," I said. "It felt real, Alex. The boundaries were gone. The stupid touching rules were gone. We were actually making love—" I gestured in a circle. "—all over the room. Or some kind of room."

"Want to go back to sleep?"

"Completely."

He laughed. "So what was the best part?"

"All of it. Maybe riding you in that chair."

He looked back at his chair and made a little groan, rubbing his face.

"Except it was red."

His gaze stayed on the chair a few more seconds before he turned back to me. "Red?"

"Yeah, and other things were a little different, but dreams are like that."

Something flickered in his eyes, but he blinked it away. "What was different?"

I shrugged. "Just—I don't know. I had on a yellow halter dress, which I have never owned, but I think I need to go find one now." I laughed. "Oh, there was a swing." I felt the heat again. "It all started on a swing."

His expression locked in place, and he only blinked once before he licked his lips and sat back a few inches. "A swing."

"Yeah. That's a new one. One of those big flat plank things with heavy rope from a big tree. I don't know, that one's kinda vague." And it started with Jason. But I wasn't going there.

He nodded, and something in his face changed. Like it got far away.

"But if I had to pick something," I continued. "It was— I've—never been kissed like that."

He met my eyes then, heat for heat. "You should be. Every day."

I swallowed hard at the fire in his eyes. It wasn't just physical. He was fighting something.

"Alex, last night—"

"You need to be careful," he said, his voice low.

"What? Why?"

"This thing with Nazi boy."

I blew out a breath. "Really? You're gonna kill this mood with that?"

"I'm just telling you, the guy's got issues. And he lives on a boat."

I laughed at that. "Yeah, I know."

"It's not solid. It's not stable. It can float away."

"And if it does, I'll wave from the dock. I don't care where my boss lives."

"Please," he said. "We both know that's becoming more complicated."

I sat up in bed and crossed my legs, since the sensual part of the evening was clearly over. "And how do *we* both know this?"

He paused for a moment. "I was on the porch when you got home."

I narrowed my eyes. "No, you weren't. Riley and Grady were there. She would have seen you. I would have felt you."

"Okay, I wasn't on the porch, but I did see you after they went down to the dock."

I felt like I was in trouble, and it grated on me. "Okay. But, Alex, nothing happened." I twisted a piece of hair. "God, this is so warped."

"What?"

"I feel like I'm—cheating on you or something."

He blinked and backed up a bit. "Why?"

"Because I just had sex with you," I said, bringing a grin back to his face. "And we're talking about me being interested in another guy."

With the air lightened up a little, he shook his head. "I don't mean that."

"I know but I can't help it," I said. "You've been like— my man. For my whole life. At least in my head you were."

He locked in on me again, and I was unable to look away. "I know." He paused again without blinking. I hated it when he did that. "And I know it's time for you to find that in someone real."

"You are real," I said, the sound of the words fading off.

He held the rose against my shoulder and trailed it down my arm and back. "Who can touch you with more than this."

I felt a knot in my chest that burned.

"I'm sorry I asked too many questions last night."

Alex looked at the flower in his hand, and appeared to get lost in it as I watched him.

"It was called the Sarah Alyssa."

My brain backpedaled, spun, cartwheeled, tried desperately to align that sentence with something I knew to make sense.

"What—was called—"

"The boat."

"The—oh, the boat you built at your dad's shop?" I asked, and he nodded. "You named it after your wife?"

"And my little girl."

His voice all but disappeared on that sentence, and it broke my heart. I suddenly wanted him to keep it private.

"It was a gorgeous afternoon, and we wanted to take the boat out for a celebration." His voice took on a haunted tone, almost as if it were someone else talking. "It was finished, Sarah had gotten a raise, and Alyssa had straight As on her report card."

I smiled. I could picture them as a family, celebrating the basic successes like Riley and I did.

"We dressed up a little. A lot, by Key West standards." He tugged on his jacket for emphasis. "Alyssa made it a big deal. She was so enamored with her name painted on the side, she thought we needed to make it a formal occasion."

"Hence, the black clothes."

"Yes." His expression went dark, and I knew the bad part was coming. "We were having a good time and I lost track of how far out we were. The sky got dark and the storm was on us before I could even register it. Looked like the claws of hell."

I closed my eyes so I couldn't see his pain. I hated to see him like that. He stopped for a bit, tracing a pattern on a quilt with the rose stem.

"I lived my whole life on that coast. Knew the tides, the wave patterns, how to read a storm. I knew better than to lose track of captaining my own boat. I can even see now how that storm was telegraphed in thirty different ways."

"You were enjoying time with your family."

"And it got them killed," he said flatly. He spread his left hand and touched his ring finger. "They depended on me, and I let them down."

Tears sprang to my eyes as I visualized the little girl.

"We were broadsided by a rogue wave and rolled."

"Oh God."

Alex got up and went to the window. "I heard Sarah scream Alyssa's name once, and then she disappeared. I got to Alyssa and tried to hold her and look for Sarah, too—but she was panicked, and it was everything I could do just to keep her above the waves."

"Could she swim?"

He looked out into the yard and nodded, but saw a different scene, I was sure. "We lived on the coast; she could swim before she could walk, but it was fifteen-foot waves. There's no swimming in that. She kept saying, 'Don't let me go, Daddy. Don't let me go.'"

His voice started to break up. "I told her, 'I've got you, baby. I'll never let go.' I held her up for almost two hours in brutal waves and sideways rain, waiting. I prayed. I begged someone to come. My legs went numb. I rolled on my back to float and laid her on top of me. Nothing stayed. It was too rough."

I felt frozen in bed, wishing so badly I could go to him. Hold his hand. Give him a hug.

"She finally gave out and started to sink and I yelled at her to keep kicking, but she couldn't. She was done. I dove under her to push her back, but—"

He broke. So did I. I'd never seen Alex cry. He grabbed the wall like he wanted to snap it.

"I held her up over my head like that till everything just went quiet. No more wind. No more fighting. No one came.

Not even God. My wife was twenty-nine. Alyssa was eight.
And beautiful. And trusted me—"

He walked around the corner of the room and disappeared.

"Alex, wait."

But there was no one there.

Chapter 11

WHAT do you say to that? I sat there in bed still wrapped around my pillow, almost wishing I hadn't asked. But I marveled at the selfish, tunnel-visioned person I had clearly been to have never asked before.

I couldn't comprehend losing a child like that. Especially fighting so hard for it and then losing. I also couldn't stand to see Alex like that. A broken man. He was always the pillar of strength, with the killer smile and kick-ass attitude. This was the Alex he hid from me. The one with the cross to bear.

Oh, man, it ripped my heart out. I got up, wishing Riley was home so I could hug her. I felt like I needed to do something productive to offset feeling like a complete ass, so I decided to go downstairs and clean something. The living room, I noticed, was pretty good. Bathroom was good—much cleaner than mine. The kitchen still had food crumbs and dirty dishes left from earlier, so that was the winner.

Some people find it therapeutic to hand wash dishes. The warm soapy water and the transition from dirty to clean—

all that. I'm not one of those people. I feel strongly that dishwashers should experience that magic and provide us with the mystery.

When we first landed back at Dad's, I was happy to dive into that sink out of sheer gratitude. Over the weeks since, I found reality and reintroduced his dishwasher to the world. I was loading up this marvel of technology when he walked in with Bo, who made a beeline for my crotch before I diverted him with a spatula.

"What's up?" Dad asked, pulling out a chair with a scrape.

"Nothing. Just antsy today, I guess."

"What for?" He laid out his newspaper across the table like he'd done my whole life.

"I don't know," I said, cramming a meatloaf pan between two plates. "Thinking of things I know I should do, versus— running off to Disney World."

He chuckled. "You used to want to adopt Pluto. Said he got a raw deal since Goofy could talk."

That made me grin. "Yeah, I guess even the happiest place on earth has its issues."

"Guess so."

"Oh hey, Riley had an album the other day that I've never seen before. An old yellow one with black and whites of you and Mom."

Dad peered down his glasses at the paper. "Yeah."

"Have you seen it lately? I wanted to look at it."

"Hmm. No, don't think so."

I went back to loading. "Riley said she put it in my room, but it wasn't there. Oh, and neither is my picture of me and Mom."

He frowned and looked at me over the top of his glasses. "What?"

"The picture of Mom holding me—it wasn't in my box."

"Oh," he said quickly. "I took that a while back to have copies made." He winked and went back to his paper. "Kinda wanted one myself."

"So, where's mine?"

"I guess I forgot to put it back. Maybe I stuck it in that other album instead."

I laughed and put a hand on my hip. "Which would be where?"

He looked up again like one waiting for the inquisition to be over. "I don't know, sweetheart. But I'll look around, okay?"

"Okay."

I went back to the dishwasher, thinking that was an odd conversation. Odd enough, that after he left for a drive into Restin, I went on a mission. I looked through every cabinet and shelf in the living room. I went to his room but just stood in the middle and scanned, unable to bring myself to invade his privacy. The picture of my mom and me was in a frame on a bookshelf, and it pulled me closer.

I felt the familiar pang of loss and distance mixed together that I always felt. As if I were looking at someone else's photos. And it struck me for the first time how much she looked like Riley. Same mischievous smile.

There was only one other place to look, and that was the attic, which seemed a highly extreme thing to do for a photo album. Still, something was driving me to find it. I pulled down the hide-away stairs and peered up into the darkness, sure that I was crazy.

I looked down at Bo next to me, who gazed from me to the stairway and swung his tail like a baseball bat.

"You gonna come with me?"

His eyebrows did a little Groucho Marx thing, and his tail got a little less enthusiastic as the oppressive attic heat poured down.

"Yeah, that's what I thought."

I trudged up the stairs as they creaked and wiggled under my weight and grabbed the flashlight my dad kept on a hook at the top. Just in case. Daylight poured in from a dusty window, but it didn't make it to the corners.

"Whew, it's hot up here, Bo," I called down.

But it wasn't just hot. It was crackly. Like if I rubbed my hands together, I'd ignite a spark. It made my skin itch. And it was an odd sensation in contrast with the mugginess everywhere else.

I scanned the room, turning in a circle with my beam as it landed on boxes and plastic tubs and black plastic garbage bags labeled in tape and Magic Marker. My Big Wheel was there, as well as a pogo stick and a crib that had slept my dad, me, and Riley. Lead paint and all. There was a big box of wooden crafts that I'd started and never finished. My old rock collection, including the polisher that was all the rage when it came out but in reality only held up through one batch. My grandfather's old wooden rocking chair with two different-sized rockers that always listed to one side.

And a big treasure chest. I laughed when I saw it because for one it looked like something you *would* find in an attic in the movies. And second, my dad and I made it together for a school project about pirates. Except him being him, it wasn't made out of cardboard and glue. We made an actual treasure chest of treated wood and heavy-duty hardware that he had to put on rollers so I could bring it into the building, and it will probably outlive Riley's great-great-grandchildren.

Inside, I knew there was old "stuff," so I headed that way and pulled up a stool that I had painted eyes all over when I was six. I unlocked the fake padlocks and lifted. Right on top. There it sat. I stared at it for a minute, at first startled, then confused, then annoyed. I picked it up and turned the first couple of pages as a wave of dizziness hit me. I closed my eyes and shook my head, thinking that was happening way too often. I blinked and focused.

"You have no idea where it is, huh?" I said out loud. "Can't imagine how it got locked up here."

There were some pictures I'd seen before, which now I knew had just been pulled from their little corner-piece holders, because they were all in their places. Others were new to me.

Snapshots of my mom, young, maybe even Riley's age, acting goofy and looking full of life. At the beach in pedal pushers and an oversized button-down shirt, throwing sand at whoever took the picture. She and my dad, smooching upside down from tire swings over by the old dock. I recognized the cove. Even Jiminy, young and unwrinkled, holding a bottle of Falstaff up for the camera as he and my dad perched on an old car and grinned the carefree expression of kids with no worries. My dad, whom I'd never known to be skinny and beardless, looked to be about eighteen.

The heat settled on me, making my clothes and hair wilt and stick, but I hardly noticed it. Everything was captioned, and my hands shook as I read the handwriting. All the times I wanted something new of her. And here it was. Funny little quirky comments that were so her style.

Then interspersed with other pictures of them in action were some odd ones of seemingly nothing. A tree. My favorite old dock in its better days. A porch. An old car. But it wasn't the pictures that made my skin crawl. It was the captions. I read them again and again.

Henry. Tried to capture him, he's walking away with a cane.

Do you see her sitting cross-legged there? So sad for such a pretty girl.

Her name was Carrie, she's holding fingers over Jiminy's head.

Every nerve ending in my body stood up on full salute, as the ringing in my ears rocketed to a deafening pitch and the words swam in front of me. I felt hotter than before, and

I pulled at the neck of my T-shirt like it was cutting off my air.

"Are you kidding me?" I choked out as I touched the faded black print.

She was like me. My mom was like me.

And Dad knew.

"Oh my God."

I flipped page after page, only half seeing the images, looking for the ones that had no images. There were only a handful of them, but it was enough. As I turned the last page, there was my picture, tucked loose into the back cover. Me and my mother.

"My moth—" I sobbed on the word and touched her face. "You knew this world. You knew how hard—why—why didn't you come help me?"

I tossed the book aside and buried my face in my hands. All those years of feeling cut off from her. Of needing a mother. Of feeling like an outcast. Treated like a freak.

She was a freak, too.

But—I raised my head—she didn't come across that way. She tried to take pictures of them, for one thing, and then put them very publicly in a book just because *she* knew they were there. She didn't have to do that. She could have hid them or thrown them away. She chose to write about them, and—

"Oh my God."

Riley looked at that book. But said nothing. Did she not understand? Maybe she didn't read the captions? Or just thought old people were odd and blew it off. I swiped at my eyes and sweaty face, and then saw something else. Clipped together in a box next to some old framed school photos were a group of folded papers. I pulled them out and unclipped them, the old faded paper retaining the indention. I opened one, and my breath caught as I saw my mother's handwriting.

Nate,
I can't sleep tonight so I thought I'd write you. I
kind of hoped you'd come to the tree again, and I
keep going to the window just in case, but I guess
you are one of the lucky people sleeping right now.
Hope you are dreaming about me—HA-HA! About
the other day with Jiminy, we were just talking at
the dock. He thinks it's interesting—the things I
see—and it's nice to be able to talk about it.
That's all. I know it makes you uncomfortable, so
I try not to say much around you, but sometimes
that's difficult. Please understand that sometimes
it's confusing for me and I need to be able to tell
someone. And Jiminy is a good friend to both of
us. You're the one I love, forever and always. I'm
gonna go back to bed now and think of you.

Love, Nadine

I ran my hand over the faded ink, trying to feel her. I couldn't believe it. I couldn't believe it took forty years to find it out. I folded it back carefully and opened two more, which only talked about school and graduation and not having to work at the drive-in for a week because she had a sprained wrist. And little hints about their sex life, which was more information than I needed, but even that I soaked up because it made her more real to me. She was human in those letters. Not just captions under pictures.

There were many generic ones that I scanned, and then the last letter I opened slowly, not wanting it to be over where I'd be searching for more again.

Nate,
Tonight was so amazing. And I love you so much. I
can hardly believe you actually asked my parents

*and all of that! I cannot wait to start planning our
life together! I don't want you to ever replace this
ring. I don't care what you say, it's beautiful and
you bought it for me and proposed to me with it,
and I'll wear it forever. Till the day I die and then
after! I love you and I love that you accept me the
way I am. We have come such a long, long way. I'm
so proud of us. And Jiminy looked so giddy when
you asked him to be best man. I thought he was
going to goof himself right into the river. When you
told me that you'd love me and our children and
grandchildren no matter what "sight" we might
have, my heart soared. Because I know I can trust
you to make our family-to-be strong and secure.
Look at me, talking about babies already! Geez,
maybe I should concentrate on a wedding dress
first! HA-HA!*

*Love you always and forever,
Nadine Danielle Simon
(soon to be Mrs. Nathaniel Shane!)*

I felt light-headed. I carefully folded each letter back up
and replaced the clip, just as I heard the footsteps on the
wooden attic stairs.

"Hello? Dani, you up there?"

"Yeah," I called, but my voice sounded odd and weirdly
pitched.

Dad's heavy footsteps made the trek up and stopped at
the top.

"Whatcha doing, sweetheart?"

I couldn't turn around. Everything inside me threatened
to ooze out my pores and scream. He walked up next to
where I sat, and I heard him let out a defeated sigh. I could
imagine him scratch his beard as he took in the album and

the group of papers I still held in my left hand. I suddenly felt oddly guilty for having read his letters, but not enough to stem the flow of anger that poured from my eyes.

Without a word, he walked to the dirty window and stood staring out of it, hands shoved into the pockets of his blue jumpsuit.

"You need to tell Riley," he said without turning around. "Don't make the same mistake I did."

Then he walked back to the stairs and went down and outside. I heard the screen door close behind him. I sat there, unable to move, wondering if there was more to be found. I rooted around halfheartedly but saw nothing else. So I grabbed the album and picked up the letters, then stopped and put them back in their place. The album was fair game, but the letters didn't belong to me. And they were forever burned into my brain anyway.

I spent the next hour in my room, studying that album like the little kid I used to be, trying to grasp some little new piece of my mother. But I had gold now. Getting to read actual thought processes in her letters was just short of a video for me. Which *really* would have been awesome, but that wasn't happening in the sixties.

I was so glad that Riley wasn't home. My brain was too swirly with secrets to be able to piece any kind of logic together.

But I did need to go face one person.

I wandered out onto the porch with two orange sodas in my hand. Dad was in the porch swing, staring off at nothing.

I took one of the big chairs and pulled my feet up with me, as we popped the tabs on our sodas and I marveled at how big a sound that makes when you're dancing around silence.

"When I first met your mother," he began, "I knew something was different, but I didn't know what. I just knew I was completely in awe."

"She was beautiful."

"She was more than beautiful. She had a presence. An infectious laugh. And nothing bothered that girl; she embraced everything as a gift."

There was a moment of silence, and I didn't know if I was supposed to fill it, but I couldn't.

"The first time I found out about it was by pure accident. Walked up on her talking to someone." He stopped and took a long swig of his soda. "I thought she was joking, but she spilled it all. I wasn't sure I believed it. I mean, to the outside eye, it just looks like you're talking to yourself."

"Guess so."

"But Jiminy—he thought it was cool, or he just thought *she* was cool, or probably a little of both. I couldn't blame him. You couldn't help but love Nadine."

"He's never said anything like that."

"And he won't. But he was a better friend to her on that subject. He listened to her. To be honest, it creeped me out a little bit, watching her talk to nothing, whereas Jiminy was all into it."

Well, at least he was honest. Now.

"And when people looked at her funny, she didn't care. She laughed it off and people loved her regardless. She just had that way."

"Unlike me."

My dad looked at me straight on, and I winced a little at his pained expression.

"Exactly. Honey, when your mother died, I was a wreck. But I went on the best I could because I had someone counting on me. I had this precious little girl that grew to be quiet and thoughtful and watchful and more like me than her outgoing mom."

I nodded.

"When you started showing signs of—seeing people—" He shook his head and faced forward. "I thought, oh, hell no. Not this girl, please. I was so afraid for you. You didn't have the thick skin that she did."

"Like Riley."

"God, I'm telling you, Riley is so much like her, it's eerie sometimes. Such a free spirit and doesn't care."

"And I'm scared for her. I mean, she's strong, but she's also new here. Her roots aren't deep enough."

"You're gonna have to trust that she can handle it, Dani. I screwed up, pretending I didn't see it half the time, thinking it would go away if we didn't acknowledge it." He blew out a breath. "I was wrong."

My eyes burned with the unspoken subject. "Okay. I can understand that part. But—" I stopped and tried to get it together so it wouldn't sound angry. He beat me to it.

"Why didn't I tell you about your mother?" He closed his eyes and scratched at his beard. "I don't know. I guess because you and I never talked about it, and after a while, too much time had gone by."

"But—" The hot tears spilled over. "Do you know how alone I felt? I was a freak, Dad. A complete outcast. I still am. Do you realize people threw food on me last night?"

He flinched. "What?"

"Yeah, it hasn't changed." I rubbed at my face. "Do you know how much easier life would've been just to know I wasn't the only one? That I had something in common with her?"

His eyes filled with tears. "I'm sorry, baby."

"Why did you keep that from me?" I cried.

He shook his head. "I was wrong."

We sat in silence for a while, till I got myself under control. I thought of what he'd said about Jiminy, and his relationship with her.

"So—" I began, then having to clear the crying from my throat. "Is that why you and Jiminy grew apart? Because of him and my mother?"

"Not really," he answered, his voice quiet as he sat back and rocked the swing gently. "I was okay with that. It was more after she died that we didn't see eye to eye."

"What do you mean?"

He breathed in slowly and released it even slower. "He took it pretty hard. I don't think he was ever quite the same without Nadine to light things up." A silent chuckle came with a small smile. "And she did. She made everything—glow."

"So being around you, I guess that made it harder?"

"I guess." He took a long swig of his soda and wiped the orange out of his white whiskers. "Things got more normal later on, we started hanging out a little again. But when you started seeing ghosts, too—and I asked him to keep a lid on it—it all kind of went south."

I traced the wet on my can, watching the drops creep down in scraggly lines. "He thought what—people should know?"

"He thought you should know. He said Nadine would want it that way, and that it wasn't something to be ashamed of." He shook his head and rubbed his eyes. "Of course he was right, but I was a pigheaded fool running on little sleep and even less money. I met myself coming and going half the time; I thought all that was foolishness."

The things you don't know about your parents. Like that they're real people with crap on their plate just like you. My dad had quite the double helping.

"He stopped coming around after a while, and that just became the new normal."

"That's sad." I thought of Alex. "Friendship is important."

"Yeah," he said, barely putting sound to the word.

I looked at him, taking in the weariness on his face. It wasn't fair to beat him up for this. He'd done everything alone. I, for one, knew all about that.

I took a deep breath and blew it out, finishing off my soda. Time to change the direction. "So, how do you bring this up to a teenager without them thinking you're certifiable?"

"Do they have reflections?"

I looked at him, unsure. "Do—what—have reflections?"

"The—people. The spirits."

"No."

"Then have your friend stand in front of a mirror."

THAT was a great idea. I hoped. In all honesty, I could see it going either way, and that had me up all night. I didn't grab the opportunity when she got home, because she was in a great mood and I hoped it wasn't "first sex" kind of great mood. Regardless of that, I had trouble getting my mind around the new idea that evidently the women in my family have a secret club. Besides, Alex wasn't around.

And then there was that. Alex had spilled it all to me and then left distraught, which had me concerned for him. And Jason would be there tomorrow and would it be different? Had he talked to his son? Did he think about me? Yeah, I was pathetic enough to latch onto that last question, too.

Miss Olivia was at the shop bright and early Monday morning, actually before I was.

"Hey, Dani girl," she called out as she climbed out of her blue Cadillac.

"What on earth are you doing up this early?" I asked as I climbed out of my creaking tub that ten minutes earlier had lost electric window capability. How I wished for that old-fashioned crank.

"Dropping off some soap before I head out for a couple of days."

I caught up with her in all her green-and-yellow glory. Green top with yellow pants and, of course, the straw hat.

"At six in the morning?"

"Afraid so. Going to see one of my brothers for a week or so, leaving Grady here—so heads up on that, by the way," she added with a wink.

"Good to know."

"I'm glad they're bonding," she said. "He may be going to school out here this year."

"Really?"

"His mother's a wuss."

I laughed. "Well, bonding is fine. As long as mating is out."

"I hear that. I love you but I don't need to be related."

She linked her arm with mine to go in, and I had to admit that it did take the edge off seeing Jason after the hot dream from hell. There's a reason girls travel in packs.

"Hey, I heard that you and this one hit the nightlife the other night."

I heard the inner groan in my head. "No."

"No?"

"I was there. He was there. We ended up at the same table and we ended up dancing."

"Ah, so yes."

"Well, Blaine Wilson threw shrimp on me, so by that definition he bought me dinner?"

She held on to her hat as she got tickled. "Touché, my girl."

The bell jingled overhead and we walked in to the familiar sight of Jason behind the counter. He did a double take when he saw Miss Olivia and put on a charming smile.

She chuckled and hauled her bag on top of the counter. "Marg wanted some more in the inventory."

"And good morning," Jason said, still smiling.

She swatted at him. "Oh, quit flirting with an old woman, Jason."

"I know where they go," I said, digging in the bag.

"Okay."

The two of them struck up a conversation and I couldn't help feeling a little anticlimactic. He could have at least said hello.

"Well, I'll be back in time for the party next weekend," she said, poking me.

I looked at the two of them. "There's a party next week-end?"

Miss Olivia shook her head like I was so wearing. "The July Fourth party on the square, girly girl. Actually they still call it 'party on the square' but it moved to the river a couple of years ago. Over by where Ella's is now."

I checked Jason's expression for any kind of reaction to the mention of Ella's, but he didn't bite.

"Well, I guess I'll see you there. Be careful driving."

And she was gone. And Jason was left with me.

"So, if you can get those put away, and the tide info ready," he said. "I'm going to go finish cleaning up the back."

Well, of course. Aye-aye. "Oh, how did the bait room make out?"

"Fine. I came in yesterday and swept the last of the funk out. Good call on leaving the fan. That helped."

I nodded. "Okay." Yay for me.

He went in the back. I continued to nod like a bobblehead doll. This is what I worried about all night (partially) and put on makeup for at the crack of dawn?

"Damn, I could have slept another thirty minutes."

I did as I was told. I arranged the soaps, I pulled the tide reports, I called Jiminy and Hank and gave them their tour schedules for the week. I called the feed suppliers, I stocked the new Chinese yellow-bellied wigglers we got in that were supposed to make the fish offer themselves with a smile.

Jason walked from the front to the back three more times while I did all that, and I watched him. So methodical. Like a robot. Like he'd been at first, before he learned to relax.

"You okay?" I asked him on a fourth trip up front.

"I'm fine," he said offhandedly.

"What are you doing?"

"My job."

Oh honey. Hot dream or not. Hot moment or two on a

dance floor or not—that was nasty and arrogant and—ugh! Men are freakin' pigs.

I plucked his half-eaten blueberry muffin off the counter, and dropped it into the garbage can.

"Oops."

I snatched a rag left over from Saturday's cleaning and blindly wiped down the counter till you could probably eat off of it. Too bad he didn't have anything left to try that out with.

And I didn't have time to get any angrier because the bell jingled and in walked Riley and Grady. I looked at my watch, then back at her.

"Something blow up?"

"Ha-ha," she said, making a face.

"What on earth are you doing here?"

"I have to ask Mr. Miller something," Grady said, stepping up with a grin. A sweet, cute, melt-your-pants-off grin that made me want to tell Riley to run. Fast.

Instead, I just eyeballed him a second or two, hoping it intimidated him. Probably not. Crap.

"Hang on."

I turned to go get Jason, and I'll be damned if he wasn't right there. Again.

"God!" he yelled as I landed on his foot. "What is with you and running into me?"

"I'm sorry!" I said, backing up, but the laugh came up anyway. A giggle I couldn't contain.

He looked at me like I'd lost my mind as I stood there and laughed like a fool, and then Riley got in on it.

"Sorry—" I tried to think of something horrible to make it quit. Cleared my throat. "Sorry. Grady needed to—talk to you."

"Come back here," he said to Grady. "It's saner."

Riley raised an eyebrow when they had made it to the back. "What's with Mr. Roboto?"

"I told you he wasn't all that."

"He seemed cool the other night."

Yeah, he did. Night after that, too. "The other night was different—but he's evidently over it."

"So, did y'all step it up?"

I frowned. "Did we what?"

"Did y'all do anything to make it awkward now?"

"No! And so not your business. And no."

She snickered. "You said that."

"Okay."

"No kiss good night or anything? I mean, I did leave y'all alone—"

"Oh my God, we are not having this conversation. But let's talk about you being up at seven thirty in the morning."

"So?"

I raised an eyebrow. "So, are you attached to his hip now?"

"Please."

"I'm serious. Are you 'stepping it up'?"

She rubbed her eyes. "You did not just say that. I'm so never saying that again."

"Riley."

"Mom."

Oh, standoffs were cooler when she was six. Sixteen gave me a headache.

"Miss Olivia is out of town. Where are you two hanging out?"

"I was gonna help him over at Mr. Personality's boat till I have to go to work."

"Oh no."

"What? Why?"

"Because no one is there, either."

There came the look and the disgust. "We don't need a babysitter, Mom."

"You don't need to be alone where there are bedrooms, either."

"Oh my God. You are such a spaz."

I shrugged and held my hands up. "Call me whatever you want, you aren't doing it."

"You know, there's a big flat rock down the street that would work just as well. You gonna go dig that up or just forbid us to sit on it?"

Everything in me went still, and she knew it. It wasn't our first rodeo.

I took a deep breath and lowered my voice. "Go park yourself on that bench outside until it's time for you to go to work."

"Mom!"

"Now."

She narrowed her eyes and jutted out that famous hip. "You can't put me in time-out like I'm a child."

"You get up from that bench, you'd better be bleeding from the eyes, otherwise you'll be grounded to the house for a week."

"What's going on?" Grady asked as they emerged from the back.

"I'm grounded to a bench all day so that we don't accidentally trip and fall into a bed and have sex," she spat, glaring at me.

It was Jason's turn to snicker, and he turned around.

"What? I'm—never mind." Grady cut himself off when he saw my expression. A smart choice that Riley had yet to learn.

"God, I knew better than to show up here and try to hang out with you," she said, fighting tears I knew she hated.

"Save the drama. Go."

She wheeled around and knocked over a map stand on her way out. Probably on purpose. It didn't really matter. I turned to the two men who stood bewildered behind me.

"Sorry you had to witness her sweeter side like that."

"Ma'am, we weren't gonna do anything—" Grady began, but I held up a hand.

"It wasn't about that, Grady. She got in trouble for her mouth, that's all. It overrides her brain sometimes."

"Yes, ma'am."

The kid had manners, that's for sure. He left, after a few words with Riley outside, not lingering long. He probably didn't want her bad luck to rub off. Jason stood next to me, as we watched Grady walk down the street and Riley sulk.

"He wanted to borrow my keys so he could fix them something to eat."

I must have sported a crazed expression because he added, "I told him no, too."

"Lord."

"Of course, I didn't banish him to a bench for it."

I closed my eyes and sighed. "She got 'banished' for—"

"Her mouth, I know." He nudged me with an elbow. "I was joking."

Now he was joking? Who the hell could tell?

Chapter 12

THE morning went on like any other morning with Jason, which irritated the hell out of me because it wasn't supposed to be like any other morning. It was supposed to be electric and full of innuendo. Wasn't it? I mean, who was I to guess at that? I wasn't exactly dripping with experience.

And I was clearly focused on the wrong person, because then he asked, "Who is Riley talking to?"

My head jerked to follow Jason's gaze, and there was Riley still perched on the bench out front. Chatting it up with Alex. Laughing. Great.

"Does she have a Bluetooth or something?" I heard him ask from behind me because I was already under the counter and halfway to the door.

"She's just—" I flailed a hand in his direction as I walked outside.

They both looked up at me as I waited for the door to fully close. Alex was at a far end of the bench to avoid contact, and he rose to his feet.

"No, sit back down," I said as I held a hand out and made sure I faced Riley.

"Mom?"

"What are y'all doing?" I felt my last nerve begin to shred.

"Talking," she said, the toxicity back in her voice. "Is that against—"

"Don't finish that sentence," I said, locking eyes with her. "Put the attitude to rest, I'm telling you now."

"Fine," she said, visibly pulling inward. I could see all the little doors latch up. "It's almost time for work; can I go now?"

Her face was blank. It broke my heart just a little to see her know how to shut down like that. I saw my reflection in the window behind her, and then immediately dismissed the idea as soon as it came. It wasn't the place.

"Sure. But we have to talk tonight." Oh, that made my stomach hurt.

"Bye."

She got up and left, and I took her spot on the bench, mindful of what Jason could see out the window.

"Why do you keep putting me under the gun like that, Alex?" I said in a low voice. The street wasn't crowded, but there was enough foot traffic to notice a woman talking to herself.

"I was coming to see you. I didn't know Riley'd be standing guard."

I looked his way, then remembered to face forward again. "Coming here why?"

He ignored that as he watched a kid walk by with an ice cream cone.

"If I could be alive again for one day, I'd eat thirty of those."

"I'd think you would be more concerned with other things," I said with a smirk, and it pulled an intense sensual

expression from him. Enough to make my insides go all
liquidy.

"I'm good at multitasking."

"Dani?"

Jason's voice came around the door I didn't even hear
open, and I jumped like I'd been shot.

"Hey," I said, popping up.

"Now *you're* talking to yourself. Where's Riley? What
are you doing out here?"

I felt like I was being torched, I felt so overcome with
heat. "Just taking a break. Riley went to work."

Alex stood up with us and stood next to Jason, looking
from him to me. It was disconcerting to see them like that,
and even weirder was Alex's expression. Like he was fighting something. Sizing him up.

Jason waved a hand. "Dani, where are you?"

I blinked. "Sorry."

"Ask him," Alex said, his voice barely audible.

He stared at Jason so hard, I couldn't believe he didn't
feel it. I wanted to ask "what?" but I couldn't, and I started
to sweat.

"Ask him what you want to know. If the other night was
something or not."

How did he know that? Why did he know that? He
wouldn't blink and it was freaking me out and Jason was
about to call the loony bin on me, I was sure of it.

"Whatever," Jason said then, stepping away.

"The other night," I blurted, stopping him. "Was it—I
mean—"

Crap. I sucked at that even more than Jason did. But I
looked at his face, and it told me he could read past the babbling.

"Was it just a—I don't know. It seemed like there was a
moment."

That last sentence trailed off to a whisper, as Jason didn't jump into the conversation with me. And how the hell was I supposed to do it with Alex hovering? And not just hovering, but glaring. Almost like he was daring Jason to be good enough to replace him.

Jason looked around him, looking very uncomfortable, and just as he opened his mouth to probably suggest medication, someone walked past us and into the store. He turned and followed them in.

I just wanted to stand there, very still, and I flashed back to feeling that way every day at school. Fantasizing about being so still that I could disappear.

"Why did you make me do that?"

Alex moved slowly, coming to a stop in front of me. His eyes looked troubled. Conflicted.

"I'm sorry."

I rubbed my arms and tried to shake off the humiliation.

"Have to go back to work." I breathed in deep and let it go slowly as I walked back under the jingle.

DAD and I sat at the kitchen table, each lost in our own thoughts as we waited for Riley to come home. I hoped that Alex would come around. But I felt like at least having Pop verify it might give it more credibility.

I looked at the round-faced clock above the door and sighed heavily to realize it was still thirty minutes till she'd get off, and another ten home. I was antsy, and I got up and hugged his shoulders.

"I'm gonna go upstairs and surf the internet or something non-productive till she gets here."

He chuckled, but it was kind of a sad sound. I pulled out my laptop, perpetually plugged in but rarely visited. I have always thought my life was interactive enough without adding the internet to it.

But occasionally, I'd wallow in it. Check on my old company, see what else was going on in the world outside Bethany. Sometimes I'd even play games. Google things just to see what I'd find.

I Googled "Jason Miller" and found more than a few, but he was in the mix. Nothing more exciting than a camera bought on eBay. Then I thought of something I was surprised never occurred to me before.

I Googled Alex.

I typed in "Alex and Sarah and Alyssa Stone Key West Florida" and then held my breath as the links came up. As usual, there was a multitude of web garbage and the link up of every plausible match of "stones" and "keys."

But just before I moved on, there was a sentence that caught my eye because of the date.

Key West: Monroe County School District presents honorary diploma for deceased Alyssa Stone on April 16, 1980. (read more)

Well, of course I wanted to read more.

Archive: April 16, 1980. Mayor Sonny McCoy presented an honorary diploma to longtime friend Charles Alexander Stone, in memoriam of his granddaughter, Alyssa Stone.

"Alyssa would have been eighteen this year, graduating no doubt with honors," he said in a brief acceptance. "I may be biased, but she was a bright, bright girl, and the shining star of our family. This means more to me than you could possibly know."

It was ten years ago on this date that eight-year-old Alyssa and her parents, Alex and Sarah Stone, were drowned at sea while on a boat outing. Reports said a freak storm with beach-damaging waves came out of the Atlantic, causing natives to scramble at the last minute with very little warning. Several vessels were casualties, and the Stones were three of five lives claimed that day.

I know I read it again. I'm sure I read it three or four more times. The ringing in my ears got so loud, I wasn't sure anymore.

Alex and Sarah and Alyssa died on April 16, 1970. The day I was born. The day my mother died.

"No."

That couldn't be right. I went back to Google and typed in "Key West boat accident April 16, 1970 storm" with shaky fingers. Six unrelated matches, then the seventh said "Key West Citizen Archive." I clicked on it and held my breath.

It was an Adobe pdf file—a scanned image of a newspaper article depicting the storm. Same details. Except at the bottom, there were fuzzy black-and-white newsprint photographs of those that died. Two individuals, and one family photo.

My heart threatened to knock right out of my chest, and the image swam before me. Alex and Sarah and Alyssa. Alive. Smiling for the camera. I shut my eyes tight and started to cry, and I heard them. I heard them laughing. Then I heard them screaming. My eyes shot open and I gulped for air; it felt like I was underwater.

"What are you doing?"

I jumped up so hard, the chair fell down behind me, and I struggled to my feet as I coughed and gagged to catch my breath. Alex was staring at the image on the screen, transfixed, with eyes full of tears and anger.

"What—" he repeated, his voice choked. He held one hand close to the screen, almost touching it. "What—oh my God," he whispered.

His knees buckled under him and he went down on one, his face crumpling as he absorbed the image. I stepped backward, reeling from the mix of betrayal and compassion for him. I'd never seen him like that, and it dawned on me that he hadn't seen anything—not even pictures—of his family since that day.

"Why, Dani?" he said finally, his voice raspy and strained. He didn't take his eyes off the photograph. "Why are you doing this?"

"Why have you lied to me all these years?"

He tore his eyes away from the screen to turn to me. Tears streamed down a face so tormented, it made my stomach twist. Hot tears burned the backs of my eyes, and suddenly I didn't know what to think.

"All these years, Alex, through everyone else's bullshit, you were the one thing I could count on, the one person I could trust." My voice cracked and wobbled. "I thought you were my friend."

His eyes flashed, and he shoved a finger toward the screen. "I thought you were mine."

"You lied to me!"

"That's my baby girl—" he yelled back, through a throat that betrayed him. "How could you? That's—" His jaw twitched and he shut his eyes as if that would shut his mouth, too. "You don't understand—"

"Hell, no, I don't. How many times have you stood with me at the cemetery looking at that date? How many times have I talked about it?" I stopped to grab a hiccupping breath. "And you never found it relevant to mention that you died that day, too?"

Alex didn't speak, he turned his head back to the picture, as if it called him in. The pain and the longing in his expression was heartbreaking, like he wanted to jump in there with them.

"Wait—" Little puzzle pieces flashed in my brain. Flashes that I could only glimpse for a second. "You came directly here, you said, when you died. Was I born yet?"

"Yes," he said, his voice rough, as though he wanted me gone so he could be alone.

But my thoughts reeled. I reached out blindly until my hand found the big chair, and I went to it, leaning on the arm. My heartbeat thundered in my ears.

"Did my mother talk to you?"

It was barely more than a whisper, but he heard it. He knew it before I even asked. Just as I already knew the answer. He turned back to me and I saw it.

"Oh my God."

I left the spot I had been rooted to and walked across the room and back again, sinking into the chair and burying my face in my hands.

"How could you keep that from me? You of all people know how that would have changed my life. How could you do that?"

"I had to."

"Bullshit!"

"You have to trust me."

"Trust you?" I rose to my feet. "Turns out, I don't even know you. All this grief about coming clean with Riley, and look at you."

"Coming clean with me about what?"

Alex and I both head-jerked at her presence in the doorway.

"What are y'all talking about? And why are you up here?"

It was the eleventh hour, there was nowhere else to go, and I'd never felt more trapped and overwhelmed. I met Alex's eyes once more as they burned into me. Telling me something. Begging me for something. Showing me something I couldn't grasp.

He looked back at the photo as if trying to burn it to memory, then he walked off without another word, around the corner of the room. I held my breath as Riley did a double take.

"What—where—" She took a few steps that direction, and then whirled around. "What the hell?"

I held out a hand. "Come here."

"No!" She backed up and her voice rose two octaves, and the wild look in her eyes was pure fear. "What is going on?"

She turned back to the wall he'd disappeared into. "How—" She shook her head and looked back at me. "Why is this okay for you?"

I swiped at my eyes, trying to push everything I'd just learned to the background. That wasn't as important as what was in front of me.

"You might want to sit down," I said and heard the shake in my voice.

"I'm good."

I looked in her suddenly distrustful eyes and realized that Alex and I had just done this same dance. I was no better than he was.

"Alex is a spirit. A ghost. He's not alive."

She didn't move. She didn't blink. I licked my dry lips and kept going.

"I can see them. They look like we do mostly. My mother could see them. And evidently you can, too."

Riley shook her head. "You're crazy."

"Honey, you saw for yourself," I said, gesturing at the wall, and she shut her eyes as two big tears fell. I walked toward her but she held her hands up.

"No. Don't."

"It's not a big deal, boog, you learn to—"

"Not a big deal? You're talking about seeing dead people and it's not a big deal?"

My dad appeared in the doorway, and it occurred to me that this was the most bizarre interaction I'd ever had in that room. And there had been a few.

"Did you know this?" she asked him.

He nodded, looking almost apologetic.

"God, you're both crazy. You're all crazy," she said, storming from the room.

"Riley, wait," I cried, following her down the hall, but she was already halfway down the stairs.

"Get away from me," she yelled. And then she was out the front door.

"Well, that went well," I said, my voice shaking.

"Give her a little bit," my dad said from behind me. "Let her get her head around it."

I stopped and wiped my face and dropped cross-legged to the floor, right there at the top of the stairs, sobbing like a baby. I had nothing left. My dad sat on the top step and rubbed my back, like he'd done a thousand times when I was little. Back when that's all it took to make things better.

I heard her when she came home, a little over an hour later. Went straight to her room and locked the door. I ambled down the hall and knocked, but she didn't answer, so I went back to my room and stared up at the ceiling fan.

THE next morning I knocked again, to no answer. "I love you, boog," I said to the paneled door. The door didn't respond, so I left for work.

I hadn't slept well, trying to process too much information. The date thing had me crazed, but Riley had me worried. Had I done the wrong thing, telling her? Not that there had been much of an option, given Alex's exit. Did I wait too long? And Alex—I just couldn't go there yet.

Then I walked in the shop, and there was Jason looking very Jason-esque in his faded jeans and pullover shirt. He looked up from paperwork when I walked in and lifted a finger.

"Hey."

"Back atcha," I responded, and kept on going.

I saw from the corner of my eye that he watched me with curiosity, but I didn't have it in me to deal with my Jason issues, so I figured why bother. It had evidently been a spontaneous moment brought on by the atmosphere and—two swallows of beer. Nothing more significant than that. Not worth stressing over. I had bigger fish to fry.

Every single person that came in had something to say about the upcoming party. The music, the food, the crafts, the contests, the fishing tournament, who was doing what, and who would be with who. I wondered if any of these people had jobs.

Jiminy came in to pick up his list and wait for his appointment to arrive, and I had a hard time looking at him.

"What's the matter?" he asked finally, on my third dodge.

"Nothing."

"Don't lie to an old man, girl, it's bad luck."

I looked into his twinkling old eyes and then around me to ensure that we were alone before casting my eyes back down again.

"You didn't just know my mom, you knew *about* my mom."

Some of the smile left his face. "That's some old ancient history there, Dani."

"Maybe to you, but it's pretty new for me. Any reason you chose not to share it with me?"

He shook his head. Removed his cap and scraped through what was left of his hair and put it back on.

"Wasn't my place. I made a promise."

I looked him eye to eye. "But you didn't agree with it."

He half shrugged. "My word is my word. Agreeable or not."

"Hmm."

"What's brought all that up, now?"

I looked around to check that Jason wasn't coming back in. "It's evidently a club membership in my family."

Jiminy frowned, then narrowed his eyes. "Riley?"

I nodded. "She's overjoyed."

He leaned against the counter. "She should be. Your mother was."

I looked at him, surprised. "It's not an easy life, Jiminy."

"It's not a death sentence, either," he said, patting my hand. "Nobody's life is easy. Lighten up."

His group arrived and he tapped the counter in a good-bye as he moved on to make some money. The bell jingled again and I groaned inwardly as I watched Shelby excuse herself around the other group, holding her hands to herself as if she might get infected. The smug look she gave me didn't help my opinion any.

"Dani."

"What can I do for you, Shelby?"

She made a *hmph* sound. "Is Jason around?"

I smiled. "Of course."

I headed down the hallway to the bait room and stuck my head in. "You're wanted out here."

The irony of that wasn't lost on me. Jason came out less than a minute later, and the look he gave me when he saw it was Shelby was like, *why?* I got a little kick out of that.

"Hey," she said, much perkier for his benefit, arm touch and all.

"Hey, Shelby, what's up?"

"Well, I think my freezer went out. And I thought you probably are all mechanically inclined, since you live on that boat. Matty's truly not, and he's out of town today anyway, so I was hoping you could take a look at it."

All in one breath, she said that. But Jason shook his head.

"Honestly, I wing it, Shelby. I pay a teenage boy to work on my boat. I've got a broken water pump here that he may have to look at, too, because I suck at it."

Her face fell, as her plan to get Jason to her house flopped.

"Hey, I'll bet Grady would be happy for a few extra bucks," I said. "Or Bob."

Jason turned to me with the corner of his mouth twitching. "That's a thought."

"Who's Bob?" she asked.

"He's the bait guy next door," I said. "I'll ask him when he gets in."

"That's okay," Shelby said, suddenly interested in a brochure on rabbit pellets. "I'll just check around."

I saw Riley outside the door then, and all other thoughts went away. Shelby followed my gaze, as Riley came in looking all sullen, and she lit up all over again.

"Well, hi there again."

"Hey, Mrs. Sims."

"Are you looking forward to the festival next weekend?"

Riley looked at her like you would an annoying bird. "Sure."

"Micah and her friends will be there, that will be a great time for you to meet some people before school starts."

Then Shelby looked at me and the expression on her face set off alarm bells in my head. I almost wanted to duck. "So are you and Jason going together?"

Jiminy came back in and stayed to one corner. I didn't look his way but I knew he was watching.

"No," I said, without looking at Jason. I didn't want to see that rejection again. "Are you and Matty going together or will he be otherwise occupied again?"

Even the smirk fell that time. That one almost hit bare bone. She ignored the question.

"That's a shame. Y'all looked so snuggly and cute the other night before Blaine's unfortunate little trip up."

I caught Jiminy's eye, and he grinned at me. *Your mother was happy. Lighten up.* I smiled, too. For the first time, that kind of comment didn't fluster me. Even in front of Riley.

"Yeah, you're right. We were having a good time." I braved looking Jason in the face and was surprised to see a smile in his eyes, if not on his lips. "Until your friends decided to be twelve."

I raised the counter and walked out front, slinging an arm around Riley. "If you'll excuse me, I'll be right back."

We walked outside and waited until the door closed all the way, then she sat on the bench and looked up at me.

"Is that what I have to look forward to?"

THAT nearly broke me. I felt very heavy and old as I sat down next to her.

"No, boog. Because you're stronger than me."

"That's why you didn't have friends here, isn't it? Why you didn't want to come back?"

Nothing like having it nailed down for you. "Yeah."

"So people knew?"

I shook my head. "No. Mine started young, Riley. I saw things I didn't know I wasn't supposed to, so I'd be talking to people no one else saw."

"And mine just popped up when we got here?" she asked. "Seriously?"

"I don't know," I said. "Maybe? Maybe you've been seeing them all along and just didn't know it."

She covered her eyes. "God."

"And I wasn't looking for it, either," I said. "I never noticed until suddenly you were talking to Alex in the front yard."

"What if people see me?" She slapped her hand back to her lap. "If this town already knows—"

"They don't," I said, careful to keep my tone calming. She looked ready to run again. I knew that feeling. "No one ever knew except Miss Olivia. Everyone else just thought I was weird."

"Now that will be me."

"No." I touched her arm. "Look at me. No, it won't. If there's one thing I've learned since being back, it's how to embrace this. I didn't have my mom to help me, but you do. And I'm telling you like someone told me. Lighten up about it. It's not that bad."

"But if people are already looking for something weird—"

"Baby, you'll be fine. Because you won't give them anything. I'm told my mother was outgoing and vibrant and didn't care what people thought. And they loved her. You are like that."

She looked forward. "If I hadn't walked in last night, would you still keep it from me?"

Oh, déjà vu.

"Last night, I told you we needed to talk, remember? Pop and I were waiting for you to come home so we could tell you."

She shook her head. "How am I supposed to trust anything? Anyone? How the hell do I know who I'm talking to?"

"You have me to show you. To tell you the rules."

She got up. "I don't want this. I don't want to know any rules. I don't want this freak show."

"There's not much choice, sorry."

She deflated and sat back down with a thump. "This is messed up. And I knew something was off with that Alex guy."

"That Alex guy—was my best friend." Is? Was? I was on that uncomfortable fence of defending someone you're mad at.

"That's pathetic."

I got up and stared her down. "And that's beneath you. You can leave now."

Her face instantly changed. "Mom, I—"

"I said leave."

Shelby walked out at that moment.

"I'm sorry, did I interrupt something private?" she asked, her sarcasm barely disguised.

"Get a life, Shelby," I said, swinging the door open. "Go plug your freezer back in. You're not getting laid today."

I heard Riley laugh in spite of being mad at me. That darn fence again.

Chapter 13

Alex didn't come by that night. Riley stayed in her room, wanting privacy, not even wanting to go see Grady. Dad was into some westerns, looking for normalcy I suppose. I sat on the porch, feeling that article calling to me. I never did click it off. I knew it was still up, under the screen saver, and the memory of the last reaction I had to it still burned in my brain. What the hell was that about? I finished my tea and headed up there, knowing it was inevitable.

I sat down and skimmed the touchpad, and felt my stomach wrench again at the sight of Alex and his family.

Absently, I ran the cursor in a circle around Sarah. She was beautiful. A natural smile that radiated love. I could almost imagine her kiss him and laugh just before the picture was taken, teasing him about an inside joke. Alyssa making faces until her dad poked her in the ribs, making her giggle for the camera. *That's my baby girl . . .*

I blinked and sat back, feeling disconcerted. I scrolled back up and reread the article, word for word, and filed it in

my head with what Alex had told me about the storm and
how they had died.

While I was born.

Or not totally. Alex said that I was already born when he
got there, and my mother was alive. A flash of light burned
across my vision, followed by a wave of vertigo. I closed my
eyes and felt my fingers grasp the desk, but it was like it was
someone else doing it. I heard the wind again, roaring over
something. Water? My chest tightened as I heard a scream—

My cell sang, which made me jump and gasp for air as I
yanked myself out of my thought process. It was a text message. From Jason. Jason had my cell? Oh yeah, the car.

Yes. There was a moment. A good one.

My jaw dropped. And I felt sixteen. Or maybe I just felt
forty because I didn't get to experience that at sixteen.

I looked back at the article and took some deep breaths.
Something was seriously messed up there. I had to get away
from it, and I was just given the perfect diversion. I would
take a shower and bask in my first text message from a guy
telling me there had been a moment. I was pathetic, as Riley
would say, but I didn't care.

Tomorrow he'd probably be distant again, but right then
was good. Even with an unanswered something nagging
behind all the puzzle pieces and those last tortured burning
looks from Alex. Right then was okay.

THE next morning, I woke up with thoughts of Alex, and
instantly pushed them aside for thoughts of Jason. I had to
focus on something; the schizoid life was making me nuts.
No pun intended.

So I took extra care getting ready. Still jeans and a
T-shirt, but my best T-shirt, good hair, and a little makeup.
High fashion at the bait shop.

I pulled up at the shop, with butterflies in my stomach.

His car wasn't there, but sometimes he walked, so that didn't mean anything. I took a deep breath before I opened the door and walked in with a smile.

"Hey there."

I stopped short. "Hey, Marg. I thought you were gone till Monday."

"Didn't want to miss getting ready for the festival next week. Lot of things to prepare."

My God, what was with this freakin' festival? You'd think it was Mardi Gras.

"Oh, okay." I went behind the counter and started my normal routine, grabbing a cup of coffee. "Jason here yet?"

That sounded nonchalant, right?

"No, I called him and let him know I'd be here. So he won't need to come till noon."

Everything flopped. I felt like Shelby. I wanted to throw my coffee in the air and cry.

"Gotcha," I said instead.

I'd smell like shrimp by noon. Groovy.

"So did y'all miss me?" Marg asked, as she opened a crate of lures I'd put off till I could find a spot for them. Or till she got back.

"Of course; how was your vacation?"

"Hot. Don't go to Colorado in the summer. Freaks don't have air-conditioning."

I laughed. "What?"

"Seriously. My brother-in-law says they don't need it most of the year, because the humidity's so low." She dumped the crate over on the floor. "Whatever. All I can say is the summer is god-awful brutal with no air. House bakes all day and heat rises. Bedrooms are upstairs. You do the math."

The rest of the morning wore me out, waiting six hours to find out which one would show up—Jekyll or Hyde. Which was harsh, I knew, but the man was moody. And I found out in a way that only I could. Coming from the back, rounding the corner of the hall, yelling something back at Marg, I stopped just short of colliding with him again.

He grabbed my arms as I teetered on momentum.

"Oh!" I started laughing. "I'm sorry."

"We need mirrors and traffic lights in here."

We were awfully close, like body-heat close, and I found myself struggling to remember what I was yelling to Marg.

"Eight dozen," I said.

He blinked. "What?"

"Excuse me." I pulled free of him and wound my way up front. "Eight dozen, Marg. That's all we have left."

"All right, I'm posting that up front," she said. "Bob said it's tapped out. When they're gone, they're gone."

"Got it."

"Now I'm out of here. Try not to flood the place, will you?"

"Yes, ma'am," Jason answered, and a smile played at his lips. He might own the place, but he was still a newbie. Margie Pete ran that particular ship for too many years to answer to an outsider. She turned to look at both of us as she reached the door and chuckled.

I frowned as she left. "What was that?"

But Jason had already dived into a box of hooks and weights.

"Been busy?" he asked.

"People are lunatics today," I said, trying to get a read on his mood by staring at the side of his head. "Everyone is doing practice runs for next week's fishing tournament."

"Don't knock it—it means more business."

I nodded. Not that he saw it. He was elbow deep in merchandise. I headed to the back, wondering why I'd bothered with anything this morning. He was all business. Evidently, moments—even good ones—were few and far between. Or maybe he had just meant to acknowledge that yes, that moment was nice, but wasn't implying any future ones.

"Maybe he was just being nice," I muttered as I picked up an empty box and tossed it to the big garbage bin, narrowly missing the shrimp vat. "Maybe I imagined the whole mess, text and all. Maybe I need to quit analyzing it."

"Maybe you just need to turn around."

I whirled in place, uttering a yelp that probably wasn't the sexiest, and found myself looking right up into his face.

"Oh—hey!"

"Hey."

His eyes were playful and sweet and hot all at the same time, and I didn't know whether to jump him or shake his hand.

"You—shouldn't sneak up on people when they're—babbling to themselves." Oh God. Just shoot me.

He jutted a thumb behind him and backed up a step. "Should I go? Do you need to continue?"

"No—no, no," I said, laughing. I prayed for something witty to say. "Come back—where you were." Yeah, that wasn't it.

He stepped closer again, and it became painfully obvious that the two of us combined had the romantic social skills of a tree. We stood there looking at each other waiting for—something.

"So, where've you been lately?" I asked.

Thank God he knew what I actually meant by that. A small silent chuckle crossed his lips.

"Wondering if this is a really bad idea."

I nodded as my stomach fluttered. "Wow, that—"

"Sounded horrible, I know."

"No, I know what you mean."

"Thank God." He rubbed his eyes and I had to smile. "See, that's just it. I can talk to you for some reason. That blows my mind."

"Why?"

"Because I don't do that. Talk."

I nodded again and pretended to consider that as I watched his lips form words.

"So what was your conclusion?"

He inched closer. "That it's still a really bad idea."

"And yet—" I gestured around us. "Here we are. In the bait room."

"Yeah, I can pick a hot spot, can't I?"

I started to laugh, and his hand came up to my face and into my hair, and I found it interesting that I could laugh without breathing. His face came down, mine tilted up, and I was reminded of that night on the dance floor.

"Relax," he whispered so close to my lips that I felt the word.

Then it was on. As soon as his mouth landed on mine, my body remembered what to do. His lips were soft and searching and mine were hungry. He pulled me in, kissing me deeper. I wound my arms around his back and pulled him to me in response.

He made a little moan in my mouth, and I got a rush of liquid heat that I hadn't felt in years. Not in real life—with another person. The thought whizzed through my head that I was being way too easy, but the one that chased it off said that I was forty and tainted goods and too horny to care.

He backed me up to the bait table and before I knew it, I was lifted and sitting on it, looking him eye to eye. Our hands shifted roles. I wound my fingers into his hair while his worked from my waist down my legs and back again. Over and over. It was everything I could do not to wrap my legs around him and hump him like a dog.

Then he moved his mouth down the side of my neck and I thought I was done for. A little noise escaped my throat as he slid his hands around to my ass and tugged me against him.

It was crazy. Something in my head knew that. But my body was starved for the attention and judging by his reaction to my touch, so was his.

Then the bell jingled up front.

We both jumped as if we'd been hit with electric shock,

and Jason backed up a step. He rubbed at his face with a shaky hand.

"I'll um—" He gestured toward the front. "I'll go see."

I just nodded. Talking was out of the question. He backed up, not breaking eye contact with me until he left the room. It was like being an awkward teenager, except that I had one of those and she was much more together than me.

I closed my eyes and fanned my hair out for air. I knew my chest had to be bright red and my face and neck were on fire.

"Oh my God, what am I doing?" I said, pushing off the table onto shaky legs.

Making out with my boss in the back room. He was right. Nothing about it was smart. So then why was my entire body in heat, recalling every place he touched like memory foam?

Hearing voices, I decided to suck it up and go be a grown-up. I fluffed my hair out and swiped under my eyes, checking my reflection in an old glass poster frame advertising tackle boxes. I just hoped my chest and neck weren't glowing, but that thought alone brought a fresh wave of heat to the surface. I needed to go stick my head in a freezer.

The walk up front gave me a second to hold my head up, just in time to see Matty Sims turn around. I almost groaned. He gave me a once-over.

"How's it going, Dani?"

Well, I was getting lucky till you showed up. I chanced a look at Jason, ignored the flutter in my belly, and pasted on a smile. "Great, Matty, how are you?"

He had a different sidekick with him, one who looked familiar. And not in a good way.

"Dani Shane, wow," the new guy said, and the voice brought me all the way back. Back to the snotty doctor's son he was and the gropes in the hallway when Lisa-do-you-remember-me wasn't looking. Carson Marlow, Lisa's now-husband. The guy who pretended to like me and invite me to my one and only party. That got me wasted and then threw me out when I still had enough snap to turn down him and his friends. The night I met Alex.

Before I could open my mouth, the door opened again and a big teenage boy walked in followed by another slightly smaller one. I recognized the bigger one from the bait shop as Lisa's bag-hauling son. The other looked to be a younger brother.

"What can I help you with, besides the lures?" Jason asked.

Matty smiled at him and then at Carson. "We want to sign up for the tournament next week. The boys, too."

"No problem." Jason pulled some forms out from a drawer. "Fill these out and it's fifteen each."

"Oh, come on," Carson drawled, throwing what I assumed to be a charming look my way. His eyes were red and floating in scotch. Charming had left the building. "For old friends of Dani's? You could waive that, couldn't you there, big guy?"

My mouth went sour. Jason actually laughed out loud.

"Yeah, I've seen how close you are. Sorry, guys. Tournament rules."

Matty leaned his big arms on the counter, and Carson followed suit, taking my left hand in the process.

"No ring, Dani?"

I yanked my hand free before Jason could swoop in. Assuming he had swoop intentions. Truth be known, I had no idea what his intentions were. If he would be jealous, indifferent, angry, possessive—I had no clue what the hell we were outside that bait room.

"You know, boys, your dad and I went to school with Miss Shane, here," Matty said, not turning around. "Come say hello."

They looked at each other with that unmistakable tolerance of those forced to live with assholes. That look of going through the motions to keep the peace, as they ambled up behind Carson.

"My sons, Drew and Derry," Carson said. I held out a

hand and both boys reached around their dad, who was planted firmly.

"Are you Riley Shane's mom?" Drew asked. He was the one I'd seen before and was already taller than Carson.

"Yes, I am. You know Riley?"

"Kinda."

I blinked at the short answer. Okay.

"I think we'll get some live shrimp, too, just in case they don't bite on artificial. See what the trend is before next week," Matty said.

"How much?"

"Four dozen or so."

I headed to the back to count out "or so" as the two boys headed out and around to meet me with a bucket. I opened the back door and grabbed the net off the hook as I waited.

"Hey, you seen that Riley Shane chick?" I heard the younger one ask, and I held my breath in anticipation. I heard the zipping sound of a lighter, and realized they were grabbing their thirty-second smoke break.

"Riley? Yeah."

"She's hot."

A snorting laugh. "She's out of your league, dude."

"Yours, too."

"Bullshit."

A laugh from the other one. "You're full of it, Drew. You'll never hit that."

"I'm telling you, once that guy she's been hanging with goes back to wherever he came from, that tight little ass is gonna be mine."

I almost dropped the net. I lost feeling in my fingers.

"You think he's doing her?"

"Hell yeah. They were all over each other the other night when we were skinny-dipping."

I covered my mouth before I could cry out. Skinny-dipping? With Grady? I saw red and purple and five other colors.

"You saw her naked? Damn."

"Nah, just to her underwear. But it got see-through real fast." He laughed. "Man, I'm telling you I'd have thrown Micah aside in a heartbeat to have that wrapped around me like he did."

"Mom would have a shit fit if you came home with her. Remember she said they're weird."

"Who's talking about bringing home? I've got Micah for that."

There was the scrape of snubbing cigarettes out on concrete so they could pocket them for later. I was glued to the floor. And sick. I wanted to run, grab Riley, and drive as far from there as possible. Drive till the land ran out.

Instead, I slowly released the breath I'd been holding and swiped at my eyes as they strolled in. The tall one, Drew, stopped a little short when he saw how close to the door I was, and gave me a polite smile as he handed me the bucket. I clenched the bait net as hard as I could to stop the trembling, or to keep from beating him with it.

I turned to the shrimp vat and had to close my eyes for a second or two and breathe. When I opened them, it was still there—the fantasy of drowning him in there with the shrimp. Holding his pretty head under the water until the bubbles ceased and the quiet lights came. I cleared my throat and started scooping. Drowning wasn't nice. It wasn't a good way to die. *Where did that come from?*

Besides, the little brother would rat me out.

When they left, I didn't go back up front. I couldn't. I sank onto a stool, instead, and leaned over on my knees. How could I have brought Riley here? To this particular portal of hell where history was determined to repeat itself. Where fathers passed down their toxic waste like baseball cards.

"You okay?"

I turned to focus on Jason, but all I could see was the image of Riley and Grady skinny-dipping in the lake.

"Yeah, sorry, I'm just—"

"A million miles away."

"Somewhere in that area."

He rubbed at his neck, looking awkward, then pulled over another stool, sitting far enough in front of me that we couldn't touch. I was glad of that. Sort of.

"Look, Dani, I—" Jason shook his head. "I didn't mean for that to happen earlier."

His earnest innocent expression made me chuckle in spite of the turmoil boiling through me. He looked like he'd been caught with his dad's *Penthouse* magazine.

"You accidentally fell in my mouth?"

He gave me a look. "No, I meant—I just—"

I laughed lightly and held a hand up. "I know what you mean. I—didn't mean to get all carried away like that, either."

He looked relieved. "I don't know—what came over me. I guess it just felt—" He stopped as he made eye contact.

"Really good," I finished.

"*Really* good."

I caught my bottom lip with my teeth, still tasting him. The memory of that made my stomach do a little shimmy.

"Look, I can't deny I've wanted to kiss you since the other night," he said, stopping to breathe in deeply. "And I really want to do it again. But I never planned on all those fireworks. That's not what I want."

I raised an eyebrow.

"Okay, of course that's what I want," he continued. "But I guess what I'm not saying very well is I don't just want to bang you on a bait table."

"Really?" I said, tickled at that. "Because if that asshole hadn't come in, we'd be—"

"Please don't. I might cry."

I burst out laughing. He was funny? Who knew? I felt a little of the tension release. A little.

"Oh lord, Jason," I said after the giggles subsided. I looked away and scooped my hair back. "What are we doing?"

"I don't know." He laughed to himself, looking at the floor. "God knows I'm nobody's catch. I've got a mountain of baggage and I suck at this."

"You do better than you think," I said softly, bringing his gaze back up to me. "And your little baggage has nothing on my steamer trunks."

"Steamer trunks?"

"*Titanic* worthy."

"Okay, you win."

I smiled, then felt it fade as reality crept back in to settle in the crevices. "Jason, there are things—" I paused, startled at the sudden urge to confide in him. I'd never felt the desire to do that before, and it was foreign. Scary. "Things you don't know about me. Heavy things."

My eyes burned with unbidden tears as the subject came to the brim. That's as far as I could bring it.

"And there's crap going on with Riley," I continued, diverting. I ran a quick hand under my eyes. "Probably not the greatest time."

"Hey," he said, scooting his stool forward. He leaned on his knees and took my right hand, running his thumb lightly back and forth over my knuckles. "I'm not in a hurry; are you?"

I watched his thumb, and had the most random thought that it was the most intimate gesture anyone had made toward me in a long time. That tiny touch had me more captivated than when his hands had my whole body on fire.

"No."

"Then relax."

I smiled at the word and met his eyes again. He leaned in so I matched him, and his lips brushed mine, once, twice, then claimed them. His hand never left my hand, our bodies stayed where they were, but we kissed slowly, softly, tasting

each other. I got lost in the sensation, in the intimacy of it.
You should be kissed like that every day.

I pushed Alex's voice from my head.

THAT afternoon after work, I was a useless mess. I tried to
get gas; I flubbed up the credit card. I went to the grocery
store and forgot a third of my list. I didn't even make it into
the house when I got home, I just flopped onto the porch
swing.

I could've kissed that man for days. And that wasn't even
counting the prior grope session that still made me tingle to
recall.

But behind all that fantasy was the reason for a mount-
ing headache. I closed my eyes and hit rewind. What the
boys had said about Riley. What Alex had said about my
mother. And how to try to have what appeared to be a relationship without any of that coming to light.

Riley skinny-dipping with Grady—oh, that just reminded
my blood to boil, as my skin burned with it and my eyes
flew open.

Alex was in front of me.

"Shit!"

He didn't flinch, just continued to lean against the railing, hands in his pockets as usual. His face was passive.
You'd never think our last conversation was so volatile.

"Seems we've got some unfinished business," he said,
his voice smooth and even.

His eyes showed nothing. It made my stomach hurt, and
a hand automatically went there. I had to look away from
the hard stare.

"How would you feel, Alex?"

He said nothing, but I saw something flicker in his face.
The hard resolve pulled back a bit.

"I need answers," I said.

"You already have them."

"What?" I had nothing. What did he think I had?

"You just don't see it, yet."

He pushed off the railing and turned to gaze toward the river. I rubbed my throbbing temples. Too much. It was too much.

"I don't have the strength for word games; please just tell me what I'm too stupid to figure out. My mother clearly said something to you. Tell me whatever it is you've spent forty years not telling me."

He turned his head to fix me with the most heart-wrenching look. Something between torn and pissed.

"Sarah died first."

It was blunt and not news. But that was supposed to do it for me, I guess, because then he turned back toward the river.

"I know that."

"Then use that information. You can—"

"Or the source that is standing here can just talk to me," I said, interrupting. "Honestly, Alex, I'm sick of this. This isn't some Nancy Drew mystery. Why won't you just tell me?"

"Because I made a promise," he said, kneeling down in front of me with a loud sigh. "I keep my word."

His eyes were soft again, and I felt my irritation dissipate a little.

"To whom?" But I knew that one. "My mother?"

Behind him, car tires crackled on the gravel. Miss Olivia's Caddy pulled in.

"Crap," I muttered.

Alex didn't turn; he stayed locked in on me. "You look different today."

"Don't change the subject."

"Miss Olivia already has. It's your lips, they're kinda puffy."

That jolted my attention back to him, who was studying my mouth as Miss Olivia made her way up to the porch. Crap.

"Hey there, Dani girl," she said, taking the steps slowly.

"Hey, what brings you back early? I thought you were gone for a week?" I asked, trying to give Alex a nod to leave. Or move. Or no, leaving would be better. "Please?" I whispered under my breath.

"People getting on my last nerve," she answered.

She made it up the stairs and settled into a big cushiony chair to my right. Alex caved to my glare, only enough to back up to the railing again. I took a deep breath and turned sideways in the swing to talk, attempting to ignore him.

"So you're going to this thing next weekend, huh?" I asked.

"Oh hell, girl, that's the only time you can see everyone at once."

I grimaced. "That's not a selling point."

Miss Olivia chuckled and adjusted her hat. "True. Sorry. So, what's going on with the girl?"

I narrowed my eyes. "Why?"

"Because I asked, young lady."

I smiled. "Try again. What have you heard?"

She winked at me and pulled a roll of Certs from her giant bag, popping one in her mouth after I declined. "Grady's smitten with her."

"I'm pretty sure that's mutual."

She dropped her big purse on the porch with a thud. "That's what I hear." At my questioning look, she continued. "You know, being an old woman, I just tend to blend in sometimes, and so I get things without people knowing."

Alex actually chuckled, and I couldn't imagine Miss Olivia ever blending into anything, either, but I just nodded. "And you got what?"

She shrugged. "Girl talk. Jealousy, mostly. Riley's new and gorgeous and she's snagged the new boy in town. But there was a comment about whether she was as crazy as her mother."

I took another breath on that one and fought back the

burn. Riley was just destined to pay the price of being my daughter. I looked at Alex. "It never ends."

He was back behind them again, his eyes. Compassion and depth radiated from them. My voice shook as I said the next sentence, locking eyes with him.

"She knows now."

"Really? How did that come about?"

"She saw Alex disappear into a wall."

I watched his jaw flex and he averted his eyes. I blinked back the tears that wanted to come and focused back on Miss Olivia, who was wide-eyed.

"Well, that'll do it."

"I was telling her anyway, but that sort of hit fast-forward," I said.

"How did she take it?"

I snorted. "Not well. And she's pissed that I kept it from her, too, which I understand too well."

Miss Olivia turned sideways in her chair to get into the conversation. "Meaning?"

"Oh, that's right, I haven't told you."

"Dani," he said, his tone suggesting that I stop.

I refused to look in his direction. If he was going to stay, then so be it.

"I found out that Alex died the same day my mother did, and he didn't tell me. He spoke to her and didn't tell me. Oh, and then there's that—she could see ghosts, too, and my *dad* knew and didn't tell me."

Alex started to pace the porch in front of me. Miss Olivia looked stunned. "Holy smokes, girl, how long have I been gone?"

I rubbed my forehead and blew out a breath I felt like I'd been choking on. "Yeah, sorry. Didn't mean to unload all that."

She reached across with her speckled old hand and squeezed mine. "No, you need to or you're gonna fall over."

I laughed. "Well, enough of that. What brought you over here?"

She chuckled. "An old lady's curiosity, originally. But it seems you've got bigger fish to fry than a new romance."

My smile faltered as Alex stopped pacing. My peripheral vision registered every move he made as he came back to kneel directly in front of me.

"What romance?" I attempted, sounding weak even to me.

Miss Olivia guffawed. "Save it, Dani girl, I went by the shop first, and asked where you were, and Jason Miller lit up like a Christmas tree." She pointed at me. "And you're doin' the same thing."

I scooped back my hair and fanned the front of my shirt out. Not from the muggy, mucky air. No, that would be the heat from the scrutinizing eyes of Alex Stone.

"Your lips," he said again, his voice soft and faraway sounding. I sucked my bottom one in between my teeth.

"Dani girl, it's a good thing, you and Jason. He's a good man."

"It's complicated."

"Bullshit," she said, working her way back up out of the chair. "People always say that when they're chickenshit. It's what you make it. Don't be a fool."

Alex stood and backed up to the rail, and as I got up, I took a quick look at him. I wished I hadn't. His gaze was directed back at the river, but there were tears in his eyes. My breath caught in my chest, and it was everything I could do to not say something to him.

I walked Miss Olivia to her car instead, just as Riley walked up the drive.

"Hey, Miss O," she said, giving her a hearty hug. "How was your trip?"

"Peachy, how was the swim?"

Riley's jaw dropped, as did mine. Although I don't know why I was surprised. Leave it to Miss Olivia to know everything about everything and usually before the body was cold. And then not mince words about it.

"Um—what?" Riley attempted, giving me a this-old-woman-is-off-her-rocker conspiratorial look. I just smiled sweetly.

"People talk, sweetheart. And in this town, if you aren't one of the chosen ones, they don't talk nice. Think with your head, child. Not your hormones. And if I hear more crap like that, I'm cuttin' you both off."

Riley turned as red as a tomato, eyes and everything. Her chin even quivered. She wasn't used to that kind of bluntness, and I loved it.

"Yes, ma'am."

"Okay, love y'all. Gotta go."

Bing! Change of subject, and she was gone. Riley walked straight to the house and up the stairs. I decided to let Miss Olivia's words work their magic and give Riley the shock effect she needed. Let her sweat out me knowing, with a little cold shoulder. I totally sounded like I knew what I was doing. How hysterical was that?

Miss Olivia was gone. Riley was upstairs. And I stood in the yard, facing the porch. Facing an empty porch. Alex was gone.

Chapter 14

No guilt there. The man of my dreams—literally—can only stand by while another man steps in. That sucked. Alex had always been my soul mate. It was palpable from the moment we met. Granted, I was a bit young then, but I knew him. I knew him instantly.

But reality was reality. Alex and I could never be together. Not until I died. Which made me wonder why he wasn't with Sarah. *Sarah died first.* Why did he come here? *Not like there was a choice.*

So if he came directly here, did Sarah and Alyssa do the same? Did they cross over or go somewhere else? And then what did he promise my mother? And why?

I lay on my bed that night, staring at the ceiling fan again. Asking my mother things I knew I'd never get answers to, but I'd done that for so long, it was just rote. The questions had changed, though. It used to be about why she never came. Why everyone else in the world came but her. Why she didn't want to see me, talk to me, help me.

Those were the standard questions of my life. Now it was

just—why? Why anything? I swung my legs down and went to the computer, telling myself I'd surf around and check e-mail that no one would send. But I knew where I was going.

I pulled up the site off of history and quickly scrolled directly to the photo. All three of the Stones smiled at me through their grainy window.

Alyssa's mischievous grin drew me in, making me smile. The warmth and love spread through me as her laughter bounced off my ears. Knowing she had peanut butter crackers in her pocket struck a funny bone and I felt the giggle bubble up as Alex poked her in the ribs. The laugh fell out of my mouth, loud in the quiet room, and I sucked in air with such a violent start that I felt dizzy for a second. I blinked and gripped the desk with hands that were suddenly sweaty. My breaths came in short bursts.

"What the hell?"

I stared at the picture, Sarah smiling. I'd felt that smile. Inside me.

"Jesus Christ," I muttered, scooping back damp hair.

"Mom?"

I jumped a mile and sent a cup of pens and pencils flying. At Riley's alarmed look, I held up a hand.

"Sorry, I was just—somewhere else."

"God, Mom, you look sick."

I felt sick. "I'm fine. What's up?"

She pointed at the computer screen. "That's Alex."

I looked back at it, still gripping the desk. "Yeah."

She walked forward. "His family? He was married?"

"Yeah," I repeated.

She frowned. "What happened?"

"They died in an accident."

She turned to meet my gaze. "The little girl, too?"

I nodded, looking from Riley to the mottled image of Alyssa.

"That sucks. Where are they now?"

"I don't know."

"I mean, why aren't they—" She gestured in circles. "Hanging out with him?"

"I don't know."

She turned her frown to me. "What do you know?"

"Not nearly enough." I got up and walked to the bed, flexing my fingers.

"What got you all wigged out over here?"

"Nothing, Riley." I sat down and tried to refocus. "Did you need something?"

She ignored me. Nothing like normal. "Do you think he misses them?" she asked, pointing at the picture.

I let out a long sigh. "Yeah. If something happened to you, I'd miss you every minute."

Riley let a small smile tug at her lips. "Even when I'm being an ass?"

"No, but I'd focus on the good times."

She threw a stray eraser at me. "Nice."

I flopped backward onto the bed, and she slung herself down next to me. I turned to study her as she picked at old fingernail polish.

"This is weird," she said after a bit. Her voice sounded soft and childish.

"Which part?"

She widened her eyes. "That's what I mean. *Everything* is so bizarre now. We talk about dead people like that's normal. What happened to the *real* normal?

I pulled a pillow to me, feeling the regret burn inside my chest. "That's why I didn't want to tell you. I wanted you to have a normal life as long as possible. I never had one."

She looked at me then. "If we wouldn't have come back here, would you have ever told me?"

I gnawed on my bottom lip on that one, knowing the answer. "I don't know," I lied. "Probably, if I'd noticed you doing it. I always thought it was just me."

She frowned. "You said your mother did this, too."

"Which I found out last week. By accident."

"Whoa."

"Yeah."

Her blue eyes narrowed and reality dawned across her features. "That photo album—"

"Yep, that's what did it."

She nodded and turned her interest back on her fingernails, and I watched the haughty little mask settle across her face.

"You know, what Miss O said earlier—all we did was go swimming, I don't know what she's making such a fuss about."

"I'd say it's about stripping down to your underwear and dry humping a boy in public."

Riley's eyes flew to mine, wide and startled. And busted. "What the—"

"There's not too much you can sneak by with in this town, believe me, but that little gem came straight from somebody who watched and is on a mission to be next."

Disgust replaced the defiance, as she fixed me with an expression of repulsion. "Oh God."

"Yeah, so think of all the horny eyes out there getting a thrill next time you decide to put on a show."

"Mom! God, there was no *show*." At my raised eyebrows, she added, "That I knew about."

"So you want to tell me now that you and Grady aren't doing anything?"

"We're not, Mom. I swear." Riley looked me square in the eyes, and I knew that look to be the real thing. The before-she-was-an-alien look. "Making out is as far as it's gone."

"In your underwear."

She closed her eyes. "Yes."

"That trend won't last."

"I know." She sighed and rolled onto her back. "That was stupid. I guess I thought I was being all responsible because everyone else was getting naked."

"Okay, in that situation—other than coming home—" I said with a pointed look. "You made the smart call, boog. But making out like that took the smart away."

"It just kinda got away from me."

I nodded. "It'll do that." I paused. "Were you drinking?"

She waited a beat too long. "No."

"Riley Anne."

Her whole body reacted. "I hate when you do that." She fidgeted with her cord necklace and then her hair, staring at the ceiling as if it could rescue her. "Okay, yeah, there was some beer."

"How much?"

"I don't know. It was just in this big ice chest in the back of somebody's truck."

I shook my head. "You, sweetheart. How much did *you* have?"

She shrugged. "A couple, I guess," she said, her voice trailing off. Which meant probably more.

I stood up and walked to the window and back again, my stomach propelling me around the room.

"Half naked and beer doesn't go well together, Riley. You're damn lucky you weren't raped."

She perched on one elbow. "Grady wouldn't do that."

I scooped my hair back, breathing in and out slowly. "I don't mean Grady. But even with him, that makes it a lot easier to let things *get away from you.*"

She averted her eyes. "I know."

"You know." I was frustrated and my stomach went acidic. I flopped into the big chair. "Riley, I need to be able to trust you better than that."

Defensiveness boiled back up in her face. "Okay, I get it. I'm sorry. I wasn't thinking clearly that night. I'd just seen a man vanish into a wall and was a little pissed. I wanted to be like everybody else."

"This was the other night when you left?"

"Yes."

Some of my anger and anxiety dissipated, as logic started to piece itself together. "The next day, when you didn't go see Grady—are things okay?"

Back at the fingernails again. "Yeah. I was just—I don't know. I felt kinda weird about it, I guess." Oh, thank God. "So, can I sleep in here tonight?" she asked.

A smile tugged at a corner of my mouth and I got up to pick up the pencils so she wouldn't see. If I appeared to enjoy it, she'd yank back the request.

"Because there are bugs in your room?"

She twisted a piece of hair and then tucked it behind her ear. "Possibly."

"Well, that can't be good."

She climbed under the covers, taking a lack of a no for a yes.

My cell chirped that I had a text message at precisely 11:48 p.m. I knew this because I'd seen that minute and every preceding one tick by since I'd turned off the lights.

I couldn't get it out of my head. What the hell was going on with that picture? It was like I was there. I fumbled for my phone, marveling at who would be texting a psychotic freak like me at nearly midnight. Jason.

Are you asleep?

Really?

Yes, I typed. *I'm sleep-texting.*

What are you wearing?

I blinked and put the phone down, then chuckled and picked it back up. Sliding carefully out of bed, I moved to the chair and hit the call button.

"Hello?" he answered.

"Are you serious?"

His rumbling laugh sounded warm in my ear. It was comforting, familiar. Oddly so, for not knowing him that long.

"I always wanted to ask a woman that," he said. "Thought I'd give it a whirl."

"Well, keep on whirling."

"Why are we talking so soft?" he asked, almost whispering himself.

"I have company in my bed tonight."

"Really?"

I pulled my feet underneath me and snuggled into the chair, refusing to look in the direction of the computer. Even with the screen off and dark, it gave me the creeps.

"Yeah, my daughter thinks she loves me on occasion. She's having a weak moment."

"Do I need to let you go?"

"No, she sleeps like the dead." Which I found ironic to say since the dead had never once slept or been quiet around me.

"So, were you were really awake, or did I wake you up?" he asked.

"I was counting the ceiling fan revolutions. And you?"

"I've been up and down eight times, and then tried to think of something good to fall asleep to, so I went to making out with you."

Stomach flip. "And what I was wearing?"

"No—clothes weren't in there."

"Oh, wow."

"Yeah, so that really did nothing to help me get to sleep."

I laughed softly. "Yeah, I guess not."

"I keep remembering that my hands were on your ass today."

Goose bumps trickled down my back. "I think there was even a boob hit-and-run at one point."

"I was thinking that, too, but I didn't know if that was real or just my embellishment."

I giggled. "Your embellishment?"

"My play-by-play is always on a plane just above reality."

"Well, our planes were flying together then."

"I really am sorry about all that."

"Mmm—not really. 'Fess up," I said.

"My heart is. My body's a heathen."

I laughed out loud and then clapped a hand over my mouth. All this funny coming from Jason was something no one would expect.

"So, tomorrow," I said, not a clue what I really meant by that.

"Tomorrow, my son is visiting."

Boing! Whiplash. I was still on the kissing. "Really? How did that come about?"

I heard a deep sigh in the phone. "I texted him. Figured I might get a better response that way. Guess so, because his mom is dropping him by the shop tomorrow."

Oh wow. Jason's son. "That's great! Are—you nervous?"

"Completely. And that's so messed up. Nervous about seeing my own son."

"It'll be good. It'll even out and feel normal again, you'll see," I said, trying to be helpful.

There was a pause. I got the feeling he wanted to say something but didn't. "Well, guess I'll see you in the morning."

"Yes, you will, so go back to bed and quit thinking about my ass."

I crammed a fist into my forehead. Really? I think he laughed and I think we said good-bye. I was wishing for a different mouth at the time.

The chair was squishy and comfortable and Riley had since spread out like an octopus across the queen-sized bed. So I curled up in somewhat of a fetal position in Alex's—in the chair—and tried to close my eyes. My brain still wouldn't shut down. My daughter's reputation was at stake, my computer was haunted, my mother bailed on me, I felt like I was cheating on my dead best friend—who lied to me for decades—and evidently I had a boyfriend.

The really sad part was that the last one was the scariest. I could deal with the rest. Kinda.

THE next morning, I was surprised as I walked under the jingle to smell coffee. I raised my nose to see if it was a cruel joke.

"What's this?"

Jason gave me a look and poured me a cup as I raised the counter. "Stepping outside my box."

"Wow." I added my generous helping of creamer and stirred as I noticed his restless feet. "What time does he get here?"

Both our heads turned toward the bell, which wasn't supposed to ring yet.

"Now," he said.

A dark-haired boy in jeans and sporting a camouflage backpack, and a woman with short brown hair stopped in the doorway. The boy ambled in looking around him, taking in the busy clutter.

"Hey, Dad," he said, his arms flopping loose at his sides as he touched this and that.

"Hey, Connor."

Jason raised the counter so the boy could come back, and Connor's expression said that was pretty cool. The woman stayed rooted to her spot against the door, as if she might break some kind of treaty by stepping any closer. She was pretty, I noticed, and I was weirdly surprised by that. Why wouldn't she be pretty? She had dark eyes but fair skin, and her hair flipped softly at the ends.

"Okay, Connor," she said, getting the boy's attention. "I'll be back to get you day after tomorrow."

"Okay," he answered, already busy checking out a box of artificial worms.

I watched as Jason gave her a quickly mouthed thank-you. She halfheartedly flicked a hand and backed out the door before it could seal itself shut with her inside. I busied myself with my coffee, wincing at the strength of it—*wow*.

Jason's phone sang at his hip, and he held up a finger as he was pulled into a conversation with what sounded like a supplier.

"Ever seen live bait?" I asked Connor.

He looked over at me as if I'd just appeared there and shrugged. Okay.

"Come on," I said, walking down the hallway, hoping I wasn't talking to myself.

I turned in time to see the facial reaction to the smell as he entered the bait room. That was a reward all in itself.

"Man!"

"Yeah, you get used to it."

He was already moving from one vat to the other. "Cool, I've never seen live shrimp before. Like swimming around and everything. Look at their eyes."

"Yep. Want to hold one?"

He looked back at me with something between horror and fascination. "For real?"

"For real."

I retrieved the green net from its hook and scooped one out, holding it out for him as he gingerly picked it up with a finger and thumb. It squirmed around, unhappy with the sudden turn of events, and Connor laughed at all the legs and eyes moving at once. He looked so much like his dad when he laughed.

Jason walked back there and Connor grinned at him as he held up the shrimp. "People fish with these, huh?"

"Yep. Fish around here love them."

"Can we go? Fishing?"

His eyes sparkled like a Christmas tree, and I saw Jason's mind working, trying to pull that off.

"We can go tomorrow night, maybe—"

"Aw, come on, let's go today."

"Shop's too busy for one person, bud, we have to wait till after—"

"Four," I interrupted. Jason looked at me. "Take off at four, I've got it the last two."

He tilted his head slightly in question. "You sure?"

"Positive." I widened my eyes to make my point.

The back door swung open as Bob ambled in, his unshirted hairy torso already shiny with sweat and river water. I watched Connor's mouth fall open at the sight of him.

"No bait runnin' today," Bob said, grinning and showing off all his gaps. "So top-feedin' lures won't be much good if anyone asks."

"Okay," I answered, as if I really knew what to do with that information. No top feeders. Check.

"Hey," Bob said, nodding toward Connor. "You got yourself a helper today, Boss?"

Jason beamed and laid a hand on his shoulder, which Connor avoided by leaning out to put the shrimp back. The light shone a bit dimmer after that.

"My son, Connor."

"Well, that ain't no shocker there, he's all you," Bob said with a smoker's laugh. He passed a lanky hand across his dirty jean shorts and stuck it out.

Poor Connor did his best to act unfazed and put his hand out as if he might not get it back.

"Bob. Nice to meetcha, Connor," Bob said, pumping Connor's hand till he pumped back. Making him a man. I bit my lip.

"Nice to meet you, too, sir."

Bob guffawed. "Do I look like a sir to you?"

Connor laughed at that and his body went loose again.

"I'm just Bob, bud," he said. "But I 'preciate that. Your daddy raised you right."

Connor learned about unpacking boxes and putting away merchandise and how to wield a broom. Things I didn't find particularly exciting but he seemed to enjoy. I noticed he was happy while piddling around the shop, even talking with his dad, unless Jason tried to show any affection or talk about anything too personal. Then he would shut down.

Four o'clock came, and they headed out on a boat Bob had gassed up and stocked with rods and bait and life jackets. Connor surely had to be rethinking it once he realized the intimacy of a few hours trapped alone with his dad, but when they walked out he didn't show it. He was all boy, his nerves itching with the want to get in that boat.

JASON didn't call that night. That was okay; I knew he was busy with his son. A text letting me know they made it back would have been nice, but it was okay. Really.

Riley and Grady hung out in the yard playing washers while Bo ran back and forth thinking they were throwing them for him. Dad sat on the front porch working his crossword puzzle till it was too dark and there was no plausible reason to stay. Alex didn't come by, either. And I refused to turn the computer on. In fact, I didn't even go to my room until it was time to collapse. I flopped on the couch and watched mindless TV until I could stand it no more.

The next morning, I walked into the shop as a purple wiggly whizzed by my head. I jerked a little to the left, and snatched the worm off the floor. Connor's laughter filled the room.

"So close," he said from behind the counter, perched on a stool.

"Too early," I replied, sniffing the air. Damn. "Where's your dad?"

Connor shrugged as I tossed the worm back into the box he held. He plucked it back out and stretched it. I chose to ignore it and headed to the coffeepot instead.

"Dad said you might come with us out on the boat today."

I turned, empty carafe in hand. "Dad said what?"

He shrugged again. He needed to quit doing that.

"Connor."

He finally turned to face me.

"Why am I coming?"

"I don't know. He just said you might. Said you know some cool places."

Ah. Tour guide. Gotcha. "We'll see. How was the fishing yesterday?"

That woke him up. His eyes lit up as he dropped the worms and shifted on his stool to face me. "That was awesome! I caught a bunch of croakers, and since there wasn't a size limit on them, we kept 'em. Dad said they're good when you do something like a—fish boat or something?"

I smiled at that and went back to scooping coffee. "Yeah, you put it with peppers and onions and butter—and shrimp if you have any—and wrap it all up in foil and broil it." I'd told Jason about that in passing one day, and he'd remembered it?

"Like a Boy Scout thing?"

"Kinda. Are you a Boy Scout?"

He shook his head and looked away. "Nah. But my friend Riley is. He's shown me some stuff."

"My daughter's name is Riley."

He gave me a scrunched-up look. "Riley is a boy's name."

I laughed. "Not if a girl is wearing it."

His eyebrows raised a little as if to tell me that was really stupid, so I bit back the urge to tell him I knew a girl named Connor once.

"What else did y'all catch?"

"A flounder but we had to put it back, a bunch of catfish my dad said wasn't the good kind—"

"Hardheads."

"Yeah," he said, pointing at the word. "And then when it started getting late he caught two specs. Keepers! I caught a spec, too, but it wasn't big enough. Man, like just by an inch."

"That's really cool!" I didn't even know Jason could fish. "Did you use live or artificial?"

"Just shrimp and minnows."

"Well good, I'm glad you had a good time."

"We're gonna do the fish boat thing tonight after we get back, in case we get some more to add in."

Fishing and dinner. Or was I only on the tour part of the evening? Part of me wished to be invited, and part not. It was way early to be introducing his son to anyone, especially with the tension already between them. And I didn't know what I was to him yet. Not really.

I turned then as I heard steps behind me and looked into a face that didn't know I was there yet. The things his eyes did when he saw me—kinda told me what I was to him. And made my knees wiggle.

He looked down at the steaming coffee in my hand as I stirred in the creamer. "Mmm, sorry, forgot about that today."

"Heard about the big catch yesterday," I said, trying to include Connor before he got weirded out.

Jason laughed. "Yeah, we did pretty well."

The bell jingled and in strolled Jiminy. Introductions went around, Connor bragged about his fishing trip, and Jiminy kept glancing at me. I pretended to busy myself with pulling tide reports.

"We're going again tonight," Connor said.

"You should go with them, Dani," Jiminy said with a shit-eating grin.

Jason paused. "Actually I was going to see if you wanted to," he asked, his eyes questioning.

"Do you really know places to go?" Connor asked, looking doubtful.

I opened my mouth to answer all three of them, but then just smirked. "Jiminy knows more. And he has hats."

Jiminy's eyes sparkled. "I'll throw in the hats. You can handle the rest."

"As long as I drive," Jason muttered, stepping just outside my reach to pop him.

"Well yeah, that, too," Jiminy said, chuckling. "Basically, you'd just be going fishing."

I shook my head. "Y'all are just too funny. Maybe I'll just stay home and eat chocolate ice cream and let the guys hook the fish."

"Or you could bring the ice cream and come eat the fish with us?" Jason asked. And there it was. I looked at Connor and saw a flicker of disappointment fly through his eyes. The evening must have gone well; he wanted more private time.

"I tell you what," I said finally. "I'll go fishing, then leave the stinky bloody part to the men. Save me some of the fish boat, I've already got plans with Riley tonight."

Which I didn't, and Jason looked a little disappointed, but Connor looked happier, so all was good. Right?

I ended up bucketing the bait, since Bob was off somewhere in his golf cart. And I figured the rods were ready except for mine. I set myself up one with a weight and swivel, amazed that I still remembered how to do that. Jason looked amazed, too. He hovered nearby, watching me tie a hook on with my teeth and clip the excess line.

"What?"

"You never cease to surprise me."

I chuckled. "Yeah, thank God Riley wasn't a girly girl, because I wouldn't have known what to do with a Barbie."

The water was like a sheet of glass. No waves, thank God. But I knew the tide would be coming in soon off the pass, bringing a current and hopefully some fish. The boat was a nice one, the better of the four rentals we had through the shop. Bigger than my dad's aluminum side console, that's for sure, but not as nice as Jiminy's or Hank's boats.

I stashed my rod in one of the ports and took a seat on the side while Connor played king of the world at the front. I held on like it was a roller coaster and forced back the bile that rose in my throat. I was getting better. My skin wanted to crawl away, but I was in the damn boat so I was pretty proud.

"Sit down, Connor," Jason said as we took off.

Yes, sit down. Please sit down.

Connor zipped and unzipped his life jacket absently as he lowered himself to what could just technically be called sitting. In a flash, an image of a child hurtling over the edge into monster waves and sideways rain tore across my brain, along with a scream that stopped my blood.

"He handles that wheel better than you would."

I jolted toward the voice as my little old lady friend positioned herself across from me, trying gingerly to put her legs up longways on the bench as she held on to the rail handle.

I felt a fine sheen of nervous sweat break out. Shit, double hell. What was all that and why the hell was she back?

I looked at Connor and then back at Jason, noting even through my panic that he did look good at the wheel. For a midwestern boy.

"Please sit, Connor," I said with a jerky smile. "Please." He looked disgusted but complied.

I gave the old lady a pointed look that I hoped asked her in great detail why she chose that particular day and time for a boat ride. Now that would have been a good trick to give me while weird gifts were being doled out. Telepathy.

But she wasn't paying attention to me. She was too busy laughing at the way her feet bounced against the bench seat when we ran across the wake left by another boat.

"Sweet Jesus," I muttered.

"Whoo-hoo!" Connor said, holding his arms up as Jason sped up.

"I'm with him," the old lady said, doing the same. "Whoo-hoo! It's like being on a carnival ride. Except I never rode one."

I felt hot, despite the air rushing past me, and my stomach churned. *Why?* I mouthed at her, cutting my eyes to each side.

"Why not?" she said, laughing and subsequently coughing. "I missed my ride last time." She looked back at Jason, giving him a once-over. "This one has more potential."

"Hey, aren't we fishing in there?" Connor asked, pointing at a cut in the trees off to the right.

"Thought we'd ride around awhile first, maybe find another spot," Jason answered.

Great. My friend's short gray curls spun wildly, kind of like my head.

"So talk, girl, don't mind me," she said.

I took a deep breath and closed my eyes, making a wish. I opened one—nope, still there. Still grinning like a kid.

"Dani? You okay?"

I started at Jason's voice, pasting on a smile. "Great. Something in my eye."

She laughed. "He's cute." Then she winked at me. "The boy, I mean. But his dad is, too." Her expression went drifty as she gazed out over the water. "Need to get my grandkids back out here."

I rubbed my face, wishing she'd quit rambling. It was hard to ignore, even for someone like me.

"Didn't see any alligators yesterday," Connor yelled over the noise as he turned around. "Aren't there supposed to be alligators here?"

"They're around," I called back. "You have to look close on the edges, they sleep in the tall grass and just under the surface." I held a hand toward Jason as I kept a death grip on the side of the boat. "Can you slow down a little, please?"

He looked concerned. "You okay?"

"Mmm." I smiled and hoped I wasn't green.

"Man, I wanna see one." He swung his head from side to side.

"Used to be a big one that lived right over there." I pointed to a cove. "I named him Herman Munster when I was little."

Jason slowed down and headed that way, I presumed to fish. I took some easier breaths once the nose was down and concentrated on talking to the right people.

"Herman who?" he asked.

"Munster. Like the TV show?"

Blank look. "I'll ask my Grandma Helen about it," Connor said, reaching for the bucket with the anchor.

"Helen?" The lady said. She grinned and then snorted. "That's *my* name. Well, sorta."

"Sorta?" I asked, then wanted to swallow my tongue as I felt the heat rise. I was slipping. That was a rookie mistake. I blamed the boat.

"Huh?" Connor asked.

I watched both of them as she babbled on. "—hated that name."

I coughed and pretended to swallow a bug or something.

"You okay?" Jason asked again.

I held up a hand. "I'm good."

"I swear, my kids had a good laugh putting that on my gravestone. They knew. Hell, I wrote it down. I said I'd gone by June all my life and to put it in the paper and everything as June, and I'll be damned if they didn't put Helen June."

I leaned on my knees and massaged my temples. Not for long, though. Connor already had the anchor out ready to throw like a pro. Jason cut the motor and glided into the spot he wanted.

"Hang on, Connor," he said. "Dani, come steer a second."

My head shot up. "What?"

He sighed. Loudly. "There's no motor. Just keep us to the left of that tree."

I jumped up and traded places, just as Connor moved

backward and Jason had to step to the right. Into Don't-Call-Me-Helen.

She gasped, cleared her throat, and disappeared. Jason went woozy on his feet for a minute and grabbed the console behind him.

"Jason?"

He shook his head. "Just got up too fast, I guess." He sniffed. "You smell cigarettes?"

Chapter 15

"WHO was the top dog?" Bob asked as we shuffled into the back door of the bait room.

I held all the gear and Jason and Connor carried a large cooler between them. Connor cut his eyes toward me as they set down the chest and I opened it and pulled out a thirty-one-inch speckled trout.

"That would be me," I said with a smile.

Bob nodded approvingly. "Nice."

"That's a girl's luck," Connor said. "We caught all the rest, she catches *one* and it's the biggest."

I laughed and pretended to toss it to him so he'd flinch. He smirked and backed up a little. I could tell he didn't quite know what to make of me. And I knew Jason had no idea how to help with that.

"Connor did catch the most," I said, smiling at him. "He is the croaker expert."

"Nine of 'em," he said, standing a little straighter. His hair poked up on top where he'd taken his cap off.

"Croaker—that's good eating," Bob said, looking in the cooler. "You got yourself a good haul, there."

Connor beamed.

"Well, let's get this haul cleaned so we can eat sometime tonight," Jason said, heading to the big sink.

Connor grabbed the filet knife like he'd been doing it for years instead of two days. It was good, him being there. Good for him and good for Jason. The next day would not be good. I had the feeling moody Jason would be back in residence.

I stood awkwardly to the side. "Y'all need my help?"

Jason turned with a skeptical smirk. "Seriously?"

"No."

He laughed. "Want your fish? We can do it first."

I waved a hand. "Nah, just add it to your pile. Y'all enjoy."

I turned to head down the hall to the storefront, but I heard a whisper. "Go ask her."

It was Connor, and it made me look back. Jason was looking at him funny and then he cut his eyes toward me. I suddenly felt awkward again, and Jason looked stuck.

"You could come eat if you want," Connor said, looking at me quickly, then back at the fish. "I mean, you did catch the biggest one and all. Kinda sucks to just go home now."

"Connor," Jason admonished.

"What?" he said, looking up at him. "Suck isn't a bad word."

I laughed to myself and walked back, taking a chance and giving Connor a sideways hug. He didn't pull away but he didn't look at me, either.

"Thank you, Connor, I appreciate that. But I have to go see what my family is up to tonight."

He nodded. "Oh yeah. The girl with the boy name."

I laughed. "Yeah, her."

When I looked up to catch Jason's eye, my laugh caught in my throat and made my skin tingle. The expression in his eyes was almost physical in its power. His son had invited me over. Relief, joy, happy. That's what it was. His happy was showing. I licked my lips nervously and then got sidetracked again when his eyes dropped to watch that. Had to blink that away, and I gave Connor's shoulders another squeeze.

"See you in the morning."

"See ya." His face went blank.

He was like Jason that way. Show a feeling. Take it away. Act like nothing matters.

THE next morning felt like coming home from a vacation. Depressing. Connor was moping and grumpy. Jason grunted one-word answers and his face was dark. I made my coffee and tried to make small talk.

"Well, how was my fish last night?"

"Awesome," Connor said, flopping onto a stool. "Dad saved you some."

"Oh cool."

He fiddled with a zipper on his backpack. "I wish we could go fishing every day."

I chuckled. "Nobody can do that, babe. That's not reality. But you can probably go each time you come here. I'm sure your dad can swing that." I hoped so, or I just sold him out.

He nodded. "Yeah, maybe."

"I enjoyed it though," I said. "Haven't gotten to do that in years."

"Really?" His face scrunched up in surprise. "Why not?"

I shrugged. "Just got busy, I guess. I should do better about that."

"Wish I could stay for the festival," he said, his eyes clouding again. "My mom is such—"

"Don't finish that sentence, Connor."

We both turned our heads as Jason entered the room.

"Sorry," Connor whispered.

"Let's just take this one visit at a time, okay?" Jason said, his expression softening. He put a hand in Connor's hair. "Maybe she'll let you come for longer next time. Before school starts."

"Yeah."

A car pulled up out front, and I knew by Jason's face who it was. I took my coffee and went to the back to avoid the awkwardness. The minnows needed to be checked. I could do that. But shortly after the jingle, I heard steps behind me. I turned to see Connor stop a few feet from me.

"Hey—just wanted to say bye."

I took a step forward and held out my right fist. His face relaxed and broadened into the smile that so resembled his dad's, and he knocked his own fist against mine.

"See ya next time, Connor."

"See ya."

He ambled out, leaving me blinking and trying not to let that go to my heart. But when the bell jingled again, it did. For Jason. I walked slowly down that hall, not wanting to get there, slower with each step. Jason leaned against the counter, staring at the door.

I stayed back, suddenly unsure of my footing, not wanting to intrude. He heard me and swiped at his eyes as he turned away. I saw it morph in front of me—the moody withdrawn Jason I'd first met, with the tight jaw and angry eyes.

He busied himself with some papers, and I went to the computer to pull the tide report. Two clicks in, stupid hit me in the head. What was I doing? Exactly what I'd always done. Taken my cue from other people's moods and wimped out. His back was to me when I turned around, so I watched him. Watched him operate on robot mode, shutting down all the parts of him that made my heart race.

"Hey."

"Hmm," he responded, not turning.

"Hey," I repeated.

"What?"

I paused, but still he kept flipping through papers.

"Please look at me."

He set down the papers with barely disguised irritation. I saw the man on the houseboat that told me to leave. Same guy. More clothing.

"Dani, it's not a good time."

"Yeah, I get that." I walked the distance between us and put a hand on his arm. Feeling the tightness of him, like a spring bolt. His eyes flickered at my touch.

"I know you're sad, Jason. It's okay to be. Talk to me."

He closed his eyes. "I don't want to."

I don't know where the boldness came from, but I moved his arm so that I had access and wrapped my arms around him, holding tight. He didn't move, didn't respond, didn't say a word, and I just shut my eyes tight and hoped like hell it wouldn't backfire on me.

The doubt hit me like bullets. Was I being presumptuous? Did I cross a line? Did I feel more than he did? What did I know about losing a child? My head started to spin and I started to pull away—when his hands came up my back.

I held my breath as one slowly moved upward into my hair, as the other one pulled me tighter against him, so tight it was hard to breathe. But I didn't care. I hugged him back, wanting to take the hurt. I felt his breathing quicken, as if maybe he was working not to cry, but I didn't look up in case he was. I just let him take what he needed.

Several moments later, he moved his hands up to my face and lifted it to his. I caught a glimpse of reddened eyes before he kissed me soft and slow, long and deep, melting my insides and sending heat to important places. That kiss went on for days, it felt like. Till we heard a truck door creak shut outside and we pulled away, both of us in a hazy fog.

Jason backed away and disappeared down the hall as the bell jingled.

* * *

"I want some boudain balls. And shrimp on a stick. And cheesecake on a stick."

Riley's head was on a swivel, taking in all the food kiosks at the festival.

"Your mother was always about the cotton candy," Dad said, pointing at a small girl smeared in sticky blue. "I always wished they'd make a white one. She'd always end up blue or pink."

I handed her a twenty. "Take it one at a time, boog," I said, glancing around. We'd been there for fifteen minutes and there was no sign of Jason. Not that I was really looking. Or worried about it.

"Ooh, funnel cake," Riley said, sounding six instead of sixteen. Then she caught sight of Grady and Miss Olivia and waved.

Oh sure. She saw *her* man.

"Hey, Dani girl," Miss Olivia said as she ambled closer. "Nathaniel, you look better every day."

"Are you flirting with me?" he asked.

"Am I?" Miss Olivia chuckled. "It's been so long, I have no idea."

My dad laughed—a deep warm sound that instantly made me relax. Grady looped an arm around Riley and pulled her in for a hug. She hugged him back and then pulled back to stand next to him as her blue eyes scanned the crowd. No floor shows today.

Bob slow-rolled by in his golf cart, his head swinging from side to side, taking it all in. It was the first time I'd ever seen him with a shirt on, and he almost pulled off normal till he swung his metal leg out the side as a wave to me.

"Every year, it's hot enough to fry eggs on the street, you hear me?" Miss Olivia said, fanning out her yellow-and-white muumuu.

I nodded and checked out the sky, the familiar thickness tickling my skin. A storm was brewing. The quickening of my pulse told me that. "It's muggy, though. Air's heavy."

"Choke you if you breathe too deep." Miss Olivia adjusted her straw hat. "Rain's on the way, the weatherman said. Was supposed to be here early this morning, but it's waiting, I guess," she said, laughing. "Could blow this whole little party off the street. Y'all get something to eat yet?"

Yeah, it's waiting. I closed my eyes for a second and breathed in the wet air. It was for me, somehow. I felt the energy of it on my skin.

"Not yet, but I'm working on it," Riley said.

"Well, I'm going to see what's happening on the fishing board," Dad said, already heading toward the giant stat board used to track the tournament. And Jiminy, who nodded at him and said something they both chuckled at. The two of them slapped each other on the shoulders and ambled off together. My heart warmed instantly at the thought that maybe—just maybe—they were finding that place again.

"Bye, Pop!" Riley called out, and he raised his right hand in a wave, not looking back.

"We're going for a stroll," Grady said as he took Riley's hand. She looked up at him with a smirk.

"A stroll? Really?"

"Thought it sounded nice," he said, defending himself. "Old-fashioned."

I patted his shoulder and leaned in closer. "Just keep your clothes on, that's as old-fashioned as I need."

Miss Olivia snorted, Riley clapped a hand to her eyes, and Grady turned five shades of red.

"Yes, ma'am."

"Mom."

I fixed her with a smile. "That's me."

"Let's go," she said, tugging on his hand.

"Riley," I said, stopping her.

She turned around, exasperated. "What?"

I paused a second, staring hard into her eyes. "Don't talk to strangers."

Grady chuckled but Riley's annoyance faltered, and she just nodded. I watched them walk away. *She's gonna be okay. She's gonna be okay.*

"She's just walking around a festival, not Europe," Miss Olivia said, leaning into my line of vision.

A laugh escaped my throat, but I didn't really feel it. "Europe might be safer than Bethany."

She squeezed my hand. "Take a breath, girl. Let's go look at that jewelry over there."

I followed her gaze to a kiosk filled with silver everything, appropriately bannered SILVER EVERYTHING, then back to the retreating figures getting swallowed by the crowd. I had the weirdest urge to run after her. Instead, I followed Miss Olivia as she made her way over to the bling.

There was an index card marked up in red Sharpie, ALL STERLING SLIVER 50% OFF! A sweating bald man with a goatee readied himself for a "sliver" sale as Miss Olivia perused the selection. As ringed and braceleted and adorned as she was, he probably figured an easy sale.

Not to be the case. Fifteen minutes later, Miss Olivia had him down to around 90 percent off a whole bucketload of jewelry. I tried on a few rings, a few bracelets, but put them all back. Riley had all the cash I could afford to blow, and I was saving my last five dollars for an Italian sausage po'boy sandwich I'd passed.

There was a pair of brushed silver fleur-de-lis hook earrings that kept drawing my eye, though. I picked them up and glanced at the tag. Twenty bucks. I grimaced. Even at half off, and giving up my sandwich, I didn't have enough. And I wasn't going to use Miss Olivia to get it cheaper. The poor guy was frustrated already. Still, I had to hold them up to my ears and check it out in the smudged mirror he had there.

"Those are nice," said a familiar voice behind me.

I turned to see Jason half grinning down at me, and I chuckled as I put the earrings back, marveling at the heat to my face that had nothing to do with the temperature.

"Hey there."

He frowned. "You're not buying them?"

"No," I said, waving a hand in their direction. "I was just messing around."

He reached around me and picked them back up.

"Jason—"

"Hush."

He held them up to my ears again for the mirror, standing behind me so close I felt the goose bumps tickle my skin. "Have you bought yourself anything since you've been back here?"

"Hmph," Miss Olivia said loud enough for me to hear.

"Yep, bought some toothpaste day before yesterday." I turned so that his raised eyebrow of disapproval was up close and personal.

"Cute."

"Yeah, she's irritating that way," Miss Olivia said, shoving plastic bags of her purchases into her giant pink one.

I tried a loving glare, but she just smiled and leaned against the table.

"I'm good, Jason. I don't need earrings."

"Your earlobes might disagree." He touched my earlobes as he said it and I thought for a minute they might ignite into flames.

"Well, they'll just have to suck it up."

He laughed and handed the earrings back to the guy, leaning into me as he did it. I got a delicious whiff of him that made my insides go a little wiggly. He hooked an arm around my neck and led me away, squeezing Miss Olivia's hand as he did. She winked at me. Oh lord.

"Subtle," I said softly.

"What?"

"You just slipped her money to buy them."

He looked wounded. For about two seconds. "You make it really tough to do something nice for you."

I laughed. "Sorry. Guess I'm not used to it."

Jason pulled my head to him and kissed the top of it. It stopped me. Intimacy in public was something way outside my box. My feet stopped and I looked up into eyes that already had me figured out.

"Relax," he said softly.

A thumb ran across my cheek, and I couldn't look away. He understood me. And yet he knew nothing about me. He dropped a soft kiss on my lips followed by the sexiest grin I'd ever seen.

My stomach flipped over, and I tried not to want to do the girly scream as we walked on. There were children around, after all. But my giddiness was short-lived. Because right in front of me, sitting on the hood of an old car, was Alex.

I never expected him to be out there. Too much contact potential. I must have tensed or stopped or choked or something, because Jason's head turned quickly.

"You okay?"

My mouth worked and I couldn't quite form the words. Alex's expression hit me to the core. Raw. Pain. The last time—the only other time—I'd seen that on him was when he was talking about Alyssa's death. My head suddenly filled with that loud wind again, and I shook it away and pleaded with my eyes for him to understand.

"Dani?" Jason said, shaking my shoulder.

"I'm—sorry," I managed, breaking eye contact with Alex. "I—"

"Well, wasn't that sweet?"

It was a smart-ass drawl I knew in my sleep just by the level of skin crawl. Shelby and her equally obnoxious husband approached, her carrying a bag of jar candles, him carrying a beer.

"I had no idea y'all were a couple now," Shelby said, smiling with all but her eyes. They darted back and forth between us, pissed off.

"I could say the same," I said, glancing around them. Alex was gone. Damn it. "Never seen the two of you actually together."

Matty ignored us and scanned the crowd, letting his eyes fall to the ass of a twentysomething walking by. Always after the strange.

"I thought you were fishing the tournament," Jason said, pulling Matty's attention back.

"Fish were crap the other day," he said. "We decided it wasn't worth the time."

"The boys, either?"

Matty shrugged. "Not sure what Carson's kids are doing, they probably bailed, too. Storm's coming, anyway."

Yes, it was. I rubbed my arms, suddenly itchy as uneasiness blanketed me.

Shelby caught a glimpse of someone better and excused herself. Matty turned to follow her, but not before giving me what I'm sure he thought was a sexy once-over. I pulled Jason away before Matty's slow response time could even register I'd vacated the spot.

Dad and Jiminy walked up to our right, and I couldn't miss the expression of curiosity on my dad's face.

"Nathaniel Shane," he said as they approached and I said nothing, reaching across me to shake Jason's hand.

"Oh my God, I'm sorry. Dad, this is Jason, my—" I looked up at him, looking for a description. "Boss?"

Jason laughed and pumped his hand heartily, thank goodness. "Jason Miller, good to meet you, Mr. Shane."

"You must be the new honcho at the bait shop that Marg has told me about."

"Uh, I'm pretty sure Marg just humors me, sir. She lets me think I'm the boss, but we all really work for her."

Jiminy chuckled. "Isn't that the truth?"

Dad laughed, his eyes lighting up. "Where's Riley?" he asked me. "She hanging out with her *boss*, too?"

"Cute."

He winked at me and gave Jason an approving nod. The best he could do, I'm sure. Meeting up with my love life wasn't something he'd had much experience with.

"She's with Grady."

I pulled my hair back and twisted it up with a hair band I had on my wrist. It was hot, yes, but it was more about stress. It felt like my blood was on a switch that someone kept flipping, changing the direction at will. I ran a hand over my face, wiping away the light sheen of sweat.

I was uneasy. Alex had seen me kiss Jason. That hurt my heart and I felt the urge to talk to him. And not just for that. For whatever else was going on. Whatever the hell else was behind the secrets and the walls and the noises and the feelings I kept getting and my feelings for him that kept igniting in weird ways and Sarah and my computer and my mother. There were just so many unanswered questions. And besides all that, I missed him. I missed my best friend.

And something was bugging the crap out of me with Riley. Something familiar. It was making me a nervous jumping bean that she wasn't in my sights. And that wasn't normal. Nothing was normal.

Jason and I walked along, but I didn't register much. I kept looking for either of them, Riley or Grady. Something to ease the acidic dance my stomach was doing. Then I heard it. What my subconscious knew was coming, but I'd forgotten the signs. The feeling of everything being off.

The laughter. Not happy laughter or even an emotional release. But the bitter, evil, merciless sound of group hate. My eyes and skin burned in unison as I jolted toward the sound and left Jason behind. Not far.

I rounded the kiosk selling the sandwich I'd never see and nearly took down a small redheaded girl watching from outside a circle of people. She wasn't laughing with the others. She was tearful. And she was dead.

The brief contact with me made us both gasp. Kind of like sticking a paper clip in a light socket, and I had to catch my breath. But I'd seen her confusion and regret in that instant, and I knew she'd asked Riley for help.

Don't talk to strangers.

Seven or eight teenagers were gathered to pounce on my girl with the taunts and ugly ignorance I knew too well. She was alone; I didn't see Grady anywhere. She was standing stiff and defiant, jutting that chin out and flashing her eyes, but it got quiet when Carson's son Drew zeroed in.

"I'm sorry," the redheaded girl said softly, backing away. I held a hand up.

"It's okay."

Five heads swiveled my way as I let my guard down by speaking to the girl they couldn't see.

"What's okay?"

I turned to Jason's questioning gaze, then back to the group in front of me that for a moment forgot about Riley.

"That's her mom," whispered a pretty brunette to a girl I recognized as Micah, Shelby's daughter. Micah nodded but was less interested in me than she was in the fact that her boyfriend was making a spectacle of hitting on Riley.

"Drew, come on," she said, scooping a stray blonde lock behind her ear. Her eyes darted to a few of her friends and there was a crinkle above her nose. "Who cares what she did. Let's go."

He was clearly oblivious to her request, because as Riley attempted to walk around him, Drew stepped in her path, grabbing her around the waist and whispering something that included a tongue wag.

In that one action, I flashed backward twenty-five years. To Matty in the nurse's office. Blaine behind the stairwell. Carson and his groupies at the party, and nightmare school days too numerous to count. Everything glazed over, coupled with the whispers echoing in my ears. I rushed forward to stop history from repeating itself. But Riley beat me to it.

She slapped his face so hard, even I jumped, stopping in mid-step. Wow. I never did that. Micah sucked in an audible breath at the sharp pop of hand against face.

"Get your fucking hands off me," Riley said, her voice low and trembling.

Drew's face twisted in shock and embarrassment, and he grabbed Riley's arm and yanked her against him.

"What the hell's going on here?"

I turned toward the voice I recognized as Carson's, but the view of him became a blur as Grady morphed from behind me, newly purchased pork kabobs and boudain balls flying in his wake as he lunged at Drew. He had him pinned against the back of a giant wobbly plastic ice cream cone before anyone could react.

"Touch her again, and I'll break your fucking hands," he spat.

Drew's face mirrored Riley's for shock value. Shrieks and oh-my-Gods charged the air and pulled him back into action. Red-faced, he shoved back at Grady, moving him a foot or so with his bulk, but that just gave Grady leverage to slam Drew backward again.

"Drew!" Micah cried.

"Bring it, pretty boy," Drew hissed. "I'll mess up that face of yours. See if she wants to fuck you then."

Grady grabbed him by his neck, but Drew slammed a hand up under Grady's jaw. Jason was suddenly there, pulling them apart, and I realized I hadn't moved.

"Come on, Grady. It's not worth it," Jason said through his teeth.

But Drew was hell-bent on making it worth it. As Jason pulled Grady backward, Drew blew a kiss to Riley.

"Yeah, I'll show that cunt what a real man is."

"Drew!" Micah yelled, this time in anger.

She looked like she wanted to pelt him herself. Grady broke free, however, and beat her to it, coming across Drew's face with a hard right hook. Jason scrambled to restrain Grady as all hell broke loose. Girls screamed, Carson rushed in to extract his moronic son, and I yanked Riley by the arm and pulled her out of the way just as Drew spat blood in Grady's face.

"Jesus, Carson, control your kid!"

It was out of my mouth before I could put any logical thought behind it. Carson had Drew around the chest, straining with the exertion, but he had enough energy to fix me with a sneer.

"Control yours, you bitch. She started this."

"What?" Riley yelled.

I held on to her and she was trembling. I saw Grady's eyes glaze over and Jason tighten his grip.

"She can't help it, Carson."

It was Matty's voice. We all wheeled around as Matty and Shelby Sims strode up like king and queen of the prom. Shelby went straight to Micah's side.

"Coach, he jumped me," Drew slurred through his bloody mouth.

"It's okay, son, he's trash," Matty said, smiling and patting Drew's shoulder. "Just like what he hangs with." He took a swig of his beer.

"Excuse me?" My voice didn't sound like mine, but all eyes turned to me so apparently it was.

"Exactly," Shelby chimed in. Micah looked at her with confusion and unmistakable embarrassment.

"Watch your mouth, Sims," Jason said through his teeth to Matty. "This doesn't involve you, but if you keep talking about Riley like that, it will."

Matty laughed. "I'd say it doesn't involve *you*, but I forgot you're banging her mother." He took another swallow of beer and I felt my ears go hot. "Like I said, the little whore can't help it, it's in the genes."

Everything boiled and a lifetime of repressed rage bubbled to the surface. I was around Riley and smashing my hand across Matty's face before I even realized it. I heard Riley gasp along with about twenty others, but no one had time for a second one because Jason shoved Grady aside and slammed a fist into Matty's nose.

"Shit!" I yelped as blood spurted everywhere, jumping back and pulling Riley with me.

"Oh my God, Mom," I heard her whimper, but I didn't have the chance to look at her.

Matty's bottle hit the ground and shattered, he swung back and missed, and Jason hit him again, bringing him down.

"You asshole!" screamed Shelby, running to her husband. "He's unconscious! And you!" she continued, thrusting a finger at me. "This is all your fault. You and your psycho babbling to people that aren't there. You're a fucking lunatic and she is, too."

"Mom, shut up," Micah said, tears in her eyes and in her voice.

I felt like I was in the center of hell with Riley, and everyone around us had torches. Carson released his son in the chaos, who then shoved Grady from behind. Grady whirled around and it was about to be on again when a voice boomed across the ruckus.

"Enough!"

It was like God commanded the air, and everyone jumped. But I knew who possessed that voice. And that tone.

Chapter 16

"Pop," Riley whispered, and she ran to him, her eyes red with tears and fury. He wrapped her up in his arms and kept moving, pointing at Carson with his free hand as he nodded toward the dysfunctional family scene on the ground.

"Get that idiot up and out of here," he said, his voice gruff.

Carson grabbed his son by the shirt and half dragged him behind him to help Matty up as he stirred. A whimpering Shelby moved out of the way. Drew tried to help Micah up and she elbowed his hand away.

Matty wobbled to his feet, shoving hands aside. "You son of a bitch," he growled, heading toward Jason. But my dad moved Riley behind him and stepped in front of Matty, making him stumble back a step. Matty pointed around him at Jason.

"You're mine, Miller," he croaked. "You broke my fucking nose. I'll sue you for that."

"I don't think so," Jiminy said, walking up next to Dad.

Matty gave him a look. "What?"

"You heard me," Jiminy said, his voice flat. For a small man, there was power there.

Dad pointed at Matty. "You and your pathetic wife." Shelby scoffed and he turned then to include anyone in his line of vision. "All you people. You're toxic."

My eyes burned, and I pulled Riley to me. She felt stiff. I looked at her and she looked numb.

"My family has never done a thing to any of you, but you've made my daughter's life a living hell from the time she was old enough to remember." He spun around. "Now you're poisoning your kids to do the same thing to Riley. They have a gift. So what."

I felt Riley suck in a breath and I was already holding mine. We were being outed. Behind an enormous ice cream cone.

"They can see people after they die."

"Oh shit," Riley muttered, and I closed my eyes as the murmurs hummed.

When I opened them, Jason and Grady were staring at us, questions and surprise on their faces. Dad turned to us with tears in his eyes, the white of his beard in sharp contrast to his flushed skin. He wasn't one for the spotlight.

I felt the familiar prickle on my skin, one that I instantly knew wasn't the redheaded girl. But I was too stunned by my dad's expression and Jason's eyes boring into me to look for Alex.

"Who cares?" Dad said softly. "You'll pay to see movies about things like this, but when it's real people, you treat them like lepers? Are you that small-minded?"

The whispers stopped. It felt like the very air stopped—heavy and thick. I couldn't look at the faces. I couldn't focus on anything but my dad and the shaking that I wasn't sure came from me or from Riley. Then the droplets began, echoing on the metal roofs around us. It seemed to break the shocking quiet and even diffused the charged heat of the moment.

People started to move again. Quieter, as if sound might bring attention to them instead of us. Micah left her parents and walked away. Matty and Shelby went the other direction, not looking at each other. Everyone else wandered off, trying not to make eye contact with me.

Everyone except Dad, who looked defeated. And Jason and Grady, looking stunned. Jiminy stood with his shoulders spread and his back to us, staring everyone down as they walked away, like a guard.

The raindrops became steadier, drumming out a dance around us, causing steam to rise from the hot pavement. Riley pulled free and pivoted to face me, anger and hurt in her reddened eyes. Her face was wet with rain and tears.

"We have to leave here," she said, her voice hoarse.

I blinked free tears that had been burning and took a couple of steadying breaths, not trusting my voice.

"It doesn't stay in Bethany, Riley. It comes with us," I finally said.

"The people don't."

She stormed off, pulling away from my grasp.

"Riley."

But my voice was lost behind the frogs in my throat, as stuck as my feet were. I could feel eyes on me. Eyes I couldn't meet yet. I was too afraid of what I'd see. And there were whispers in the raindrops, falling from those heavy clouds. Whispers I couldn't make out.

"Let her go," Dad said softly.

I looked at him as his eyes followed her. He looked all wise with rain dripping off his hat, but his shoulders gave him away, stooped and spent.

"I'll go after her," Grady said. I touched his arm as he tried to pass me without looking my way.

"Grady, are you okay?"

"I'm fine," he said gruffly, then he faltered. His eyes met mine only for a second, then all the anger, hurt, and bewilderment were turned back to the pavement. "She could have told me, you know. Why didn't she tell me?"

He cut off his words and his expression crumpled.

"Baby, she just found out herself. Cut her a little slack."

He ran a raw-knuckled hand over his blood-spattered face and walked off quickly, away from remaining stragglers, in search of his girl. In that instant, I loved him for that.

"And your excuse?"

I closed my eyes and slowly turned back to the voice. To suck up what I deserved. But when I opened my eyes, Jason was shaking his head as though pushing that thought away. Wishing he hadn't said it out loud. He ran fingers through his wet hair, and I flashed to the day he'd come out of his bathroom wet and half naked and bared his soul that day and night about his son.

He wiped his hand on his jeans, leaving a bloody smear. With his other hand, he touched my dad's back.

"Sir, I'm sorry about all this."

"Nothing to be sorry for, son," Dad said, looking ten years older. "Thank you."

Jason tried to walk past me but his feet failed him. He stopped in front of me.

"I didn't know how to—" I whispered, my words falling away.

He shook his head slowly. "It's okay, Dani."

But I knew it wasn't. I watched the old Jason morph back in front of me, doors and walls and locks slamming shut and sealing up tight. I could hear the clanging. My eyes burned with familiar pain. He wanted no part of this. Well hell, who did?

"So, I'm a freak now," I said under my breath as a statement, not a question.

His expression was a mix of irritation and hurt. Tiny droplets dripped from his hair and eyelashes.

"So, I'm that shallow now," he shot back.

With that, he walked away. I watched him go, my feet still rooted to the same spot, my mind reeling with uncertainty.

"Sweetheart, I'm sorry."

I turned to face the only man who'd ever stood by me unconditionally. He hadn't moved, either. My dad stood soaking up the falling wetness as if he weren't aware of it. I shook my head and looked from him and Jiminy to the retreating figures of everyone else.

"No more secrets."

Jiminy nodded, his eyes warm. "No more secrets."

BACK at home, I made a pot of coffee and kept watching the window. The rain fell soft and steady but didn't get bad, so I gave Grady the benefit of the doubt and resisted the urge to go all Mommy-crazed and head off on a Riley hunt. Still—my body was on fire, head to toe. This storm—this rain—it was different, somehow.

I poured a hot cup of black and set it in front of my dad, giving his shoulders a hug.

"Quit worrying."

He slid me a look. "Hypocrite."

"Yeah, I know." I pulled out a chair and sat down. Then got back up and sat down again. "She's not mad at you though, Dad. She's mad at the situation. At me for *giving* it to her."

I traced a long, deep groove in the old wooden table with my fingernail. One I'd made with a butter knife when I was eight and had lost Saturday morning cartoons for two weeks over.

"And I made it public."

"It's okay, Dad," I said, poking his hand. "They caused that cluster today, not you. The same people throwing the same stones. They were ready to crucify Riley. You shut them up."

He took off his blue fishing hat and scratched his head, causing his thin white hair to poke out in all directions before the hat plopped down and hid it all again.

"But spilling the goods wasn't necessary. I don't know what I was thinking."

I stared into my cup, "Maybe you were thinking that it has to stop." I looked up and met his tired blue eyes. "This witch hunt needs to end."

No more secrets, I'd said. That called me outside, somehow. To the rain. I got up, leaving my coffee untouched, and kissed the top of his hat.

"I'll be on the porch for a bit."

Bojangles came with me. He loved a good storm. I didn't like this one; it had me antsy. It was noisier, but yet there wasn't much movement in the trees. Nothing to match the wind that was singing steadily louder in my ears. The weather-vane plane propellers turned steadily, but nothing crazy. Something was off. I felt Alex then and pivoted to see him walking across the yard.

Bojangles sniffed the air and ran in his direction, taking on the yard as a mission as he always did when spirits were around.

Alex seemed oblivious to the water, as he stopped short of the steps that would carry him out of the rain. He stared up at me, his eyes boring deep into me as the rain pelted harder. I shook my head to clear the roaring in my ears.

"Had quite an afternoon, didn't you?" he asked.

"I've had better. Riley went off upset—"

"I know."

"So do you know where she is?"

"Not at the moment."

He stood in the driving rain, hands in his pockets as though it were a sunny day.

"Alex, what's going on with you?" I yelled it, feeling like my ears were stopping up. "I'm—I'm sorry you had to see that today. You have to know I never want to hurt you."

But he was shaking his head. "It's how it's supposed to be, Dani. Life with the living, remember? He took care of you today."

There was a small smile to go with that, but his eyes looked sad. My feet pulled me down the stairs into the giant raindrops that had me soaked to the skin in seconds. I didn't have a choice; his eyes pulled me there.

"You look beautiful in the rain."

My head spun and I shut my eyes tight to it as another image swam over the roar in my ears. Alex smiling—but different, somehow. Different clothes. Touching my face and saying, *You look beautiful in the rain.*

Wait—*touching* me? I shook my head and blinked him back into focus. The sad Alex in front of me.

"Alex, what the hell?"

"Things are waking up," he said softly. "Coming full circle." He closed his eyes. "God, I'm so sorry, Dani."

"What? Waking *what* up?" I wanted to shake him till his teeth rattled. "Alex, enough!" I grabbed my head as the words echoed back at me. "No more secrets."

"Sarah died first."

"Oh God, this again." I threw up my hands.

"No, *listen* to me."

His tone caught my attention. Sharp. Painful. Things he didn't want to say. Suddenly I wasn't all that sure I wanted to hear them. Not if it made him look so tortured. Then the roaring stopped and all I heard was the rain.

"Sarah. Then Alyssa—" His voice cracked. "She crossed over. But Sarah—"

He stopped and drove his eyes into me, hard, as if we were taking turns and I was supposed to finish the thought. A gust of wind slapped wet strands of hair into my eyes and I yanked them away just for them to blow back again.

"What?"

"She came here."

My focus returned for a second. "Here? With you?"

"Before me."

He looked at me so warily. I felt obligated to try to sort the freaking puzzle. But the roar had returned, and although the wind had kicked up, flapping his jacket around him, it didn't sound like wind. It sounded like water. I put my hands over my ears.

"Please, Alex, no more riddles." I turned to see the river and my stomach knotted. The water had turned into a churning, boiling mess. "I've got to go find Riley."

"Dani!"

I whirled back around impatiently. "What?"

"She came here—as you—were being born."

I stared at him, oblivious to my hair whipping around my face, little bells going off somewhere but not quite reaching me. My body went hot, as if my insides were baking. Alex looked at me as though memorizing me, like the next moment might suck me away.

"You were born in this house. In your room."

"I know that."

"When I got here, it was chaotic. I was looking for my family, didn't know where the hell I was, and besides that, your mother was dying."

I sucked in a breath, ignoring the increasing sound of water and what sounded like people yelling.

"Your dad left the room and she died."

"I know," I croaked.

"I saw her spirit leave her, but she kept looking at you, like she didn't want to leave."

The hot tears fell down my face, mingling with the warm rain. "Why didn't you tell me this before?"

"Because she asked me to take care of you."

I felt like the breath was pulled out of me. "But I didn't meet you till—"

"Until I was ready to show myself. Until I knew I could see you as your own person."

My head spun. "What?"

"Your mother crossed over." Alex's composure finally broke, and tears fell freely. "But only after she promised to take care of my little girl. She'd watch over mine if I'd watch over hers."

I shook my head. "That's crazy!" My voice sounded hoarse and unfamiliar to me. "Why would she think you'd stay? Why wouldn't you cross over, too?"

Alex closed his eyes and dug angrily at his face, opening them again to give me the most gut-wrenching, tormented, please-don't-make-me-say-this look.

"Alex?" It was more a token effort than any real sound.

"She knew I would stay."

"Why?"

But I knew why. In that instant, with the sound of water rushing in my head, the sound of screaming over wind, with the rain now pounding nearly sideways against me, I knew. *Sarah died first.*

"Because Sarah did."

The horrid reality settled on my skin with an icy cold. Sarah was—"No," I sobbed, clutching my middle. Weird flashes danced around my brain like a slideshow. Images of a life I didn't recognize. Of a child that wasn't Riley.

Alex cried, too. "I'm sorry, Dani."

"Dani?" I laughed bitterly. "Is that a joke?"

He shook his head. "You *are* Dani. You became your own person—"

"With your *wife* along for the ride?" The sound was deafening, maddening. I doubled over, grabbing my head. "God! How could you play with me like this all these years?" I yelled. "You were my best friend."

"You're mine."

I stood back up. "Yeah, I'll bet. Two for one." Then another thought seared across my brain. "Oh my G—" I said, half laughing, half crying. "That night I dreamed about—about us—about you." The tears burned so badly I shut my eyes tight.

"Dani." His voice sounded choked.

"The dress, the chair—the swing." I turned in a circle and held my head together as if it might fall apart otherwise. "It wasn't a dream, was it?" I yelled over the wind. "It was a fucking memory. It was Sarah's mem—"

I couldn't finish that sentence. It was too insane, even for my life.

"Parts of it, probably, but that doesn't change what—"

"Bullshit!" I screamed hoarsely. "It changes everything."

"Dani!"

I turned to see Jason in full run, almost busting it in the mud.

"Jason—" I trailed off, weakly. Why the hell not.

He reached me in seconds, and Alex sidestepped to avoid the collision, backing away slowly, as I continued to look at him, struggling to process what I'd learned.

Alex just nodded. "Go."

"Dani!"

Jason's voice pulled me back. He looked around in the direction of my stare, breathing hard, looking distracted.

"Grady just called me—they're out in *that*, and in trouble."

Jason pointed at the river. My river, that was always my solace, now looked more like the Bering Sea, rolling with rage.

"Oh my God, why?"

"I don't know, he lost his cell in midsentence. Come on!"

I turned to follow him, never looking back at Alex. Something in me ached at that choice. But I had bigger problems.

"Wait, my dad's boat is right here!" I yelled through the wind. I looked back at the angry white caps ripping at our dock. "Or no, it wouldn't make it in this."

"That's what they're in."

"Oh my God."

In the next moment I was running down the driveway, raindrops stinging my eyes, flying leaves and sticks scratching my skin. Bojangles barked in the distance, following us. I knew Jason was behind me, but I didn't know how close till I slipped and went down and he caught me by one arm, hauling me back up and setting me in motion without ever missing a step.

"Shit!"

Jason's expletive was nearly swallowed up by the wind. But my stomach jumped anyway when I saw what he saw. His houseboat was dancing on that water like it had legs, slamming repeatedly into the dock, sending wood chunks flying. There went our best option. There was no lassoing that thing. I focused on the evil body of water that had my Riley.

"Can you see them?" I yelled. "Did he say where they were?"

Jason swiped at his face and shook his head. "I don't know. Something about an old dock, then I lost him."

My dock.

I tore off to the right through the woods instead of back up the road and around. Like I wasn't forty years old, fighting gale-force winds. Like I was eight and knew the way with my eyes closed. I jumped over logs and rocks, hurdled over downed tree limbs and vines, and slung through underbrush completely oblivious to the thorns and tree limbs that ripped at my clothes and scratched my arms and face. Bo was right on my heels, like he knew it was serious.

I slid into a slushy bog when I hit the spot. The low-lying land was taking a beating, and what was left of the dock was in and out of visibility. Light was fading, too, as the storm hovered dark.

"Shit!"

I pulled myself up from the sinkhole I landed in, and Jason and I waded to the old dock, fighting the waves that drove us back.

There it was—my dad's boat. Hurling around the waves like a stray stick. And upside down. My breath left me. The wind and water noise was nothing compared to the crazed storm I heard in my head.

"Jason."

"I see it."

At that second, a head popped up as a wave slammed into a post. I sucked in my breath and strained to see.

Grady.

"Help!" he screamed, his voice tiny and nearly lost.

Jason was there, scrambling across what was left of the dock. He snatched him up in seconds, pulling him up on the stable side.

"Get her!" Grady said, fighting at Jason even as he fought for air. "Get her! I can't find her!" He rolled over, coughing up water and crying uncontrollably. "Please, God, I can't find her."

I felt nothing but boiling fear and it came screaming to the surface in one violent raging wail.

"Rileeeyyyyy!"

The sound of her name filled my ears and went on forever. But the crushing sickness that threatened to overtake me wasn't going to win. This water wasn't going to take my baby. *Not this time.*

Fresh sobs overtook me at that thought, but ones churned from adrenaline. I ran to the end of the dock and jumped with everything I had, hearing Bojangles barking frantically and Jason yelling my name as I went under.

I groped in the angry water, unable to see anything but brown and bubbles. I surfaced with Riley's name already bursting from my throat.

"Riley!"

I barely caught a breath before a wave went over my head, shoving me down, knocking that breath clean from me. My feet hit bottom, and I pushed off, letting the water's motion spring me back up.

I came up screaming her name again. I could barely see the dock, the rain was so thick, and I'd been thrown out more than I thought. I turned to see another mean-looking wave bearing down, and I dove down to beat it.

There was nothing. I groped blindly through the blackness, praying for contact, begging for it. Trying to stay calm. Trying to hold my breath through the screaming sobs racking my body. My heart felt like it would burst through my chest. And the sounds I'd heard in my head had been this. The screaming was me. I'd been here before. I had to find her. I had to find Riley. *I had to find Alyssa.*

Then suction pulled at me, opposite from the direction I was trying to go. My strokes were futile. Back and upward I went, popping to the surface with a huge gulp of air, but just in time to see the dock rushing at me.

"Dani!" I heard Jason's hoarse scream just as I slammed into the dock. My yelp was silenced as the right side of my face met wood.

The noise quieted as the same wave that drove me there rolled me down under its belly and began the pulling process all over again. The bottom came sooner in that shallower point, and I found it almost peaceful to bounce along it. *Where were they? Where was my family?* I saw the quiet lights and wanted to reach out to them. I'd been there before. My delirium was short-lived.

Hands grasped my waist, contact that was nothing short of putting a key in a light socket. My brain buzzed with instant energy, the peacefulness left and images of a life flashed before me. Sadness, hurt, joy, pain, happiness—it washed over me in a flood of nonsensical heat. Images of a woman at the other end of a church, making love on a beach, laughter, sorrow, and the horrible deep residing ache of losing a battle with life underneath a child that was still breathing.

I was shoved upward and popped to the surface gulping air, into another pair of hands that hauled me up.

"Shit! Dani!"

My body was still buzzing as I choked and coughed up water, still trying to call out for my daughter. I fought at their hands and struggled to get to my knees, as Jason pulled me back.

"You'll die out there, damn it!" he screamed against the wind.

I whirled on him. "My baby is out there!" I yelled back, not much left to my voice. "Get the hell out of my way!"

A roar of unmistakable pain jerked our attention back out to the crazed river, and my heart stopped at the sight of Alex emerging from the water with Riley in his arms, just twenty feet from us.

"Holy shit!" Grady yelled.

Alex's face was tight and he fought to keep them above water as he held my Riley limp in his arms.

"Oh my G—" I began.

"Who the hell is that?" Jason yelled as he leapt into the river toward them.

"Alex!" I finally managed. I tried to jump in, but Grady held me back. "Riley! Oh my God, is she okay?"

"Get her, she's dying," Alex croaked, his face twisted in pain.

"No!" I screamed, and as Jason reached them through the waves, Alex's head dropped.

"I got her," I heard Jason say as he took her from Alex. "I got her."

Jason immediately floated her on her back and started rescue CPR on her as he swam her in. I was on my hands and knees on the dock, reaching out to them, praying, my whole being shaking with fear and dread. Grady positioned himself next to me, ready to haul them up.

For a moment, Alex looked up at me with effort, and we locked eyes. In that moment, all was clear. He'd done it this time. This time, he'd saved us.

He closed his eyes and sank back under the surface as hysteria and Riley reached me at the same time. Grady and I pulled her up as a wave drove them in, and Jason latched onto the post he was rammed into.

"Riley?" I yelled, pulling her limp weight into my arms. I touched her cold face. There wasn't a scratch on her, she looked like an angel. "Baby, please breathe."

Grady pulled Jason up and he instantly snatched her from me and laid her out, pumping serious air to her lungs. Her arms flopped to her sides like a ragdoll.

"Please, God," I begged. I looked upward at the raging water pouring from the sky. "Please, Mom!" I sobbed. "You owe me this!"

"Breathe, damn it!" Jason yelled in between breaths. Grady cried next to me.

Then my miracle happened. My baby girl threw up.

I'd never been so relieved to see anyone hurl in all my life. Water and everything else came up as she coughed and retched and cried. I pulled her back into my arms and held her as I cried into her hair. I wasn't aware of the storm anymore or the biting rain, or the waves beating over the dock at us. I rocked her in my lap and she clung to me as if she were six, while Jason flopped onto his back, exhausted, trying to catch his breath.

"Mom—" she choked out. "Alex—"

"I know, baby." The realization made my head spin.

"Hey, where'd that guy go?" Grady asked.

Jason sat back up with a start, as if just remembering the man in the waves. "Shit! Did he go under?"

"Yes," I said. "That was Alex."

"Al—Alex. Your *friend*?" He jumped to his feet, looking at me as if I were a loon. "I have to go after him, he'll die out there."

"He's already dead."

I continued to rock my girl.

Chapter 17

I F rain showers wash the earth down, then we were about as squeaky clean as it gets. My dad's dock looked mostly the same, if not a little pressure-washed. Minus the boat that once hung out there. Dad joked that it was down somewhere making a really good fish harbor if he could just find that sweet spot.

I sat down at the end, leaning against a post and fiddling with a cracked plank. Bo lay with his head in my lap, nose twitching and little eyebrows bouncing back and forth at the dragonflies that skimmed the water.

The river was glass smooth. The slightest insect touch made ripples you could see all the way across. It didn't even resemble the monster that tried to kill us a week earlier.

The buzzing was gone. The wind, the sounds of fear and pain and water rushing—all gone. I could only guess it was because we'd lived it again, Sarah and I, and survived. *Sarah and I.* That was weird. But nearly losing my Riley had put that little gem of information in perspective. It didn't matter who was hanging around in another realm, outside my reach. What mattered was right here.

I turned at the sound of feet on the creaky boards, even though Bo's tail thumps told me it was Riley. If it had been Dad, he would have gotten up. Respect for your elders.

Riley sauntered down, hair pulled up, no makeup, bare-footed and wearing a T-shirt and sweats she'd cut off into shorts. She looked young and innocent. But she wasn't. She sat down opposite me, Indian style, and snatched a stick out of the water. I watched the concussion of that ripple spread out for half a mile before she spoke.

"You still mad at me?" she asked softly.

I met her eyes. Eyes so much like my own, it was eerie. They held and hid so much, and yet could touch your soul.

"I'm not mad at you."

"Lie."

"I'm not." I shook my head and rubbed my eyes. "Just—" I looked out at the water and blew out a breath.

"Disappointed."

I was so many things, I couldn't even pick one. I felt like a ball in a pinball machine, bouncing from one emotion to the next.

"I don't know what I am, boog. That's the honest truth."

Her eyes watered. "I told you I was sorry."

"I know, Riley, and—and that's fine. But you don't understand what it was like to think you were—dead." I nearly choked on the word.

She lowered her eyes and two tears fell.

"You nearly got yourself killed. And Grady. And me. I have never been so sick, so devastated in all my life, as I was thinking I'd lost you. And for what?"

"Mom—"

"For sex."

And that was the kicker. Once we'd finally gotten back home from getting a clean bill of health, we talked.

"I told you, it wasn't a plan, Mom. I had to get away. Grady caught me trying to take the boat out and said he'd drive." Tears fell freely. "I couldn't even look at him. All I wanted was to be normal. Make him see *me* as normal."

"He already did."

"I know." She wiped her face. "But I wasn't thinking that then. I begged him till—" She didn't go further. She didn't have to. I'd already been floored with it in the first round, when I tongue-lashed her about irresponsibility and unprotected sex. I wasn't going there again. And I wasn't buying the begging part.

"Okay."

"I'm serious, Mom, it was me. He actually said no for a while." She frowned. "It was really weird."

I closed my eyes. Something inside me felt closed up and hurt. It wasn't really logical. Like my little girl was gone. Like—that part of her—of us—had died. And too soon. It had been taken too soon.

But it was done. *Move on.* I looked back at her.

"How do you feel about it now?"

"About doing it in a boat? It sucked."

I dropped my head. "Don't ever say that out loud again. Pop would have a coronary."

"Sorry."

"How do you feel about *yourself*?"

She paused and dragged her stick in the water, focusing on the patterns it made. "I don't know. Weird, I guess. Wasn't what I expected."

"What did you expect?"

"I don't know. Love and glowy romance, I guess. All I got was panic when the wind kicked up. I was pretty lucky just to get dressed."

"Well, here's a tip. Even when *not* in a boat, if the glowy romance isn't there already—sex isn't gonna bring it."

We sat in silence for a little while, each lost in our own thoughts.

"So—have you seen anybody?" she asked finally.

I looked over at her. I hadn't left the house since we came home from the hospital. Hadn't gone to work. Jason made sure we were okay and hadn't been back or called since. Couldn't really blame him. Swimming out to take Riley from a talking dead man was probably disconcerting. For a newbie.

Grady hadn't quit calling or coming by, much to my annoyance, so he was clearly not as bothered by it.

"No."

"Me, either."

Then I realized what she meant. Alex hadn't been by, either. And although I couldn't talk about it, it was eating me up. Tears sprang to my eyes as I recalled his face as he told me his secret. The torture in his eyes. And then right before he went back under the water—that one was for Sarah. I'd seen all his demons when he touched me. That last look was for her.

As anxious as I was about seeing him again, I had a gnawing fear that I wouldn't. What if that was it? What if that was the closure he needed to move on? What if he just didn't want to face me anymore? Or worse—and what kept poking at me—what if the strain of holding Riley's dying body took too much?

I knew how that worked. That each felt everything the other had. The shock I received when he pushed me up confirmed that. But holding someone whose life force was nearly gone—would that feel like dying all over again?

"Do you think he'll show up again?" Riley asked, her voice sounding small. "I mean, I'd like to thank him at least."

I gave her a shrug and a small smile. "I don't know, boog." I watched her as she looked far off. "What do you remember about it?"

Her eyes filled up again. "His family. He—drowned underneath his daughter, Mom. The little girl in the picture."

My skin felt like it could move on its own. I'd never told her that.

"Yeah," I breathed.

"And he loves us."

That took me off guard. "What?"

She looked back at me. "He really loves you."

I blinked fast so I wouldn't cry. "Well." I cleared my throat. "We've been connected for a really long time."

"Do you love him?"

Damn it. I let out a breath and swiped at my eyes as a little laugh escaped my throat.

"Always." Lord, she didn't know the half of it. "But obviously that's not a workable situation."

"That's sad."

"It's reality. Or, at least *our* reality."

"What about Jason?"

"Mr. Miller," I corrected.

"He gave me mouth-to-mouth, Mom. I think we're on a first-name basis." She gave in to a laugh as my face contorted. "Just kidding. Sorry, I couldn't resist."

"Try."

"So what about *Mr. Miller*?"

I sighed and scooped my hair back. "I'm not sure. He may not be interested anymore."

"You just gonna sit around and wait to find out?"

I gave her a look. "As opposed to what?"

She shook her head, exasperated. "Going to the source."

I looked down at Bo and scratched his neck till he smiled. Oh, for life to be that simple.

"He knows where I am, boog."

"Ugh, that's so old school!"

"And we're old," I said pointedly. "It works for us."

"Whatever," she said, rising to her feet in one motion. "But you'll get old alone with that attitude."

I saluted her. "I'll survive."

She turned to walk away, but two steps in, she turned back around. "Mom—I love you."

I looked up at my baby girl and got up—*much slower than she had*. I slung an arm around her and we walked back toward the house, Bojangles reluctantly coming to his feet to follow. I kissed the side of her head, since I couldn't reach the top anymore.

THE ground under my feet was dry and dusty, no traces left of the deluge. I kicked a rock in my path and recalled a similar stroll I'd taken with Alex. The night he'd told me Sarah's name. So many things made sense now. His reluctance to tell me any details about his family.

My anger was gone. As much as part of me—the *me* part of me—wanted to be hurt and angry, the memory of his face after saving Riley melted me to the core. Would we ever be the same? Probably not. But we could still be okay. Assuming I ever saw him again. And the possibility of that going negative made my stomach hurt.

What started out to be a random walk brought me within throwing distance of the Bait-n-Feed. Well, within someone else's throwing distance. I'd need another twenty or thirty feet.

I hadn't gone back to work initially to make sure Riley was okay. After that, it was pretty much my own chickenness. I knew I needed to be a big girl and go back to earning a paycheck, but the thought of dealing with the people in town made me nauseous. And yes. There was the Jason issue. As long as I didn't see him, I could tell myself he was just working through it. But what if—what if I made eye contact and saw *that look*. The one I'd seen all my life. I knew it would crush me, and so avoiding it seemed the logical choice. Until Riley pointed out my spinster potential, that is.

So I stood there in the middle of the road, the sun cooking my shoulders, playing with a smooth clear rock I'd picked up for luck, staring with anxiety at the building. Miss Olivia's car was there—that was good. Diversion. Because Jason's was, too. Bob ambled out of his trailer next door and waved, grinning as he made his way to a giant pot of something cooking on a propane tank. Knowing him, it was best not to ask what.

"Okay, wuss," I muttered. "Time to put that thick skin back on."

I got my feet moving again and took a deep breath as I opened the door. *Please don't let him be standing there.*

Miss Olivia and Marg both turned my direction as the bell jingled overhead. I smiled warily and tried not to do the five-second room scan.

"Hey, my Dani girl!" Miss Olivia said, her straw hat bobbing as she made her way around a barrel of mousetraps and bar bait. I looked down at the new display all front and center.

"Somebody have issues?"

"Whatever," Miss Olivia said, waving at that barrel. She gave me a giant hug. "Glad to see you out and about. Where's that girl?"

"She's at home. Going back to her job at the store tomorrow."

Miss Olivia and Grady had been at the house together three times since the "incident," as it had come to be called. I had all but ignored Grady, but I was starting to soften a little after the talk with Riley. And the fact that he called and tried to come by in some way every single day. He was persistent. And after what he'd seen and learned, that said something about him. More than I could say for some people.

"Good for her."

"What about you?" Marg asked, leaning on the counter with her typical no-nonsense stare. "When are you coming back?"

Involuntarily, I looked toward the back hall. "Um—"

"He's out at the dock, playing with the boats," she said dryly. Miss Olivia chuckled. I smiled and cast my eyes down, releasing a breath I'd been holding.

"I guess in a couple of days—" Why? What was I waiting for? Jason to call and make it all cozy?

Yes.

"Can you be here Wednesday? I'm supposed to be— somewhere."

I raised my eyebrows. "Somewhere?"

Marg blushed, which made me even more curious. "Yes, somewhere," she repeated. "Can you be here?"

"Yes, ma'am."

That gave me two days to gear up for seeing Jason again. Assuming he didn't drum up a road trip once he heard I was back.

"Good. I'm tired of hanging out with his grumpy ass all day," she said, hitting a button on the register to run the hourly report. "Thinks he runs the place."

I held back the urge to laugh.

"By the way, you conjure up ghosts at will?" Marg asked, turning to face me openly with her ice-blue eyes.

My mouth dropped open and some little squeaky noise came out. I wasn't used to conversing in public about it. Blinking in succession was as good as I could do.

"No, she can't," Miss Olivia said, jumping in there for me, giving me a second to find my tongue. "I've asked her that since she was a little skinny thing snapping beans on my front porch."

Thank you, Miss O. I let a forced little laugh out. "Um, no, they come to me. I don't go looking for them."

"Hmm. So they just pop up out of the blue?"

I nodded. "And usually at the most inopportune time."

She chuckled, nodding. "Cool."

And then she went back to her work, done with me. Well, that went okay. One down. Then the bell jingled and in walked Lisa Marlow. Her mouth dropped open as whatever she was going to say fell away when she spotted me. I had the urge to snap it shut but smiled instead as I clenched my fingers tightly together.

"Dani," she said awkwardly, averting her eyes as she passed me.

Oh yes, don't look, you might catch it.

But then she surprised me as she slowly turned around.

"Um, Dani—I—" She stopped as her eyes met mine. And I saw something there I'd never seen. Not ever.

Regret.

She looked down at her hands, and back to me. "I wanted to apologize for my son's behavior with your daughter. I—heard about some of the things he said." She closed her eyes. "I'm just mortified. I'm sorry."

My thoughts went straight to high school. *You did the same thing back—*

"It—it kind of brought some things home to me as well," she said, glancing toward Miss Olivia and Marg. Miss Olivia turned and busied herself with a pack of gardenia seeds. "We—we did some pretty awful things to you, years ago." She shook her head. "I don't know what to say."

I blinked a couple of times. "I don't know, either, Lisa. But thank you."

She nodded and then turned uncomfortably back to the counter. Miss Olivia strolled up to me and wiggled her eyebrows.

"Got one of them baits stuck up her ass, that one does," she whispered.

I pushed Miss Olivia out the door ahead of me. "You're bad! She was trying. She was actually human there for a minute."

She waved that off and adjusted her hat back a little before she got in her car.

"Just words, Dani girl. Let's see what she does when she's with the pack. But you're right." She swung her legs in and made sure her dress was in there with her. "Sometimes people have to say what needs sayin'. Tomorrow might not be around to get another chance."

She was smiling, but her eyes were fixed on me when she said it. I let the words bounce around my skull a little. *Say what needs sayin'.*

Hmm.

"Dani."

I turned toward the voice, already yelling *Oh crap!* in my head as my stomach shimmied.

"Jason."

"Hmm," Miss Olivia said as she shut her door. I looked at her with what I knew was a deer-in-the-headlights look, but she just winked at me and left.

Crap.

Jason waved at her, standing there with a rag in his hand, grease on his hands, in a muscle shirt and dirty cargo shorts. I'd never seen him that casual. Well, except for that day in the towel. His hair was sticking up in back. And he'd never looked hotter.

I really wasn't ready. I was supposed to have two more days. So I stood there with all the grace of a fourteen-year-old girl, wondering what a grown-up would say. My relationship experience consisted of a ghost and someone who vanished like one. I licked my dry lips and attempted coolness.

His eyes were intense on me, as he nodded casually toward the door.

"You back today?"

"No, um, Wednesday. Marg—she has to be somewhere. So—Wednesday."

Somebody please tape my mouth shut.

His eyebrows rose in what I knew was amusement. I knew the look, I'd been stupid around him way too much.

"How's Riley?"

I nodded, thankful for something solid to talk about. "She's good. Has her strength back, going back to work tomorrow."

"That's good." He smiled and it made my breath catch in my chest for a minute.

"Yeah," I managed.

It was contagious; I felt myself smiling, too. And then Miss Olivia's words nagged at me. Damn it. Say something. But as the seconds ticked by into awkwardness, the window of possibility started to close. Jason broke eye contact, studying his greasy rag. My stomach fell. There hadn't been the look of shame, but he wasn't jumping through hoops for me, either.

"How's the boat? And the dock?" I threw out quickly.

He nodded, meeting my eyes again but this time he looked troubled. "Not too bad. I've been working on it in the evenings."

The distance suddenly felt solid, like concrete. My heart pounded, and I felt the hurt filling up my chest. I suddenly wanted to be anywhere else. I wanted to go cry in a pillow like a kid. And I had to make my exit before he saw it.

"Well—I'll let you get back to work. I'm just gonna—" I pointed at the road and gave my best smile.

"What are you doing for supper?"

My mouth dropped like Lisa's had moments earlier. The temperature change was boggling. Then I remembered this *was* Jason.

"Uh—I don't—"

Then Lisa walked out and stopped short when she saw us. She looked uncomfortably from me to Jason, and then settled on the ground as she made it to her car.

Jason glared at her although she didn't see it. I had to smile again. He could definitely hold his own here. He took a few steps closer, fiddling with his rag again, before looking at me again. He wasn't going to repeat the question. I knew that.

"Probably a bowl of cereal. It's on-your-own night at our house tonight."

A small smile tugged at his lips, and I suddenly wanted to kiss them. Two-day growth and all. "Meet me at Ella's?"

In public. I took a deep breath. "Our last experience there wasn't so good."

"Part of it was." I looked in his eyes for that memory. They were soft again. "Relax."

I got goose bumps. Yeah. I was a wimp.

"Okay."

"Six thirty?"

"Okay."

He nodded, backing up a few steps. "Okay."

"Okay."

I turned and walked away before either of us could say "okay" again. I refused to look back to see if he was watching. I just pretended he was and didn't breathe until I was around the corner.

THE walk back home was slightly more optimistic. I both looked forward and dreaded the evening, because I knew those damn "things had to be said." I was going to have to come clean about everything, in order to be fair to Jason. Well—maybe not everything. But he'd seen Alex, for reasons I couldn't explain since Alex hadn't come around to fill *me* in.

It was going to be a conversation. That much I knew. What I didn't know was why Micah Sims was sitting on our porch banister.

"Hello?" I announced as I approached.

"Oh—hi. Riley's getting us drinks," she said while pointing at the door, as if I would throw her off the banister otherwise.

"Okay, no problem."

Riley emerged holding two Cokes and a bag of chips, and chin-nodded at me.

"Hey, where'd you go?"

"To see if I still had a job."

"Do you?"

"Yeah."

"Was he there?"

"Yeah."

Riley shook her head with a look at Micah. "And she calls me cryptic."

They chuckled together in the bond of all things parentally stupid, as I raised my eyebrows at this new duo. I gave them another once-over, then went inside. My guard was up—I didn't trust that girl. But I didn't know if it was because of her or her parents. I couldn't sink her on that relationship alone, so I tried to give her the benefit of the doubt. Riley had to make her way here now just like I did, so I mentally backed off.

And thought about my date. Oh lord.

Which I must have said out loud when I went in the kitchen, because Dad walked in from the opposite doorway asking, "What's the matter?"

I grabbed a glass and filled it full of ice and sweet tea and plopped down in a chair.

"You notice we never sit anywhere else?" I asked.

He shrugged. "Close proximity to my favorite pastime," he said as he slathered two pieces of bread with butter and sprinkled a liberal dose of sugar on top. Then he poured a little Steen's into a saucer and brought it all to the table, handing me a piece.

We munched in decadent silence for a moment.

"Riley tell you Micah Sims was here?"

He gave me a curious look. "Stranger things have happened. I think she'll be okay. What about you?"

"Go back to work on Wednesday."

"Oh? Good. You went down there?"

I sighed. "Yeah. Sorta."

"Was he there?"

"What is it with that question?" I slugged back some tea. Dad chuckled. "I take it he was."

I blew out a breath. "Yeah, it was—awkward. But we kinda have a date tonight. I think."

"Well, hey, that's good," he said, popping a hand down on the table and making me jump. "You look so gloomy, I thought it went badly."

"Well, I mean, the reality is this may not be a big ball of laughs, Dad," I said, soaking up the syrup into my last bite of sugar bread. "I've got to talk about things I've never talked about. I have to explain the unexplainable."

"You think he won't understand?"

"I think he would have understood better before he saw it in person. I think that wigged him out."

"You really think that's what it's about?" he asked, giving me his furry-eyebrowed eagle eye.

"Okay, what do you think it's about?"

Dad sat back in his chair, all happy on his sugar high. "Well, if it were me, I'd be pretty ticked off to find out I wasn't worth trusting."

I stared at my groove in the table. "It's not that simple, Dad."

"Not for you. But for him, it's probably very simple." He scraped his chair back. "Men aren't complex creatures, sweetheart. We depend on the basics. Trust. Loyalty."

He rinsed his plate and then turned back to me, leaning against the counter. "But also we want to take care of the people we love—make them feel safe. I failed at that. Made your mother feel like she couldn't talk to me about it. Don't put that assumption on Jason. He seems to be okay. Give him a chance to do better than I did."

I got up and let him wrap me up like he did when I was little. I didn't tell him about Mom and Alex and Sarah and all that. I figured Mom could drop that particular bomb on him one day, up there in the happy place.

"I think you're wonderful," I said.

"That's why I keep you around." When I laughed, he continued. "Hey, since you'll be working Wednesday, you probably won't miss me much, but I'll be out all day. Probably pretty late getting home that night."

"Okay, where you going?"

"Spending the day in Spring."

I backed up and narrowed my eyes at him. "A whole day in an antiques village? You?" Spring, Texas, was antiques heaven—if that was your idea of heaven. "Since when?"

He shrugged. "Trying new things?"

"Since when?" I repeated. "By yourself?" Then my eyes flew open wide and I pointed a finger at him. "You're going with Marg, aren't you?"

He feigned ignorance but he blushed. "Don't you have a date to hyperventilate over?" he said, putting up the syrup.

"Oh my God!" I said, laughing. "Not when I can talk about yours."

"It's not a date."

"Please! A whole day of antiquing? That's such a date."

"Told you. I'm trying new things."

I tossed a dishrag at him. "Marg is nice. And she's got it bad for you." Which was a very weird thing to fall out of my mouth toward him.

"Next subject."

"Hope you have fun," I prodded.

"You first."

"Ugh."

Chapter 18

I stood in my closet, flipping through the same old clothing that wouldn't change no matter how many times I started over. I didn't have date clothes. Not anymore. Not much use for pencil skirts and heels in Bethany. I still had a few really dressy things in case someone died or got married, but those would be overkill at Ella's. Especially if I ended up wearing dinner again. The other 90 percent of my wardrobe was jeans and T-shirts and tank tops.

"Dilemma?" Riley asked as she came in and flung herself across my bed.

"I'm such a guy," I muttered.

She laughed. "Want something of mine?"

"I only wish I could fit in your clothes." Riley rolled herself back up and wandered over to stare with me. I laughed. "It doesn't help to wish it, I've tried."

Her eyes narrowed as she studied my meager choices. "No, I'm looking for how to mix it up."

"Mix what up?"

She thumbed through a few shirts, pulling out a stretchy silky black tank top with tiny black spaghetti straps.

"I'm not—"

"Hang on."

A few hangers down, she gave something a look-see, then pulled it out. A deep blue fitted silky vest that I'd never worn because I never knew what to do with it.

"With a tank top?"

"Just try it on." She went to my dresser and riffled around. "With the black jeans," she added, tossing them at me. "And your silver wedges. And I have a belt that'll go."

I put it all on, and stood in front of the mirror, amazed. The blue vest worn open was perfect with the tank top. It hugged my body without showing my flab, and made my boobs look fantastic. The studded belt gave it a modern kick. I actually looked sexy. It had definitely been a while.

"Wow."

Riley stood next to me, hand on hip. "Do I need to do your hair and face, too, or are you good with that?"

I gave her a look. "Don't get cocky."

"Well, you've got the potential to look hot if you work it right," Riley said, then rubbed her eyes. "And I can't believe I just said that."

"I feel your pain." I went in my bathroom to plug in things and see what I could do to step up my "hot" potential. "I basically told Pop to party it up with a woman earlier."

Riley's expression was priceless. "Oh my God."

"Yeah, I kinda had to shake it off."

"What woman?"

"Does it matter?"

She grimaced. "No, but it's like I can't stop."

I chuckled. "Marg, from work."

Riley slapped a hand over her eyes. Things were good here. In our little isolated world where no one could hurt us, life was getting back to normal. But there had been no spirits all week. It was like they were all on vacation. Like regular people live. But living like regular people meant no Alex. And my insides were pining for him.

"What's the deal with Micah?"

"I know, right? She knocked on the door and I was like 'holy hell.' But she just said she wanted to apologize for her boyfriend—or ex-boyfriend, rather—and for her other friends. She said she thought they were being stupid and she should have said something, but then it all got so crazy."

"Yeah, it did do that."

"So anyway, no big deal." Riley pulled her hair down, fluffed it in the mirror, and then twisted it back up again.

"Do you trust her?"

She did a face shrug. "No reason not to, yet. We hung out and talked for a little while. She's okay. Hates her parents. I felt kinda sorry for her."

I clipped my hair up in levels. "Why?"

"Because her parents don't even notice her unless she wins something or does something they can brag about. As far as just talking about stuff, she doesn't have anybody."

Oh, thank God, maybe I was doing something right.

"Can I get a tattoo?" she asked then, pulling up her shirt and circling her hipbone with a finger.

After the pause I needed to recover from the proud-parent moment, I said, "When you're grown and paying your own rent and health insurance, you can do whatever you want."

She grinned. "Carmen has one."

"Well, there's a selling point."

"Just saying."

"Carmen has—issues." When Riley laughed, I added, "Don't pick up any of them."

She sighed as she grabbed the straight iron from me and started on the back of my hair.

"Seriously, I've got this," I said.

"You keep missing the same spot and it's bugging me."

I gave up and let her make me pretty. "So, what are you doing tonight while Mommy's out having a meltdown?"

"Grady's helping Miss O with some stuff, so I'll probably go over there or just watch TV or something." She finished that level and pulled another clip down. "And don't have a meltdown, you'll mess up the outfit."

I debated whether to walk or drive. It was close enough, but the fifteen-minute walk to Ella's would have me arriving a sweating un-fresh mess, so I opted to drive the silly thirty seconds instead. I laughed when I saw his car, especially since his was about ten. But when I got out and walked up to the boardwalk, I wasn't laughing. I was looking for my tongue.

Jason stood leaned up against the building, arms crossed, wearing dark tight jeans and a black button-down that was a little snug on his upper arms, freshly shaven and looking good enough to lick banana pudding off of. Even better was his expression when he saw me.

He pushed off the wall and looked me up and down like I was chocolate. Or maybe that was my perspective. Him being a guy and all, it was probably more like prime rib.

"Hey," I said, trying to sound casual.

"Hey."

I blinked and licked my lips when his gaze didn't waver. "You're staring."

"You're stunning."

I willed my knees not to buckle and mentally thanked Riley. "Well, back atcha."

There was a thickly charged moment in which I thought my blood might catch fire, then he finally said, "Hungry?"

Not even if it had been a month of tree bark and seawater. "Sure." I gestured toward the door. "You waited out here for me."

"I asked you here. I'm not gonna make you walk in there alone."

His hand came up under my hair and rested on the back of my neck as we walked in. Looking like a couple, my girly mind squealed. Micah looked up from a clipboard and did a double take. Giving me a small smile, she grabbed a bucket and two menus.

"Hi, Ms. Shane. Y'all eating here?"

"Yes, ma'am."

"Band's playing tonight. Want a table in there?"

Did I? Dancing close to Jason would be so good. Rowdy crowd—not so much. But it was Monday. How rowdy could a Monday be?

"Sure," he said. I guessed he was hoping for a grope, too.

I followed Micah, feelings of trepidation washing over me mixed with excitement over being with Jason. What were the odds that we could ignore all that mess and just start from right now? We sat and Micah hovered for a second.

"Um," she began, her eyes moving from me to her hands and back again. "Just so you know—" She looked around her. "My mom might be here later with her friends."

Great.

"Okay."

"Doesn't matter," Jason said, opening a menu.

"I just—I don't like how she is sometimes and I'm sorry for all that."

I smiled at her. "It's okay, Micah. Thank you."

She left, and unfortunately that put Jason and me right smack in the middle of the crap I had wanted most to avoid. I saw it in his face. He put down the menu he wasn't really reading since he knew it by heart, waved down the waitress, ordered us two beers, and sat back to look at me.

I met his intense gaze and tried to appear calm, to breathe normally. I refused to just start babbling. He was going to have to lead this show.

"Damn, you're beautiful tonight," he said, his voice low like he wasn't sure it was out loud. Heat rushed to my head and made me dizzy. Wasn't expecting that. "I'm—you know I'm not good with words. But I've gotta tell you, I forgot how to breathe when you walked up."

A nervous laugh fell out of my mouth. "No, that's—pretty good."

"Made all my thoughts leave me for a minute, so bear with me if I ramble."

My heart was thumping so hard, I had to take a deep breath and let it out slow. "Say whatever you want. I know—you have questions."

He closed his eyes and shook his head, as if trying to get the jumble back in order. "I don't even know what to ask you, because I don't know if I have the right to know." He toyed with a spoon in front of him. "I guess that's my dilemma in a nutshell."

Okay, wasn't sure where to go with that. "What is?"

"What are we doing? Because if we're gonna be together, I have a son who will eventually ask questions, and I need to know what the hell is going on." He looked at me hard. "And even if Connor doesn't ask, I need to know anyway."

I took a breath. "Okay."

"Unless we're not together," he added quickly. "And that's a question. Because I feel like we are, but if we aren't, then I guess you don't have to tell me anything."

I suddenly felt sweaty from the rambling outpour. My beer arrived and I took a swallow gratefully, letting the icy bitterness sink through me. I took another deep breath and blew it out.

"I've been hoping we still were."

"Then why didn't I know any of this?"

"Because I—I've never been able to do that. I mean, Riley's dad was around for a year, I *lived* with him, and he never knew. I don't go around inviting reasons for people to push me away."

Jason frowned. "Is that what you think I would do?"

"Where have you been this week?"

His expression relaxed and he looked down. "Okay. Touché. I'm sorry." He took a long swig of his beer. "Can you tell me about it, now?"

I looked in his eyes for a moment. "I've never done this."

He leaned forward on his elbows. "Relax."

I smiled involuntarily and averted my eyes, feeling some of the stress recede. Just relax. Let it all tumble out. Good lord.

"When people die, sometimes they don't leave just yet. And for some reason, I can see them. They come to me on their way to other places. I don't know why." I picked up a napkin and began tearing tiny strips. "When I was little, I didn't realize that other people couldn't see them, too, so I became the town freak, talking to people who weren't there."

I looked up and saw some puzzle pieces fall into place for him.

"And now?

I gave a small shrug. "It's a small town, Jason. Most people just avoided me growing up, but Matty and Blaine and that crowd—they were the worst. They had to get in my face every day." I laughed bitterly. "Well, you've seen that hasn't changed much."

"I'm sorry, Dani."

His eyes were soft and sincere. "I'm used to it. It's Riley I'm concerned about."

"And she can do this, too?"

I nodded. "But I didn't know that till the day we got here. I never saw it till—till she saw an old friend of mine." I swallowed hard.

He blew out a breath. "The guy in the river."

I met his eyes. "I know this is a lot to process. I know it's hard to buy into."

"It probably would have been. But I saw it."

"And I can't even explain that, because—I haven't talked to him since."

He rubbed his face. "Talked to him—see that's the—is this all the time?"

I felt my heart sink, and I sat back and traced lines in the condensation on my mug. "Jason, if this is too much to deal with, I get it. I've been alone for most of my life for that reason. I understand. Really."

"No, you don't get it."

The sharpness in his tone made me look back up.

"Dani, did you hear me earlier? I wouldn't be sitting here if it was too much. Truth is, you scare the hell out of me."

"What?"

"And long before Superman came up out of the waves, believe me. Nothing to do with that. What terrifies me are secrets."

Okay, Dad, I hear you.

"It's been a long time since I trusted anyone. But I've let myself trust you. With my son. With—" He stopped and took another swallow. "I just don't do that. And that scared me, already. Now, finding out that the woman I'm—that you have this whole life I didn't even know about."

"I'm sorry. Look, I understand not trusting. I've never been able to do that. Ever." I sat back in my chair and scooped my hair back. "This isn't like saying 'hey, I used to shoplift candy bars.' People don't understand this. They'd rather burn me at the stake than try. My whole life has been a secret."

He was quiet for a minute. "And now?"

I looked around the room. "Now, it's everybody's business." I waved a hand. "And I'm not blaming my dad. He'd had enough. He's seen and heard so much crap because of me, it was time." I closed my eyes. "I just don't want Riley to have the life I did."

"Maybe it not being a secret anymore will help."

I shook my head. "Closed minds will stay closed. I'm not naïve."

"Hey, Dani," someone said to my right, and I turned to see a woman and her husband passing on their way to the bar. Her smile was open and I recognized her from the bait store. They both raised a hand. Wow.

I turned back to see amusement in his eyes. "What?"

"Maybe they aren't so closed."

I chuckled and shook my head. "Don't let them fool you."

He leaned forward. "Don't let them in, right? Because they might fool you?" He reached for my hand, and his was warm. "I know that game, too. It's safe, but it's pretty lonely there."

I opened my mouth but there weren't words. He knew me. Somehow, he knew me. And was blindly trusting someone for probably the first time in his life, and look at the circus he chose to start that with.

"You're right. And Jason, it was never that I didn't trust you. We're just new. I wanted this so badly, and I—I was so afraid you wouldn't want me back anymore."

He leaned closer across the table. "You have no idea just how much I want you."

The double entendre made me relax and smile. "You know what I mean."

"And you don't have to worry," he said, sitting back. "But I'm curious, if all this hadn't come to light like it did, would you have told me?"

No.

"Yes." I laughed lightly. "With two of us talking to thin air, I think it would have been hard to hide long term."

"And Alex?" My insides tensed at just the mention of his name. Jason's eyes recorded it all, and the playfulness pulled back as he nodded. "That's what I'm talking about. Dani, that's the same response, the same look in your eyes as the other night when you saw him." He rubbed his eyes, and then let his hands fall to the table. "I'm honest with you. What are you still hiding?"

I felt the burn in my throat, in my chest, in my eyes. Alex was hard to talk about. And to tell him everything?

"Alex is—"

"Are you ready to order?"

My thoughts were interrupted by the jovial, round-faced girl standing next to us.

"Bring us some chips for now, we're not ready yet," Jason said quickly. The girl bounced away on her chiply mission.

I inhaled sharply and tried to clear my head. My napkin was beginning to look like it had gone through a shredder. I focused on the fibers, not able to look at Jason while I talked about Alex. I just couldn't.

"I met Alex when I was sixteen," I said softly. "After Carson and Matty and their buddies tried to pass me around as a party favor one night."

"What?"

I lifted a hand to wave it off. "Carson acted all nice and invited me, then they got me drunk and tried—well, they tried. I wasn't drunk enough." I felt the testosterone level rise in the air, but I didn't look up. "Alex was at my car and wouldn't let me drive home. We got to be friends that night." I smiled. "My only friend. Didn't matter that he was a spirit, he was all I had."

"So he's looked out for you all these years?"

How deep to go? "Yeah."

"What else?"

"What?"

"I can tell there's more." He sat looking so patient. Damn it.

I was his wife in another life. "He died—" My chest got tight. "He and his family died in a storm very much like— the other day." I felt my resolve go down and my voice with it. "He drowned trying to hold his little girl above the water."

"Damn."

"Yeah." I couldn't look at Jason. I focused on keeping myself together.

"And since then, he's been keeping *you* above water."

I looked at him and my eyes filled with tears. God, I'd never thought about it like that.

"I guess so."

"So saving Riley from drowning—"

My tears spilled over and I tried to say it. I tried to say

that it was significant. That he saved another of my children, that there was more to it than that, but I couldn't form the words. The emotion overwhelmed me like a flood coming up from my core. I put a hand over my face and tried with all I had to stop it.

Jason got up and came to sit by me, putting his arms around me. "Hey, it's okay," he said, pulling me to him. "Baby, it's okay."

I wanted to crawl in a hole, crying like that on a date. No wonder I never had any. But bringing that up had opened a door that I couldn't close. He pulled my hand away from my face and made me look at him.

"I'm sorry, I didn't mean to make you cry."

"Oh God, *I'm* sorry." He thought he'd done it. I clenched my fists and tried to think of Shelby or Matty or things that would make me mad so I'd quit. I wiped at my eyes and tried to laugh. "Not looking so hot, now, huh?"

He pulled my face to his and kissed me, soft and tender. And again. And again. Till all my muscles were relaxed and I was mush.

"I think you're gorgeous," he whispered against my lips. The sensation sent tingles to every nerve ending. He leaned back a bit so he could look at me. "I get it, okay? You don't have to explain anymore. I know how close we came to losing her."

And saying "we" was just about the coolest, most endearing thing he could say to me. But there was no way for him to really understand, while I kept him out of that particular loop. It was about Riley, but also about Alyssa. About Alex. About Sarah. About my lifelong connection with a man I could never have but would always be tied to because of her. I couldn't say any of that. I could only grab on to the Riley issue and ride that out, because the truth was I was falling for him big-time. And telling him the truth about Alex would drive him away, no matter what he said earlier. Jason was stealing my heart and I wanted him to.

"You saved her, too." I touched his face and watched his eyes flicker. "You were my hero, too. He pulled her out and you breathed life back into her." I felt my eyes burn again. "And if we keep talking about this, I'm gonna cry all night."

The waitress brought our chips and gave us a questionable look, hovering for a second then moving on. Jason wiped the remaining tears off my cheeks and kissed me again.

"Then let's talk about something else."

Oh, thank God I passed.

"Well, let me go find the ladies' room, and then we can talk about anything you want."

He pointed the way, squeezed my hand, and went back to his seat. I rounded the corner through a hallway marked with neon people wearing pants or dresses and shoved through another old wooden door. I glanced at myself in the mirror and groaned on the way to privacy.

Wasn't private long. The second I sat down, the room was full again. With Shelby-ites and the queen mother. Crap. Where did they morph from?

"—Saw it, but my husband's too damn cheap."

"No shit," another one said. "We never have enough money for what I want, but if it's flat and plasma or cold and in a bottle, funny how the coins fall out his ass."

I recognized the voice as Lisa's. Female laughter echoed through the bathroom, and I heard Shelby's flat sarcastic cackle. There were two options. I could stay in the stall till they left or go throw myself in the fire. I got out my compact and did quick eye repair in case I never made it to the mirror.

"I saw Jason's car outside; did you see him?"

"No, but I'm sure he's here," Shelby said, sounding flippant. "He's always here."

"Wonder if that psycho is with him. What's she, a witch now or something?"

I opened the stall and strode out, smiling ear to ear. "Or something."

Lisa and another woman I remembered as Aliciasomething pivoted in place, eyes wide. Shelby at least had the presence of mind to stay facing the mirror, staring at me with hatred as she fixed her lipstick. It was like high school all over again. I suddenly pitied all of them, still living that same life, and that one moment lifted all the intimidation.

I looked at Lisa and thought of what Miss Olivia had said. "Excuse me," I said, and she and the other girl parted like the Red Sea so I could wash my hands.

"Well, well," Shelby said, taking her time messing with her purse. "If it isn't our own little Charmed One."

"Shelby, quit," Lisa said, her voice so tiny it was almost a whisper.

Shelby swung her are-you-crazy gaze her way, and Lisa looked like she wanted to duck. "What? After what Carson and Drew went through because of her? Seriously?"

Lisa busied herself with her hair, not meeting Shelby's eyes. "Drew was a jerk, and Carson taught him how to be that way. Look how he was treating Micah! They put themselves there, nobody twisted their arms." For just a microsecond, her gaze flickered to me.

Shelby scoffed, looking royally pissed. "Well, you be all bleeding heart if you want, but I know what I know."

I looked her way as innocently as I could, and gave a small smile. "Whatever."

As I walked away, Shelby said, "Dress her up, she's still a freak."

I stopped. Not because of what she'd said, but because Micah had walked in, and her face was priceless. And I was sad for her.

"Mom."

Shelby's eyes jerked her way, surprised, and then her demeanor settled back into her normal haughty way. "Micah, go back to work, baby."

"No!"

I held my breath. All three women's faces reddened, but Shelby's was in anger.

"Micah—"

"What is wrong with you?" Micah's voice was trembling. "Mom, you sounded just like the bitches at my school. How can you be such a horrible person?"

I stared at her in shock. Shelby's offspring was taking up for Riley and me. The earth felt like it wiggled a little. As much as it was like watching a train wreck, I really wanted to get out of there.

I made my feet move. "Micah, it's okay," I said as I tried to pass her.

"Don't speak to my daughter," Shelby piped in, following me. "Don't even look at her."

"Mom!"

I turned with the intention of saying something equally as hateful, but somewhere in that two seconds a peace settled over me. Micah's expression was etched on my brain, and by the time I was eye to eye with Shelby, all I could do was pity her.

"I hope my daughter never looks at me the way yours just looked at you," I said softly, and then I walked around Micah, patting her arm, and made it out the door.

Somehow, I got to the table without ever exhaling, and when I sat down I let it all go. Jason looked at me funny, then looked up as the parade came out, and his expression changed to wary.

"That can't have been good," he said under his breath.

"It was sad, actually."

"Sad, how?" he asked, but had to do a double take as Shelby planted herself tableside. We both looked up at her.

"Don't you ever talk to anyone in my family again," she spat. Her face, I noticed, wasn't actually pretty anymore. Up close, she had the age that comes with the party life. "Do you understand me, *freak*?"

She leaned down a little in order to make the word land on me harder. But it was different. Clarity had beamed down on me, and all I could do was touch Jason's hand so he wouldn't use it to hit her, look at him as if she wasn't there, and smile.

"Ready to order?"

There was a second of surprise in his eyes, but then he recovered and went with it.

"Absolutely."

We grinned at each other as Shelby marched away, her puppets faltering and going a different way. Lisa met my eyes for just a second and I felt the tide change.

Jason looked at me with curious eyes. "Do I get the play-by-play?"

The band came and started their set and I smiled at him. "Later. Let's just enjoy this, now."

"Oh, I almost forgot." He reached into his back pocket and pulled out a tiny bag, handing it over to me.

I took it tentatively. "What's this?"

He nodded at it. "Just open it and then don't argue with me."

Well, that sounded appealing. I unfolded the paper edge and peeked inside, then put it down and gave him a look.

He shook his head. "You heard me."

I sighed and pulled out the fleur-de-lis earrings I'd seen him conspire to buy with Miss Olivia. I traced the pattern with my fingertip. It was ridiculous, but no one had ever bought me anything. Riley's dad only bought household things, and then he'd taken them with him.

"You're amazing," I said, not really trusting that my voice would come out. "Thank you."

"No big deal." But he was beaming.

"It is to me."

I put them on, and held up my spoon to see the reflection, smiling like a teenager. My first gift from a man. Well, other than a baby.

We ate chicken fried steak and mashed potatoes and summer squash baked with cinnamon. And banana pudding. I really tried not to think about my earlier fantasy with the pudding. But the kissing had flipped that switch, and it kept jumping in there. We laughed and people-watched and ignored Shelby's friends, who were there without her then and looked lost and confused.

People still looked at me—at us—but mostly me. They'd look and then look away and say something discreetly to whomever they were with. Wasn't new, but yet it was. They knew the real deal now, and I guess that made it different. There was eye contact, though, and occasional smiles. I guess that was something. Or maybe Jason was right. Maybe it was me *allowing* it to be something.

As we sat there, fat and happy, a slow song came on, and Jason stood up.

"Going somewhere?"

He smirked and grabbed my hand. "You're coming with me."

I followed him to the dance floor, weaving around the other touchy-feely couples, and as he turned, he pulled me tight into his arms. There wasn't the polite starting distance of the first time. When I wrapped my arms around him, we were moving as one. And as I closed my eyes and felt his hands on my back and in my hair, everything dormant began to stir.

That song ended, and thankfully another slow one followed, because I wanted to stay like that forever, molded to Jason. Enveloped in the warmth and aroma and feel of him.

My face was in his neck, and he smelled delicious, like sweet wood. I wanted to kiss him there, so badly, but I was afraid we'd end up on the floor. Then he moved my hair and kissed my ear, sending sparks to everything hidden, and I figured all was fair.

I let my lips land where they wanted to, and I tasted him, getting a charge through my body when I felt him suck in a breath and pull me even tighter. He kissed my ear again as we moved to the music, swaying together. I kissed him back, trailing my lips a little farther. I felt his chest rumble as he made a tiny groan, and my breathing quickened.

His hands started to roam as he kissed the side of my face, my nose, my mouth, and then he held the back of my head as he deepened his kiss, exploring my mouth. I wound my fingers in his hair and kissed back with all the passion I had, feeling like I would erupt into flames any minute.

He pulled back slowly, his hands in my hair, breathing fast. "Dani—"

"Want to leave?" Did I just say that? I was about to be easy. I'd never done that. But I'd never been with a man like Jason, either.

"So much."

Chapter 19

H E threw three twenties on the table, which was way more than the bill would ever be, but he clearly didn't care. I didn't, either. My blood was boiling and everything else was buzzing and certain places were teetering on feelings I'd become accustomed to experiencing alone. Or in dreams. *Not going there.*

He took me by the hand and led me out, thanking Micah, and opening the door for me. We stood outside, looking at both our cars. He looked at me as if afraid I'd change my mind if I got in my own car.

"I'll be right behind you," I said, meeting his eyes.

And I was. Nothing was going to deter me. Not even if Alex was in my car. Which I prayed he wouldn't be. Not that I didn't want to see him so badly it hurt, but it would have kinda washed out the sex drive with Jason.

It took longer to start my piece of crap than it did to drive to his boat, but I made it there and parked behind him, where he stood waiting for me again. My heart thumped even harder at the sight of him. I was going to have sex.

"Shit, Dani, grow up," I breathed.

He opened my door for me, and I laughed nervously, suddenly wishing we were back on that dance floor where everything was hot and clear and easy and I didn't have to think.

But he surprised me again. He didn't grab my hand and lead me into the devil's den. He just hugged me. Really good. Really warm. Burying his face in my hair, and kissing it, and melting my bones.

He slid his hands up my arms and back again, leaning back to look at me. In the darkness, his face was just lightly lit by the glow from his "porch."

I smiled, but I felt like my insides were quivering. He moved his hands slowly up to my neck, my face, and then kissed me. Soft, slow, tantalizing, and delicious. *You should be kissed*—No. I *was* being kissed. I wasn't going anywhere else in my head. This was about Jason.

"It's been a really long time," I whispered.

He nodded and kissed the tip of my nose. "For me, too."

I smiled. "I bet I win."

He chuckled. "Okay."

I felt his fingers trembling as he stroked my face, and I pulled him closer. "You're shaking."

"I'm nervous," he said, inhaling deeply. "I want you so badly—but I haven't—I haven't loved anyone like this—not this fast." My skin tingled. *Did he just say*—"This matters, Dani."

I looked into his eyes that I really couldn't see well, but I hoped he could see mine. See everything. I reached for his face and pulled it down to mine, kissing him like he'd kissed me. Slow. Long. My heart raced as his words rolled in my head. I kissed him with my whole body, until he responded with a noise in his chest and his hands on the move, and liquid heat spread to all things important.

He picked me up and carried me inside, miraculously not hitting anything on the way in. When he set me down on my feet, I went straight to work on the buttons of his shirt and he made quick work of discarding my vest. He kissed my shoulders, my neck and worked his way down as he sat on the couch. Then as I looked down at him, shirt open and looking tasty, he lifted up the bottom of my tank top and kissed my stomach as if he were making love to it.

"Oh my G—" My voice went away. I closed my eyes and I had no idea if my legs would hold me up. It didn't matter. I twisted my fingers in his hair as he continued to raise my top up and follow with his mouth. I yanked it off the rest of the way and he popped the front clasp of my bra in a mini-second and landed there with his mouth, warm and wet, as his hands came up my legs.

I couldn't breathe. I was one giant nerve ending, feeling sensations I couldn't remember ever feeling. Not like that. Jason rose from the couch, taking me with him in one motion. I wrapped myself around him and he carried me to his bedroom.

JASON even slept sexy. I lay curled up hugging a pillow, watching him. No drool, no slackened open mouth, no snoring. Just gorgeous. And at peace. One arm slung above his head, the other one under my pillow, left over from when we were snuggling.

I was basking. Running over the moments again and again. The feel of his hands on my body, the feel of his skin under my fingers, the heat. The way he moaned my name when he came. The endless kisses that had my lips feeling like they'd been pumped with collagen. His eyes taking me in, the slow sexy way he'd made love to me—the second time. After we'd gotten the mad monkey sex out of the way.

The silliness and the laughter and the serious moments. Like when he said—at least I thought he said—that he loved me? Wow. But I hadn't said it back. It was simmering there, I knew. I wouldn't have spilled my guts to him if it wasn't.

But I still had unfinished business lurking somewhere in the realm between here and another place, and that was pulling me two different directions.

I leaned over and trailed my lips lightly down his chest, circling his navel till he stirred.

"Mmm," he said with a smile, his eyes still closed. "Keep going, you might find the prize in the Cracker Jack box."

I laughed, and then peeked under the sheet. "It's already bigger than the box."

"Your fault."

He pulled me back up, and kissed me, then we lay face-to-face.

"So, why are you awake?" he asked. "Did I not exhaust you enough?"

I smiled. "Most definitely. I just have to go home in a little bit."

"Am I hogging the bed?"

"No. I just live with my *dad*."

"Ah. Forgot."

I closed my eyes and smirked. "Really don't want to have that conversation with him."

"I understand."

I scooted up to bury my face in his chest. "Mmm, but you smell so yummy."

He pulled me tight to him and let his right hand wander from my ass to my breast. "You feel so yummy. And I don't think I've used that word since I was six."

I kissed his chest and his arm, loving the tightness of his skin over muscle. "Can we play again tomorrow night?"

"It already is tomorrow so how about tonight?"

"Sold."

"You really have to go right now?"

I looked at the clock on his dresser. "I have about two hours before my dad gets up."

He lifted my face and kissed me, rolling me over. "I only need one of those."

*   *   *

I closed my car door with just a shove to make it click, and walked across the gravel, hearing the crunch and the crickets. Feeling thoroughly worn out and giddy, till the hairs stood up on the back of my neck. I looked up.

"Hey."

I stopped in my tracks and dropped my keys. "Um—hey."

Alex sat on the top porch step, looking like any other time. Except it wasn't. I squatted to pick up my keys, feeling the dusty dirt on my fingers. Feeling the dusty dirt on my heart. Everything went heavy as I looked in his eyes. Even from ten feet away, I could see the sad.

"Late night?"

Punch to the gut. "Yeah," I whispered, feeling the burn. I was gonna cry again. Damn it. "Alex—"

He shook his head and looked toward the river, blowing out a breath like it was a thought he wanted to be rid of. Then he looked back at me with his trademark grin.

"It's okay, Dani." He rubbed at his eyes quickly, then smiled again. "It's how it's supposed to be."

I shook my head slowly, blinking the tears free to clear my vision. "Not for us. Not really." I wiped at my eyes but they kept coming. "It's always been you." I flicked a hand his way. "Well, now I guess I know why, but still. It's always been you."

"Till now."

Everything hurt. My chest was heavy, my head hurt, my heart hurt. "Till—now."

"Come here. Up here." He pointed at the swing as he stood.

I trudged up the stairs, feeling so bad. How could I go from being so happy to being so sad? I sat down and he kneeled in front of me, which was even worse because I was so close to him. So close to his face. I felt like an errant child. Or a cheating wife.

"I was worried about you after last week. After you saved—" I broke. "Oh God, Alex, you saved my baby."

"I know."

"She wants to thank you, too."

He shook his head. "She doesn't have to. I'd do it again a million more times."

"Did it hurt you?" I asked. "I mean, why could the others see you?"

"The steady contact, I think. I—really don't have another explanation. I didn't know he could see me till he swam out there." He met my eyes. "He's a good guy, Dani."

"I love you."

I said it. To Alex. So easily. He breathed a little faster, as if taken off guard.

"Dani—"

"Alex, I've loved you my whole life."

"And I've loved you." I sucked in a breath and shut my eyes tight to the tears that threatened to take me down. "Please don't cry, love." Oh God, it would have been better if he hated me than calling me "love." I wanted to die. "You haven't done anything wrong."

"Then why do I feel like I have?"

"Because you're falling in love. Again." As much as he fought it, tears came to his eyes, too. "And you think that's wrong. But it's not." He ran a quick hand over his eyes. "We had a life, Sarah and I. And you and I have, too, in our own way. But we—can't be that. I was the one for Sarah." He swallowed. "Jason is the one for you."

I cried harder, and he stood up as he started to, as well. He walked to the banister with his back to me for a minute, and then turned back, better composed. And holding a white rose.

"You're leaving me, aren't you?" I choked out.

He knelt in front of me again. "I have to, love."

"No."

"It's time."

"Because of Jason?"

He shook his head. "Not just that. Because of you. Because you have a chance now. The town knows. Jason knows. You have a chance at a real life, with a real man." His voice cracked on the last words, and I blinked free a whole new wave of tears.

"Where are you going?"

"I don't know. Whatever's next."

"But—"

"Listen to me, Dani." He closed his eyes for a second, as if to get his thoughts together. When he opened them again, I saw it was to get his heart together. "I need you to know that it has been you. You." He touched my cheek with the flower. "Not Sarah."

"What do you mean?"

"I stayed here for Sarah, years ago. I thought you'd be her, but you weren't. The girl and the woman that became my best friend—" He stopped, breaking under the emotion. "Was you. I will never—ever—let that go."

I was a mess. A sobbing, wet mess. "Alex, please don't go."

"Stand up."

"What?"

He stood and motioned me to do the same. I stood, facing him, only inches away.

"You felt a little of this the other night, so you know—this will jerk you around a little."

My head spun. It was all happening too fast.

"What? What are you—"

"I have to kiss you good-bye." I was speechless. He was serious. "I'm not supposed to. I wasn't supposed to push you up or pull Riley out of the water, either. But I—can't leave without it. And I'm just letting you know it's gonna hurt a little."

"Wait!" I cried. "Not yet. Can't we do this later or tomorrow or—" I scrambled for more time.

"No."

"Why?" I whined.

He ran the rose under my chin. "Because Jason is coming. And you're his now."

I looked around. "What?"

"Make it count, love. It's all we've got."

"Wait, Alex—" I croaked, my voice all squeaky. But there was no more time.

Alex crossed the inches, gave me one split second to look into his eyes, then his hands cradled my face at the same moment his lips touched mine. It was a jolt, like before, but different because I was trying to feel him. Electricity and light and emotion and memories flashed through my body like bombs going off. I couldn't breathe. I felt his mouth soft on mine, over and over; I even felt his tears. I also felt the most overwhelming love. For Sarah and for me. He was bidding us both good-bye.

My legs started to give way, and he lowered me to the swing, kissing me one last time. I wanted to see him, to look at him again, but I couldn't seem to open my eyes. Everything was swimming in a haze of lightning.

Then I felt his lips against my ear. "I love you, Dani."

And he was gone.

I lay on the swing trying to catch my breath, trying to open my eyes. It felt like when your arm goes to sleep and everything is dead, then the pins and needles come. Except it was my whole body coming back.

Including the realization that Alex—

"No!" I wailed, trying to scramble up, but I fell flat. "Alex! Don't leave me!" I sobbed it to the not-quite-dark-anymore night. To the crickets that were going to sleep. To anything that could possibly hear me. "I love you—" I cried into my hands.

I tried to get up, but my legs were weak, and I stumbled. But not before I saw Jason standing in the yard, toward the far end of the porch. Looking like he'd seen a ghost. Again.

Chapter 20

"JASON."

He turned slowly and started to walk back the way he'd come.

"No—Jason, wait. Please!"

I tried to follow him, but my feet weren't back yet, and they buckled, sending me sprawling down the steps and landing hard on the gravel.

That turned him back, and he jogged over to me. "Jesus, Dani, what the hell?"

My hands were scraped and had little pieces of rock stuck to them. My elbow was bleeding. It wasn't a good time.

"Alex was here."

"Yeah, I got that."

"Well, that's 'what the hell.'"

Jason helped me up, and walked me back up the steps where I sat down. He stood. I dropped my face into my hands.

"Are you okay?"

I shook my head and let a bitter laugh out. "Not really."

"Well, you were thirty minutes ago. Before—"

"Before Alex showed up?"

He didn't fire back, and I looked up. He was pissed. But right then, I wasn't feeling all that zippy, either.

"Yeah. Guess that tells me what I need to know." He turned to leave.

"No, actually, that doesn't tell you shit, Jason."

He wheeled back around. "What?"

I held my head, which was pounding, and tried not to think about what I probably looked like. "You'd rather jump to whatever conclusion justifies walking away. How about *asking*."

"What I saw doesn't require asking. And look at you now."

I narrowed my eyes. "What did you see?"

"Enough. And heard words you certainly couldn't say to me," he said, the last sentence full of acid and hurt.

I closed my eyes. "You saw him."

"Yes."

The logic started to click. "You saw him in the river because he was holding Riley. You saw him here because he was holding me."

"Kissing you."

My stomach clenched again at the memory. "Kissing me good-bye, Jason. He's gone." New tears came, and it wasn't a good time for that. "Contact like that knocks the nervous system out. I'm sorry I'm not all up to par right now."

"You're in love with him."

"Jason—"

"Dani, don't. It's all over your face. I know a broken heart when I see it."

I tried to stand, but everything went woozy so I sat back down. "Damn it, he's my best friend. He was the one constant and basically the 'man in my life' for lack of anyone else. And now he's gone." My voice rose as my head pounded harder with the adrenaline. "So yes, I'm a little upset."

"Well, then I'll leave you alone."

"Jason!"

He turned again and jerked his hands in the air. "What?"

I pleaded with my eyes for him to understand. To go back to the loving guy he was before, instead of the brooding jerk standing before me. Which something back behind the pain was telling me wasn't fair, but I couldn't focus on that.

"He's gone. He left to get out of the way. But he's a ghost, Jason. He was never competition."

Jason walked back to stand right in front of me. I could smell the faint woodsy smell still on him, and I wanted to be wrapped up in that warm aroma again.

"I came over here to surprise you. To be romantic and spontaneous and—something, I don't know. Because I suddenly couldn't stand to be away from you."

I reached for his hand. "I feel—"

He shook his head and pulled away from me. "Don't. The fact that he knew he was *in the way* should tell you something, Dani. I'm grateful to him for everything he's done for you, that's the truth." Jason scrubbed his hands over his face and through his hair, making it stand up. "But you're lying to me and to yourself if you think he wasn't competition." He laid a finger over my heart. "In here." He pointed up at the porch. "You don't look at me like that. And I'm not settling for less."

I watched him walk away. I didn't have anything left to argue with. How could I? He was right, wasn't he? I was in love with Alex, as warped as that was. I crawled to the swing and climbed on, picking up the rose where it had fallen. I lay down and let the movement lull me.

"MOM?"

Riley's voice pulled me from the cobwebs. I opened my eyes but I felt like I'd pulled a massive tequila night. My head throbbed and my stomach threatened to rebel.

"Mom? You okay?"

"Mmm." I sat up and clapped a hand over my mouth, then bolted to the railing and horked the previous night's dinner. I just lay there, half flopped over afterward, too spent to move. The activity didn't help my headache any.

"Wow, that must have been some night."

"You have no idea," I croaked.

"Probably don't want to," she said with a chuckle. "Need some coffee?"

"Please."

I managed to get myself on the top step and leaned against the banister post, feeling the still-cool surface against my temple. It wasn't dark anymore, but it didn't feel late, either. Riley came back with a steaming mug of coffee and set it beside me as she sat on the other end of the step.

"You been crying?" she asked, leaning forward to look at me better.

"Am I all swollen?"

"Pretty much." She turned my right hand over to view the mess that matched my elbow. "My God, what happened?"

"Great." I picked up the mug carefully, since my dexterity wasn't the best.

"Well?"

"Thought you didn't want to know."

"Well, you've got me all curious now. Crying and sleeping on the porch with a hangover and what looks like a brawl." She pointed to the rose in my hand. "And a flower. There's got to be a major story there."

A bitter noise came from my throat. "Not what you'd think." I took a swallow and relished the burn.

"So a bad date with Satan?"

I had to laugh at that, in spite of none of it being funny. "No, actually a great date. More than great. The best ever."

"This is 'best ever' results?"

"No, this is 'Alex is gone forever and Jason witnessed my meltdown and left me, too' results."

Riley just stared at me. "Drink some more coffee."

"I'm not drunk, boog," I said with a wink. Oh God, I winked. I was losing it.

"Yeah, okay."

I shook my head and patted her arm. "I'm coming down off contact with Alex."

"What?"

I rubbed my eyes and grimaced at the black on my fingers. I probably looked like a deranged raccoon. "He was here when I got home. To tell me good-bye."

"But he's like your best friend."

New tears. Was that possible? I was going to dehydrate. "I know."

"And you love him."

"Seriously?" I took another swallow of the hot coffee. It was black and I didn't care. It could have been purple.

"What?"

I flailed a hand. "Jason walked up in time to witness the big exit and me losing my sanity. Wasn't one of my finer moments."

"And he said—" she prompted.

I wanted to squeeze my skull. "Basically that he won't settle for less than undying love. I guess."

"You guess? Well—I mean, what can he say about anything? He hasn't professed any *undying love*, has he?" I looked at her, and her eyes shot open wide. "Holy crap, he has?"

"Told me he loved me last night."

"Oh my God! What did you say?"

I winced and shrugged. "It's complicated."

She jumped up and stood in front of me. "Mom. Snap out of it. You've got a hot guy who loves you, who—okay, may or may not be the devil—but he seems to treat you good. And I've seen you around him, you light up." She leaned over to make me be eye to eye. "He's a real live flesh-and-blood person, Mom. I know you have a thing for Alex, but that's not reality. He can't show flaws, he can't burp and fart and leave the toilet seat up and steal the remote and do all the real-life things to piss you off. This guy is real."

I watched her rant in awe. "That was supposed to be a selling point?"

"Seriously, Mom."

I sighed and scooped my matted-up hair out of my face. "Where'd you get all this wisdom about men?"

She shrugged. "TV."

I smirked. "Well, as long as it's reliable."

"Okay then, think of this." She put a hand on her hip. "If Alex were alive and breathing, standing next to Satan—and you didn't have five hundred years of back history—" she added quickly. "If you'd just met *both* of them when we moved here, who would it be?"

She left me with that. Well, hell.

I went to Miss Olivia's, nodded at Grady as he stumbled over himself to be nice to me, and dumped the whole story on her. All of it, including Sarah and little baby me. She was the one person who wouldn't be damaged by knowing.

"I'll say this, Dani girl. Nothing about you is boring."

"I'd love boring."

She handed me a potato and motioned for me to peel it. I looked around for a peeler or a knife, and she pointed to a contraption on the counter to my left.

"What the heck is that?"

"You stick the potato in there, and push down the lever, and it skins the thing clean. Turn it sideways and it slices it."

"Really?"

"I'm telling you I do everything easy now. Got that off TV."

"Huh." I did what she said and tentatively pushed the big black lever down. It cut into the skin but just started mangling it and stuck. Miss Olivia came over and nudged me aside, whacking the lever down like a ninja.

"You gotta put some oomph into it, girl."

I eyed the machine and its naked potato guts. "Got it."

"So what are you thinking?"

"That I'd rather have a potato peeler and a paper plate."

She waved a hand at me. "About Jason."

"I hurt him. Not meaning to, but I did." I sunk into a chair. "I don't know if there is a Jason to consider anymore. He seemed pretty done with me."

"Seems pretty smitten to me. Sounds like he just wants you to love him back."

"I do." I did? I just said that? Miss Olivia stopped sorting tomatoes and looked at me and I blinked. "Um—I think."

She laughed and pointed a tomato at me. "I think you know."

"How would I know? What do I have to compare to? Riley's father? Hell no. All I've ever known about love is from Alex. And since Riley pointed out that's all based on a non-farting environment, what kind of expert am I?"

She chuckled. "That Riley. She's got some thoughts beyond her years, that's for sure." She pulled up a chair across from me and settled into it. "You want some serious advice about love?"

I nodded.

"That 'love is perfect' drivel from the Bible is only for God. Not people. Love is messy, complicated, irritating, gut-wrenching, and all about giving up something for someone else. There are no rainbows and roses. There's piss on the toilet and razor stubble in the sink."

I laughed as I recalled having stubble and piss once. I was left with nothing but the damn sink and toilet. "You and Riley sell from the same book."

She pointed at me again, then tapped her fingernail on the counter. "And when it's the real deal, honey, it's like nothing else. You grab on and ride that ride."

My smile faded. "Alex said we had that once."

"No, he said he had that with Sarah." I stared at her. She

was blunt as always, but she was right. I hated that. "What you've had is the shadow of that, like light from space."

I frowned. "Come again?"

"You know—light from the stars. What we see, by the time we see it, doesn't exist anymore." She smiled, her old eyes crinkling at the corners. "That Jason is the real deal I'm talkin' about."

I felt the burn in my stomach as I thought of my history with Alex. He was forever inside me. Flashes of a life that wasn't even mine to remember, intertwined with a friendship that defied death.

"And Alex?"

"Did what you couldn't do, baby girl. He cut the ties."

I gave the little bell on the string a look, then walked past it, taking a deep breath and knocking on the wooden door. The last time I'd crossed this space I was being carried in with Jason's tongue in my mouth.

Now I stood in ratty sweatpants and a Hello Kitty faded tank top at one in the morning with no makeup and my hair yanked up in a crooked ponytail. Who on earth wouldn't want that?

I'd flopped in bed long enough, thinking of Miss Olivia's words, of Riley's words. Staring at my phone, willing Jason to call me. Refusing to call him. Wishing Alex was there to talk me down, and then pushing that thought away. It was time for action, and while that thought pumped me up on the way there, the simple act of knocking deflated all my bravado.

I held my breath when I heard movement and tried to remember to let it out when he opened the door. His eyes were barely open and his hair was spiky and he wore sweatpants and a T-shirt with holes and I went weak at the knees.

"Dani—what—what are you doing here?"

"I love you."

He blinked and rubbed at his eyes, then focused on me, not saying anything for what felt like eternity. "What are you doing?"

"Telling you that when I wake up every day, I think of seeing you at work. When I come home, I think about seeing you the next day and stress out over it."

"Um—"

I had to keep going. "My relationship with Alex was easy. He'd always been there, always been my best friend. He was all I had. But it could never be more than it was."

"But you wanted it to be."

"Yeah," I said, nodding. "I did. Even though I knew better, I'm human. He was the only man I ever gave my heart to. It was perfect and easy and no mess." I inhaled and let out a shaky breath. "And then came you."

He blinked at me. "And now you want mess?"

"Yes!"

He scrubbed at his hair. "Dani, it's the middle of the night—are you still dazed from—"

"No. I'm telling you that yes, I did love him, Jason, but not like this. My feelings for him were about a long— loooong—friendship, that probably crossed some boundaries, but not like this." I pointed down at the ground. "Here, right now, this."

Jason inhaled slowly and let it out, looking at me seriously finally. "And if he comes back?"

"He won't. But if he did," I paused as I felt my voice catch. "He'd be happy for me." I inched closer. "He told me that I was falling in love with you. And he was right."

Something in his face flickered. "You're—in love with me."

"I believe I said that when you opened the door."

"I still thought you were insane then."

I chuckled. "Not the first time today."

He reached out as if to touch me, then pulled back. "How often is this going to happen?"

"What?"

"Are there any other invisible boyfriends out there?"

"None."

"But lots of other just random people."

"Everywhere."

He nodded. "Will you tell me when they're there so I don't look like an idiot or think you're talking to me or something?"

I smiled. "I promise."

"There's no more secrets?"

I only blinked once, as I folded that one up and put it away. Deep inside a chamber of my heart that could never be touched. "None." *I'm sorry.*

"I love you, Dani."

My insides quivered, and I suddenly couldn't feel my feet. "I love you, too."

"Come here."

I walked into his chest and let him wrap me up in his arms, in his old ratty clothes. Nothing ever felt so good.

"Can we go to bed or do you have to report back home again?"

"I'll text Riley to cover for me."

"That's twisted, you know that."

We walked inside, hand in hand. "Twisted doesn't even come close to our lives. Do you have razor stubble in your sink?"

He stared at me. "I—don't—is that important?"

"Not really."

He frowned at me. "You're a little weird, you know that?"

I reached up and kissed him softly. "But you love the weird lady."

He sighed, which made a low rumble in his chest. "Yeah, I do." He kissed me back and shut the door.

My dad once asked me if seeing ghosts like I did messed me up when I was young, or changed my life. Since I've only had one life to compare, I don't know if it was messed up or not, but I know I can't imagine what it would have been otherwise. Without Alex. Without knowing him. Loving him. As warped and twisted and bizarre as that may sound, my first love was a ghost. The first, most intense feelings of my life were for a man I could never touch, never kiss—except once. And in that instant, I knew more about him than if I'd spent ninety years with him. I know he loved me. I know he will always love me. I know that at the end of my life, he will be there to smile at me as I cross over. I'll get to see Alyssa and tell her all about her dad.

And I know that on the day I married Jason, somewhere in the back of the crowd that I never thought I'd have, he was there. I didn't see him, he made sure to blend, but I felt him when the back of my neck tingled. I knew it was him. And when we got to the cake fiasco, there it was. One single perfect white rose, lying in front of the cake. Jason is the second and greatest love of my life, my future, my best friend. He's my everything now. Alex gave me that gift.

Jason didn't notice the rose; there were so many flowers around. But I knew. I didn't even bother to look around, I knew I wouldn't see him. I picked it up with my hands shaking a little. Just held it to my lips and closed my eyes, saying good-bye. Again.

Turn the page for a preview
of Sharla Lovelace's next novel . . .

BEFORE AND
EVER SINCE

Now available from Berkley Sensation!

THERE is a moment when you know that your day has gone down the toilet. Mine was before lunch, and after my fourth cup of coffee, when an unexpected knock on my front door brought me face-to-face with my ex-husband.

Not that he was a horrible troll, or lying in wait to machete me in a weak moment, but he just wasn't one to just drop by and say hello. Which was good with me. Child support and visitations came to a legal end three years prior, so daddy-pick-ups were off the table. So I stood in the doorway, self-consciously running a hand through my unbrushed hair and then crossing my arms over my chest to disguise the no-bra action I had going on.

He gave me a once-over and frowned. "Are you sick?"

I started to protest that not having to get dressed was a perk of working from home, that until someone wanted to look at a house, talking to potential clients on the phone didn't require me to brush my hair or put on shoes. But I didn't feel like having that long a conversation with him. So I fake-coughed into my hand.

"Little bit. What's up?"

He shrugged. "I was wondering how much she's selling it for."

I blinked a few times, thinking I'd missed something. "Um—she, who?"

He tilted his head with widened eyes like he was humoring me. "Your mother?"

I opened my mouth, but just air came out. Maybe it was the coffee. Maybe I needed to eat something or go for a walk. Use the treadmill that was collecting dust in a corner of my office.

I shook my head. "I—I give up, Kevin. What about my mother?"

"Her house, Emily," he said, impatience lacing his tone. "How much is she selling her house for?"

I laughed then, which I knew would piss him off. "Selling her house? What kind of crack are you smoking?"

My mother would sooner sell one of us than sell that house. She and my dad lived in it their whole married life. Raised two kids there, multiple dogs, a couple of birds, and I think there was even a brief stint with a ferret. She didn't leave after my dad died in the living room, and if anything could have shoved her out, it would have been that.

Kevin's dark blue eyes glazed over at my comment. He held his hands up in front of him and shook his head as he turned. "Never mind. I forgot how crazy y'all are."

"Whoa, whoa, wait," I said, still laughing. "What are you babbling about?"

He took the steps two at a time, and waved a hand behind him. "Never mind, Em. I'll just call Dedra. That's who it's listed with, right?"

My smile started to fade, and I felt it stick at the confusion point. Something was off. Something didn't make sense. Starting with him saying that sentence.

"*Dedra*?" I said. "What are you talking about?" My tone combined with her name was enough to tweak his attention because it turned him around. His expression changed to wary and unsure.

"Your mom's house? It's for sale with her." He looked uncomfortable and pointed randomly at the air behind him as if to prove it. "I had nothing to do with it. It's on the sign; I passed it this morning on my way out."

Another leftover piece of a laugh kind of popped out, but with much less confidence. I shook my head as I turned around, knowing he'd follow me.

"That's crazy," I said. "Has to be a joke or something. I just had lunch with my mom last week. I mean, come on. Don't you think she'd have mentioned that? She talked about her garden."

I landed back on the squeaky swivel chair in my office, as Kevin found a spot on the couch among scattered manila folders. He moved a few aside, turning one over to read the name.

"829 Montgomery—why does that sound familiar?" he asked.

"It's one street over from my mom's," I said, clicking through the links that would bring me to the multiple listing database. "And quit snooping, it's not listed yet."

"Oh yeah. The Landry place," he said, and I ignored the snide change of tone.

"Yep."

"Bobby's finally unloading it, huh?"

I blinked and sighed and continued to ignore the shiny object he was dangling to get a rise out of me. "Guess so."

"About time," Kevin continued. "It's been one strong breeze away from blowing over for years."

"Oh, it's not that bad," I said, scoffing. "Just needs a little attention. Vacant houses get that way."

"Well, I don't blame him," he said. "Ben left him high and dry with that place back when their mom died. Never even came back for the funeral."

The old dig that used to stab me barely felt like a pin-prick. "You don't know that."

"And you do?"

I cut my eyes at him. "This town can make a lot of noise when it wants to. You believe everything you hear?"

Kevin tossed the file over with the others, and I was grateful for the change. I watched him take in the overflowing bookshelf, the three different-colored jackets hanging on the treadmill, the row of file boxes stacked against one wall.

"I assume there's a method, as usual?" he asked.

"Ha ha, very cute."

In our eleven years of marriage, he'd never learned to appreciate my version of décor or organization. Kevin preferred empty space. Like moving into a house with no stuff, kind of empty. No pictures, no decorations, no curtains, no coasters or vases or magazines. Give him a chair and a rug and a TV and he's good. In fact, the rug would probably be pushing it.

"So, dating anybody?" he asked.

I hit a button and gave him a look. "Really?"

His face went all innocent. "What?"

"You really want to know about my love life?"

He looked away with a smile. "I want you to be happy, Em."

I coughed again, this time for real. "So, what's the deal?" I asked, changing the subject as I waited for the zip code filter to update. "You looking to move again? Sherry wanting to simplify and rub elbows with the common folk?"

He gave me a look and leaned back, his brown leather jacket making noise against the wannabe leather of my couch. "I'm thinking about buying some rental property."

"Ah, you want to be a land baron now."

"It's easy money," he said with a shrug.

"Not with old houses like—"

My words died on my tongue as the page populated, and there it was. Three listings down. A familiar address and equally familiar picture of my mother's house. Listed by Dedra Powers.

"You've gotta be shitting me," I said under my breath, and I heard Kevin and his jacket sit forward.

"So, how much is it listed for?"

I tore my eyes from the screen to glare at him. "Seriously?"

He lifted a hand. "What?"

I swiveled around in my chair to find my phone, and leapt up to grab it off the top of my treadmill, hitting speed dial number two. Three rings led to voice mail and my mother's voice telling me how sorry she was that she couldn't answer my call.

"Mom!" I yelled, then bit my lip and let my mouth work for a second. "Mom?" I tried again. "Please call me."

I hung up and stared at the listing again as I hit speed dial numbers one and three, both of which went to voice mail as well. "Jesus, where is everybody today?" I muttered as I tossed the phone to the couch next to Kevin and smiled not-so-patiently at him.

"I've gotta go change clothes and—interrogate my mother," I said. "So—" I did a little hand flourish that I felt encouraged his exit.

"You didn't know."

"That's pretty clear," I said, not enjoying his smirk.

He stood up and leaned over to view the page on my laptop, which I then flipped closed.

"Ninety thousand," he said, narrowing his eyes in that financial thinker's expression of his, and I shook my head before another second could pass.

"No."

He blinked and met my eyes. "What do you mean?"

"I mean, no," I said. "I don't know what's going on with this, but regardless, you aren't buying it."

"Why not?"

My head was spinning. I wanted answers and I wanted Kevin to be gone so I could go find them.

"Because." He tilted his head again, and I made a sound

of disgust. "God, you look like such a girl when you do that. Stop it."

"You aren't answering my question."

"And I'm not going to right now," I said, taking him by the arm and walking. "Come on. I have to leave. I have to get naked first. And unless Sherry-bom-Berry is okay with that, you probably shouldn't be here when I do."

We made it to the door and I pushed him gently out. Just as he turned back around. "Oh, I almost forgot. Do you know if Cassidy sent in any of those business school applications yet?"

I sighed and gave him a look as I slowly guided the door closed. "She's twenty-one, Kevin. She doesn't run her day by me anymore. Call her."

"I have, and she doesn't call me back."

Shocking. "Gotta go."